A STRUGGLE FOR NORMAL

A NOVEL BY

RICHARD K. MOORE

authorHOUSE®

AuthorHouse™
1663 Liberty Drive, Suite 200
Bloomington, IN 47403
www.authorhouse.com
Phone: 1-800-839-8640

This is a novel in which the author has fictionalized the involvement of imaginative characters in a number of historical events. Any resemblance of these fictional characters to actual persons, living or dead, is entirely coincidental. It is not the author's intention to denigrate the involvement or conduct of any individual in any of these events.

First published by AuthorHouse 9/16/2008

ISBN: 978-1-4389-0158-9 (sc)

Printed in the United States of America
Bloomington, Indiana

This book is printed on acid-free paper.

DEDICATION

For my beloved Willis
Friend, lover, wife, mother, grandmother

INTRODUCTION

In this sequel to the author's first book, *A Loss of Freedom*, Thomas O'Roark returns home from the mud and blood of World War I badly wounded and disillusioned. His main wish is to get back to normal.

But first it's his mother, then the Ku Klux Klan, then a former girlfriend who challenge his happy homecoming. His mother, ostensibly too busy with her Red Cross work, fails to meet his train. Before he leaves the station, he gets into a fight with a bunch of Klansmen harassing a Negro soldier. Later, he is confronted by the girlfriend, claiming he's the father of her baby.

These conflicts take place against a background of America still in turmoil after the war. It's a world with multiple labor strikes, a hysterical government campaign against 'Reds', pending Prohibition and rampant inflation. The Ku Klux Klan, an extension of widespread wartime persecution, is growing rapidly.

Thomas again tangles with the Klan when he goes to the aid of a new neighbor, a Russian immigrant family. He later defends his own home against the

Klan, intent on harming an old Negro soldier he has hired as a helper. He confronts his mother over her plans to start a birth control clinic, and eventually marries the girlfriend, entering into a union that leads to more conflict.

Things come to a head when, returning from flying, Thomas finds the Klan again attacking the family farm. He buzzes them to frighten them away, then inadvertently crashes the plane. Recuperating in the hospital, he learns that one of the Klan members is the German sympathizer who impregnated his sister before being deported as a spy. He also finds that prior to being deported, the sympathizer hid out with the in-laws and could have fathered his new wife's child.

The wife eventually contracts smallpox and dies. This sets the stage for the surprise discovery of who really has been leading the Klan attacks against Thomas. The story ends with him finding a newspaper article quoting presidential candidate Warren G. Harding promising a 'return to normalcy'.

CHAPTER 1

As the *California Limited* sped southward through the long, flat San Joaquin Valley, Thomas O'Roark struggled to stay awake. One moment he was scrunching around in the unrelenting mohair seat, his head bumping against the mahogany window frame, trying to get comfortable; the next he was sitting up massaging the bullet wound in his leg, attempting to ease the pain.

When the train lurched through a switch block, he rubbed his eyes awake and leaned forward to stare through the window, streaked with rivulets of moisture and partially blackened by smoke blown back from the big Baldwin four-eight-four locomotive. The view into the gathering dusk revealed a seamless green landscape of winter wheat, pock marked by an occasional vineyard or orchard, the limbs of its vines or trees barren and scraggly in their winter dormancy. Here and there, a lonely farmhouse and wisp of fireplace smoke offered the only evidence of life. In the distance, the familiar snowy carapace of the Sierra Nevada Mountains was hidden by a mantle of gray tule fog settling inexorably toward the land.

Thomas was returning home with the Great War in Europe now over, battered and disillusioned, his once youthful patriotism broken on the reality of mortal combat. His muscular young body had been ripped open twice, leaving him with a jagged shoulder scar and a leg wound that would impact the rest of his life. He had killed and seen his close comrades killed.

Uncertainty over his future left a sunken feeling in his chest. He was apprehensive over who would meet his train, the mother who had disowned him for abandoning the family farm to go to war, or Brenda Stuckey, the girlfriend who claimed he was the father of her child. Or would it be Becky, the faithful older sister, the one person he trusted and who seemed to understand him.

He was brought back to the moment by the hollow rumbling of the train's wheels crossing the high wooden trestle over the San Joaquin River. He sat up and pressed his face against the window, cupping his hands over his eyes to shut out the reflection of the interior light, striving to see some familiar landmark in the deepening dusk.

As the train slowed for the outskirts of his hometown of Fresno, he flexed his travel-weary shoulders and impatiently reached for his Army-issue cane. When the train stopped, he clapped his campaign hat on his head, struggled into his heavy Army overcoat, and slung the strap of his *musette* bag over his shoulder. He joined several other returning soldiers moving expectantly toward the exit and what they hoped would be a return to a more normal life.

He stepped down onto the platform and into the encroaching fog that was becoming a cold drizzle. He moved under the wide protective eaves of the big chateau-style station and glanced around uncertainly. A Red Cross tea wagon was parked under the pale, misty lights. It was staffed by four smiling, matronly women, stamping their feet and rubbing their hands against the cold, and serving a mixture of soldiers, sailors and Marines. He peered at the women, and determined that his mother was not among them. He turned in the opposite direction and caught his breath at the sight of a lone woman standing under the overhang. This one was smiling, waving to him and carrying a baby.

He started forward when he recognized his tall, willowy sister, even with a cloche hat partially covering her reddish-blonde hair. He hobbled to her and wrapped his arm around her, knocking her glasses askew. Becky squealed in delight as she pushed the glasses back in place, the little one started wailing and Thomas stepped back, tears welling in his eyes.

"Oh, God, I'm sorry," he said, patting the baby uncertainly.

Becky cuddled her son closer, "Don't worry. He's just not used to big bear hugs."

Thomas pulled out a handkerchief and wiped his eyes. "He's sure a little fellow. What's his name?"

"Richard…Richard Thomas. Everyone calls him Ricky."

"Oh, yes. I remember from your letter." The baby was starting to calm down, and Thomas lifted his little bonnet for a closer look. "Man, look at that blonde hair…and…and the blue eyes!" He blew his nose and stuffed the hanky in his pocket.

Becky sighed. "Think you can stand a little German in the family after all you've been through?"

He nodded and frowned as his mind flashed back to Werner von Karman, the Normal School professor who had gotten his sister pregnant and subsequently been deported as a German spy.

"Want to hold him?"

"Uh, not sure I'm steady enough to try that just yet. Maybe when I'm sitting down."

He continued balancing on his cane and good leg as she examined him more intently, commenting, "You look different…older, I guess."

He shrugged, "Guess that's what war does for you."

"You look like you lost weight, too."

"Yeah, I lost quite a bit after too many missed meals. But I'm about one-hundred-eighty pounds now, almost back to normal."

She reached to lift his hat, exposing his wavy brown hair. "And your wave's starting to grow back."

He grinned sheepishly.

"What happened to the leg? We got word you were seriously wounded, but the Army didn't give any details."

He started to reply, but cocked his head at the sound of shouting coming from the opposite side of the station, "What's that noise?"

Becky shook her head, "Don't know. Maybe it's a parade."

"Let's go look." He led the way around to the front of the building where, in the small park across from the station, they could see several individuals struggling with a Negro soldier. They were clad in white robes and cone-shaped masks with cat-like eye slits, and were trying to drag the soldier toward a big Chandler motorcar parked at the curb, its engine idling.

"Who the devil's that?" Thomas asked.

His sister shook her head, "I don't know...looks like some of that Klan bunch. They've gotten real big around here since the war."

Thomas turned to several doughboys standing next to him at the curb. "You guys got any fight left in you?"

They nodded and followed him as he dropped his *musette* at the curb and hobbled across the street, shouting at the Klansmen to leave the soldier alone. When they told him to mind his own business, he plowed into them, flailing away with his cane. The others joined in the fray, punching and kicking wildly until the attackers dropped their victim and retreated toward their car. "We'll get you for this, you damn Nigger lover!" the apparent leader shouted in a high-pitched voice as he shook his raised fist and jammed the car into gear, and they sped away.

Thomas turned to help the Negro soldier untangle the ropes loosely wrapped around his arms and shoulders and get to his feet. "What the hell was that all about?" he asked as he caught his breath and straightened his tunic, then leaned down to retrieve his hat and cane.

"Doan know, Sergeant. Ah was jus' walkin' down the street mindin' ma own business, and they jumped me. Reckon I'm in the wrong part of town?"

Thomas shook his head, "Maybe you better find out before you get into more trouble. We might not be around the next time."

"Yessuh."

Thomas thanked the other soldiers for their help and turned to his sister,

"Shall we head for home?"

She led the way toward the family Maxwell, commenting, "I hope you didn't get yourself in trouble with the Klan."

He shrugged, "They looked like a bunch of cowards to me, hiding under those robes and masks."

"They've been causing a lot of trouble with people who don't cow-tow to them. Been picking fights, tar and feathering, burning crosses and stuff like that."

He changed the subject, "So how's the car been running?"

"Pretty good. Had a little work done on the motor and bought two new tires about a month ago, but otherwise OK." She moved toward the passenger side, asking, "You remember how to drive?"

"Er, believe so, but not sure I can with my leg."

"I hope you can because I have something to tend to. Ricky is ready for his supper."

Not sure he understood, Thomas helped his sister into the seat, closed the door, and hobbled around to the driver's side. He tossed the *musette* bag and cane onto the rear seat and eased in behind the wheel. He tested his injured leg against the brake pedal and winced at the stab of pain, but started the engine, turned on the headlights and backed away from the curb.

As they pulled away from the station and turned into the downtown area, he was plunged into something he had forgotten; the cacophony of city life. The brightness of street lights, the clanging of streetcars, the honking of motorcar horns and the low background hum of Saturday shoppers and office workers scurrying for home was something he had forgotten during his fourteen-month absence.

He turned to his sister, "So, how did the town get along during the war?"

"OK. We bought Liberty Bonds, and collected old shoes and clothing for Belgian Relief. And we knitted socks and sweaters for soldiers, and learned to live with Hoover's wheatless Wednesdays and meatless Mondays."

"You look like you survived OK, but you look skinnier."

"You forget, I was pregnant the last time you saw me."

"Yeah, but seems like your hair was longer. You cut it shorter?"

She poked at the tufts of hair around the edge of her cloche, "Oh, yes. All the girls are wearing it this way now."

He fell silent as they left the macadam of city streets and bounced onto the muddy, corrugated surface of the farm road. Becky settled into the seat, pulled back her coat and suit jacket, unbuttoned her blouse and nestled her baby into the crook of her arm. Thomas stole one glance at him suckling noisily at his sister's partially exposed breast, then stared straight ahead, struggling to see beyond the headlights barely penetrating the deepening darkness.

A few minutes later, as they turned into the familiar driveway, he could see the ghostly outline of the dark farmhouse and the big, bare-leafed sycamore hovering sentinel-like over the middle of the yard. The headlights briefly illuminated the roadside mailbox, and the dead cornstalks and snap bean poles standing askew in his mother's neglected vegetable garden. The small combination barn and bunkhouse, once a respite during his unhappy teenage years, hunkered shadowy in the left background. It was made slightly more visible by a pale light from the single window. An Overland automobile was under the tree.

"Who does that belong to?" he asked as he cut the engine.

"Don't know. It doesn't look familiar."

He climbed out of the car, retrieved his cane and *musette* bag, and limped around to open the door for his sister. They were interrupted by someone running toward them from the bunkhouse and yelling, "Hey, Boss, welcome home!" It was PJ Sloan, the wiry little farm manager Thomas had hired during the first summer of the war.

He reached out to shake the hand of the older man, who responded with a hearty slap on the back that almost knocked him off balance. PJ enthused, "Jeez, you sure whupped the snot outa them Heinies!"

Thomas smiled weakly and nodded toward the automobile that started to look vaguely familiar. "You buy a car?"

"Er, naw," PJ replied, shuffling his high-heeled, pointy-toed cowboy boots and glancing away. "That belongs to Missus Harrington. She's just visiting. Her old man's still in prison, you know."

Thomas looked away, partly embarrassed, partly annoyed. "I'm pretty tired, PJ. We'll see you later."

As he and Becky and the baby headed for the house, he muttered sarcastically, "Looks like someone enjoyed the war."

He entered the house and felt along the rough surface of the plaster wall to flip on the light switch as Becky followed along, carrying the baby. He blinked as his eyes adjusted to the bright light, then turned slowly to scan the room. The clamminess of an area that had not been occupied for a couple months washed over him and caused him to shiver. His gaze paused at the cold, blackened hearth of the large stone fireplace. In front of it, seemingly out of place, was the old spindle-back Boston rocker he never felt comfortable sitting in; even after his father's death it seemed to reek of the old man's body odor and the smell of his pipe. His eyes wandered to the overstuffed sofa with the lumpy cushions that relentlessly pushed an occupant to one side or the other. His mother's glass-enclosed bric-a-brac cabinet stood silently in the corner behind him with several of the pieces tumbled over in disarray. Turning to his right, he observed the stove and the icebox, still anchoring the end of the kitchen counter, a water stain on the floor where the ice drip pan had overflowed.

Becky carried the sleeping baby into the back bedroom and laid him on the bed surrounded by pillows, then removed her hat and coat. Thomas tossed his hat, bag and overcoat on the sofa, and headed for the bathroom.

When they rejoined each other in the all-purpose living room, she asked, "Want something to eat? Maybe some soup?"

"That sounds OK. Got anything to drink, like beer or wine or something stronger?" He limped to the fireplace, crumpled in old newspapers, added kindling and a log, and struck a match.

"No. But I think there's apple cider in the icebox. Undoubtedly warm since the ice is all melted." Without waiting for a reply, she pulled out the jug, poured them each a glass and put them on the kitchen table. He peeled off his Marine tunic, reached in the pocket for his smoking materials and tossed the garment on the sofa next to the overcoat and hat. He moved to the table, pulled one of the ladder-back chairs up beside another, sat down in one and lifted his aching leg up on the other. He rubbed his hand across the cool, slick surface of the red and blue plaid oilcloth table cover, asking, "This new?"

"Yeah. I bought that last year to hide all the scratch marks."

While his sister turned to opening and heating a can of *Campbell's* tomato soup, he curled a cigarette paper partway around his left index finger, tapped in *Bull Durham* from its little cotton sack, closed the yellow strings with his teeth and free hand, and sealed the paper with a lick of his tongue. He scratched a match along the underside of the table, lighted up and took a long drag. He followed that with a drink of the warm cider as his mind tumbled back to his days on the farm prior to his enlistment.

As America edged closer to war early in 1917, he seemingly had everything a young man of his time could ask for: a good job with a supportive boss, new friends, his first car, a room in town and a willing girlfriend. Then tragedy struck when his father died on the eve of America's declaration of war. This forced him to return to the farm and the life he deplored under the wing of his overly demanding mother.

His painful daydreaming was interrupted by Becky placing a bowl of soup and saucer of crackers in front of him. As he picked up his spoon and blew on the steaming liquid, his eyes turned warily toward the rocker and he asked, "Is something different about the furniture?"

She sat down across from him and replied, "Yeah, the Morris chair is gone. That old verdigris upholstery was so ugly and worn out that I let PJ take it to the bunkhouse and moved Father's rocking chair in from the bedroom."

He took another drag on his cigarette and blew the smoke toward the ceiling. He sampled a spoonful of the hot soup.

"I gave the rocker a couple coats of *Murphy's* varnish and Brenda helped me make new covers for the seat and back cushions so they match the curtains. Don't you like them?"

He ignored the reference to Brenda, and again eyed the chair, "I see one of the back spindles is still missing."

"Yeah. Been that way as long as I can remember."

Morosely, he took a bite of cracker and slurped up several more spoonfuls of the soup before asking, "You see much of her during the war?"

"Brenda? Oh, yes. We got together to knit for the soldiers, and we read and ate together sometimes. Then she had her little boy in September, so I helped her with him."

He didn't respond as his sister continued, "She claims you're the father, you know."

"Yeah, you told me in your last letter." He shifted uncomfortably, took a final puff on his cigarette, stubbed it out in a saucer and finished his glass of cider.

Becky went to the ice box to get more cider, and when she returned her brother commented, "I've been admiring your outfit, but isn't the skirt kinda short?"

"Oh, this is the newest style!" She was wearing a wool suit in a blue and white nailhead pattern, and paused to lift the tight-fitting skirt as she turned in a half pirouette. "See, it's supposed to be six inches above the floor, and they're talking about hems rising to nine inches next year."

"And what's that on your face?"

She touched her hand to her cheek. "Oh, that's my new rouge and lipstick. Don't you like it?"

"Um, I guess so."

"I'm a working girl now, you know. Have to look stylish." She sat down at the table to finish her soup.

"Working girl?"

"Yes, I've started by own cosmetics business."

"What kind of business is that?"

"I sell lipsticks, rouges, perfumes and things like that. I just started last month."

"So, who's been taking care of the farm?"

"PJ and the Mexican family."

When they were finished, Becky gathered up her coat and hat and baby to return to her apartment. Thomas bid her goodbye and turned to washing and drying the dishes. Then, finding himself surrounded by an unfamiliar quiet, he locked the kitchen door, banked the fire and wandered into his old bedroom. He pulled back the faded yellow, chenille bedspread, wool blanket and top sheet, and sat on the edge of the bed. He removed his clothes down to his underwear, turned out the lamp and eased his six-foot, three-inch frame into the enfolding softness of the feather mattress.

He relaxed with his hands behind his head, reveling in the almost forgotten comfort of his old bed, the fresh-washed smell of the muslin sheets and pillowcase. His mind drifted away to the war and the American Hospital in Paris where, during treatment for his leg wound, he had reconnected with Lillian Branson. She was the nurse he had met the first summer of the war on a train trip to Tacoma to recover his brother's body, and had introduced him to a night of lovemaking he would never forget.

But then his eyes popped open and he stared unseeing into the blackness of the night. He began to feel uncomfortable in the softness of the feather bed. He had gotten used to sleeping on the firm mattress of a military barracks or hospital, or even on the cold, muddy ground of the battlefield. In a few moments he was startled by a rifle-like crack from the fireplace when the flames bit into the sap of a log. Next came a random popping, similar to that of *Very* signal lights arcing over the battlefield, as the bedroom windows contracted against the cold of the night. Finally, the skittering of mice through the attic over his head reminded him of the huge trench rats he had encountered in France.

He sat up abruptly as the sounds carried him to the final day of the war. His feet started feeling cold when he recalled sloshing across the *Meuse* River on a partially submerged pontoon bridge with the icy water sluicing into his boots and leggings. He shuddered at the memory of Corporal Tim Cambell, his best buddy, being knocked into the river by enemy artillery, and his inability to save him.

He jumped out of bed, stumbled barefooted into the dark living room and dropped tentatively into his father's old rocker with his feet resting on the warm hearth. He added a couple more logs to the fire and watched idly as the flames licked around them hungrily.

CHAPTER 2

Becky phoned Thomas the next morning, a Sunday, to advise that she and their mother would be coming to the farm with his favorite meal, pot roast with all the trimmings and rhubarb pie for dessert. They would motor out separately in Emma's Red Cross car and the Maxwell so they could leave the latter for his use.

He awoke to this news reluctantly. His mother's failure to meet his homecoming train added to his annoyance over her abandonment of the farm after he enlisted in the Marines. She had communicated with him only once during his absence, exaggerating Becky's illness during the 1918 flu pandemic in an effort to get him to return home. While he recognized most mothers would oppose a son going to war, he felt her decision to take a full-time job in town rather than manage the farm represented selfishness on her part.

Still clad in the underwear he had been sleeping in, he limped across the cold living room toward the bathroom to relieve himself, then returned to build a fire in the fireplace. As the pile of crumpled newspapers and kindling crackled to life, he pulled on pants, shirt and shoes and turned his back to the welcoming warmth. He added a couple of logs to the fire and moved to the kitchen where he scrounged around in the empty cabinets until he found a box of leftover cereal and can of stale coffee. He boiled a pot of coffee and ate a few handfuls of the dry cereal while browsing through old issues of the *Morning Republican.*

Later he stepped outside where he found the cold drizzle of the night had turned into a damp, dreary tule fog blanketing the area just above the tree line. Moisture was dripping from the sycamore limbs and eaves of the house. The Overland motorcar was gone, and the only sign of life from the bunkhouse was a thin trail of gray smoke bumping up against the fog. He scanned the exterior of the farmhouse, the yellowed board siding and loose battens, the cold, silvery limbs of the purple sage around the foundation. He returned despondently to the warmth of the interior.

It was almost noontime when he heard a vehicle pull into the yard. He went to the door and watched a woman climb out of a Red Cross Ford and approach the house. Dressed in a full-length motoring coat, hat, gloves and patent leather boots, she didn't look like the mother he had left in December 1917, garbed in an old housedress and sobbing over his imminent departure.

He opened the door and spoke, "Er, hi, Mother."

She responded ebulliently, "Welcome home, Thomas!" and reached out her hand so he could help her up the stoop. She threw her arms around his neck, kissed him on the cheek and, much to his annoyance, ran her fingers through his hair, "Oh, heavens, it's good to have you home again!"

He grinned tolerantly.

"But you look like you lost weight."

"Yeah, but I'm getting back to normal." He pulled away from her embrace.

While she peered around the room as if to refresh her memory, he glanced at her uncertainly, taken aback by how young she looked, so stylish in her motoring outfit, seemingly changed from the overly dependant mother he once knew. He asked if he could take her coat and hat.

She nodded, peeled off her gloves, unbuttoned the coat, removed the pins from her hat and handed it all to him. Without her coat, Thomas observed, the hem of her white linen shirtwaist dress, like Becky's the night before, was some six inches from the floor. She plumped up her hair and turned toward the door, commenting, "That sounds like Becky now."

Thomas, relieved to get away from a mother he hardly recognized, carried her coat and hat to the bedroom, then went to the door to greet Becky. With a potholder in each hand and dressed in a blouse, wool skirt and pale blue sweater that complemented her hair and skin coloring, she was carrying a roasting pan. She called out, "Morning, Thomas. The pie's in the back of the car along with milk and eggs and other stuff and a block of ice. Can you bring those in for me?"

"Sure. Where's your little guy?"

"Oh, I left him with a neighbor lady so we could relax."

He grabbed the tongs hanging on the wall, limped out to the Maxwell, staggered back to the house with the twenty-five-pound block, and slipped it into the icebox. Then he returned for the other items and the pie, still warm from the oven.

Emma had started the roast at her apartment, so all Becky had to do now was add the potatoes, carrots and onions and slip it into the oven to finish cooking. Thomas rummaged in a drawer for eating utensils to set the table, poured glasses of water and took a seat at the table. He turned to his mother, who was sitting on the sofa, and asked, "Whatever happened to that bank job you started just before I left?" he asked.

Emma replied, "Oh, I quit that after a couple weeks. I didn't really like that kind of work."

Becky spoke, "Don't forget, the Red Cross was begging you to return."

"Yes, they offered me a salary and motor car to take charge of their new Home Services division."

"So, how is everything at the Red Cross?"

"Pretty good. We've been quite busy with all the troop trains returning home."

"Mother's responsible for over thirty volunteers now," Becky said from the sink, where she was cutting up lettuce for a salad.

"What do they do?" he asked.

Emma sighed. "Well, we're responsible for helping families whose menfolk are overseas, like when they don't hear from a son, father or husband, or their allotment checks haven't arrived, or maybe they run into some legal problem, that sort of thing."

"But, you've been serving hospital trains lately," Becky added.

Emma shifted uncomfortably. "Yes, that part has been more difficult, especially when they're carrying so many sick and wounded, or...or the dying." Her voice turned sorrowful. "The train yesterday evening was especially bad, with over one hundred fifty wounded on their way to the military hospital in San Francisco. We had to transfer several flu cases to the Barnett Sanitarium and two dead bodies to the morgue."

Thomas was puzzled. "The Red Cross is responsible for that?"

Emma shook her head, "Oh, yes. That's part of our job."

Becky placed the bowl of salad on the table and glanced toward her mother, "I understand Major Brown was there to help?"

"Yes, thank goodness."

"Who the heck is Major Brown?" Thomas asked.

Emma replied, "He's the new Western division chairman for the Red Cross. He's a wounded veteran just like---" She stopped when she noticed her son staring at her.

They fell silent for a few minutes, watching patiently as Becky removed the roast from the oven, arranged it and the vegetables on a platter and placed it on the kitchen table. They pulled up chairs and waited while Becky served, then dug in eagerly. After a few minutes of eating and idle conversation, Emma retrieved her purse from the sofa and handed Thomas his bank deposit book. He opened it to see a balance of over seven thousand dollars.

"Good grief! Where did all this come from?"

"That's your share from the 1917 and 1918 raisin crops. Didn't we agree to split it three ways while you were in the service?"

He nodded vaguely, still dumbfounded over the large total.

Becky said, "We had record crops and received high wartime prices of almost two hundred dollars a ton while you were gone."

Emma added, "Of course, expenses went up too." She turned to her daughter, "What did you have to pay for pickers, and pruning, and fertilizer and all that other stuff?"

"About sixty dollars a ton," Becky replied as she passed the gravy.

Emma reached across the table and pointed to an entry in the booklet. "That two thousand dollars is your share of the second payment on the 1918 crop, which came in last week. The final payment is due this summer."

His sister continued, "We bought Liberty Bonds and paid our Income Tax, but the rest is in your First National account drawing five percent interest."

He glanced at his sister, "Income Tax?"

"Don't you remember? Congress increased that two years ago to help pay for the war."

He shook his head in annoyance and stuck his fork into a piece of roast. Chewing solemnly, he pointed to the deposit booklet, "Well, with this kind of money, it seems like someone shoulda been taking better care of the farm."

Becky and Emma, taken aback at the remark and caustic tone of his voice, glanced at each other. "What do you mean?" Becky asked defensively.

He waved his hand around, "The inside is a mess, covered with dust and cobwebs. Mother's bric-a-brac is all tumbled around…icebox water stains on the floor." He paused to catch his breath, "And that Morris easy chair I used to like to relax in. You said you moved it out to the bunkhouse and replaced it with Father's old rocker. Seems like if you were gonna do that you could have at least fixed the missing spindle."

Becky glared at him and replied sarcastically, " I'm sorry, dear brother. As I told you, I moved into town and took a job and just didn't have time---"

He interrupted, raising his voice, "Why'd you do that anyway? With all this money, you surely didn't need a job...you...you coulda stayed out here and taken care of things!"

Becky's eyes flashed in defiance and she put down her fork, "It just got too darned lonely, Thomas. I couldn't stand not having anyone to talk to, and sometimes at night I got, well I got scared." She started to mention the rainy night arrival of the one-legged Negro soldier begging for food, but Thomas cut her off---

"And the outside looks terrible too. Dead sycamore leaves blowing all around, the vegetable garden neglected and full of weeds, and...and...the house needs paint real bad."

Becky shook her head in frustration, "I raked and burned a bunch of leaves in November before I moved to town, but you know how the darn things just keep falling."

During the argument, Emma had stayed quiet with her head down, but now she looked at Thomas, "Well, maybe if you had stayed home and hadn't gone off to war, you could have---"

"Mother!" Becky stared at her Mother and shook her head in disbelief. Thomas glowered at her, too dumb-struck to respond.

Emma kept boring in, "Well, I'm just telling the truth. You could have had a farm exemption and... and raised food for the soldiers...and...and taken care of things here."

Thomas just shook his head in frustration. He remembered from prior experience that when his

Mother got her head set in a certain direction, it was pointless to argue. He resumed chewing silently while Emma pressed on, "And the house never was painted, Thomas. When Father finished building it, he just ran out of money. Besides, he didn't see much value in paint."

He sighed before finally replying, "With all that money in the bank, it looks like we should do something to spruce the place up."

Becky smiled and reached across the table to pat his arm. "I agree, you should do whatever you want, don't you think, Mother?"

Emma nodded.

Thomas, now feeling embarrassed over his outburst, fell silent.

Emma stuck her fork into a potato then paused, "Don't forget, you have to live on that money for a year and pay for this year's water and fertilizer and pruning…and…and next fall's harvesting."

He ignored his mother's reminder, and they continued eating pensively. After a few minutes, Emma started asking questions for which her son as yet didn't have answers. "Are you happy to be home?" she asked as he ladled more gravy on a second helping of meat and potatoes.

He shrugged, "Guess so. At least I'm glad to be out of the war."

"That's what all the boys on the hospital trains say. They're sure glad to be returning to their loved ones."

He continued chewing silently.

"Are you anxious to get to work on the farm?"

He replied glumly, "Not sure I could handle it with my leg."

Emma reached for her water and took a swallow. "Maybe you'd prefer to try something different like manufacturing artificial limbs, or moving picture operation, or…or making jewelry."

He glanced blankly at his mother, "What the heck are you talking about?"

"Those are some of the new trades the Red Cross Cripple Institute has identified for returning doughboys. They'll be training them free of charge."

Becky squirmed in her chair. She could tell by the way her brother started stabbing into his meat and potatoes that he again was becoming annoyed. She tried to dissuade Emma from further questions by complimenting her dinner.

But their mother just smiled and pressed on with Thomas. "Maybe you would like to join one of our Cripple Parties. The Red Cross is organizing them all over the country."

He bristled, "What the hell's that?"

She looked momentarily confused at the sharp response, but persisted, "They're groups of wounded veterans who get together to cheer each other up and talk about their successful return to civilian life. We have the nicest bunch of young men. One carries a jar of paste so he can mold himself a new ear when he needs it. Oh, and one of the farm boys has an artificial leg with an extra large wooden foot so he can walk on plowed ground."

He responded sarcastically, "My, that sounds like fun."

His mother looked a little hurt and puzzled, but continued wistfully, "Maybe you could bring your banjo and play for the others. One used to play in a band... you probably knew him." She paused and sighed, "But he lost his arm, so he can't play anymore."

Thomas jumped up from the table so violently he sent his chair crashing back to the floor. "Jesus Christ, Mother! What are you talking about? You think I'm some...some pathetic cripple...or...or an invalid? Leave me alone, for Christ's sake!" He threw his napkin on the table, stalked into the bedroom and slammed the door.

Emma glanced at her daughter in shock and confusion. Becky just shook her head in disbelief, "Mother, I was hoping you might be more understanding. Can't you see he's going through a difficult time?"

Emma started pouting, "I was just trying to help. I didn't mean to---"

Becky interrupted, "I know you meant well, but maybe it would be best if we just left him alone. He'll let us know if he wants help." She reached to pat her mother's arm.

Becky rose to clear the table and wash the dishes while her mother retreated to the rocker and one of her *Ladies' Home Journal* magazines. They returned to town later that evening, each silently lost in her personal thoughts, and the rhubarb pie remained in its bakery box uneaten.

CHAPTER 3

Thomas felt pretty depressed after his mother's visit and remained cooped up in the house for several days. Deterred in part by the omnipresent February fog and cold weather, he found it preferable to indulge his still painful leg in front of the roaring fireplace or listlessly scan a book or one of his mother's old magazines prior to dozing off.

It was early March before he decided to brave the weather and venture outside to work on the Maxwell. He had bought the car in the fall of 1917 when his mother was out of town, using part of their prior year's crop payment and reluctantly trading in his Ford Torpedo roadster. He also used some of the money for a down payment on an abandoned forty-acre vineyard located along the south side of the farm road.

Recognizing that the vehicle had been neglected during his absence, he started with the engine. He adjusted the tappets, cleaned the high-tension magneto, re-gapped the spark plugs, tightened the fan belt and changed the oil. He rummaged around in the storage shed for his old grease gun and lubricated all the fittings, paying special attention to a squeaky rear spring shackle. He brushed the bird droppings and other dirt from the mohair top, wiped the leather upholstery, and washed and polished the black body.

Near the end of his morning's work, he was interrupted by the 'putt-putt-putt' sound of the *Trak-Pull* returning from the vineyard. He looked up to see PJ driving the little field tractor and pulling a small, two-wheel wooden cart carrying the mysterious Negro man Thomas previously had observed from the house. He vaguely recalled Becky's description of how he had stumbled up to the door one rainy night begging for food, and subsequently became PJ's helper.

"Morning, Boss," PJ called out as he pulled up beside the Maxwell and cut the motor.

"Hi, PJ."

"Good to see you out and about. Been wonderin' how you're fairin.'"

He didn't reply, but peered suspiciously at the black man, dressed in a loose-fitting Army uniform and battered campaign hat tipped part way up on his forehead. He recognized the red and gold braid of the French *Croix de Guerre* draped through the left epaulet of his shirt and the American Victory and Good Conduct ribbons on his left chest.

This was the first time Thomas had seen him up close, and his stomach muscles tightened as he quickly scanned the gaunt stranger sitting in the cart with his right leg dangling over the side. His left pant leg was pinned up above the knee, and a pair of Army-issue crutches lay beside him in the cart. There was something about the broad forehead, the thick lips and wide nose, the brown, wooly hair visible around the edges of his hat, the bushy brows shading dark bottomless eyes that were trying to trigger his memory when PJ interrupted---

"This here's Erasmus Jones, my new hand."

The old Negro nodded and shifted his weight.

Thomas asked, "Where's he from?"

PJ related the story of how Erasmus had appeared at the farm begging for food and how he was letting him stay in the bunkhouse in exchange for the odd jobs he could handle with only one good leg.

Thomas repeated his question.

"He says Virginnie." PJ turned and grinned at the old man, who returned the grin.

An awkward silence was broken in a few moments by PJ. "I was wonderin' if you want to have a look around the old place."

Thomas didn't respond.

"We could carry you in the cart if your leg's troublin' you."

He felt annoyed and insulted that his hired help was proposing to haul him around like some invalid. He hadn't realized PJ even knew about his wound and felt patronized that he was worrying about it. Before he could speak, the farm manager pressed on, "We've got most of the vines caned and pruned, and Erasmus is gonna clean up Miss Becky's vegetable garden next week and git it ready for spring plantin.'"

Thomas opened his mouth to reply, but PJ interrupted, "We've still got a couple piles of trimmin's to burn, if you feel like helpin' with that."

Thomas bristled, "Christ, PJ. I just got home, give me a break!"

PJ, seldom at a loss for words, hesitated. Finally, he responded with a shrug, "OK, sorry, Boss." Surprised by the outburst, he started the tractor and putt-putted away to the bunkhouse. Thomas, embarrassed and chagrined at his response, threw his washing cloth in the water bucket and limped into the house.

That night, in the first recurrence of the nightmares that had bothered him in the Paris hospital and on the homeward-bound hospital ship, he had frightening visions of the German soldier he had bayoneted to death on the final day of the war. Thomas could still vividly see him charging toward him ghost-like through the battlefield mist and the feeble thrust of his bayonet. His own desperate parry, the crunching of his bayonet as it tore through viscera and bone, the dark eyes of the old man pleading in disbelief and the moan of death as he fell to his knees swirled in and out of his subconscious like a windblown fog.   He yelled out at the stab of pain when the enemy bullet tore through his right leg.

He awoke wide-eyed, bathed in sweat, grasping at his throbbing ankle, feeling the warm, sticky pus oozing through the bandage.   He sat up on the edge of the bed, struggling to catch his breath, waiting for his heart to stop racing.   He rose and limped to the bathroom, peeled off the sticky bandage, rinsed his leg off under the spigot of the tub, and gently dried the wound.

After wrapping his leg with a clean bandage, he returned to the living room, poked the reluctant embers in the fireplace back to life and added a log. He hobbled over to the rear door and peered through the window into the stillness of the night, then moved to the stove and poured a cup of stale coffee, sat down at the kitchen table, rolled a cigarette and lit it.   He tossed the tobacco sack and papers on the table.

With the cigarette dangling from his lips, he stood up and fruitlessly rummaged around in the kitchen cabinets and pantry for whiskey or some other form of alcohol.   Finally, afraid to return to his bed, he flipped his half-finished cigarette into the fireplace, stretched out on the sofa where he could elevate his leg on the arm, and dozed off to the comforting sound of a surging fire.

But that didn't work either.   He soon was wrestling with another recurring nightmare, the one where he was sleeping in an underground bunker that took a direct artillery hit and caved in on him and his buddies. When he awoke with a start, he had rolled off the sofa and was gasping for breath and flailing his arms to push away the imagined dirt.

He lay on the floor in the dark for a few moments, trying to collect his thoughts, straining to bring his mind back to the reality of where he was. A glance toward the kitchen door window, outlined by the pale light of a full moon settling toward the western horizon, told him it must be early morning. Struggling to his feet, he turned on the kitchen light and noted from the wall clock that it was a few minutes past four o'clock. He warmed up the rest of the stale coffee on the stove, poured a cup, smeared some jam on a cold biscuit, and sat down at the kitchen table. He eyed his cigarette makings on the table, but didn't reach for them.

When dawn finally broke through to another cold day, he decided that a hot bath would comfort his weary body. As he struggled to soak away his troubles, he realized his general discomfort stemmed in part from his confusion over the old Negro and embarrassing blowup with PJ. Later that morning, in an effort to make amends, he pulled on his heavy winter coat and cap, and hobbled out to the bunkhouse to find the farm manager in the tiny kitchenette making sandwiches.

"Morning, PJ."

"Oh, howdy, Boss. How'r you feelin'?"

"Pretty good. Whatcha' doing?"

"Fixin' lunch for me and 'Rass.'"

An awkward silence followed during which Thomas peered around the interior that brought back many unwelcome memories. His eyes fell longingly on the tattered upholstery of the old Morris easy chair and saw the twin bunks, separated by a partition, that once were occupied by him and his brother Patrick. Off to one side, he admired the toilet and shower he had installed before going to war, when he also added the kitchenette, an electric floor heater and small icebox. The faint odor of damp straw and stale manure wafted in from the adjoining shed, where his parents once kept a horse and cow.

"Sorry about blowing my stack yesterday," he said.

"No problem," PJ replied as he smeared butter on four slices of bread.

"Afraid this damned leg just got the best of me."

"Yessir. Reckon you've been through a lot."

Thomas paused, then changed the subject. "Guess the old Negro's a good helper?"

PJ nodded, "Carries his part, and does what I tell him."

Thomas' eyes fell on a picture of Jesus tacked above the black man's neatly made bunk and a Bible lying on top, "Looks like he's pretty religious."

PJ turned to remove a chunk of baloney from the icebox. "Yeah, I reckon. Prays ever' mornin' and evenin' and hums them hymns when he's workin'. Says it gives him a feelin' of freedom." He chuckled as he sliced off some meat and placed it on the bread.

"When he gits goin' with one of them catchy tunes and choppin' weeds he's pretty hard to keep up with."

"What are you paying him?"

"Just grub and bed.   He ain't asked for nothin' more."

"Gosh, that doesn't sound fair.   How much should we pay him…a dollar a day enough?"

PJ finished the sandwiches and reached into the icebox to pull out a couple of *Nehis* as he replied, "That might make him kinda upitty.   Where I come from black folks never git mor'n two bits."

"How's fifty cents sound?"

The farm manager shrugged. "Sounds fair."

"When did he start?"

PJ thought for a moment.   "Reckon it was November, 'bout the time the war stopped."

"OK.   We'll count from the first of November, and I'll get the money soon as I can go to the bank. How about you, what are we paying you now?"

He shrugged, "Well, it was two dollars.   But hain't been nothin' since December when Miss Becky moved to town."

"Oh, Jesus, that isn't right!   How about if I raise you to two-fifty, and I'll pay you and your helper through the end of March.   That sound OK?"

PJ grinned. "Yessir.   That sounds mighty good."

"How's Pedro been doing…still taking care of the West Forty?"

"Yessir, got her fixed up right nice."

"He been getting paid?"

"Don't reckon."

Thomas shook his head, "I'll talk to him this afternoon to make sure we get him caught up."

They shook hands and stepped out of the bunkhouse. As Thomas headed toward the house, he hesitated, "Oh, and thanks for raking up the yard and all the sycamore leaves."

"Rass' done that. He's pretty reverent toward that tree…says it's written up in the Bible."

"That a fact?"

"Yeah, seems like some sinner couldn't see Jesus in a crowd so he climbed up in a sycamore for a better look. Jesus told him to git down then bunked at his house that night…somethin' like that."

Thomas chuckled, "When I was a youngster, I used to climb in it to hide from my Father when he was ranting after me. But he always found me and made me come down for my whipping. Jesus or nobody else ever came to my rescue."

PJ smiled at the childhood reference, then added, "Rass' also likes to mix them leaves with that old cow shit. Says it's good for the vegetable garden."

Thomas grinned. "Yeah, guess it makes 'em taste better." He turned to leave and PJ climbed on the *Trak Pull* and headed for the vineyard clutching two sandwiches and two *Nehis*.

CHAPTER 4

Over the next few nights, Thomas' nightmares continued and he finally concluded they were sending him a message; he had to do something to put the war behind him and move on with his life. His first worry was the obligation he felt to meet with Earl Fenton's parents to try to ease the pain of their son's death. He and Earl had been friends before the war and had joined the Marines together.

Then, he was going to have to find a job, something he could manage with his wounded leg. He wasn't interested in returning to farm work, and didn't feel he could handle the hard labor anyway. His initial thought was to rejoin the First National Bank where he worked before the war, but wasn't certain they might still have an opening for him.

He finally was stimulated into action one morning when he was awakened by beams of bright sunlight poking around the window shade directly into his eyes.

After a bath and quick breakfast of *Kellogg's* corn flakes and dressing in his Marine uniform, he limped out to the Maxwell. As he motored through the warm morning, he tried to think ahead to how he would handle the meeting with Earl's family. The facts were that his friend, contrary to his bravado and sometimes bullying personality, had not behaved bravely during his first exposure to combat. He had refused to go over the top and remained cowering in the trench, only to be ignobly suffocated when the parapet was caved in by enemy artillery. How could Thomas possibly relate this bitter reality to his bereaved family?

He had met Earl's father once briefly before the war and remembered he owned a lumber yard and paint store and was involved in some new housing development north of town. He found the Fenton house, a palatial two-story structure, at the northern extension of Van Ness Boulevard, out past the Normal School. He parked at the curb, grabbed his cane, climbed out of the car, and started walking up the half-circle driveway past a Ford flatbed truck and Overland touring sedan parked under the *porte-cochere*.

He was met by a young man who came out to greet him. He apparently was the younger brother, whose wide-set eyes, broad forehead and black hair combed straight back made him look much like Earl. The main difference was that this one, whom Thomas guessed to be two or three years younger than he was, wore steel-rimmed glasses.

"Hi," he called out, "I'm Ernie. You must be Thomas O'Roark."

"That's right," Thomas responded as he limped forward smiling, leaning on the cane in his right hand, and thrust his left hand forward in greeting.

"We didn't know you were home yet."

"Yeah, got back a couple weeks ago."

The father stepped out on the porch, and Thomas could see the shadow of a woman behind the screen door. "Howdy, son," the older man called out amiably, "come on in."

He climbed the porch steps to a hearty handshake and backslapping, and was escorted into the spacious living room. He was directed toward a Queen Anne chair where he sat down, hooked his cane over one arm and removed his campaign hat. Mister Fenton, dressed in white carpenter's coveralls, was a heavyset man with thinning gray hair and a large round belly. He had dark bottomless eyes shaded by heavy eyebrows and a pair of malformed upper canine teeth that made Thomas uncomfortable when he smiled. He eased himself into one corner of the sofa, and the son sat next to him.

The woman, who neither the father nor son bothered to introduce, also was on the plump side and was wearing a pale blue cotton housedress partially covered by a flowered apron. Her weary smile reflected an inner grief as she asked Thomas if he would like something to drink, coffee or tea perhaps?

The father interrupted, "Naw, he's been killin' Krauts, he needs somethin' stronger. How about some of my good brandy, nice sippin' stuff?"

Thomas demurred, "Guess I better pass on that. Maybe something cold?"

"We've got lemonade," the son piped up, and headed for the kitchen without waiting for an answer.

"Sure you won't join me in a little brandy?" the father repeated.

Thomas shook his head and Mister Fenton struggled up ponderously from the sofa and left the room. He returned in a few moments with a snifter of brandy, and Ernie brought in two glasses of iced lemonade and handed one to Thomas.

The father lifted his glass toward Thomas in a toast, "Here's to the great job you boys did beatin' up them Heinies."

Ernie raised his glass and added, "Yeah, wished I coulda joined you but they wouldn't take me with my eyes." He pushed his glasses back up on the bridge of his nose.

Mister Fenton continued, "We did a pretty good job takin' care of a bunch of them hyphenates around here, too. Put some of 'em in jail and sent a few back to Germany. Now we need to take care of all the damn Commies in this country so we can get back to normal."

Ernie added, "We hassled the Catholics and Jews, too. Makes me mad the way they get those extra school holidays."

"Niggers are the worst," Mister Fenton growled. "They're lazy and can't be trusted, and they steal from white folks."

Embarrassed and taken aback by the intense language, Thomas shifted uncomfortably while the son added, "Shoulda strung up that Seattle gang a couple weeks ago, too."

The father, responding to Thomas' perplexed look, added, "Maybe you weren't home yet, so you didn't hear about the big Seattle strike?"

He replied vaguely, "Guess I saw the headlines in the <u>Republican</u>, but it didn't mean much to me." He took a swallow of lemonade.

The son explained, "Bunch of Bolsheviks and 'Wobblies' in the shipyards struck against reduced wages. The mayor finally called in troops and busted up their little party."

Thomas cringed inwardly as the reference to the Industrial Workers of the World brought back painful memories of his older brother and several of his IWW friends being killed by the Tacoma sheriff in the early days of the war.

They sat awkwardly avoiding each other's eyes until the mother, who had remained standing in the kitchen doorway, asked plaintively, "You were with our Earl when he died?"

Thomas was surprised by her directness. He had thought about this moment for several days, trying to anticipate what their questions might be and how he would answer, but now he stumbled as a ghostly vision of Earl cowering in the trench flashed before his eyes. "Uh, well, we were in different parts of the battle, Missus Fenton. I didn't actually see him get hit."

"Did he suffer much?"

"No. I believe it was rather sudden. I doubt if he suffered." Thomas struggled to swallow more lemonade against his tightening throat and bit his lower lip as he wondered what it was like for Earl to suffocate under the dirt of the collapsed trench.

Ernie interrupted his thoughts. "Did he kill lots of Germans?"

"We all did, Ernie. They were attacking across a wheat field in front of our trench and we shot lots of them."

"Did you see what they did with his body?" Missus Fenton asked.

The question scratched a particularly painful part of Thomas' memory as he recalled burying dozens of bodies and body parts after that first bloody battle at *Belleau Wood*. "Well, Ma'am, we buried quite a few in temporary graves after that first day."

"They haven't sent him home yet," she said wistfully, looking down at the floor. She pulled a hanky from her apron and dabbed at her eyes.

Thomas squirmed uncomfortably, not knowing what to say or do to ease her pain, wishing he could get away. He looked at the father, hoping for support, but all he did was stare back unnervingly and continue sipping his brandy. When his wife broke into quiet sobs, he left the room and returned with a refilled glass.

Ernie spoke, "Can I see your wound?"

"Earnest!" his mother admonished, wiping her tears with her hanky.

Thomas, at first startled by the request, replied, "I'd rather not unwrap the leg, but here, I'll show you my shoulder." While he unbuttoned his collar and loosened the top of his tunic to expose the jagged scar across his left shoulder, Ernie moved closer and pointed to his sleeve. "What are these?"

"Those are my wound chevrons."

The younger man reached down and touched the varicolored ribbon bars on the left breast of the tunic. "What are these for?"

Thomas pointed to each. "This is the Victory Medal, this is my Marksman Badge and this red one with the narrow blue stripe down the middle is for Good Conduct."

"What's this one?" Ernie asked, touching the red, white and blue bar.

"That's the Second Division medal. The Marines served with the Army's Second Division in France."

"Will we get my brother's medals?" he asked.

Missus Fenton spoke up, "Earnest, stop bothering Mister O'Roark."

Thomas ignored her as he replied, "I don't know. I would think the Government would send them to you sometime." They all watched silently as he downed the rest of his lemonade and reached for his cane as if to leave.

Suddenly, the father, his heavy eyebrows beetling over his bottomless eyes, peered suspiciously across his brandy glass, asking, "How come Earl was in the trench by himself? Didn't others get hit by the same shell?"

Caught off guard, Thomas stammered, "Well… er…as I recall, Mister Fenton, others were hit by the shrapnel. But…but I guess it was just bad luck".

The father stirred uncomfortably, then asked, "Did Earl fight and die like a man, Sergeant?"

As a bead of sweat trickled down his back, Thomas hesitated, trying to frame a response he could live with. "Yes, Mister Fenton. I believe they all did."

Fenton sighed and seemed anxious to change the subject. "Whatcha planning to do now that you're home?" he asked.

Thomas shook his head, "Don't know for sure. Need to find something I can do with this bad leg."

"I can give you a carpenter job…got lots of houses to build out north. Or maybe you'd rather work behind the counter selling paint and building supplies in my lumber yard."

"I appreciate your offer, Mister Fenton. But don't believe I could handle anything that strenuous." He reached for his cane, donned his hat, struggled to his feet and started to hobble toward the door when Ernie called out, "Wait, I have a present for you." He ran from the room and returned in a moment with a photograph of the 1913 varsity football team at Fresno High School. Tears welled up in Thomas' eyes and his throat tightened as he recognized his old friend Earl standing bravely in the front row.

Impulsively, he reached down and unpinned the ribbon bar of his Second Division medal and handed it to Ernie. "Here, you can keep this until you receive your brother's."

"Oh, boy, thanks!" Ernie took the bar, examined it closely then pinned it to his shirt.

Mister Fenton had disappeared quietly and returned now carrying a paper sack with two bottles of brandy. "Here, you're gonna need this when that damned Prohibition starts. This is some of my best stuff."

Missus Fenton showed up with another paper bag. "These were Earl's favorite cookies. I just baked them this morning." She reached up and kissed him on the cheek.

Thanking them profusely and fighting back tears, Thomas cradled the two sacks under his left arm, gripped his cane in his right hand, eased himself out the door and down the porch steps, and returned to his car. The Fentons were still waving as he headed toward town, barely able to see through his misty eyes.

In town, he ran into a bustling crowd of Saturday morning shoppers, drawn out in part by the first sunny, fog-free day they had seen in weeks. He parked the Maxwell and headed for the bank, bumping along against the throngs seemingly unmindful of his uniform or his cane.

When he reached the bank's familiar exterior of glass and beige-colored tapestry brick, he paused to look around, then stepped inside. The interior was unchanged from his days of working there. The counters and desks of solid oak backed by oak paneling on the walls and around the wickets all bespoke security. The marble floors added to the sense of solidity, and the steam radiators welcomed him with their timpanic clanking and popping.

He scanned across the central open area toward the employees he could see. None of them seemed to notice him and he didn't recognize a single one, including the partially bald man sitting at his old desk. He had a sudden urge to leave, but then recognized Mary Wilson, the president's secretary, waving to him. She was still guarding the boss's corner office and keeping her matronly eye on everyone moving in and out of the facility.

She started moving toward him and as they drew close, he thought for a moment she would forget her innate reserve and throw her arms around him. But she paused at the last step and offered a demure handshake and a cautious smile, "My heavens, Thomas...we...we were so worried about you!"

He grinned and tried to sound nonchalant, "Worried? It was nothing but a little old war."

"But the paper listed you as severely wounded!"

"I took a pretty good hit all right, but it's getting better."

He looked up to see Emmett Johnson stepping out of his office and calling his name. He hobbled over and extended his left hand, which his former boss grasped enthusiastically in both of his. "My God, it's good to see you!"

"Thank you, sir. It's good to be home." Thomas averted his eyes for a moment, trying to mask his surprise at how much weight the older man had gained. His face was jowly and he looked like he was carrying over two hundred pounds on his five foot, six inch frame. He was wearing an expensive-looking silk suit that, along with the unbuttoned vest and stiff shirt collar, appeared a size too small.

Johnson turned and escorted Thomas into his office, held a chair for him and squeezed into another one beside him. "How's the leg?" he asked.

"It's coming along. Still hurts and drains sometimes, but it seems to be improving." He laid the cane across his lap.

"Guess it was pretty bad over there, huh?"

"Wasn't much fun."

"You young fellows did a hell of a job taking care of those damn Germans. We're sure proud of you."

Thomas smiled tolerantly and, anxious to get away from the subject of the war, asked, "How'd the town get along?"

"Pretty good. We over-subscribed the Liberty Bond campaigns, tried to do our part saving tin foil and conserving food, even put a few radicals and German sympathizers in jail."

"And the bank?"

"About the same, couple of new employees been added. We lost old McIntire about six months ago. Had a heart attack."

"Sorry to hear that."

"We replaced him with a fellow named Ray Benson."

Thomas shifted in his chair. "Well, that's what I came to talk to you about, Mister Johnson, is a job. I need to find some kind of work."

The bank president looked puzzled, "Er, how about the farm?"

"Don't think I can handle that heavy work any more with my leg."

"I see. Any thoughts on what you'd like to do?"

"How about here, got any openings?"

Johnson squirmed a little and looked even more uncomfortable in his corpulence. "Afraid not right now, Thomas. We've got all the people we need. And we're having a rough time trying to compete with that new Bank of Italy."

"How's that?"

"Had to lower our loan rates down to seven percent to match them, really cutting into our profits."

"I see they've moved into their new building."

Johnson sighed, "Yeah, in January. One good thing is that with over eighty-five million in deposits in their statewide system they have the money to make those big packing house loans in the fall. Remember how we used to struggle to find enough funds?"

Thomas nodded. "So, you know of any other work around town?"

"Looks like things are pretty tight." As if to demonstrate his point, the banker ran his finger around the inside of his collar and added, "As you've probably heard, the Red Cross is appealing to the community to find four thousand jobs for returning doughboys."

Thomas suddenly felt very depressed. He wasn't sure what he really expected to gain by visiting the bank. After all, he had left there almost two years earlier to take over the farm after his father died, so he really couldn't expect them to have held a position for him. At the same time, Johnson was one of the city's business leaders. You would think he would have a few suggestions for where he might at least look for work. Thomas was starting to recognize what his buddies had cynically alerted him to even before he left France; back home he would be just another veteran whose sacrifice soon would be forgotten.

When their meeting concluded, Thomas stepped up to one of the tellers and drew six hundred dollars from his account. That would be enough to cover back pay for PJ, Erasmus and Pedro, and give himself a little pocket money. He then departed the bank and, realizing it now was almost one o'clock, headed toward the Oyster Grotto and Chop House for lunch.

As he entered the restaurant, the sight of the familiar red leather banquettes brought a wave of nostalgia. Before the war, it had been one of Jack Lewis' preferred eating places and the scene of much envy on the part of Thomas as the older friend boasted about his latest female conquests over platters of oysters, shipped in fresh daily by rail from San Francisco.

Thomas had hardly taken a seat and placed his order for a beer and ham sandwich when someone stepped up beside his table. He looked up to find the bald-headed man from the bank, who smiled and stuck out his hand. "Hi, I'm Ray Benson from the First National."

Thomas returned the handshake.

"Mind if I join you?"

Thomas motioned to the seat across from him and Benson eased his big frame down and opened with the obvious, "Back from the war, I see."

"Yep."

"How'd you get in the Marines?"

"Signed up."

"I tried to enlist, but they turned down my flat feet."

Thomas didn't comment. He guessed Benson to be about his own height and in his late thirties, although the baldness made him appear older. He carried himself like a man in reasonable physical shape, except for the apparent softness in the belly. He speculated that, like the bank president, Benson hadn't missed too many meals during the war.

The waiter delivered his beer and Benson ordered a beer and sandwich before continuing. "You guys sure did a good job taking care of those Heinies."

Thomas nodded vaguely as he unbuttoned the collar of his tunic and took a couple swallows of beer.

"Now we gotta get rid of our other enemies and we'll have a lot better country."

Thomas squirmed uncomfortably and against his better judgement asked, "Who you talking about?"

"Commies, Jews, Romans, all the goddamn foreigners."

Thomas was perplexed. He had heard of communists and Jews and was familiar with the on-going resentment against all immigrants moving into the United States. "But who are the Romans?" he asked.

"Oh, you know, the Catholics." Benson leaned forward, elbows on the table, arms across his chest, and lowered his voice. "In case you haven't heard, the Pope's planning to move his headquarters to Cleveland so they can take over our whole country."

Thomas sat back in the booth, struggling to control the urge to laugh. "No shit! All the way from Rome?" He ordered another beer when the waiter brought their sandwiches.

Benson ignored Thomas' response as he took a swig of beer, but as soon as the waiter departed he continued, "We got that information straight from our Imperial Wizard."

Thomas chuckled, thinking his unwelcome companion was initiating some kind of joke. But then he noted the serious facial expression and became annoyed. He was being confronted by a nut case. He took a long drink of beer and bite of sandwich before mumbling testily, "Who the hell's that?"

Benson peered around the room and again lowered his voice, "You haven't heard of the Ku Klux Klan and the Imperial Wizard in Atlanta?"

"Yeah, I tangled with some of those goons the night I returned from the war. Wasn't much impressed. Who the heck are they anyway?" He finished his second bottle of beer and motioned to the waiter to bring another.

"We're a good Protestant organization that believes in one hundred percent Americanism; no niggers, no foreigners, no Catholics, no liquor, no---."

Thomas interrupted and pointed at Benson's beer bottle. "How come you're drinking that?"

Benson glanced over his shoulder to see if anyone was looking, "Well, a little three-point-two once in awhile don't hurt."

Thomas finished his sandwich and motioned to the waiter to bring his check as he tipped the third bottle of beer to his lips. It was the most alcohol he had consumed in a long time, but he was feeling defiant. "So what's all this got to do with me?"

"You oughta join. We're getting real big in California."

"How big?"

"The exact numbers are secret. But a lot of important people are members. Mister Johnson is the Exalted Cyclops for our Fresno Klavern, and I'm a Kleagel, and the sheriff and police chief---"

Thomas interrupted again, "Emmett Johnson, the bank president?"

"Yes, and several of our Protestant ministers are members."

Thomas shook his head in disbelief. "So what's a Kleagel?"

"I sell memberships. It's only ten bucks."

"Man, that's a lot of money. I sure don't have that much to spend on some crazy organization."

Benson frowned, "Well, part of it goes to the Imperial Wizard."

Thomas slugged down the last of his beer, trying to soothe the agitation he felt building up.

His companion did the same before suggesting, "You should join and come to our big meeting next week. We've got the Odd Fellows Hall reserved."

Thomas had had enough. He burped noisily, rose woozily from the table, paid for his lunch at the cash register, and headed to his car. He drove home silently, morosely, trying to focus his boozy vision on the road ahead. He wasn't sure why he was feeling so irritated.   Had he expected a bigger welcome home, or maybe that someone would hand him a nice new job? Or was he beginning to realize that after all his fighting for freedom and personal sacrifice, he had come home, not to the relatively comfortable, normal life he longed for, but to more turmoil and prejudice and persecution?

When he pulled into the farm driveway, he peered ahead to see an unfamiliar motor car parked under the sycamore.   Staring more intently, he saw that someone was sitting on the running board, huddled up against the returning afternoon fog. It was Brenda and she was cuddling a blanket-wrapped bundle in her arms.

CHAPTER 5

After Thomas' depressing meeting with Earl's parents, his tentative and fruitless search for a job and the annoying confrontation with Ray Benson, the sight of Brenda waiting for him was almost too much. He recognized they would have to meet sometime, but had hoped it would be at a time and place of his choosing. But there she was, sitting patiently with the baby in the cold and semi-dark. "Hi, Thomas," she called out, sounding much too cheery.

"Hi," he responded warily as he stepped out of the Maxwell, picked up the bags of cookies and brandy and moved closer to her.

"How are you feeling?" she asked as she rose from the running board of her father's Chandler touring sedan and cuddled the baby closer. In the waning afternoon light, his tiny white face was barely visible in the folds of the blanket.

"OK, I guess," he replied. Actually, he was feeling quite uncomfortable, and not just from this encounter with Brenda and her baby. His bladder was about to burst from the beer he had been drinking in town. He shifted his weight to ease the pressure and stumbled slightly on the uneven ground, but caught himself with his cane and mumbled, "You wanna come in?"

She smiled, retrieved a canvas bag from inside the car, and followed him toward the house. He opened the door, flipped on the light, set the bags on the kitchen counter and wordlessly hobbled across the floor toward the bathroom. When he came out a few moments later, Brenda was seated at the kitchen table still holding the sleeping baby. Thomas crossed the room, sank into a corner of the sofa and tossed his campaign hat to one side.

After an awkward silence, she asked, "What've you been doing since you got back?"

He sighed, "Not much, I guess."

"I imagine you're glad to be home?"

He nodded and tried not to be too obvious in his efforts to get a better look at her now that they were in a lighted room. She had let her wavy brown hair grow out from the boyish bob he remembered when he had last seen her over a year earlier. It now cascaded down to her shoulders to frame her soft face with the sensuous hazel eyes and full red lips.

"We were sure happy to see you back, safe and sound---" She caught herself and blushed as she forced her uncertain gaze away from his legs.

He turned sideways on the sofa and stretched the wounded leg out on the cushions, leaned back against the arm, unbuttoned the top of his Marine tunic and pulled cigarette makings from an inside pocket.

As he rolled the cigarette paper around his index finger, she interrupted. "What are you doing?"

"Making a smoke."

"You shouldn't do that with the baby in the room."

Reluctantly, he put the makings down on the table as the baby started to stir. Brenda pulled the blanket from his face and rocked him gently in her arms. "Looks like he's ready to eat. You want to hold him while I warm a bottle?"

"Uh, yeah. I guess so."

She stood up and carried the baby to Thomas and placed him in the crook of his arm.

Thomas squirmed uncomfortably and looked down suspiciously at the pale blue eyes staring back at him. He wasn't sure if he saw as much of himself in the eyes, the small shock of wavy blond hair and the squarish forehead as he did of Brenda's German lineage. "What do you call him?" he asked.

"Thomas Eugene."

He looked up at Brenda, "Where'd you get a name like that?"

"Thomas?"

"No, Eugene."

She smiled, "Oh, that's becoming a very popular name for boys. It means 'well born.'"

The baby started to whimper and Thomas rocked him uncertainly as Brenda removed a nursing bottle from her canvas bag, filled it with milk, placed it on the stove in a pan of water, and set it to warming. While waiting, she filled the sink with hot water and soap and started washing the pile of dirty dishes Thomas had neglected over the past couple of days. When the bottle was ready, she brought it to the baby, who grasped it and started sucking noisily. She made no move to take him, and returned to the sink.

Thomas ventured, "How old is he?"

"Six months."

"Where was he born, the hospital?"

"No, no. The hospital was overflowing with flu patients. Papa called an old German midwife, the same one who brought me into the world over twenty years ago."

"He looks like a healthy little tyke."

She turned toward him, smiling, "Like I said, 'well born.'"

"What's that mean?"

"It means he has a healthy mother and father, strong enough to have survived the war."

Thomas sensed the implication of her response, but ignored it. The baby soon finished the bottle and was making gurgling noises, causing Thomas to again stir uncomfortably. "What are you supposed to do now?" he asked.

"Burp him," Brenda replied as she moved to the sofa and showed him how to place the baby over his shoulder and pat his back. The little one obliged with a gurgle of sour-smelling milk down the back of the Marine uniform. She picked him up and retreated to the bedroom to change his diaper and lay him out on the bed for a nap, then returned in a few minutes to finish washing and drying the dishes.

Thomas went to the bathroom for a damp cloth to sponge off his tunic. When he returned, he tossed it on the sofa and turned to her, "Watching him eat made me hungry. You want something?"

"Sure. What do you have?"

"Not much." He opened the door to the pantry and peered inside, then turned and started rummaging around in the icebox. "Well, I've got a can of *Heinz* pork and beans and a chunk of baloney and a bottle of fresh milk. How's that sound?"

"Sounds good. Shall I fry the meat?"

"Sure. I'll take care of the beans." He opened the can and emptied the contents in a saucepan while she cut off a couple slices of baloney and dropped them in a frying pan. He sliced some bread and set the table with silverware, and poured her a glass of milk. Then he moved over to the fireplace and built a roaring fire against the cooling afternoon air. "You care for a drink?" he asked.

"A drink?"

"Yeah. Earl's father gave me some brandy. Afraid I don't have any of your father's good wine."

"Thanks. Guess I'll pass."

He got a glass from the cupboard, chipped in some ice, and pulled the cork from one of the bottles. He took an exploratory whiff of the unfamiliar liquor, poured a couple fingers in the glass, added a little water and took a tentative taste. The sharp tang of the brandy caught in his throat and made his eyes weep, so he diluted it with more water. He returned to the stove to ladle the pork and beans onto two plates. She added the meat and they took seats at the table.

As they ate, he told of his trip to town and uncomfortable meeting with the Fentons and with Emmett Johnson and the poor outlook for finding a job.

"Your friend Earl was killed?"

"Yeah, when an artillery shell blew a trench in on top of him." Morosely recalling the incident, Thomas smeared butter on a slice of bread, cut off a piece of baloney and stuck it in his mouth.

She did the same and they chewed silently for a few moments until she spoke again. "Guess we lost over a hundred of our local boys, plus the wounded."

He spooned up some pork and beans without responding and took a few more sips of his brandy. They continued eating silently, awkwardly until he asked, "What'd you do during the war?"

She didn't answer for a few moments, then replied wistfully, "Not much. I read some, and we kept to ourselves mostly. We stayed away from town. German-Americans weren't welcome, you might remember."

He nodded and swallowed more brandy.

"I couldn't visit with friends in town or go to parties or dances. We were even afraid to go to church after someone smeared yellow paint all over it. And we were always on the lookout for vigilantes after they painted 'hyphenate' on our house one night."

"Why'd they do that?"

She shrugged, "Prejudice, I guess. We tried to do our part, conserved food, bought bonds, saved tin foil and old shoes for Belgian Relief, stuff like that." She added plaintively, "I got pretty lonely, especially when you didn't write."

He replied defensively, "I did write to Becky a couple times before I went overseas. After that it seemed like the Marines kept me pretty busy."

She ignored his response, adding, "I also cooked and kept house for Papa and Emil and helped with the farming as best I could. Mama died in the flu epidemic, you know."

He shook his head. "Guess I didn't know that. How'd your father take it? Seemed like they were pretty close."

She reached for her glass of milk and sighed, "Yes, he took it very hard, especially since we had to bury her in a wooden coffin instead of a nice bronze or copper one."

He glanced at her, puzzled, "How come?"

"War restrictions on metal."

His look turned incongruous as his mind clouded over with ghostly visions of the fellow Marines he had helped bury, some wrapped in the luxury of ponchos or blankets, others in the bare ground with body parts missing, or guts or brains spilling out.

She spread butter on a slice of bread and continued, "I've also been trying to get Papa to learn more English."

He reached for his glass of brandy. "Why's that?"

She sighed, "It doesn't look like German will be a very popular language anymore, especially since the government is trying to ban it. I just believe he could get along better in the world without it."

"So how's he doing?"

"Not so good. He keeps slipping back into German. I think it's part nostalgia...reminds him of Mother and their early days in the old country."

Thomas fell silent as he buttered another slice of bread, took a bite and chewed idly. Then he asked, "How are your brothers?"

"Ivan's home from the Army. He didn't have to go overseas. When he left, Emil had to come home from the university to help Papa with the farm, but he's back there now."

They continued eating quietly until she said, "I also got together with your sister and some of the neighbor ladies to knit and sew for the war effort and talk about babies."

He ignored the reference to babies. "Speaking of neighbors, what ever happened with the Maloney place?"

"We heard some Russkies bought it."

"Russkies?"

"Russian immigrants. Understand they moved up from Los Angeles. Emil says they're probably Bolsheviks."

"Why's he say that?" During his convalescence in France and return home on the hospital ship, Thomas had heard much discussion among fellow soldiers about the Russian revolution and Bolsheviks. But the impact the event might have on his future had not yet registered on his consciousness.

Brenda responded with a shrug. "Not sure, maybe because of the way they're living. Their house is an old boxcar, and we've heard they have four kids."

Thomas finished his supper, pushed the plate away and downed the last of his drink. Then he belched loudly. "Oops, sorry. Bad habit I picked up in the service." She smiled indulgently as he went to the counter to pour himself another brandy. He opened the bag of cookies Missus Fenton had given him, put some on a plate and carried it to the table.

"You say you've been reading…what?"

"Oh, lots of things, like bulletins from the Children's Bureau."

"What's that?"

"A government agency in Washington. They publish information for expectant mothers on how to take care of themselves, like getting plenty of rest, eating vegetables, and drinking water and avoiding alcohol. They sent me another one on how to take care of the baby; give him pure milk, sunshine and fresh air and teach him self-control and discipline."

Thomas munched absently on a cookie.

"But mostly I've been reading about the science of eugenics."

"What's that about?"

"It's a program to improve the human race by controlling who people mate with." She blushed and looked down at the table.

He stared at her blankly. "You mean like...like horses and...and pigs?"

Her eyes flashed in defiance. "No, no. This is just for humans. The idea is that if two healthy people have babies they'll be healthy. But if the feeble-minded or imbeciles have them, their babies will be imbeciles."

Thomas, too nonplussed to react, drank some more of his brandy.

She reached for a cookie then continued, "Other characteristics are hereditary, too. Like height, or color of eyes, or hair."

He shook his head in disbelief, stood up and retreated to the sofa to rest his leg and finish his drink. But Brenda wasn't through. "Did you notice the baby's thick wavy hair?"

He nodded vaguely.

"Where do you suppose he got that?"

Thomas sensed where she was leading him but, not knowing how to respond, he avoided looking at her. He drained the last of his drink and set the glass on the end table.

Her voice softened, "Don't you remember that night we were together out by the river, before you went away?"

He did indeed remember that long blissful night of lovemaking, even to the extent that it now brought a tingling sensation to his loins. He looked across the room at her. "You trying to say I'm the father?"

"Can you deny it when you look at him?"

"But I seem to remember you saying not to worry, you were using something."

She shook her head. "I did, but obviously it didn't work."

He got up and went to the bathroom to relieve himself of used brandy. He also hoped the movement would ease the throbbing in his leg. When he returned, he poked at the waning fire, added a log and plopped down on the sofa. He picked up his makings, rolled a cigarette with deliberation, stroked a match against his pant leg, and lighted up. Ignoring her stare, he inhaled deeply and tried unsuccessfully to wave away the sulfur odor from the match.

"You don't care about the baby?" she asked petulantly.

"He's back in the bedroom, for Pete's sake!" He took another defiant drag and blew the smoke toward the fireplace.

Brenda returned the defiance, "According to eugenicists, smoking reduces a person's sexual power and...and shrivels up your organs!"

The unexpected reference to his manhood stirred up memories of his rendezvous with Lillian Branson in Paris before he returned home and his initial inability to perform. Taken aback and embarrassed by the remark, he angrily flipped the unfinished cigarette into the fireplace and started massaging the throbbing in his leg. He fingered the empty glass on the end table, toying with the idea of getting another drink. But he was not used to the strong liquor and already was feeling light headed and having trouble focusing his eyes.

"Alcohol's not good for your body either."

He glared at her furtively, then turned away as he struggled to control his frustration. Finally, he asked, "So, what do you want to do about the baby?"

"I don't want to raise him alone, Thomas. He needs his father."

"But, my God, Brenda, I don't even have a job. I don't know how I'm gonna support myself, let alone a wife and child!" He reminded her of his disheartening meeting with Emmett Johnson and the indications that jobs were mighty scarce, then added with a wave of his arm, "Hell, we wouldn't even have a place to live. This house belongs to my mother, you know."

She glanced around, "Well, it's a nice little house, but probably could use some paint."

He didn't get a chance to respond as the cry of the baby drew Brenda out of the room. She returned in a few moments with him wrapped snugly in his blanket and commented, "I noticed in the <u>Republican</u> that the Post Office is looking for help. Maybe you---"

He interrupted with a sardonic chuckle, "Good grief, what are you thinking? I couldn't carry a sack of mail a block with this leg!"

"No, no. They're hiring clerks to work inside and giving preference to veterans. They're expanding the Postal Savings department, or something like that. Seems like with your banking experience, you would fit right in."

He sank back into the sofa without replying. Somehow, Brenda's persistence was starting to sound like his mother.

"I understand they're paying a thousand dollars a year."

That number caught his attention. It was almost double what he had been paid at the bank prior to the war. "Where'd you hear that?" he asked, somewhat in disbelief.

"Read it in the paper."

He didn't respond further but turned to stare at the fireplace.

"Well, I have to go now. Papa will be worried about me."

When he escorted her to the door, she stepped closer and kissed him on the cheek. He blushed and patted her and the baby on the back, then said,

"Uh, wait. I have a present for him." He reached to the sofa for his tunic, unpinned the ribbon bar of his Good Conduct medal and handed it to her.

"What is it?"

He chuckled, "My award for being a good soldier."

"What's he supposed to do with it?"

Thomas grinned sheepishly. "Maybe it'll remind him to always be a good boy."

Brenda smiled and stuffed it in her bag. "I'll see you later," she called back as she walked toward the car. Thomas locked the door, returned to throw more wood on the fire, sat down on the sofa and started digging through the pile of old newspapers.

CHAPTER 6

On the last day of April, Thomas awoke to a spectacular spring day. A soft, warm breeze, still damp from an overnight sprinkle, was wafting through the open windows, twisting the curtains into graceful curls. The rays of a bright sun were cutting zigzag patterns across the foot of his bed.

He stretched lazily, then sat up on the edge of the bed, reminding himself he had promised to meet Becky in town to attend the Raisin Day parade. With the Armistice now five months behind them and the influenza pandemic a worry of the past, Fresno's leaders had decided the parade would be a proper celebration to welcome home veterans and kick off the nation's final Victory Loan campaign.

After breakfast, Thomas dressed in his Marine uniform, stepped outside and breathed deeply of the fresh spring air. He called 'good morning' to PJ, whom he had promised to take to the parade, waiting beside the Maxwell. They climbed into the vehicle and started toward town, quietly relishing the beautiful morning, until they passed the O'Roark's forty-acre vineyard. PJ broke the silence, "Just look at them vines tittin' out. Pedro's really been takin' good care of that place."

Thomas glanced at the rows of greening vines stretching back from the roadside to his left, then turned to the horizon ahead. Once-vacant land now was covered with newly planted vineyards and orchards, their thin trunks and scraggly stalks poking hopefully out of the ground.

"Reckon you noticed, lot of raw land's been planted since the war," PJ continued.

"Yeah, but why aren't there more houses?"

"Land's been bought by city slickers think they can live in town and make a killin' with these war-time prices."

"That right?"

"Yeah, I heerd some vineyards been sellin' up to a thousand an acre."

The earlier reference to Pedro had reminded Thomas of PJ's Negro helper. He asked, "How's your new hand working out?"

"Old 'Rass'? Just great. Worked real good last month when I was prunin' vines and burnin' all the trash. Been helping me drive grape stakes."

"What do you call him?"

"I call him 'Rass', short for Erasmus.   We're good buddies."

"He can drive stakes with that leg missing?"

"Yep. Just props hisself up on that crutch of his'n and holds the stake while I climb up on my box and pound her in the ground."

Thomas, recalling that the helper was about a foot taller than PJ, smiled at the incongruity of the scene as he commented, "He sure reminds me of someone. Can't recall who, though.   Where you say he's from?"

"Said he ran away from some hospital in Virginnie 'cause they were fixin' to cut on him. "

"His leg?"

"No, his privates.   Told him they didn't want him makin' kids 'cause he's too stupid."

Thomas squirmed, "You mean castrate him?"

PJ nodded grimly.

Thomas, too mortified to probe further, turned back to watching the road.

The bumping of the Maxwell over the Santa Fe tracks, followed by the confluence of automobiles and horses and buggies bound for the parade, signaled their arrival in town. Thomas slowed down as he continued along Ventura, then turned north on Van Ness toward Court House Park.   The traffic soon became too heavy, so he pulled into a side street and parked.

He stepped out of the car, slipped into his Marine tunic and buttoned it up the front. He donned his campaign hat, grabbed his cane and limped up the street. As he and PJ struggled to make their way through the happy, jostling crowds, he grinned appreciatively as the little man, almost a foot shorter and about half his size across his chest and shoulders, was trying to run interference. He leaned more and more on his cane as well-wishers, acknowledging his uniform, slapped him on the back and reached for his free hand.

When they reached Fulton Street, Thomas stopped and stared ahead. As far he could see, the street was overhung with an archway of red, white and blue banners spelling out WELCOME HOME DOUGHBOYS! Lampposts, standing sentinel-like along the sidewalks, were brightly festooned with matching bunting. His chest swelled involuntarily and his eyes misted when the feeling of patriotism he had lost in the mud and blood of France surged back unexpectedly.

As he moved toward the reviewing stand, he looked across the crowd to see Becky holding her baby and waving for him to come forward. Their mother and an Army officer were next to her. PJ excused himself, advising he would go his own way and meet Thomas at the car after the parade.

Thomas limped ahead, paused to shift his cane to his left hand, and saluted the officer. He returned the salute with a thin smile, reached to awkwardly shake hands, and introduced himself as Major Mark Brown. He was almost as tall as Thomas, but more barrel-chested. His appearance mirrored his name with brown hair and eyes and a thin, brown mustache bristling across his upper lip. He was dressed in an officer's uniform with a Sam Browne belt, gold oak leaves on his shoulders and crossed pistols on his collar, signifying Military Police. Thomas took an instant dislike to him.

He greeted his mother and sister, dutifully patted the sleeping baby and followed Becky's lead toward the grandstand. Emma and the Major departed since they were among those representing the Red Cross in the parade. Becky and Thomas took their assigned seats, and he turned to look around the stands. He soon found the surroundings a gruesome reminder of his hospitalization in France. Some of the doughboys had one or both arms or legs missing, a few had their eyes covered with bandages and were being led to their seats, and several sat slack-jawed staring blankly into space. Others were in wheelchairs, olive-drab blankets covering their missing legs. Another was sitting beside the grandstand on a makeshift board mounted on skate wheels, attempting to sell pencils from a campaign hat upturned in his lap.

The festivities opened at nine-thirty with the firing of a cannon and fly-over of military aeroplanes. The parade, which stretched out for some three miles, featured flag-bearing marching units, high school bands from around the Fresno area, wheeled exhibits representing the town's major merchants, carloads of community and political leaders, a float promoting the current Victory Bond drive and another honoring the allied countries that participated in the war.

When Becky called out excitedly, "Here comes Mother!" Thomas followed her gaze down the street to see the Red Cross van approaching, followed by the horse-drawn ice cream wagon the agency used to welcome home returning troops. The van was being driven by Major Brown with Emma in the passenger seat waving gaily to the crowd. A dozen or so volunteers, dressed in their white uniforms and caps, were walking alongside the glass and wood-framed wagon and passing out ice cream cones to children. When they reached the reviewing stand, they paused and distributed cones to many of the veterans.

An especially painful moment for Thomas came near the end with the arrival of Fresno's own Company C, Sixth Battalion of the California National Guard. The progress of the guardsmen toward the viewing stand generated a wave of cheering as onlookers recognized the remnants of the hometown group, now numbering just half of its pre-war strength of sixty men. Thomas fought back tears and the cramping of his gut as he remembered his friend, Jack Lewis, the first local soldier killed in the war.

But as the soldiers paraded proudly by, the crowd suddenly fell quiet, some murmuring, a few idly clapping, everyone seemingly unable to comprehend the spectacle now passing before them. Some thirty members of the Ku Klux Klan, hidden under their white masks and robes, were marching along, swinging their arms, appearing to mock the guardsmen. Suddenly, one of them turned back and plowed into the Klan, swinging with the butt of his rifle. He was followed by another, then several others as a grand melee erupted in the middle of the street.

Several veterans scrambled from the viewing stand to join the fight and Thomas, oblivious to his sister screaming and trying to hold him back, grabbed his cane and stumbled forward. He lunged into the center of the mob, punching at the robed figures, swearing and swinging wildly with his cane and knocking several to the ground. Someone slugged him on the side of the head, knocking him down, his cane clattering off to one side. He grasped at a white robe hovering over him, and rolled from side to side trying to protect himself from painful kicks to his ribs.

Then his attacker was sprawling on the street, a victim of PJ's pointy-toed boot, and the farm manager was helping Thomas to his feet. He led him away from the fight, ducking past policemen trying to restore order with their whistles and billies, and helped him make his way through throngs of onlookers toward the Maxwell. His leg wound had broken open and the drainage was soaking into his uniform. One sleeve of his tunic was partly torn, his shoulder wound was throbbing, and he had lost his hat.

He finally caught his breath as he hobbled along, holding PJ's arm, and spoke angrily, "What the hell were those Klan bastards doing in that victory parade anyway?"

PJ shook his head, "Beats me, Boss. Used to be a lot of 'em stirrin' up trouble back where I come from. But I can't reckon on what they're doing 'round these parts."

They reached the car and Thomas struggled out of his torn tunic and tossed it on the rear seat. He scrunched painfully in behind the wheel, started the engine and backed away from the curb. As they motored through town toward home and onto the corrugated surface of the farm road, they both remained silent, lost in their thoughts.

Suddenly, Thomas looked back then called out, "What the devil's this?"

His words were drowned out by the roar of a big, black Chandler touring sedan storming past them, showering the Maxwell in a cloud of dust and gravel. It was occupied by four Klansmen dressed in white robes and cone-shaped masks.

"Must be some of that bunch from the parade," PJ shouted, using his Stetson to frantically wave away the dust.

Grumbling to himself, Thomas pulled into the O'Roark yard and skidded to a stop. "I'm gonna get the shotgun and follow them," he said, "they might be after the Stuckeys."

He hobbled into the house and to the bedroom closet where he rummaged around for his father's old 12-guage double barrel shotgun and a box of shells.   He returned to the car where he was met by PJ strapping on a holstered pistol so big it threatened to topple the little man to one side.

Thomas tossed the shotgun and shells on the back seat, kicked the engine over, spun out through a flock of chickens, and headed east toward the Stuckey farm.   After about half a mile something caught his eye as they passed the former Maloney farm, and he slammed on the brakes.   There, about one hundred yards back from the roadway, was the mysterious Chandler.   He backed up to the driveway, pulled into the yard, cut the engine and stood up for a better view. Two of the masked men had a rope around the neck of a large bearded man and were dragging him toward their car.   A couple others were moving around an old railroad boxcar, pouring something from a can.   A woman holding a baby and three other children were cowering and crying in the background.

Thomas called out, "What's going on?"

The tallest Klansman replied in a high-pitched voice, "Who the hell wants to know?"

"A neighbor."

"We've got a bucket of tar waiting for this Commie. Gonna teach him a little about the American way."

Thomas stepped down from the Maxwell, reached into the back seat and lifted out the shotgun.   He dropped in two shells, closed the barrels and cocked the twin hammers with an authoritative 'click-click'. PJ exited from the other side of the car, his right hand resting on his holstered pistol.

"I don't think he's a Commie. Maybe you better leave him alone."

The leader shouted back at Thomas, "I think you better mind your own damn business." He and his companion resumed dragging the intended victim.

Thomas raised the shotgun and squeezed a trigger, releasing a round of buckshot whistling into the oak tree over their heads. The Klansmen ducked and yelled. Thomas popped the spent, smoking shell from the gun, dropped another into place, snapped the barrels shut and re-cocked the hammers. His eye caught a sudden movement to his right and the muzzle flash from PJ's Colt .44. A Klansman screamed in pain and grasped at his bleeding hand as his own pistol flew off into the air.

As Thomas continued to cradle the shotgun in the crook of his arm, he called out, "Maybe you gents should be leaving."

The leader hesitated, then dropped the rope and gave the old man a shove. He motioned to his followers, and they climbed into their automobile. As they roared out the driveway, their fists raised in defiance, the leader yelled, "We'll get you for this O'Roark!"

While the woman and children rushed toward the man, Thomas uncocked the shotgun, tossed it in the car and spoke to PJ, "I gather these must be our Russian neighbors."

"I reckon."

When Thomas glanced around, he was hit with vivid memories. The charred framework of the Maloney's two-story house, destroyed by fire in 1917, was still there, its remaining skeleton of empty window frames and two-by-fours leaning all huggermugger. A piece of the roof had collapsed down on itself. The remains of the entryway, through which he had crawled to rescue Michael Maloney from the raging inferno, were still partly visible.

Partially blocking his view of the original house, a faded yellow Santa Fe boxcar, missing both double-wheel trucks, sat hard on the ground. Its sliding double doors had been removed from the center section along with the ampersand of the familiar A. T. & S. F. logo. The bottom half of the resulting opening was boarded up, while a sheet of isinglass covered the upper part. One of the rooftop vents was propped open to make room for a protruding stovepipe. This structure, Thomas gathered, was being used by the Russians as a house.

When the Russian had struggled to his feet, he approached Thomas calling out "Goot friend, Goot friend". As he stuck out his hand, Thomas was struck by his stately appearance, his flat-cheeked face framed by a flowing red beard. He looked to be a few inches taller than Thomas, and stood straight-backed with a barrel chest and powerful arms exposed by his rolled-up sleeves.

The Junoesque appearance of the woman following him also was apparent. She had delicate facial features for her size, a fair complexion and flaxen hair visible around the edges of a colorful blue sarafan.

They all seemed to be heavily dressed for the warm day, the woman in a thick wool dress with full-length skirt, the man's wool shirt hanging out over contrasting pants tucked into heavy boots. The boy, who appeared to be about ten-to-twelve years old, wore a wool shirt and trousers. The two younger girls and the baby, all tow-headed, were wearing full-length plain wool dresses..

With a few words from the father, the boy ran to the railcar house and returned with a bottle of milk, another containing a clear liquid and three glass tumblers. The father took them and poured the clear liquid for Thomas and PJ and milk for himself. Then, raising his glass in a salute, he started to down the contents. Thomas and PJ took a cautious sip and rebelled at the fiery taste.

"*Goot wodka!*" the old man exclaimed in his deep voice, his grin bracketed by gold-capped teeth.

Thomas and PJ nodded, and tried another sip. They stood around uncomfortably for a few moments trying with shrugs and gestures to communicate before Thomas turned to the son. "What are you called?"

"Yoseff," he answered with a proud grin.

"How about your father?"

"Boris."

"What's your last name, your family name?"

"Menshikov."

"Well, please tell your father we have to leave."

84

The boy mumbled something, and the father grinned.

Everyone shook hands and Thomas and PJ, still carrying their nearly full glasses of vodka, drove away. They poured the contents out along the roadway.

As they pulled into the O'Roark farm, Thomas turned to PJ and asked, "I wonder how those Klan guys knew my name?"

"Dunno, Boss. Maybe they seen it in the newspaper where you were listed among the seriously wounded."

Thomas nodded thoughtfully, then changed the subject, "You or your hand know anything about painting?"

PJ chuckled, "Reckon I've white washed a few fences."

"I wanna get this place painted before it looks any worse. Think you can handle that if I get the paint?"

"Yessir. Better get some ten pennies, battens and putty, too. Looks like them boards and roof are gonna need some patchin' up."

"It's a deal…and I'll get enough paint so you can do the bunkhouse" As Thomas stepped out of the car, he paused at the sound of a motor car entering the yard. He squinted through the noonday sunlight and thought he was seeing a ghost as the driver rolled to a stop and yelled, "Hey, Thomas! You OK?" The smiling face, its eyes framed by horn-rimmed glasses, was that of Brad Simpson.

Simpson, a tall, slender man with smiling eyes and dark blond hair, had been the friend Thomas most admired before they were separated by the war. Some eight years older and better educated, he had become almost a father figure. He was a reporter with the *Morning Republican* who had joined the Government's Committee on Public Information during the war and been sent to France to disseminate American propaganda throughout Europe.

Simpson cut the engine, eased his long frame out of his Model T, approached Thomas with his hand extended and reached up to throw an arm across his shoulder. "Man, it's good to see you."

"Likewise," Thomas replied, smiling bravely against his sore ribs and aching head. He turned and motioned his visitor inside toward the sofa, tossed his torn tunic across the rocker and took a seat at the kitchen table, adding "I hardly recognized you with those spectacles. They new?"

Simpson pushed the glasses back up on his nose and sighed, "Yeah, guess that's what I get for spending too much time hunched over a typewriter." He doffed his fedora and brown tweed jacket, dropped them on the sofa and sat down. "You feeling all right? I was across the street and saw you get into that fracas at the parade."

"Yeah, I'm OK. Ribs are pretty sore and my leg got banged up. Who the hell invited the Klan to join the parade anyway?"

Brad shook his head. "Not sure. But they are getting politically important around town. Understand the police chief, a couple of preachers and a number of business leaders have joined."

"Including my old boss from the bank," Thomas said as he rose from the table, then added, "You want a sandwich or something for lunch?"

"No thanks, I've already eaten. But I could go for a cup of coffee."

Thomas moved to the stove to start the coffee. He had almost forgotten his former friend, but now began to feel uncomfortable as he recalled the last time he had seen him. That was when Thomas was in Paris recovering from his first wound. On a hot summer day, he had shown up unexpectedly at Simpson's apartment to find him shirtless with another man, who appeared to be completely undressed. Thomas had fled from the scene, embarrassed and without an explanation, and later been interrogated by Army Intelligence, who claimed that Simpson was a homosexual and his companion a German spy.

"Hey, Tom, you going deaf?" Brad asked.

"Er, sorry, didn't hear you."

"I just asked when did you get back from France?"

"February. I spent a couple months in the American Hospital in Paris before they shipped me home."

"Guess it was pretty brutal in the trenches, huh?"

He nodded silently.

"You doughboys did a hell of a job. You should be very proud."

Thomas shook his head, "Not sure how I feel, Brad. Sometimes I almost feel...like...well, betrayed."

"How do you mean?"

"Well, like a bunch of other guys, I marched off to war full of enthusiasm and patriotism and ready to do my bit to save democracy, and what did I come home to? A bunch of ignorant goons hiding behind masks and trying to take over the world!" He poured cups of coffee, carried them to the table and sat down.

Brad rose from the sofa, walked over and stared into the bric-a-brac cabinet before responding, "Guess I know how you feel. But at least you should feel proud of what you did. Not sure we can, however."

"I don't understand."

Brad moved to the table and pulled up a chair, "Maybe the CPI is partly to blame for all the postwar radicalism. We cranked out tons of propaganda and generated a lot of enthusiasm during the war. But we also stirred up a bunch of latent hatreds like we saw at the parade, and trashed our civil rights."

Thomas ignored Brad's lament and changed the subject, "So how about you, when did you get back?" He took a sip of the hot coffee.

Brad brightened, "Last month. I got to stay over to help publicize President Wilson's participation in the Peace Conference. Man, you should have seen the crowds welcome him to Paris."

They fell silent for a few moments as they tasted the hot coffee. Then Thomas asked, "So, what else is new in the world these days?"

"Oh, as you've probably read, everybody's worried about the 'Reds', the communists or Bolsheviks, whatever you wanna call them. They were a big concern at the Peace Conference, too. Seems like all of Europe is in turmoil so people are afraid their leaders will turn to communism to solve their problems."

"Well, all I want is to get back to normal. I've had enough fighting to last me for a long, long time."

Brad shook his head, "Unfortunately, we came home to a changing country. We're still overly worried about patriotism, Americanism, and all the 'damn foreigners'. And now we've got communism, Prohibition, national suffrage, and too many motor cars...and..." He glanced toward the door at the sound of a buzzing noise from outside, asking, "What's that?"

Thomas stepped to the door and peered out through the screen, "Oh, that's one of those aeroplanes from the Raisin Day celebration."

Brad shook his head, "That's all we need, a bunch of those flimsy contraptions flitting all over the sky."

"But it sure looks like fun. Believe I'd like to do that someday."

"Guess it's OK if you don't crash and get your head busted open. A few people have been killed in those rickety machines, you know."

"I'd still like to try it."

They fell silent until Brad asked, "Any thoughts on what you want to do now that you're home?"

Thomas shook his head as he carried his coffee across the room and sat on the sofa. "Afraid not. Doubt that I can handle much farm work with my leg, and banking doesn't sound interesting. Don't really know what I want to do."

"You thought any more about writing?"

He glanced at Brad, surprised that he remembered his vaguely expressed interest. "Not really. Not even sure how I might get started."

"Maybe you could become a reporter like me."

Taken aback at the suggestion, Thomas didn't know how to respond. He downed more of his coffee before venturing, "But I don't have any training. How could I find a job?"

"It's not that hard. I could teach you."

Thomas shrugged, "Guess I could think about it. Maybe some day."

Brad looked over at the wall clock. "Jeez, I gotta get to work." As he stood up from the table, he turned toward Thomas, "Could I ask you a question?"

"Sure."

"Whatever happened to you in Paris that day you came to my apartment?"

"Uh, what do you mean?"

"You were at the door for a second, then suddenly you were running down the hall."

Thomas, confused over the Army's claim that Brad was a sexual deviant, didn't know how to respond. Finally, "Well, it looked like you had a visitor---

"Brad interrupted, "Yeah, a little French guy. We were sitting there half naked, drinking *pinard* and trying to keep cool in that hot apartment."

Thomas, embarrassed, averted his eyes.

"Did someone try to tell you I'm a homosexual?"

Now feeling partly foolish, partly defiant, he looked back at Brad and nodded weakly.

Brad spoke firmly, "Let me assure you, my friend, that I am not. Never have been, never will be."

"Well, who was the naked guy with you? Army Intelligence told me he was a German spy, and…and… you were a sexual deviant, or something like that."

"Sexual invert, or gay or queer or fag. That's what they call homosexuals. As far as I know, Thomas, Pierre was not homosexual. He was a Frenchman working as an interpreter at CPI headquarters."

"Was he a spy?"

"Yes. Like some of his countrymen, he did turn out to be a spy."

"What happened to him?"

"The French shot him."

Thomas grimaced, then stood up as Brad approached the sofa to gather up his coat and hat. He stuck out his hand, "Still friends?"

Thomas smiled awkwardly and grasped Brad's hand. "Yeah, still friends."

CHAPTER 7

For several weeks after meeting with Brenda, Thomas was inclined to phone her for a date, but couldn't decide if he really wanted to do that or not. The event that finally triggered him to call was receiving his first pay from the Post Office, a munificent forty-two dollars for the two weeks he worked in May. When he finally did phone one evening, she answered brightly.

"Hi, Brenda," he said. "Hope I'm not bothering you."

"No, no. I was just finishing the supper dishes."

A quiet moment followed until he asked, "How's the little fella?"

"Oh, he's fine. He's enjoying his applesauce right now."

"Would you like to go to a moving picture?"

"When?"

"How about Saturday night?"

"Sounds good to me. Which one?"

"That *Birth of a Nation* is back at the Kinema. How does that---"

She interrupted, "Oh, I don't want to go to that, Thomas. I hear it's causing riots, and the police are searching everybody. That doesn't sound like---"

"How about the new Liberty? They're showing *Broken Blossoms.*"

"Oh, yes, with Lillian Gish! She's one of my favorites."

"OK. I'll pick you up around five o'clock. We can go to dinner first."

"Why don't I cook dinner here? Then we can go to the movie."

He agreed to the plan, but after they hung up the old self-doubt again swept over him. One moment he tried to put her out of his mind. The next he remembered their sexual escapades during that balmy night in Santa Cruz with the ocean waves crashing outside the door, or the long, cold night bundled under blankets in the car beside the Kings River before he went to war.

But she no longer was 'just a date.' She was the mother of a child, his apparently, and seemingly anxious to be married to the father so they could get on with their lives. But was he ready to make that commitment, now just a few days shy of his twentieth birthday? He had only been out of high school a little over six months when he went away to war and felt he had been robbed of his youth.

The following Saturday evening, as he pulled into the Stuckey driveway, the sight of the large two-story wood farmhouse brought back memories. Even though he had not been there for almost two years, he clearly recalled the covered veranda stretching across the front and sides. He marveled at the efflorescence of flowers in the window boxes and around the foundation.

But he also remembered the summer of 1917 when, over dinner at the Stuckey house, he had met Professor von Karman from the Normal School and Reverend Geschler, pastor of the Lutheran Church. They had engaged Thomas in a heated argument over America joining the war against Germany, their native country. Later, they had been deported for speaking against the war.

After seeing his buddies killed and wounded in the bloody fields of France, Thomas still harbored strong feelings against most things German. And he wasn't sure how the Stuckey men might feel toward him, especially now that they undoubtedly perceived him as the father of Brenda's child.

Tentatively, he walked up on the porch and knocked at the door, only to have it flung open by Brenda yelling "Surprise!" He jumped back as her shout was echoed by several more from behind her, all hollering "Happy Birthday!"

When she pulled him into the room, he caught his breath and stammered in confusion, "But…but it's not my birthday yet!"

"Just a few more days," his sister called out, stepping forward to buss him on the cheek. Baby Ricky was standing beside her, adding his little wave to the greetings.

Emma followed with her motherly kiss, and Major Brown offered a thin smile and limp handshake.

Thomas took the handshake laconically.

The Stuckeys were the next to greet him, led by Papa with a friendly one-arm hug and "*Willkommen, sohn.*" His other arm was holding Tommy, clad only in a diaper and cotton tee-shirt in recognition of the warm evening. The brothers followed with their own broad smiles and vigorous handshakes. They were as Thomas remembered from before the war, all florid of face from years of farming. Papa's hair was thinner, his frame heavier and sporting a round, comfortable belly. The brothers reflected their German heritage, both about six feet tall, square-built, muscular and flat-bellied. Ivan, at twenty-six the older, was the more friendly and open of the two, quietly in charge. Emil appeared more tightly wound, often looking like he was ready for a fight. He was nineteen, the youngest of the Stuckey siblings.

Thomas stood uncomfortably, unable to think of what to do or say next. In his nearly twenty years, he had never had a surprise birthday party. In fact, in the O'Roark family, the celebration of birthdays didn't seem very important, even to the extent that on more than one occasion, nobody had remembered his. He finally ventured, "Well, this is quite a surprise. Who thought this up?"

"This was Brenda's idea," his mother responded, sounding apologetic.

"Hope you don't mind," Brenda added, smiling.

"Oh no. It's just that I'm not used to...well..." He paused, struggling for words. "Guess I don't know what to say."

"We invited Brad Simpson, too," Ivan said. "Hope he didn't forget."

"Probably got tied up on some story," Thomas speculated.

Ivan spoke again, "Let's all go to the veranda where it's cooler and enjoy a glass of wine."

The guests followed him to where bottles of wine were chilling in ice buckets sitting on a side table. Emil uncorked one and served it around, then raised his glass in a toast. "Here's to our hero Thomas O'Roark. Welcome home and Happy Birthday!"

Thomas acknowledged the toast, though he felt uncomfortable at being called a hero. He swallowed some wine, quickly recognizing it as the same delightfully refreshing Riesling he had first tasted at that pre-war Stuckey dinner party. He offered his compliments to Ivan.

"Thank you. We'll be serving a new Zinfandel during dinner."

Brenda chimed in, "Papa cooked *hasenpfeffer*, one of our favorites."

"What's that?" Emma asked suspiciously.

"Believe that's rabbit," Major Brown enlightened everyone.

Brenda replied, "That's right.   Papa cuts it into pieces and marinates it for a couple of days in vinegar and water then…"

Papa interrupted, "*Yah, mit zwiebel, nelke, lorbeer und salz und pfeffer*."   He salivated visibly and shifted Tommy from one arm to the other.

His daughter smiled indulgently and continued, "Yes, I mustn't forget the vegetables.   After he adds those, he fries it all in butter till it's crisp and golden brown, and we serve it with sour cream and some of the marinade sauce."

"*Yah, und kartoffelbrei, krautsalat, und keks*," Papa added, patting his ample tummy with a satisfied grin.

Brenda, now looking embarrassed, explained to the guests standing with their glasses, "You'll have to forgive Papa.   He's still not comfortable trying his English in front of others."

A knock at the door broke into their conversation, and Ivan excused himself to answer.   He returned in a moment with Brad, skimmer in hand, and handed him over to Thomas for the introductions.   When he shook Thomas' hand he commented, "Happy birthday, my friend!"

Thomas smiled sheepishly.

"Sorry I'm late," he said as he gave Emil his hat in exchange for a glass of wine. "Got tied up covering a little riot at the Kinema."

"Oh, dear!" Emma exclaimed.

"They're showing that movie *Birth of a Nation* again. Some of those new Klan people turned up in their robes and masks and got into a fight with a bunch of doughboys in the audience. Someone even shot at the screen!"

Thomas stirred uncomfortably as he recalled his altercation with the Klan during the Raisin Day parade and at the Russians, then glanced at Brenda when she asked Brad, "Anybody hurt?"

"Police had to break it up with their billies. Sent about a dozen to jail or the hospital."

Brad lifted his glass in a toast to Thomas' birthday and took a swallow. Focusing on Emma he said, "Well, it looks like a new day is dawning now that Congress has finally approved that suffrage amendment. All women will be able to vote, just like you California ladies have been doing for several years."

She responded brightly, "Oh, yes! I voted for Mister Wilson already, back in 1916."

"Don't the states have to vote before it becomes law?" Thomas asked.

Brad nodded, "Oh, yes, thirty-six altogether. Probably be next year before it becomes part of our Constitution." He turned toward Brenda and Becky, "How about you ladies, will you be twenty-one by next year so you can vote?"

Becky replied proudly, "Oh, I am already!" and Brenda added, "Yes, I turned twenty-one in May. But, do we know yet who'll be running?"

Emma spoke decisively, "I'm going to vote for President Wilson again. After all, he got us through that terrible war."

Emil refilled several glasses and joined in, "Will he even be a candidate?"

"Hard to say," Brad replied. "Looks like he's heading for resistance from the isolationists over his League of Nations and the Fourteen Points."

"Including our own Senator Johnson," Major Brown said.

Thomas interjected, "Far as I'm concerned, old Hiram is right. It's time for us to stay home and mind our own business."

Brown continued, "Yes, and he's not alone. Lots of Irish-Americans are unhappy because the Brits won't give Ireland its independence under the treaty."

Ivan added, "German-Americans are upset too about the unbelievable reparations the Allies are demanding from Germany, billions of dollars and giving up their African colonies."

At the reference to German-Americans, who like the Stuckeys had suffered so much persecution and harassment during the war, Emil turned abruptly toward Thomas, "How about you, sergeant, did you kill lots of Germans?"

Thomas' face turned red and, too taken aback to think of a reply, he stared blankly at Emil.

Ivan reacted immediately, speaking sharply, "Emil, that's enough!"

"Well, I just wanted to know how good a soldier he---"

Papa interrupted, softly but firmly, "Please remember, Son. Sergeant O'Roark is our guest."

The exchange embarrassed everyone into silence until it was broken by the melodious two-tone sound of a car horn from outside. Brenda glanced out the window, "Looks like Jake's here," she called to Emil. Her brother excused himself and left the room.

Thomas looked out the window to see a Stutz *Bearcat* roadster, its brass headlights glistening against the shiny vermilion finish. It was the very car he had dreamed of buying before the war. A tall, slender young man, swarthy complexioned with a narrow face and aquiline nose, was standing beside the vehicle, peering expectantly toward the house.

"Who is that?" Thomas asked.

Ivan answered, "Oh, that's Jake Stein, a friend of Emil's. They're getting together to talk about returning to the university this fall."

Papa handed Tommy to Brenda then disappeared into the kitchen while she guided the guests outside. There, in recognition of the warm evening, the Stuckeys had set up a table underneath the dappled shade of a broad grape arbor, which extended some one hundred feet back from the house. Brenda directed everyone to their places and settled her baby into his high chair. She would be seated next to Papa at the head of the table with the high chair to her left, then Thomas followed by Ricky in a regular chair with extra cushions and Becky. Major Brown, Emma and Brad would be across from them, and Ivan would be at the opposite end from his father.

When Brenda left to help her father, Thomas took his seat, then turned to watch as Papa stepped out from the kitchen carrying the *hasenpfeffer* in a large serving platter and set it in the middle of the table. While the guests were gazing with mixed feelings at the juicy, golden brown chunks of meat, Brenda appeared with a bowl of mashed potatoes, another of coleslaw and one of sour cream. Ivan brought out a plate of biscuits, still steaming from the oven, and fresh butter. They bowed their heads as Papa gave the blessing in German.

Everyone ventured quietly into helping themselves to various-sized portions of the rich food and started eating. Papa, Brenda and Ivan dove in ravenously. Emma and Becky sampled the rabbit tentatively, while Thomas concentrated on the potatoes and coleslaw. Major Brown seemed to be enjoying his generous portions. Becky was assisting her son with some of the mashed potatoes and beets Brenda had prepared for him, interspersed with an occasional swig from his bottle. Brenda was doing the same for Tommy.

Emma looked at Brenda and asked, "What's that little ribbon on the baby's shirt?"

"Oh, that's Thomas' good soldier award!"

Thomas' face turned red as he corrected Brenda, "Good Conduct. It's awarded for Good Conduct."

Emma nodded vaguely and resumed eating. Major Brown was the next to break the concentration, "How do you like your new job, son?"

Thomas tensed up, not sure how to take the rather personal pronoun from a relative stranger. Was this a putdown or undo familiarity? He replied dismissively, "Uh, it's OK," then, poking a fork into his coleslaw, he added, "but kind of boring work."

"Pays good, though," Emma ventured, dabbing her mouth daintily with her napkin.

"You oughta keep that job. It's good dependable income," Brown added, much to Thomas' annoyance.

Ivan seconded the Major, "It's good to have that regular paycheck, especially with future raisin prices looking so uncertain now that we're going to have Prohibition."

Papa asked, "*Wann kannst du wirken deinen bewirtschaften?*"

Ivan, reacting to Thomas' puzzled look, explained, "Papa wants to know it you're going to be able to keep the job and still work your land?"

Thomas, catching the anxious look in his mother's eyes, replied, "I hope so, at least as long as we have PJ and the Mexican family."

Brown cleared his throat, "What do you think of your mother's plans?"

"What's that?" Thomas asked Emma, who looked down at her plate before replying hesitantly. "Well, now that the Red Cross is closing down operations Missus Duncan and I plan to open a birth control clinic."

Thomas bristled, but before he could reply Brenda spoke up excitedly, "Oh, that's wonderful, Missus O'Roark!"

"I agree," Becky added. "Seems like a lot of poor women sure could use some help."

Thomas, struggling to control his annoyance, asked, "What the heck's a...a... birth control clinic? Isn't that illegal?"

Becky stepped in again. "It's where they show women how to keep from having more babies than they want. And sometimes they help with abortions, don't they Mother?"

As Emma nodded uncertainly, Thomas took a deep breath then asked, "But, isn't that what women are supposed to do, stay home and have babies...and... and cook and keep house?" He glanced around the table anticipating support, at least from the men, but everyone quietly resumed eating.

Hoping to extricate himself from the embarrassing silence, he looked across at Brown. "So, what are you planning to do, Major, after the Red Cross winds down its work?"

Brown reached for another piece of *hasenpfeffer* and helping of potatoes as he replied, "I'm hoping to join the sheriff's office. Took the exam last week."

Ivan asked, "You've done that kind of work before?"

"I used to be with the police department in Kansas City before the war."

"What did you do during the war, Major?" Brad inquired.

"Military Police."

"Understand you were wounded?" Thomas asked.

"Injured. A truck backed into me and broke my leg."

Thomas' initial dislike for Brown intensified. He took a big swallow of wine and eyed him suspiciously before probing further, "Overseas?"

"No, Fort Sam Houston in---"

"What the...!" Thomas yelled and jumped up from his chair, and Becky cried out, "Oh, dear!"

Ricky, gleefully waving his tiny arm, had flung a spoonful of beets, splattering some on Thomas. As he picked up his napkin to brush the reddish stains from his shirt, Brenda cried out, "No, no, that'll just make it worse! Take that off so I can soak it in cold water and I'll get you one of Ivan's." She rose from the table and ran into the house.

The sudden commotion had frightened Tommy, who started crying. Thomas leaned toward the high chair to soothe him, remarking tenderly, "Sorry I scared you, Little Fella. You wouldn't throw beets at your fath..."

He caught himself, but not soon enough. Everyone remained quiet.

Brenda returned with a clean shirt, and Thomas stood up and slipped it on. He lifted Tommy into his arms and patted him gently as Brenda commented, "He's been a little colicky the last few days." No one spoke, and Papa started clearing the dishes from the table and carrying them to the kitchen. Thomas turned to Brenda, "What's for dessert, some of that good coffee cake you made before…er…what do you call it, cooch?"

Brenda looked puzzled for a moment, "Oh, you mean *kuchen*. No, this time I baked a special dessert just for you. But we have to go inside to get it."

The sun was settling below the vineyard line to the west and a cooling breeze was rustling the leaves of the grape arbor as Brenda took the baby from Thomas and led the way into the parlor. There, on a small coffee table in the center of the room, was a large cake bearing twenty candles. Thomas' face widened into a grin when he observed the white frosting with shredded coconut on top, his favorite cake. The guests stood around as Ivan entered to light the candles, and Thomas exclaimed, "My gosh, who told you---?"

"I've got my sources," Brenda interrupted with a grin.

He reached for his smiling sister and squeezed her hand. Then he leaned down and lustily blew out all the candles and made a wish he didn't expect to have granted that night.

Brenda motioned the guests to chairs around the room and directed Thomas to the large, leather easy chair he remembered so well from his pre-war visit. She sat on the arm next to him, and started handing him presents. The first he opened was from the Stuckeys, two of the latest style cotton dress shirts with attached collars to go with his summer suits. The next was from Becky, a new necktie and a bottle of after-shave lotion. From his mother and Major Brown he received a pair of summer slacks.

A surprise gift came in an envelope from Brad. Thomas opened it to find a piece of paper with scrolling around the edges to make it look like a certificate. He caught his breath as he read the heading, "O'Leary Flying School", and underneath, "Good For One Flying Lesson." It was signed by Kevin O'Leary, Proprietor.

"Oh, my God!" was all Thomas could say as he stared at the paper.

Brad sat across from him, grinning from ear to ear. "Just make sure you don't go out and bust your head. And remember, when you get your pilot's certificate, I get a free ride!"

Thomas, tears pooling in his eyes, rose and stepped across the room to shake his friend's hand. The others became quiet and looked confused or concerned. The concept of leaving the ground in an aeroplane was still too foreign to most people.

As Thomas wiped away tears and thanked everyone, Papa and Ivan departed to bring in coffee, after which Papa announced, "*Ich gehe schlafen, weil ich mude bin*", and headed upstairs for his bed.

Brenda responded, "OK, Papa, sleep well and thanks for all your help."

After the cake and coffee had been consumed, the party began to break up. Emma, Major Brown and Becky with her baby piled into Emma's Red Cross car and returned to town. Brad soon followed, and Brenda handed the sleeping Tommy to her brother, who left the room.

Brenda sat back down on the arm of the chair, leaned down and kissed Thomas on the forehead. "Enjoy your party?"

"Very much. Biggest and best birthday party I ever had."

"Sorry we didn't get to the movie."

"Maybe another time?"

She nodded, then asked, "Would you like to go for a drive?"

"Um, sure. But how about Tommy?"

"Ivan will take care of him."

Wordlessly, they prepared to leave. She pulled a light sweater across her shoulders as he picked up his gifts, and they walked out to the car. He helped her in, climbed behind the wheel, started the engine and steered out the driveway. As he started to turn east toward the Kings River, she put her hand on his arm. "Where are you going?"

"Out by the river?"

"Why don't we go to your house?"

The old tingling sensation, mixed with a touch of apprehension, swept through his body. "Er, why do you want to go there?"

She shrugged, "No particular reason. I just thought it would be a good place to be alone and… and talk."

He turned the car to the left and accelerated slowly as his mind tumbled about uncertainly. What did she mean by 'talk' he wondered, as they motored silently through the balmy evening toward the O'Roark farm. What was he being trapped into?

After he pulled to a stop under the sycamore, he stepped out of the car and escorted her into the house. He flipped on the lights while she moved to the sofa and surveyed the room commenting, "This used to be my favorite place on those cold winter days when Becky and I knitted for the war effort, nice and soft and warm and close to the fireplace."

He shook his head vaguely, adding, "Yeah, but it seems kinda warm in here right now." He set his gifts on the kitchen table, turned to slide down the window in the door and crossed the room to open the back window. Then he went into the bedrooms to open all four of those windows, all the while worrying about what she wanted to talk about. When he returned to the living area, she was still seated on the sofa, now with her legs crossed, the top one swinging back and forth idly. She patted the sofa cushion, inviting him to sit next to her.

He took a seat at the opposite end and reached down to unbutton the cuffs of the shirt she had loaned him after being splattered with beets. "This is a good looking shirt," he ventured as he rolled both sleeves part way up. "It was nice of Ivan to loan it to me."

"Uh huh."

"But I don't think your other brother likes me."

"Why do you say that?"

"His remark about me killing Germans."

She shook her head dismissively. "Oh, don't worry about that. Emil gets some funny ideas sometimes."

They fell silent for a few moments, making Thomas even more uncomfortable. He stretched his arms up over his head and yawned widely before finally breaking the silence with a casual comment, "That sure was a nice party."

Brenda, her body febrile from more than a year of war-induced abstinence, started swinging her leg more determinedly.

"I sure was surprised. Never had a party like that."

She just smiled.

"Great gifts."

"Yes, they were very thoughtful."

Suddenly, she uncrossed her legs, wriggled across the lumpy cushions, and cuddled against his right shoulder with her soft hair touching his cheek.

Her move caught him by surprise, and he wasn't sure how to respond. He draped his arm loosely across her shoulders and tried to ignore the warm sensation resulting from the faint whiff of her perfume. Finally, he asked, "You said you wanted to talk about something?"

She looked up at him quizzically, "Huh?"

"In the car. You said we could be alone and talk."

She sighed, "Guess I just wanted to be with you."

He felt the urge to kiss her. But he still was not certain if that was the thing to do. Incongruously, he asked, "Would you like something to drink?"

She shook her head, "Drink?"'"

"Yeah. Maybe you'd like a *Nehi* or *Jerico*...or maybe some brandy?"

She shook her head, "Oh, no thanks. I'm not thirsty."

Finally, he couldn't resist any longer, tipped her head up and kissed her tentatively on the forehead. When she responded warmly, he kissed her on the mouth then eased her against the back of the sofa and kissed her passionately on the lips and the soft concave of her throat. He could feel a warm sensation in his loins as his manhood rose to the occasion.

He whispered in her ear, "I sure would like to get you in bed."

Wordlessly, she pushed against him, rose from the sofa, took his hand and guided him into the dark bedroom where she pulled down the top bedding, sat on the edge of the bed and started removing her clothing. He eagerly peeled off his shirt and shoes and pulled off his pants so rapidly that he sent the pocket change rattling noisily across the floor.

As they slipped under the sheet and he rolled toward her, he stopped, "Oh damn!"

"What's the matter?"

He turned back to the edge and groped around in the drawer of the nightstand where he thought he had left a package of condoms before the war. He felt around until he found them, pulled one out, fumbled to remove the wrapper and struggled frantically to roll it over his erection.

"Thomas, what on earth are you doing?"

"Trying to get this damn thing on."

He then realized he had it turned the wrong way, flipped it over and quickly rolled it into place. But as he turned back toward Brenda and resumed kissing her and stroking her soft warm body, he realized he had messed around too much. Months of pent up passion were already squirting into the rubber.

"Oh, dear Jesus!" he exclaimed as he flopped on his back.

"What on earth! Oh, heavens, did you do that again?"

He nodded in abject frustration. She moved to him, laid her head on his shoulder and pulled the sheet up over both of them. They soon fell sound asleep.

He was awakened around midnight by Brenda stroking his chest and belly and kissing him on the neck, and the sensation of his penis pushing like a tent pole up against the sheet. Wordlessly, he reached for a rubber, expertly applied it and rolled on top of her. But as he entered her and began thrusting, he felt her disappear deeper and deeper into the cloud-like softness of the feather bed.

In frustration he tossed the pillows on the floor, and they tumbled off the bed to complete their mission in a burst of mutual ecstasy. He reached up and pulled the cover down over them, and they again fell asleep. They used the final rubber as the dawn's light began peeking around the edges of the window shades.

When they finished, Thomas reluctantly disentangled himself and, legs wobbly from the night of blissful exertion, struggled up from the floor and sat on the edge of the bed. He grinned weakly, "Man, what a night!"

Brenda sat up on the floor, pulling the sheet across her bare breasts and smiling, "Are you complaining?"

"No, no!"

"You liked the rest of your birthday present?"

He smiled and nodded as he reached to help her to her feet, and she grabbed her clothes and departed for the bathroom. When she returned in a few minutes fully dressed, he took his turn, deciding he would have a quick bath.

Afterwards, as he sauntered into the kitchen, he found that Brenda had picked up the papers and magazines strewn around the floor and was at the stove cooking breakfast. A cup of freshly brewed coffee awaited him on the table along with a bowl of his mother's canned peaches.   Two places had been set at the table.

"Whatcha cooking?" he asked, sitting down at the table.

"German pancakes and bacon."

"What are those?"   He tried a sip of the coffee, but it still was too hot.

"Pancakes with apple slices."

"Sounds good."   He served himself some peaches and ladled a few into the saucer at the other place setting.   She brought two plates of pancakes to the table and sat across from him.   She spooned fresh cream on her pancakes while he opted for butter and *Log Cabin* syrup, and they ate silently for a few moments until he said, "Boy, these are good."

"Glad you like them."

"Did you check on Tommy,"   he asked as he broke off a piece of the crisp bacon and stuck it in his mouth.

"I phoned Ivan while you were in the bath.   Sounds like he's getting over the colic."

He took a swig of coffee.   "I noticed yesterday his eyes have turned brown and his hair is getting darker."

"Yes, that's normal.   He's almost nine months now."

He took a bite of pancake and chewed thoughtfully for a few moments before continuing, "I really enjoyed my birthday party."

She smiled, "I'm glad."

"Eating dinner at your house sure stirred up memories, back to the early days of the war when Reverend Geschler and Professor von Karman were there."

She nodded and munched quietly on a pancake.

"Guess you haven't heard anything about them?"

She peered at him quizzically, then got up to retrieve the coffeepot and refill their cups. "Not since they were deported," she replied absently as she retook her seat.

They turned to finishing their breakfast in silence until she commented, "This is a nice little house. Now that you've painted the outside, you ought to do the interior."

He glanced around, chuckling, "These rooms never even got a final coat of plaster. Not sure they could take real paint." He took a drink of coffee.

She ignored his response. "This room would look good in a pale cream color, or an off-white. And you could paint the front bedroom in a light blue."

He turned toward the bedroom, "Blue?"

"Wouldn't that be a good color for a little boy?"

He caught the subtle reference but didn't respond.

Brenda ignored his silence and changed her tack, "You said you did a lot of work on the house before the war. What all did you do?" She sipped coffee while waiting for his reply.

"Well, I installed the new bathroom and got rid of the old outhouse. Added the storage shed in back.

And we put in electric lights and running water and a hot water heater."

She turned back toward the kitchen. "That looks like a new stove."

"Oh, yeah. We bought that and the icebox and washing machine." He paused to swallow more coffee, then a breeze wafting through the window reminded him, "New curtains, too. Mother sewed those, and I understand you and Becky made the matching covers for the rocker."

"Yes, I helped her with those during the war."

She got up, walked over and sat down in the chair and rocked several times. "This is a nice comfortable chair. Becky and I used to take turns rocking our babies to sleep."

He nodded silently, trying to ignore the reference to babies.

She stood up and reached around to push the cushion in place from where it protruded through the missing back spindle. She walked over to the bric-a-brac cabinet. "I always admired these things when I visited here," she said.

"That's some of Mother's stuff."

She leaned down for a closer look. "These cups and saucers are very pretty and valuable. They're *Chelsea* porcelain, you know."

He moved beside her. "Guess you're right. I never paid much attention."

"And the dolls. Understand they belonged to your mother when she was a little girl."

He shrugged, then put an arm across her shoulder as he pointed to two large abalone shells. "You remember those?"

She shook her head.

"I found them in Santa Cruz when I went for a swim in the ocean and then we spent the night in that ocean front cabin"

"Oh, yes. You frightened me so."

"Sorry about that."

She slipped her arm around his waist and laid her head against his chest as he patted her reassuringly.

She tipped her head back and looked up at him. "You aren't really serious about learning to fly, are you?"

He looked down at her. "Why not?"

"Oh, it just sounds so dangerous. You always hear about someone getting injured…or…or worse."

He didn't reply but leaned his cheek down into her soft hair and the faint odor of her perfume and held her close. Then, squeezing his arm around her more tightly he ventured, "You suppose we ought to get married?"

Brenda looked up at him with a puzzled expression, "Is that a proposal?"

He smiled and nodded.

"Sounds like a good idea to me." She reached up and kissed him on the cheek. He cupped her face in his hands and kissed her warmly on the lips.

CHAPTER 8

Throughout the week following his birthday party, Thomas agonized over having asked Brenda to marry him. It wasn't just that he had doubts about loving her, but he wasn't even sure if he was ready to give up his independence and freedom to get married in the first place.

By Friday, he decided to talk to the one person he felt he could confide in, his sister. He feigned a problem with his leg wound, walked out of the Post Office at noon with an exaggerated limp, and drove through the stifling summer heat to her apartment. When he knocked, Becky called out, "Who's there?"

"Your brother."

She yanked open the door. "Oh, my goodness, what a surprise! She pulled him into the room and reached for his skimmer and the coat of his Palm

Beach suit and carried them into the bedroom. He loosened his tie, unbuttoned his shirt collar and pulled up a chair. He picked up a magazine to fan himself.

The apartment was one of twelve similar units in a two-story building located on Fulton street just two blocks north of the central business district. In addition to a living room, it comprised a bedroom, bathroom and small kitchenette. The bedroom held a bed and dresser with barley enough space left over for the baby's crib in one corner. The bathroom consisted of a toilet and wash basin, but no bathtub. That was located at the end of the hall where it served all six apartments on the upper floor. The living room furniture included a Sheraton easy chair along with a couple of bentwood casual chairs and small side tables. A sink and two-burner electric stove tucked in a corner served as the kitchenette.

"What brings you to my tiny abode on this hot afternoon?" she asked softly as she returned from the bedroom. She closed the door partway behind her and, with a finger to her lips added, "Ricky's having his afternoon nap so we'll have to be kinda quiet." She closed a cosmetics case sitting on a table and put it to one side.

He nodded toward the case, "You making enough money to live on?"

"Oh, yes. Counting what I sold this morning, I'll make over twenty dollars this week."

"That's as much as I'm getting!"

"But I don't do that well every week. Usually it's less."

They fell silent for a few moments until she asked, "You want a cup of tea, and how about some leftover cookies?"

"Got anything cold, lemonade or iced tea maybe?"

"Sorry, I'm almost out of ice. Iceman isn't due until tomorrow."

"Tea's OK." He continued fanning as she stepped to the kitchenette to fill the teakettle with water and put it on the electric burner. She removed two cups and saucers from a cabinet, placed some cookies on a plate, carried them to a table and sat down across from him.

As she took her seat, he blurted out, "I've asked Brenda to marry me."

"Oh, my goodness! That's exciting!"

He shrugged, "Yeah, I guess."

"What's the matter, she turn you down?"

"Oh, no. That's the problem. She accepted."

"Don't you want to get married?"

He continued fanning himself. "Not sure. Guess I don't know what I want to do."

"Do you love her?"

"Don't know that either. What is love anyway, how do you know?"

She returned to the kitchenette in response to the whistling of the teakettle, turned off the burner, and poured the boiling water through a tea ball into each cup. "Not sure I know the answer, Thomas, but I can tell you what it's not." She swirled the ball around until the color looked right, removed it to a separate saucer and returned the kettle to the burner.

"What's that?"

"It's not making goo-goo eyes and holding hands in the moonlight. I found that out the hard way and paid the price." She gestured toward the bedroom.

He caught her reference to the moonlight night at summer school in the High Sierras when she had succumbed to the advances of Professor von Karman and become pregnant.

"I love my little boy," she added, "but wish I'd had him under different circumstances." She carried in the two cups of tea and set them on the tables, reached back for sugar and cream and again took her seat.

"That's kinda like my situation, too. I really enjoy Tommy and think it would be fun to be his father. Guess I'd like to see if I could do a better job than the one we had." He selected a cookie and pensively stuck it in his mouth.

Becky, recalling her brother's poor relationship with their father, didn't respond.

"Problem is, I'm not even sure Tommy's mine."

She looked perturbed, "What do you mean?"

He stared across the room. "How can I tell if he's really my son? He sort of looks like me, especially now that his eyes have turned brown and his hair is getting darker. But, I still don't know."

"Well, you needn't have worried about his early coloring. Lots of babies start out with blond hair and blue eyes." She chuckled sardonically, "Just look at mine, he's still that way!"

"Yeah, but his coloring is the same as the father's."

She ignored the oblique reference to von Karman, poured a little cream in her tea and reached for a cookie. "At least you don't have to worry about him being involved with Brenda because he was deported in the fall of '17 before she became pregnant."

Thomas gave her a puzzled look, took a sip of the hot tea and returned his cup to its saucer. He stood up and, still fanning himself with the magazine, walked toward the open window. He turned toward her and asked, "How do you know when she got pregnant?"

"That's easy. She carried Tommy full term until mid-September. At least she said it was full term. So, weren't you…er…you know, with her just before you went to war?"

He turned away, blushing, "Uh, yeah, a few days before Christmas."

She responded with a knowing smile.

He put the magazine on the table, went to the bedroom, removed his cigarette makings from his coat, and returned to the chair. "Mind if I smoke?"

"No, but why don't you try one of my <u>Lucky Strikes?</u>" She reached into her purse, held the package out for him, and removed one for herself. He struck a match and lighted them both, and they each took a drag before she spoke further. "I just love this new all-white package. It seemed like that old green circle design clashed with everything I wanted to wear."

He nodded uncertainly, not conscious of the fashion importance of cigarette packaging, took another puff then asked, "Do you know that Stein fellow who came to the Stuckey house the day of my party?"

"Not really. I know his family owns that jewelry store next to Gottschalk's."

"Brenda seemed to know him. Did she used to date him?"

"I believe she went with him to the New Year's dance last year."

He got up and again walked to the window, then turned back frowning, "That was about a week after I last saw her, just before I joined the Marines."

"Yes, I remember now. I saw them together again that February when I went to the Valentine's dance. In fact, that's when they got into an argument."

"Over what?"

"Over her being pregnant. Apparently he was afraid he was the father."

He took a deep drag on his cigarette and forcefully blew the smoke toward the window. "Christ, what a mess. How come she would date some Jew guy anyway?"

"Brenda told me he's German. Before they moved to America, the family name was Steinmetz or Steinberg, something like that. She said her father and brothers were trying to get her to marry a German."

He returned to his chair and stubbed out his cigarette in the ashtray. He became thoughtful, drumming his fingers on the chair arm, then suddenly resumed their earlier discussion, "I guess my main problem is I really don't know what I want to do for the rest of my life. But whatever I decide, it seems like marriage sure would tie me down."

"You're probably right about that. Look what it did for Mother and Father. They spent their life together having babies and working to feed them."

He glanced at her with a sudden revelation. "Maybe that's what's holding me back. I'm trying to judge marriage from the miserable life the folks seemed to experience."

She shook her head in acknowledgement and got up to pour more tea. "Maybe it's another woman?"

Surprised, he turned toward her, "What do you mean?"

"Weren't you involved with someone else, some woman in Bakersfield?"

"How'd you know about that?"

She filled their cups, placed the teakettle back on the stove and returned to her chair before replying. "Well, I remember your mysterious trip there in the fall of '17 and you coming home looking like you'd been in a fight. So, I put two and two together."

He smiled and stared dreamily into the distance.

Becky asked, "So, you indicated how you feel about the baby, how do you feel about Brenda?"

With the hot tea causing him to sweat, he resumed fanning with the magazine, stood up, walked to the window and stared out blankly. He spoke distantly, "Not sure how I feel about her. We seem to be compatible when we're together, and she's certainly attractive, but…" His voice trailed off as he continued gazing out the window.

"Guess that's a burden us women will always have to bear."

He turned toward her, "What's that?"

"We never know what's really in a man's heart. Is it love, or something less?"

Thomas looked quizzically at her, but didn't respond.

She put out her cigarette and took another bite of cookie before continuing, "It does seem like Brenda would make a good wife and mother. She's very attentive to her baby and she's a good cook and comes from a nice family."

"You think she'd be bossy?"

She chuckled, "Bossy?"

"Yeah, like Mother, try to run my life?"

She swallowed more tea before answering, "I don't know, Thomas. I think Mother's gotten that way from trying to manage all those Red Cross volunteers. But Brenda doesn't appear to be like that, at least not to me."

He munched on the last of his cookie thoughtfully, as she continued, "But it's obvious she's in love with you."

He brightened, "You think so?"

"You were the only one she talked about while you were gone."

"She ever mention von Karman?"

Becky stared intently at her brother, "No. Why?"

He shrugged, "I brought up his name a few days ago and it seemed like her response was kind of strange, almost evasive."

Becky was pensive for a moment. "Now that you remind me, she did express concern once about him and that preacher being deported. But I let her know how I felt about von Karman and she never brought it up again."

They finished their tea in silence. She set down her empty cup and with a sigh of resignation concluded, "Afraid I can't tell you what to do, Thomas. Marriage is something you'll have to decide for yourself."

They were interrupted by a little cry from the baby. "Sounds like someone is ready for his afternoon bottle," Becky said, heading for the bedroom.

Thomas reached into his pocket, extracted his father's old gold watch, and popped the lid. "Yeah, it's after two o'clock. Guess I'll run along."

His sister returned with Ricky in her arms, removed a bottle of milk from the ice box, and put it in a pan of water to heat. "Sorry I couldn't be more helpful with your problem."

"That's OK. I just appreciate having someone to confide with." He retrieved his hat and coat from the bedroom, kissed his sister on the cheek, patted the baby and left the apartment.

He drove home slowly, thoughtfully, relishing the cooling breeze caused by the forward movement of the car. He pulled up under the broad, green canopy of the sycamore, cut the engine and walked back to the roadside mailbox where he found a package wrapped in brown paper with foreign stamps. Recognizing Lillian Branson's handwriting, he tore the package open to find her letter:

Paris, France
February 15, 1919

My dear Thomas:

Surprise! Bet you thought I had forgotten you, but here I am.

Not only do I think of you often, but I've even remembered that June 10 is your birthday! I just hope my little gift gets there in time.

When you open it you'll see that it's an antique writing set.

I found it in one of the little shops that are all over Paris. I know it's not for the kind of writing you once talked about, but hopefully it will give you the inspiration to write to me someday soon.

I've been very busy with the rest of the Red Cross team, working primarily with refugee children. There are so many of them, all suffering from malnutrition, tuberculosis or some other terrible disease. Unfortunately, not all of them can be saved, but we keep trying.

Sick children are not the only problem over here. Many of our doughboys are behaving very badly. Some have been arrested for murder, robbery or assault, and many have been involved in bloody brawls. The Army estimates there are at least one thousand deserters in Paris alone.

But matters seem to be worse in Germany. Last week, several of us took the train to Coblenz, the American area of occupation. The trip through the countryside brought painful memories. Rolls and rolls of barbed wire were along roadsides, caved in trenches and bomb craters, farmland overrun with weeds. There were lots of signs indicating where live bombs still exist, you wonder if they'll ever be able to clean it all up.

We were told about rioting in Germany and eastern Europe. Everyone seems to blame the Bolsheviks and is afraid we're sitting on a big powder keg over here. I'll probably be coming home to Bakersfield late this summer or early fall. Be looking forward to getting away from all the reminders of this horrible war and back to a more normal life.

I do hope you'll write soon. I've missed you very much and have fond memories of our few brief moments together.

Much love,
Lillian

Thomas stood by the mailbox for several minutes, re-reading the letter, his heart racing. Finally, he walked slowly, pensively into the house and tossed the letter and package on the table. He opened all the windows to air out the lingering stuffiness from the hot day. He went to the bathroom to empty his bladder and fill the tub for a bath, then peeled off his suit and hung it in the closet.

While the tub was filling, he poured a finger of brandy in a glass, added water and chipped in some ice and rolled a cigarette. He then eased his tired body and aching leg into the embracing water, and soaked and puffed and slowly sipped the soothing liquid for over an hour.

Later, after he had completed his ablutions and wrapped his clean body in the comforting embrace of his terry cloth robe, he sat at the table and finished opening the package from Lillian. As she had mentioned in her letter, it was a writing set, all right. But this one looked pretty special. It was contained in a flat wooden box covered with a taffeta-like green cloth. The interior was silk-lined. The contents, each in its fitted slot, included a roller blotter, a letter opener, a circular stamp for wax-sealing envelopes, and a knife for scraping off a seal. The instruments were all made of sterling silver.

He sat at the table for several minutes turning the items back and forth in his hands and letting his mind and heart drift away to the blissful moments he had shared with Lillian. Eventually, he sighed deeply, returned everything to the box, carried it into the front bedroom and slid it under the bed. Then he stretched out on the bed and, clad only in his underwear, fell asleep with a warm summer breeze wafting across his body.

After about an hour, he was awakened by a knock at the screen door. He went to find PJ, dressed in a clean shirt and casual pants rather than the worn coveralls he usually favored.

"What's up, PJ?"

"Ol' 'Rass' is fixin' to cook up a mess of catfish. Wanna join us?"

Thomas, annoyed at having a quiet evening of introspection interrupted, hesitated. "Jeez, I don't know, PJ. I was just planning on a light supper---"

"He's gonna roll 'em in corn meal and fry 'em up nice and crispy."

Thomas paused as memories of the catfish he had tasted in Virginia during the war wafted back into his mind.

"And I've got some good *Southern Comfort* to wash it down with."

Thomas suddenly brightened, and the words poured out of him. "What the hell, I've got a better idea. Why don't you two come up here and cook the fish on our big stove. We can pick some greens out of the garden, and maybe your man will bake up a batch of corn bread. And…and…I've got some darn good brandy to wash it down with."

PJ, too taken aback to speak, broke out in a big grin and headed for the bunkhouse. Thomas retreated to the bedroom to pull on a shirt, pants and slippers. In a few minutes, the farm manager and his helper returned carrying three plump fish in a galvanized bucket. He pushed the screen door open and smiled at the old Negro, dressed in his military shirt and pants, as memories flooded back. He stuck out a hand, "My God, Mister Jones, you remember me?"

Erasmus returned the handshake, "Yassuh. Reckons mebbe ah does."

"It was in Virginia over a year ago. I was with some other Marines and you cooked for us at Minnies."

"Yassuh. Trouble is, ah cooked fo' lots ub dem sojer boys."

"Well, come on in." It was when Thomas reached to help him up the steps that he noticed something different; he wasn't using crutches and his left pant leg was hanging straight down, no longer pinned up. He looked down to see a foot-long piece of one-by-four inch wood sticking out from under the cuff.

"What happened to your leg?" he asked.

"Mistuh Sloan dun made me uh peg."

PJ, who had placed the bucket of fish in the sink, turned back, reached down and lifted Erasmus' pant leg a few inches. "Yeah, see, I made it from a grape stake and nailed the board on the bottom so he could walk in the vineyard."

"How'd you attach it to his...er...his real leg?"

"Made a pouch of old burlap and leather straps. He just sticks his stob in there and cinches 'er up."

Thomas shook his head. "I'll be damned!"

For a moment, they stood around awkwardly until he spoke again, "So, what'll we have with the fish?"

PJ responded first, "Greens sound good to me."

"Ah'll make uh mess uh cone bread iffen you got meal," Erasmus volunteered.

"OK," Thomas replied. "PJ, dump that fish in the sink and get us a bucket of collard greens from the garden." He turned to the pantry, "And here's a sack of corn meal. What else do you need?"

PJ emptied the bucket and departed with it for the garden. Erasmus asked for milk, lard and an egg, which Thomas produced along with a mixing bowl and baking pan. The old Negro mixed the ingredients and a little salt in the bowl, heated the milk in a small saucepan, stirred it and the egg into the bowl, and poured it all into the baking pan.

When PJ returned with the greens, Thomas removed three glasses from the cupboard. He chipped in some ice, poured them about a third full of brandy, added water and handed one to each of his guests. They followed him as he raised his glass in a toast to an anticipated bountiful raisin crop.

While PJ washed the greens and put them in a large pot with water and placed them on the stove, Erasmus rolled the fish in corn meal and started cooking them in a large iron frying pan. Thomas set the table, watching out of the corner of his eye as the tall Negro moved around the hot stove and oven, all the while balancing awkwardly on his peg with the wooden foot making a clapping sound when it hit the floor. He joined PJ at the table and asked, "When did you get called up Mister Jones?"

He paused thoughtfully for a moment, " March ub '18."

"That's about the time we went overseas."

"Yassuh."

"What outfit were you with?"

"The Buffaloes."

Thomas searched his memory, "What was that, the 367th Infantry?"

Erasmus nodded as he opened the oven door to check the corn bread and turned the fish in the frying pan. PJ got up from the table to stir the greens, then picked up the bottle of brandy and poured each of them another round.

Thomas took a swallow and continued, "Heard you guys really caught hell when the Fritzies made their final push toward Saint Mihiel."

"Thas' right."

PJ spoke up, "That where you got hit?"

Erasmus nodded.

Thomas pointed to the faded red and gold cord looped through his shirt epaulet, "That's also where he earned that *Croix de Guerre*. French awarded it to the whole damn outfit for putting up such a great fight."

Erasmus removed the corn bread from the oven, sliced it into squares and placed it on plates. He added a fish to each and handed them to Thomas to carry to the table. PJ ladled the greens into saucers and put them on the table and refilled the glasses with brandy.

As PJ sat down, Erasmus hobbled to a chair and eased into it sideways to accommodate his new peg leg. Thomas turned back to the cupboard. "Man, almost forgot the vinegar and butter."

Erasmus shook his head side-to-side and looked up with a big grin, "Now ah sho nuf 'members!"

"What?" Thomas replied as he retook his seat.

"You thu only white boy in Minnie's evah ast fo vineguh and buttah!"

Thomas chuckled, "Yeah, I finally figured it out. You were the cook at that old roadhouse near the Marine base in Virginia."

Erasmus nodded, and each took another big swig of brandy. Thomas added the vinegar, butter and salt to his greens and messed it all around in the saucer as Erasmus and PJ followed his lead. Then he poked his fork through the crispy skin of the fish into the firm white flesh and put it in his mouth, and the ghostly vision of him and his Marine buddies eating and drinking in the roadhouse returned.

He shook his head and started reminiscing. "Jeez that was quite a night, Earl and me and Bernie and Chief. Didn't realize how drunk you can get on three-point-two beer."

His companions nodded silently as they buttered their corn bread and joined him in stuffing their mouths full of the savory fish.

"Afterwards we were so busy puking and peeing we missed the last bus to camp." He wiped the mist from his eyes with the back of his hand.

PJ and Erasmus remained silent, sensing that Thomas was slipping into a moment they really couldn't share.

He looked at Erasmus, "Then you came along in your car and drove us to the gate just in time before our passes expired."

"Yassuh."

"Except for Earl. He wouldn't ride with you 'cause you're...well..."

"Nossuh. Reckon he jus didn' know no better."

Thomas went to the kitchen counter for the bottle of brandy and topped off their glasses. He took another big swallow and mumbled bitterly, half to himself, "Well, it doesn't make any difference now. Hell, they're all dead."

An awkward silence followed until he turned toward the table and asked, "How about some sliced peaches for dessert?" Without waiting for answers, he reached in the icebox for the bowl full he had sliced earlier, spooned them into saucers and carried them to the table. He sprinkled sugar on his serving, stuck a spoonful in his mouth and chewed morosely. The three of them continued eating in silence until the phone rang. Thomas stood up uncertainly, staggered toward it and picked up the receiver, "Hullo."

"Thomas?"

"Yeah."

"This is Brad. You sound like maybe you're swacked. You OK?"

"Uh huh." He turned and grinned foolishly at his dinner companions.

"What are you doing?"

Thomas chuckled, "Havin' my...'hic'...havin' my bash...bashler party."

"You're kidding! You're really going to get married?"

"Yep, in July."

"Brenda?"

"Uh huh."

"Congratulations! But, what I called for was to warn you about the Klan."

Thomas, standing uncertainly as he held the receiver and still having trouble focusing his mind, hesitated, and Brad spoke again, "You might be heading for trouble with that Negro you're keeping out there."

Thomas became defensive, "Wha' are you...hic... talkin' about?"

"The Klan's been getting a lot more active in the past few weeks. Bunch of them threatened to lynch some poor Negro in Court House Park last night. Fortunately the police got there in time."

Thomas, feeling too befuddled to respond further, sighed and acknowledged the warning. They bid their good-byes and he wobbled over to the rocking chair, picking up the brandy bottle on the way. As he nearly emptied it, he had a vague recollection of the bottle having been more than half full when they started. "Man, looks like I'm about out of booze. Wha... 'hic'...wha we gonna do during pro...probission?"

"Don't worry, Boss," PJ replied. "I know a couple good ol' boys out in Sanger promised they'd supply anything we want, brandy, whisky, gin. You just name it."

Thomas passed the bottle to PJ, took a swallow from his glass, leaned back in the chair and started rocking. When he began to doze, Erasmus spoke up. "Sho looks lak yo belongs in that chair, Massuh 'Roark."

He awoke part way and lifted his glass in a shaky salute. "Here's to the Klan. May they...may they..." He started dozing again, and PJ reached over and took his empty glass.

PJ and Erasmus silently returned the salute, downed the last of their brandy, and departed quietly for the bunkhouse.

CHAPTER 9

The wedding of Brenda Stuckey to Thomas O'Roark took place the late afternoon of July 15th as planned. It was held in the east veranda of the Stuckey home where Ivan had set up a couple of electric fans to offset the one-hundred degree temperature that continued to oppress the Fresno area. Emil was stationed next to the Victrola in the adjacent parlor, responsible for playing Lohengrin's Wedding March upon a signal from Ivan. The ceremony was presided over by the new young minister from the Lutheran Church.

After a festive dinner and dancing under the evening shade of the grape arbor, the newlyweds escaped to a passionate wedding night at the Hughes Hotel. Early the next morning, dressed in Levis and cotton shirts in anticipation of the hot drive ahead of them, they were on their way. They motored out of

Fresno to the community of Clovis where they turned onto the bumpy, unpaved route into the foot hills bolstering up against the Sierra Nevadas.

At the abandoned village of Friant, they paid fifty cents to be ferried across the river to the hardpan bluffs of the north side, and pressed on along the dry, dusty roadway. Barely more than the width of one vehicle in many places, the rutted, twisting road wound its way through undulating hills of sun-bleached range grass and broad-crested oak tress as it climbed slowly toward the pine trees and cool breezes of the mountains.

For Thomas, the euphoric anticipation of visiting an area he had never seen soon turned to frustration as he hunched firmly over the steering wheel. The struggle to avoid deep, sun-hardened ruts that could rip a tire from its rim, chuckholes that could snap a spring or axle-bending boulders was constant. The intensity of the sun, which soon pushed the temperature past the one hundred-degree mark, added to his discomfort.

Initially, Thomas had accepted the idea of camping in Yosemite with some reluctance, remembering all too well the discomfort of roughing it in the war-torn mud of France. His attitude had softened some after their day-long drive through the sun-baked foothills had carried them into the cooling breezes of the mountains and their first night stay in the comfort of the Wawona Hotel.

This morning, after a night of love-making and restful sleep, they continued their journey to the 5,000-foot elevation at Chinquapin Junction. There, after a brief pause to tighten the Maxwell's brake bands, Thomas shifted into low gear and started the long, arduous descent to the valley floor of Yosemite. As they descended slowly through zigzag patterns of early morning sunlight slicing through pine trees and the breath-taking drop-off to the Merced River canyon to the left, he began to more fully appreciate the spectacular scenery of the great national park. The potential discomfort represented by the huge wall tent, canvas cots and other camping supplies lurking in the back seat seemed to diminish against the increasing anticipation of reaching their destination.

Finally, after an hour-long struggle against the chuckholes and rock-strewn surface of the mountain roadway, they reached the valley floor. Once there, they motored along the road paralleling the river until they found a place to set up camp in a large meadow about a hundred yards from the water and near a grove of pine trees. A dozen or so campers were scattered around the area, some in tents, others spending only the day or sleeping in the open or in their cars.

It took a good deal of energy for Thomas and Brenda to wrestle the heavy, cumbersome tent out of the back seat and onto the ground and start unfolding it. When they finally had it laid out, unveiling the two support poles and bundles of stakes, he exclaimed, "God, this thing's bigger than I realized!"

She sidled up beside him and put an arm around his waist. "But we don't have to use all of it, my dear. We can just sleep in one side if we want."

"Yeah, but we still have to put the whole darn thing up."

"Maybe we could just forget it and sleep in the open under the stars."

He turned and looked up at the western sky. "We better not. Those clouds look pretty threatening."

With Brenda struggling to hold up the first support pole against the weight of the tent, he wrestled one end of the canvas into place, stretched the guy rope forward, used the head of his claw hatchet to pound a stake in the ground, and tied it off. Then he positioned the second support pole and with both of them pushing and pulling, stretched out the back guy rope and staked it down. As she strained mightily to hold up the precarious structure, he spread out one side, staked a corner and another, then went around to the opposite side.

"Hey, a couple of stakes are missing."

"You sure?"

"Yep. Hang on while I find some replacements." He strolled off into the trees and returned in a few minutes with several dried limbs. He cut them into suitable lengths and finished setting up the tent. Finally, he dug a shallow trench around the perimeter to drain off rainwater. Exhausted, and fighting the growing pain from his leg wound, he dug a <u>Nehi</u> out of the cooler and sat down on a rock.

Brenda busied herself making their temporary abode comfortable. She lugged in the food and the large duffel bag in which they had packed extra clothing, bedding and toiletries. She carried two cots into the tent, unfolded them and made them into beds with sheets and blankets. A small folding table and coal oil lantern, set up between the two cots, completed the arrangement. Lastly, she unfolded two canvasback chairs in front of the tent, flopped down in one and smiled at her husband.

Amused, he asked, "Do all German girls like to work so hard?"

She laughed, "Just when they're married to cute Irishmen."

He was energized enough by her frenetic activity to scrounge for rocks that he formed into a circular fire pit, and they sat down to consume their lunch of sandwiches, hardboiled eggs, potato salad and cold root beers. Then they climbed back in the car and spent the balance of the afternoon exploring the valley, snapping more photos with their new <u>Kodak Brownie</u>, and gawking open-mouthed at the ephemeral mists of the waterfalls and the rugged granite cliffs rising guardian-like three thousand to four thousand feet above the valley floor. They were undeterred by the heavy black storm clouds that continued to gather around the high perimeter throughout the afternoon.

By the time they returned to their tent, dusk was settling over the valley and a few drops of rain had started plopping intermittently into the dust.

Undiscouraged, Thomas started a fire, pulled out a skillet and began frying the ground meat. Brenda used another frying pan to cook up a mess of scrambled eggs, finishing just as the rain started falling with greater intensity. They grabbed the food and chairs and escaped inside the tent, uncorked the bottle of Zinfandel she had packed, and dug into their meal.

When they finished eating, they stretched lazily, lay back on their cots and listened to the background rhythm of the rain drumming against the overhead canvas. Presently, Brenda spoke, "Thomas, what was your childhood like?"

Taken aback, he hesitated a few moments before replying, "Why do you want to know about that?"

"Just curious, you never seem to talk about your early life."

He chuckled caustically, "You mean my slavehood?"

"You didn't play games or read books, things like that?"

He shook his head grimly. "I worked almost from the day I could walk. I cleaned out chicken pens, fed them and gathered eggs or helped Mother in her garden. Then when I was older, I got promoted to slopping hogs, milking cows or mucking out their sheds, or chopping ice out of water troughs at sunup."

"That took all day?"

"Yeah, with all the other chores. Don't forget, twenty to thirty cows can pile up a lot of crap."

She looked at him quizzically, "You didn't even get to read books?"

He sat up on the edge of his cot and took a drink of wine before replying. "Not much, except by coal oil lamp. When the sun went down, we went to bed; when it came up, we went to work."

She frowned, "You didn't go to school?"

"Not until we moved to California. Mother taught us the alphabet and our sums and reading and cursives." He grinned weakly, then added, "I still have my old *McGuffey* reader and a worn out *Tom Sawyer*." He looked away as his eyes started misting.

She sat up and reached for his hand, "I'm sorry I brought up an unhappy subject. Are you all right?"

He took a deep breath before replying, "Yeah, I'm OK, but my shoulder and leg are starting to bother me pretty bad. Too much driving, I guess."

"Maybe you better let me take the wheel when we return home tomorrow. I'm a good driver."

"I'm sure you are, but I don't think women should be driving on these dangerous mountain roads, especially after this storm when they're really going to be muddy and treacherous."

He stood up, walked to the tent opening and peered across the meadow toward the flash and rumble of the thunderstorm, now parked directly over the valley floor. When a blinding slash of lightning cut through the darkening sky and struck a tree at the edge of the river, she joined him to watch as the resulting flames flickered and finally smoldered down to wisps of smoke and steam against the onslaught of the rain. They shook their heads at the unrelenting downpour and the standing water building up as the meadow became engorged, and finally turned back to quietly finish their wine under the flickering light of the coal oil lantern.

She broke the silence, "Thomas?"

"Uh huh."

"You ever think about returning to farming?"

Surprised by the question, he glanced at her quizzically, then finally answered absently, "I've thought about it from time to time. I enjoy the quiet and getting away from the noise and hassle of city life. But farming's also a lot of hard work. Not sure I could handle it with my leg."

"It might be easier for you than standing around all day in that old office. You could rest when you needed to."

"But, I thought you wanted me to work at the Post Office."

She shook her head, "Not necessarily. Admittedly, it's good, steady income, not as uncertain as farming. But, you seem so interested, like when you talk to Ivan about fertilizing and weeding and stuff. It just looks like you have a natural feel for it."

He responded "Guess I really haven't thought that much about it."

"Papa and my brothers have made a pretty nice living at it. And it's such a good place to raise children."

He took a swallow of wine before responding. "To tell the truth, Brenda, I'm not happy working at the Post Office. It's pretty dull."

"What would you like to do?"

He hesitated, not certain he was ready to expose his innermost thoughts to his new bride, not sure she would empathize. Finally, his voice dry with self doubt, he cleared his throat and took the plunge, "Well, I've always thought I'd like to be a writer, or maybe a reporter."

"A reporter?"

"Yeah, you know, like Brad Simpson."

"But, do they make any money?"

He shook his head, "Don't know but, judging by what Brad's told me, it sounds like interesting work."

"When you say writer, you mean like books?"

He nodded.

"But...but can you make a decent living?"

He laughed, "You mean like Booth Tarkington... or...or Mark Twain?"

"Well, no. But how would you get started?"

"I've thought about trying short stories. Sometimes magazines will pay for them."

Brenda didn't comment further as they finished the last of their wine, stretched and yawned and decided to go to bed. Thomas reluctantly acknowledged a problem he had felt building up for some time; he had to empty his bladder. He sure didn't want to go out in the rain, and couldn't quite work up his nerve to broach the matter to Brenda. Instinctively, she came to his rescue when she started rummaging around in the duffel bag.

"What are you looking for?" he asked.

"The thundermug."

"The what?"

She pulled out a child's porcelain chamber pot. "They taught us this in Campfire Girls. Never go camping without one."

"What on earth are you going to do with it?"

"I'm going back in the corner and use it, if you'll be kind enough to turn your back."

He was too non-plussed to react. He pushed the tent flap open, unbuttoned his pants and added his stream to the nearest puddle, marveling at the feeling of abandon that came with peeing into the soft mountain air.

By the time he turned back into the tent, she was undressing down to her undies and sliding into her cot. He took off his hiking boots and outer clothes, leaned over and kissed her gently, turned down the lamp and crawled into the other cot. The thunder and lightning were more distant now that the center of the storm had passed over, but raindrops were still playing a sleep-inducing symphony on the canvas overhead. He turned toward her and called out throatily, "Aren't you going to join me?"

She yawned teasingly, "Guess I'm too tired. Can I have a rain check?"

He nodded sleepily, scrunched around trying to get comfortable in the thin cot, and soon was snoring.

But in a few moments, she was calling out, "I'm cold."

"Huh?"

"Don't we have another blanket?"

"Huh uh. You want mine?"

"No. I want you to come keep me warm."

He didn't need a second invitation. He stepped across to her, pulled the blanket back and squiggled in beside her in the narrow cot. It took only a second for him to realize she was completely naked. He eagerly squirmed out of his underwear and started kissing her soft lips and warm neck, then caressing the contours of her breasts and the flatness of her belly. In a moment, he was on top of her, oblivious to the creaking complaints of the flimsy cot.

He stopped with a shout of surprise and shock. It was like someone had slapped a cold, wet towel across his back.

"Thomas, what's the matter!"

He twisted his body against the heavy, clinging weight pressing down on him until he realized what had happened. The top and side of the tent, sopping wet with rainwater, had collapsed across him. He pushed against the soggy canvas, crawled out of the cot and stepped onto the ground, now wet from water seeping underneath. He turned the lantern back up, helped Brenda squirm out from under the sagging canvas and guided her to the opposite side of the tent, still standing precariously.

"Jesus, what a mess." He pulled the blanket off her cot and wrapped it around her naked, shivering body.

"Oh, Thomas, what are we going to do?"

"Guess I'll go out and try to tie it down."

"Better put some clothes on."

"To hell with it, they'll just get wet."

He stepped out to the sight of water-soaked meadow grass and sagging tree limbs framed by granite cliffs, now glistening under the soft light of a huge gibbous moon and shadowed occasionally by storm clouds drifting into the depths of the High Sierras.

He took a deep breath of appreciation then, barefoot and naked except for the bandage around his wound, stumbled out to the collapsed side and felt around for the support ropes. He finally found one along with its improvised peg, completely pulled out of the saturated earth. Realizing it was too weak to hold again, he hobbled across the rough terrain to retrieve a tire iron and jack handle from the car. He pushed these into the ground to serve as stakes and, pulling with all his strength and weight, finally managed to partially straighten the tent.

Resignedly he sloshed back to the car, reached into the pocket back of the front seat and extracted a pint bottle of brandy. As he returned to the tent, the wet bandage slipped down and off his calf. Back inside, Brenda greeted him with both of their towels. While she dried off his naked body, he uncorked the bottle and tipped it up for a long draft.

"What's that?" she asked.

"Pain killer," he replied and took another swig.

She pushed him toward his cot, turned down the lantern, crawled in beside him and wrapped their last dry blanket around their naked bodies. They fell into a restless sleep.

CHAPTER 10

The Sunday after returning from the honeymoon, Thomas arose with the sun as usual. He rolled quietly out of bed so as not to disturb Brenda, closed the bedroom door softly and went to the front bedroom to retrieve his new typewriter. It actually was a used *Royal* upright given to him by Brad when the newspaper bought him a new one.

Thomas carried the heavy machine to the kitchen table and sat down in front of it. He was not familiar with the arrangement of keys so started by twisting the roller forward and backward and poking at a few keys, then rummaged around in a kitchen drawer until he found a sheet of paper. He inserted it and started typing his name, laboriously hunting for each letter, and typing 'oroark' without a capital 'O' or apostrophe. When the bell dinged, he peered into the mechanism confusedly, until realizing he had reached the right margin of the page. He found the caps key and retyped his name in capital letters, and finally systematically went down the rows of keys, depressing each and admiring the number, letter or symbol it left on the paper. At one point, he hit two keys at once and had to reach into the nest of type bars to untangle them.

He was surprised at how loud the tapping noise sounded in the empty room, and turned toward the bedroom several times, hoping he wasn't disturbing Brenda or the baby. But eventually, Tommy did awake with his usual little cry and Brenda poked her head out to see what was going on.

"What on earth are you doing?" she asked sleepily.

He smiled back, "Trying out my new toy."

"You know how to use it?"

He shook his head, "Not really, but I'm starting to figure it out."

"So, what's it good for?"

"Oh, typing letters or…or you might want to print one of your menus real neat." He sighed, "Maybe I'll even type a story on it some day."

She glanced at the wall clock to see that it was six o'clock, then said, "I was planning to fix a big breakfast. I thought you would be anxious to get into the field and help PJ and Erasmus with the irrigating."

He looked up, "Uh, no. I'm sure they're taking good care of it."

She shrugged and went to the bathroom, and came back shortly to retrieve Tommy from his crib for his morning feeding. Thomas, annoyed over having his concentration broken, picked up the typewriter and returned it to the bedroom.

Seeing Brenda busy with the baby, he took over the preparation of their breakfast of bacon, eggs and biscuits. When they sat down to eat, they started reminiscing over the wedding and their eventful honeymoon in Yosemite. Brenda commented, "I'm especially proud of the sterling serving bowl Papa and my brothers gave us, aren't you?"

Thomas took a bite of egg and nodded vaguely as he glanced toward the bric-a-brac cabinet where the bowl now occupied the center position.

"It's an antique, you know. Papa and Mama brought it over from Germany when they moved here."

"Who gave us that?" he asked, pointing toward another new item, a large, wooden egg brightly lacquered with a doll's face.

"Oh, that's from that Cohen woman, Brad's new lady friend. Apparently it's some kind of Russian toy. It hardly seems like an appropriate wedding gift."

He spread butter and jam on a biscuit as he responded, "Yeah, she seems to know a lot about Russia."

"What does she do anyway?"

"Understand she runs the Americanization program for immigrants at the Normal School.

Believe she's been trying to talk Boris into signing up."

"What's that?" She asked as she fed the baby a spoonful of applesauce.

"It's that new Government program to help immigrants learn English and understand more about our customs and laws so they can become better citizens."

"Sounds like a good idea, especially for all those ignorant Russians, Slavs Italians, and…and Jews that are flooding into the country since the war stopped."

Thomas glanced at Brenda, silently swallowing his embarrassment over her remark with a drink of coffee, and observed, "Guess we can't blame 'em for getting away from that revolution over there."

"So what did you think of that woman?" she asked.

He shifted in his chair, "Seems OK to me, kinda haughty looking. Probably pretty intellectual, just what Brad needs."

"I didn't care for her hair style, all that black hair piled up on her head just makes her face appear longer. And her eyes. It looks like she uses too much of that new mascara."

"Maybe that's supposed to make her look more professional."

"Well, I think she's Jewish."

"Who cares? I'm just happy to see my friend with a woman."

"Papa always told me you can tell Jewish people from the smell of garlic. But I didn't notice any during the wedding."

He ignored her remark, stuck a slice of crisp bacon in his mouth and chewed thoughtfully for a few moments before speaking again, "It was good to see Missus Harrington again, but she sure gave me a surprise."

"What was that?"

"When we were dancing, she told me she's getting a divorce."

"Oh, my heavens!"

He shook his head, "She said Mister Harrington's gotten too radical, even become a Socialist. Doesn't have any interest in her or the boys or the farm."

"Oh, that poor woman…and…and those boys!"

"It seems like they're getting along OK without him. She bought a new truck and says the boys are making good money selling vegetables. And she and PJ seem to have found each other."

Thomas, standing up to carry the empty dishes to the sink, was distracted by the sound of motor cars pulling into the yard. He put the dishes in the sink and peered out through the screen door. "My God! What the---!"

He shouted at Brenda, "Take the baby and get in the bedroom!" He ran into the front bedroom and returned with his father's double-barrel shotgun and box of shells as Brenda, clutching Tommy, cried out, "What's the matter?"

"It looks like some of that Klan bunch. Stay back in the bedroom!" He dropped shells in the shotgun and closed and cocked both barrels.

He pushed the screen door open part way to see several individuals, their bodies and heads clad in white sheets and cone-shaped masks, climbing out of two cars. They were carrying rifles, shotguns and truncheons, and a couple had pistols strapped to their waists. He called out, "What the hell you want?"

The tallest of the group, the apparent leader, yelled in a high-pitched voice, "We're looking for your nigger."

"What the devil for?" Thomas glanced furtively toward the bunkhouse and saw PJ peeking around the corner.

"Think he mighta been messing with a white gal in town."

"That's bullshit. He hasn't been near town since he came here."

Several conferred with the taller man, then one with a holstered pistol hanging at his right side hollered, "We wanna talk to him anyway."

Another added, "Yeah, we don't like niggers living out here."

PJ, holding his big Colt .44 down at his side, had stepped out a few feet in front of the bunkhouse and shouted back, "What the hell you mean out here?"

"East of town. They belong west of the tracks."

PJ yelled back, "You can go to hell. He's staying here."

The Klansman then drew his pistol and squeezed off a quick shot that slammed into the wood frame of the bunkhouse a few inches from PJ. The little man ducked and in an instant returned fire, and Thomas gasped when the attacker crumpled to the ground, blood oozing out through his white mask.

The others stood transfixed for a moment until one raised his rifle and shot wildly toward the bunkhouse, causing PJ to grab his shoulder and yell in pain as he ducked behind the wall. Another Klansman pointed his rifle toward Thomas and squeezed off a shot. When the bullet ripped angrily past his head, Thomas stumbled back, fell down and reflexively jerked a trigger on the shotgun. The blast of buckshot was low, sweeping the ground and knocking the nearest attacker down, clutching at his legs and writhing in pain.

Thomas spun around at the sound of Brenda's scream and saw her tumble to the floor, the baby in her arms. "Brenda, Brenda!" he cried as he dropped the shotgun on the floor, scrambled to his feet and ran to her side, "Were you hit?"

She pushed herself to a sitting position, stared back at him wild-eyed and shook her head uncertainly, "I don't think so, but I heard the bullet!" She cuddled her arms around the squalling baby.

Thomas, livid with rage, returned to the shotgun, pushed the screen door open and called out quietly, determinedly, trying to mask his shaking, "Maybe it's time you bastards got the hell out of here." He dropped a shell in the empty chamber, closed both barrels, and cocked the hammers.

No one moved for a moment, then one and another Klansman started toward their cars. A couple picked up their dead member and loaded him in the back of one vehicle, while others helped the one who had been wounded limp toward the second motorcar. They jammed the cars into gear and spun out of the yard in a cloud of dust.

Thomas slumped down in the open doorway, trembling, his heart thumping in his chest. He struggled to suck air into his lungs as Brenda came to his side, holding Tommy and sobbing hysterically.

He took a deep breath, struggled to his feet, and reached out to his trembling wife and whimpering baby. He pulled out a handkerchief to dab at Tommy's tear-stained cheeks, then wrapped his arms around them and silently held them close.

When he felt them calming, he said, "I better check on PJ and Erasmus." He kissed them both, turned and ran to the bunkhouse where he found the wiry little farm manager sitting on the edge of his bunk, holding a piece of burlap against the blood seeping from his left shoulder. "Bastards nicked me, Boss."

"Let's go to the house so Brenda can bandage it proper." He helped PJ to his feet, asking, "Where's Erasmus?"

"I'se here, Massuh."

Thomas poked his head around the partition to see the whites of two big, owlish eyes peering back from the semi-darkness where Erasmus was still cowering in the corner. "You OK?" he asked.

"Yassuh, but I'se fixin' to upchuck." He leaned forward and vomited on the floor.

Thomas stepped closer and laid a hand soothingly on his shoulder. "Come on outside and get some fresh air. They're all gone now." He escorted them out of the stuffy bunkhouse and back to the house. While Brenda set about cleansing PJ's minor flesh wound, applying *Mercurocrome* and bandaging it, Thomas poured coffee for everyone. Then he phoned the sheriff's office to advise of the fracas, and PJ and Erasmus departed to take care of their chores.

When Sheriff Thorsen arrived an hour later with a deputy, Thomas met them at the door.

The lawman was effusive as he stuck out his hand, "Thomas O'Roark, my Lord! Haven't seen you since before the war. Things got pretty quiet after you and your brother left town." He chuckled at his own attempted humor, and the deputy dutifully joined him.

Thomas smiled uncomfortably, clearly recalling past altercations with Thorsen and his deputies, mostly over the involvement of his brother with the Industrial Workers of the World.

"You still messin' around with them 'Wobblies'?" Thorsen asked

Thomas glowered and replied firmly, "No, that was my brother."

The sheriff ignored the reply, "Judge up in Sacramento put a bunch of them boys in prison back in January. Reckon they need to do the same to the ones startin' all the fires and wreckin' equipment up north."

Thomas ignored the comment and invited the sheriff and deputy into the house. They doffed their Stetsons, acknowledged Brenda and the baby sitting on the sofa, and took seats around the kitchen table. "So, you think your visitors were from the Klan?" Thorsen asked.

"I guess that's who they were, damned cowards wearing masks."

The deputy commented, "Sounds like the Klan. They like to wear those robes and---"

Thorsen interrupted, "They fired first?" He used his hat to fan against the stuffiness of the kitchen.

"Absolutely," Thomas answered and described his position in the doorway and PJ's by the bunkhouse. He turned to the wall beside the bric-a-brac cabinet to point out the hole made by the bullet that nearly hit him and Brenda.

Thorsen stepped to the wall, removed a knife from his pocket and dug in the hole, causing a fine powder of plaster and lath splinters to drift to the floor. When he found the bullet, he eyed it closely and rolled it around in his fingers, "Looks like a rifle slug all right." He retook his seat at the table, asking, "So where was your farm manager?"

Thomas took a piece of paper and pencil from a kitchen drawer and sketched the layout of the yard, showing the relative location of the house, sycamore and bunkhouse. He put 'xs' where the attackers stood, another one for where PJ was when he was shot.

Thorsen, studying the sketch, said, "I want to check the bunkhouse. Maybe we can find another slug."

"Certainly." Thomas led the sheriff and deputy out to the bunkhouse. They examined the wood frame until the deputy found a bullet hole, dug the slug out with his knife, hefted it and rolled it around between his fingers, and eyed it closely. "This 'un looks like a pistol slug, Chief."

Thorsen grunted, apparently not impressed with the deputy's ballistics expertise, and turned to Thomas, asking, "Where's your manager and that nigger you're keeping?"

Thomas bristled and replied firmly. "Out doing their chores, and don't call Mister Jones that. He's a wounded veteran, just like me." The sheriff ignored the reaction, turned and led the group to the vicinity of the sycamore. Wordlessly he and the deputy examined where the pool of blood had seeped into the dirt, impressions from tire treads and scuff marks from shoe prints.

When the two lawmen ended their investigation and started toward their vehicle, Thomas asked, "Any idea who the dead one was?"

"Yeah," Thorsen responded. "The coroner identified him already. Some young fella last name of Fenton."

Thomas caught his breath, "Black hair, metal glasses, about my height?"

"Yep. Musta been in the war. Had one of them military ribbons pinned to his shirt, a red and blue one with little white stripes."

"Oh, Jesus!"

"You knew him?"

Thomas started to explain that the ribbon probably was his. But he decided the sheriff wouldn't understand and settled for a non-committal response, "Yeah, if it's the guy I'm thinking of, his father owns a lumber yard out north of town." He felt the bile rising into his throat, walked away a few steps then turned back, "How about the guy with buckshot in his legs?"

Thorsen shrugged, "Didn't hear about no one else gittin' hurt."

"Know anything about who the others were?"

Thorsen shook his head. "Hard to tell if they really were Klan, or just pretending. They've been gittin' pretty active, but this is the first real rough stuff we've heard about locally."

Thomas thought the sheriff seemed a little evasive, but decided not to pursue the matter. "You gonna need anything more from me?"

"Don't reckon. I'll talk to the DA, but looks like a pretty clear case of self defense to me." The sheriff and deputy climbed in their car and drove off with a friendly wave.

When Thomas returned to the house, Brenda rushed to him, threw her arms around his waist and laid her head on his chest. As he hugged her back and patted her consolingly, he realized she was sobbing, and his own eyes started tearing up. While the war had inured him to the sight of instant death, it dawned on him that now, in peacetime, he and his new wife and baby had nearly been shot in their own home, and someone he knew had been killed in his backyard. He didn't feel he could blame PJ; like the sheriff said, it was a case of self-defense and the little farm manager's quick reaction probably had saved their lives.

Nevertheless, the incident continued to bother him for the rest of the day. Although the killing seemed justified under the circumstances, it had happened to someone he had met, the younger brother of Earl Fenton, the friend who had joined the Marines with him. His mind returned to the mother and father and he wondered how they would bear up under this latest tragedy, the loss of their second son to a war that seemingly had not yet ended. He realized that some day, somehow he would have to help them come to terms with their loss.

Chapter 11

While Thomas and Brenda were settling into married life, the rest of the country was undergoing a period of major unrest.

Since the first of the year, there had been countless labor strikes involving nearly two million workers. Two communist parties had been formed, triggering a nationwide "Red" scare and the formation of vigilante groups intent on breaking up meetings and parades of suspected radicals. The Ku Klux Klan was expanding rapidly throughout the west and midwest. Dozens of race riots had broken out in the first half of the year, and the record of fifty-eight lynchings of Negroes set in 1918 was well on its way to being surpassed.

Among the approximately forty-five-thousand residents of Fresno, located some two hundred miles equidistant from the larger cities of Los Angeles and

San Francisco, the riots and strikes were relatively meaningless. There were no major industrial employers in the area, and prices for farm products were heading toward near records. Brenda remained at home, settling into the new life she had dreamed of during the war as a wife and mother. Thomas returned to work at the Post Office, slipping almost seamlessly into his new responsibilities as a husband, father and breadwinner.

For him, one consolation of his daily drive to and from work was he passed the aerodrome located at the fairgrounds. He usually slowed down or stopped when one or more planes were in the air, closely watching their takeoffs and landings and envisioning himself at the controls, high above the earth.

But on this particular Saturday, rather than stopping to observe on his way home, he pulled onto the dirt road that paralleled the straight stretch of the fairground's racetrack. The track, in addition to being used for horse racing during the annual fall fair, was the site of periodic automobile and motorcycle races. It also served as a runway for O'Leary's Aero Service.

When Thomas rolled to a stop next to the small wooden building on the east side of the track, a tall, slender man with pale blue eyes, a mop of red hair and dressed in a khaki jump suit stepped out and approached the car. "Afternoon, Laddie," he called out, speaking with a slight brogue.

"Afternoon, Sir," Thomas responded as he climbed out of the Maxwell and extended his hand. He noticed the flecks of gray in the man's mustache and side burns and guessed him to be in his late forties.

"Lookin' for a little spin, are you?"

"Actually, I've been thinking about taking lessons… you know… learning to fly."

"Have you now? Well, you've come to the right place." His eyes twinkled as he patted Thomas on the shoulder. "I'm Kevin O'Leary and I've taught many a young lad to fly."

Thomas introduced himself and reached into the car to his coat pocket to retrieve the gift certificate Brad had given him for a first lesson. O'Leary glanced at the paper, "Ah, yes. I remember when Mister Simpson purchased this for your birthday. How old are you?"

"Twenty."

"That's good. You need to be at least eighteen if you want to apply for an aviation pilot's certificate."

"Yessir."

"You'll have to pass several flying tests with an inspector from the Aero Club of America. Think you can do that?"

Thomas nodded a little uncertainly.

"And pass a physical. You have good eyes, hearing, heart and lungs?"

"Yessir."

"So, when shall we start."

Thomas shrugged, "How about now?"

O'Leary turned and led him into the wooden building, removed a spare jump suit, leather helmet and goggles from a wall peg, and handed them to

Thomas.   As he pulled the outer garment over his suit pants and shirt and buttoned the front, he asked, "How long you been flying, Mister O'Leary?"

"Oh, about ten years.   Took my first lessons from Orville Wright soon after I came to America."

Thomas squeezed the tight fitting helmet over his head.   "You fly during the war?"

"I was an instructor in the Army school at North Island, San Diego.   Too old to go myself but sent a lot of young lads over to battle the Hun."

Thomas followed the older man out of the building and toward the nearer of two identical biplanes parked alongside the runway.   "Ever have an accident?"

O'Leary chuckled, "Nothing I couldn't walk away from."   He proceeded to introduce Thomas to the aircraft, a Curtiss JN-4.   It was one of some five thousand bi-wing "Jennies", all carefully crated for shipment to France, that the Army had declared surplus after the Armistice.   O'Leary had paid less than five-hundred dollars for two of them, complete with engines, to start his flying service.

He led the way around the aircraft, pointing out its various features.   He lovingly rubbed his hand across the taut fabric covering and twanged one of the wire tension stays that stabilized the spruce wood struts supporting the two wings.   He pointed out the various control surfaces and ended his introductory walk-around at the engine.   He pulled two wooden boxes up so they could stand higher and peer more closely between the twin banks of cylinders, commenting, "This is an OX-5, a V-8 that puts out ninety horsepower. She's a very reliable power plant if you take care of her."

He extended three fingers as he continued, "Always check three things before you take off; the oil, the petrol and the water." He demonstrated each and slapped his hand against the radiator, adding with a grin, "And always look for leaks so you don't end up with a face full of rusty water."

Thomas shook his head attentively and responded, "Man, ninety horsepower. That's more than four times my Maxwell!"

O'Leary then guided him to the front cockpit where he settled into the bucket-shaped metal seat and dubiously eyed the joy stick rising phallic-like between his legs. The instructor showed him how to fasten the seat belt and described the function of each instrument; altimeter, compass, tachometer, gauges for oil pressure and water temperature and clock. He instructed him to rest his left hand on the joy stick, the right on the throttle so he could feel how he would operate the plane from the rear cockpit. He cautioned him to keep his feet off the rudder bar on the floor so he wouldn't put them into a spin. "I'll show you that later," he added. "Today we'll just do a few turns and light maneuvers so you can get the feel. It's probably going to be pretty bumpy because of the hot weather, so if it bothers you please use the bag." He pointed with a knowing smile to a paper bag sitting on the floor.

Thomas responded grimly, trying to hide the butterflies fluttering around in his stomach and threatening to fly up into his mouth.

"Ready?" O'Leary asked, as he summoned a mechanic to spin the prop.

Thomas nodded vaguely, and the mechanic hollered, "Switch off!"

O'Leary echoed the call and the mechanic pulled the prop through for compression, then yelled, "Contact!"

The instructor's response was drowned out as the engine roared to life and the "Jenny" surged against its wheel chocks, sucking Thomas' breath away at the blast of prop wash and castor oil exhaust sweeping over the windscreen. He pulled the goggles down over his eyes and buttoned the earflaps of the helmet under his chin.

In a moment, he could feel the airplane moving forward over the bumpy ground as O'Leary fishtailed his way to the south end of the landing strip. At the end, he spun it around and Thomas became aware of the throttle moving under his right hand as they accelerated toward takeoff. A slight movement of the joy stick and distinctive downward pressure on his stomach told him they were lifting off, and he glanced uncertainly over the side to see the ground slipping away below.

Thomas could feel O'Leary's firm touch on the controls as they banked and climbed slowly toward the east. He was just starting to relax in this strange and exciting environment when suddenly his stomach moved up to his mouth then back down to his buttocks, and he heard the words 'air pocket' through the speaking tube O'Leary had rigged between the cockpits.

When they leveled off at five hundred feet, Thomas could peer forward to the towering bulwark of the Sierra Nevada mountains seemingly moving toward them, slowly but inexorably. He barely heard the word 'maneuvers' as the instructor guided the plane through a series of gentle right and left turns. Then he pointed the nose down slightly and called out 'Sanger' so Thomas could gaze through the whirling prop to see the small farming village some twelve miles east of Fresno. His eyes traced the meandering line of the Kings River with the sunlight reflecting off the water, now reduced to its leisurely summer flow.

O'Leary again leveled off and vectored the plane into a series of steeply banked circles. Thomas looked straight down through the maze of struts and wing stabilizing wires to the multi-colored patchwork of vineyards, orchards and dry foothills twisting around like the patterns in a kaleidoscope. He reached for the paper bag just in time to catch the bitter-tasting remains of the sandwich and *Nehi* soda he had consumed for lunch.

As the instructor turned toward the west to start their return to the airport, he descended to three hundred feet and flew parallel to the familiar dirt road that ran past the Stuckey and O'Roark farms.

Thomas waved to what looked like Ivan working in the vineyard, who unwittingly waved back, then as they flew by his own home place, glanced perplexedly at two motor cars pulling into the yard.

When they landed a few minutes later, Thomas unhooked his seat belt and gingerly eased himself out to the ground. His exhilaration was tempered only by the bitter taste of bile in his mouth and a feeling of wooziness as he steadied himself against the side of the aircraft.

"So, what do you think, you still want to learn to fly?" O'Leary asked as they walked slowly back to the aerodrome office.

"Absolutely. When can I take another lesson?"

"How about an early morning or late evening next week? Shouldn't be so bumpy in the cooler air."

Thomas nodded as he doffed the helmet and jump suit, and O'Leary filled in his reservation book for the following Tuesday evening.

Thomas returned to the Maxwell and drove toward the farm, exulting over his new adventure and dreaming about being able to fly on his own. But when he pulled into the yard, he was brought down to earth by the sight of the two strange motor cars he had observed from the air. One was a Cadillac V-8 Brougham, the other a Packard Twin-Six Standard Touring car, both rather expensive vehicles.

When he climbed out of the car and walked warily toward the house, he was greeted at the door by Brenda announcing eagerly, "Your mother's here and has visitors!"

He stepped inside and quickly scanned the room to find Emma seated on the sofa with Muriel Duncan, her former Red Cross coworker, on one side of her. On the other side was a middle-aged woman he didn't know in an elegant white linen dress and straw summer hat topping her softly coifed blonde hair. Another woman was in his father's old chair, gently rocking a sleeping Tommy. This woman was more plainly dressed with olive-colored skin and her dark hair tied back in a bun. All were looking at him, smiling expectantly.

Emma spoke up, "Ladies, this is my son Thomas. And, son, you remember Missus Duncan from the Red Cross?"

He smiled and nodded.

His mother turned toward the other woman next to her, "And this is Missus Grace MacDonald." He nodded again, also observing how this visitor sat straight-backed on the lumpy sofa, crossing her legs sedately and smoothing her skirt with a certain style that, along with her blonde hair, reminded him of Lillian.

The visitor in the rocker was introduced as Doctor Rosemary Zitser.

Thomas took a seat at the kitchen table across from Brenda and turned toward Emma, "So, what brings you and your lady friends out to the farm, Mother?" He poured himself a glass of iced lemonade and reached for a cookie, noting it was being served on one of the *Chelsea* plates from the bric-a-brac cabinet, the first time he had ever seen it used.

Brenda replied eagerly before Emma could speak, "These ladies are starting a local birth control program and want your mother and Missus Duncan to manage it."

Missus Duncan spoke, "We all heard Margaret Sanger's talk last week at the Parlor Lecture Club. She was so inspiring---!"

Brenda interrupted, "Oh, did she tell the Sadie Sachs story?"

"Who the heck's Sadie Sachs?" Thomas asked irritably.

Brenda replied, "She's some poor woman who had fifteen children before she died from a self-inflicted abortion."

"But isn't birth control illegal?" Thomas asked.

Missus Mac Donald replied, "That's why Missus Sanger is promoting the National Birth Control League that she and a Missus Dennett started a couple years ago. They're trying to build public and legal support. That's why we've hired Doctor Zitser to do medical research, so hopefully the law won't bother us. She'll help us emphasize contraceptive techniques to better serve the poor and lower classes."

"And we've found an ideal location," Missus Duncan said, "on Mariposa near the Southern Pacific depot, away from so much street traffic."

Brenda asked, "You won't provide birth control information for the poor any more?"

"Oh, yes," Missus MacDonald responded, "but our priority will be on helping women prevent pregnancy for health reasons as well as financial, social or eugenic reasons."

Doctor Zitser, speaking softly so as not to wake the baby, said, "A woman with tuberculosis, heart palpitations or mental health problems, for example, probably shouldn't have babies any more than one with five or six children, whose husband can't afford to support them."

Brenda responded, "Well, I'm happy to hear you're including mental health. Maybe we'll have fewer feeble-minded in this country."

Thomas, embarrassed over his wife's remark, looked away and idly rubbed his hand against the cooling condensation of the glass of lemonade. Then he asked, "How do you feel about this, Mother?"

She nodded, a bit uncertainly. "I guess it sounds all right. I like the idea of helping all those poor women with too many children that I tried to help during the war."

Missus MacDonald spoke up. "A number of Fresno's leading women have agreed to support us financially and we've promised Emma and Muriel a starting salary of sixty dollars a month." Brenda and Thomas glanced at each other, a bit taken aback by such a significant amount, especially for women. It suddenly came back to him that Missus MacDonald's husband was a wealthy local businessman.

"And we'll have a motor car for our use!" Muriel Duncan added brightly.

Thomas took a swallow of lemonade and again turned to his mother. "It sounds pretty good to me, Mother. But, why are you telling me about it?"

Emma glanced down at her hands, then to her son, "Well, when I mentioned it at your birthday party, you were concerned about it being illegal. I...I just didn't want to cause any embarrassment."

Thomas shrugged, "Guess it looks like you're pretty safe now that these fine ladies are supporting you. So, maybe you should give it a try."

Emma smiled and the visitors clapped, and when they rose to leave, Thomas turned to Brenda, "I have a suggestion. To celebrate Mother's new venture why don't we take her to the band concert in Court House Park and finish with supper at the Hughes Hotel. How does that sound?"

Emma replied, "Oh, that sounds wonderful! I understand the Pacific Gas and Electric band will be playing." Brenda shook her head in agreement.

By the time they piled into the Maxwell, the sun was high in the sky and cooking the valley floor to a suffocating one hundred degrees. Even with the forward motion of the car and the top up, they found it necessary to fan themselves with whatever came in handy. Fortunately, the county had sprayed water on the farm road that morning so they didn't have to contend with dust.

As they approached the fairgrounds, they could see one of the "Jennys" flying about with two wing walkers waving precariously from the top wing. Thomas pulled to the side of the road and stopped for a better look.

"What are we stopping for?" Brenda asked, annoyed over the loss of the cooling forward motion.

"I just want to watch these guys for a moment."

Emma spoke up from the back seat, "Oh, that looks so dangerous. What if they fall?"

"They have ropes to hang on to," he replied.

"They'll probably get killed anyway," Brenda added sarcastically.

Thomas ignored the comments and opined, half to himself, "Looks like fun to me."

"Looks like a couple of idiots," Brenda added. "I hope you don't get any ideas about flying. It's too dangerous."

He decided not to tell about his first flying lesson, shifted the car into gear and resumed their journey into town.

When they arrived at the park, they were met by a sea of white and pastel colors clustered under the shading oak, elm, sycamore and pine trees. Hundreds of citizens, the women dressed in their summer calicos and linens, broad-brimmed garden hats and straw sailors, the men in their seersucker or Palm Beach suits and skimmers, were jammed into the wooden benches in front of the bandstand. Others had spread blankets on the grass, and some youngsters were climbing into trees for a better view. The thirty-four-piece band was tuning up on the stage.

They finally found a shady spot, spread their blanket and opened the thermos for a cooling round of iced lemonade. They struggled to their feet when the band kicked off its program with the *Star Spangled Banner*. After that, Thomas removed his coat and rolled it up for a pillow, stretched out in the shade of a sheltering oak with his hat over his eyes, and with the baby curled up in the crook of his arm, promptly fell asleep.

Later, he was awakened by someone shaking his shoulder, and opened his eyes to see Brad grinning down at him. "Hi, my friend. You're about to miss the whole concert."

Groggily, Thomas raised up on his elbows and looked around. "God, what time is it anyway…and…and where's Brenda and Tommy?"

"It's about four o'clock, and your wife, baby and mother have gone to the restroom. They said I'd find you here."

Thomas yawned and rubbed his eyes. "Man, I must have slept for over an hour."

Brad chuckled. "What wore you out, the honeymoon or flying?"

Thomas glanced around furtively, afraid Brenda might have reappeared. "How'd you hear about my flying?"

"Ran into O'Leary a little while ago."

"Please don't say anything in front of Brenda. Haven't worked up my nerve to tell her yet."

Brad nodded his understanding, removed his hat, and used his handkerchief to wipe the sweat from the headliner and his forehead.

"That a new hat?"

"Yeah, this is my new *Panama*.   Got it at Epstein's for $5.95."   He handed it to Thomas for closer inspection.

Thomas rubbed his hand around the brim, tipped down in front at a rakish angle, and felt the heft. "Feels nice and light."

"Cool too. The Indians in Central America weave them out of *jipipapa* leaves."

Thomas handed the hat back, reached for the thermos and tipped it up to find it was empty. "God, I'm thirsty."

"There's a vendor right over there.   What do you prefer, *Nehi*, *Jerico* or *Hires?*"

"Surprise me."

Brad returned in a few moments with two bottles of *Jerico*, cold and wet with condensation, handed one to Thomas just as the band started playing *The Stars and Stripes Forever*, signaling the end of the concert. He and Brad stood to welcome the return of Brenda, Emma and a sleeping Tommy.

Thomas took the baby, Brad helped Brenda gather up the blanket and thermos, and they started walking toward their motor cars. Thomas turned to his friend, "You want to join us for supper at the Hughes?"

"Oh, no thanks. Sarah and I are going to the Barton to hear Nellie Melba in *Rigoletto*."

"Who's she?" Brenda asked.

"She's an opera singer, originally from Australia. I heard her a few years ago in San Francisco. Really has a wonderful voice."

When they reached the car Thomas opened a back door for his mother, helped Brenda into the front seat and handed her the sleeping baby. He shook Brad's hand as they walked around the front of the car toward the driver's side.

Brad smiled and tipped his *Panama* to the ladies. "Thanks for letting me join you." Then with a grin, he lowered his voice to Thomas. "I'll buy you one of these hats when you get your pilot's certificate."

Thomas, nodding and smiling, climbed into the driver's seat.

CHAPTER 12

It was a Sunday morning in mid-September, and Thomas, PJ and Pedro were meeting under the sycamore, as they had earlier that week, to test the sugar content of freshly picked grapes. Pedro had brought a couple bunches of Thompson seedless from the West Forty and PJ had done the same with Muscats from the home acreage, and was gently lifting a glass saccharometer from its wooden case.

He plucked several grapes from one of Pedro's bunches, squeezed the must into the cylinder, inserted the calibrated spindle and watched as it slowly settled into the juice. He held it up to the light, studiously read the calibration and advised, "I'm gittin' twenty-two, twenty-three percent, Boss. Still a tad sour."

While he repeated the process and announced a slightly lower reading for the Muscats, Thomas and

Pedro were backing him up with the time-honored process of popping several grapes in their mouths and biting into their juicy flesh. The Thompsons, which typically matured a couple weeks earlier than Muscats, still brought a slight pucker, so admittedly could stand a few more days of ripening. And when Thomas rolled a couple of the larger Muscats around in his mouth and savored the juice, he could tell they also needed a little more maturing. He spat the seeds on the ground and glanced at his companions, waiting for their reactions.

They shook their heads, leading Thomas to ask if enough pickers would still be available if they postponed harvesting another few days. After being assured that with most of the soldiers now home and the *braceros* returning from Mexico there was plenty of help around, he decided to bow to PJ's and the old Mexican's greater farming experience. He would hold off a couple more days before making his decision. As Pedro drove away in his rattly Chevy truck and PJ wandered back to the bunkhouse, Thomas stepped out from under the variegated light of the sycamore, shaded his eyes against the bright sunlight and scanned the distant horizon. There wasn't a cloud in the sky.

But later, while he and Brenda were motoring through the hot, windless evening to the Stuckeys to celebrate Tommy's first birthday, Thomas saw something that gave him second thoughts about his decision. As they approached the Menshikov place, he peered ahead and spoke, "My God, look at that!"

"What?" Brenda replied, following his gaze and cuddling the baby.

"That's a bunch of *braceros* camped out along the road. Boris must have started picking already."

When they passed the entrance to the Menshikov place, Thomas waved at a couple of the kids playing in the yard, and remembered he hadn't seen the Russians for several weeks. He slowed to a stop as he came abreast of a dozen or so rickety looking vehicles beside the road with groups of Mexicans clustered around them. Beyond them he could see rows of freshly-picked grapes laid out on flat wooden trays and stretching several hundred yards back from the roadside. Some were even starting to turn purple, indicating they had been harvested several days earlier.

He set the hand brake, climbed out of the car, and walked across the road to an old Model T truck. A tattered tarpaulin was stretched from the roof to a couple of stakes to form a makeshift cover. A Mexican man was leaning against the vehicle lazily strumming a guitar while a woman was warming tortillas over a brazier and fanning away the blue-gray smoke with her free hand. Several kids were nearby kicking a rubber ball around in the dirt. Rolls of bedding were pushed up against the wheels of the truck.

"*Buenas tardes,*" Thomas called out.

The man stopped playing and nodded.

"*Cuando comenzar cosechar?*" he asked.

"*Tres dias*," the Mexican responded, holding up three fingers. Thomas mumbled "*gracias*", turned and stepped a few feet into the vineyard. He plucked several grapes from the nearest tray and put them in his mouth, then returned to the Maxwell.

"Looks like that wily old Russian has out-smarted the rest of us," he said, releasing the brake and shifting into gear. "He should get first crop money for those raisins."

"How much?" Brenda asked.

"The packers are estimating about two-hundred-fifty to two-hundred- seventy-five dollars a ton."

"Heavens, that sounds like a lot! How much will we get?"

"We should get that for our Thompsons, at least if we can pick 'em in time for first crop status and it doesn't rain. The Muscats will bring less, probably around two-hundred dollars."

She didn't comment further as they continued on and turned into the Stuckey yard. Papa was on the porch with Ivan, awaiting their arrival. As Thomas cut the engine, another motor car pulled in behind him. It was his mother with Major Brown at the wheel of an Overland he hadn't seen before.

"Hi," he called out as he stepped around to take the baby from Brenda. "Whose motor?" he asked.

"Oh, it's for Muriel and me!" his mother replied, a big smile lighting up her face. "The birth control ladies bought it for us." Brown helped her out of the car and retrieved a couple of gift-wrapped packages from the back seat.

Thomas, a little taken aback at such a significant benefit, didn't comment.   Brenda remarked, "My, that's quite a bonus."

"It's a second hand one," Emma added, sounding apologetic, "but it sure runs nice."

"You look pretty happy about it," her son remarked as everyone started toward the house."   He also noted that his mother was wearing a very becoming summer blouse and skirt he hadn't seen before, and he complimented her.

Ivan motioned them into the house as Brenda asked, "Where's Becky and her baby?"

"She phoned just as we were leaving," Emma replied.   "Said Ricky wasn't feeling well, but she did send a gift."

With Ivan holding open the screen door, a proud Papa reached to take his grandson from Thomas, leaned over to kiss Brenda and led the group toward the east veranda. It was the coolest room in the house, and the Stuckeys had set up a temporary dining table and electric fans ocillating at both ends. Emil, with Elsie Gross, his new girlfriend from the university standing beside him, met them with glasses of iced tea as Ivan disappeared toward the kitchen.

While they stood around sipping and fanning, Thomas eyed the Major, proudly dressed in his new cotton twill deputy sheriff's uniform, as he set his glass on the table, unstrapped his pistol and laid it up on a shelf. Then he turned to Papa to inquire about the status of their grape crop, and was advised they also were waiting a few days to harvest. In a moment, Ivan returned with a tureen of cold consommé, and Papa took his seat at the head of the table and tucked a napkin into the bib of his overalls. Emma sat to his right, then Brown and Elsie. Brenda occupied the place to the left of her father followed by Thomas and Emil. Tommy was placed in a high chair between Papa and Brenda, and Ivan started filling the soup bowls.

Everyone except the Stuckeys stirred suspiciously at the clear broth with floating dumplings until Thomas asked, "What do we have here, Papa?"

Papa, smiling and patting his tummy, answered, "*Ah, iss Markklosschen.*"

Emil translated, "It's consommé with beef marrow dumplings."

As several turned tentatively to their soup, Ivan lifted his glass of tea to toast the baby's first year and a bountiful crop. He also tipped glasses with Emil and his girlfriend, wishing them well on their imminent return to Berkeley to start their second year at the university. Then he glanced at Thomas, "Brenda tells us you had some visitors a few weeks ago. Any idea who they were?"

Thomas put down his glass and shook his head, "Not really. They were dressed in white sheets and masks like Klan members, but the sheriff wasn't sure."

Emil spoke, "I'm impressed by the number of prominent citizens who are becoming members. Makes me think seriously about joining."

Thomas eyed Emil suspiciously and said, "Not me, even though I understand my old boss at the bank is one of them."

Emma looked up from her soup, "What on earth are you talking about?"

Thomas paused in his eating to explain about the attack, leaving out the details of shots being fired and Ernie Fenton being killed.

When Brenda added, to Thomas' annoyance, that they appeared to be after Erasmus, Emma huffed. "Well, I've warned you before about those darkies. They're just like animals. They should stay among their own people."

Thomas opened his mouth to respond, but was cut off by Major Brown, "Those old Southern boys sure don't hesitate to keep 'em in their place. Strung up a couple more last week."

Emma added, "You can't trust them around white women and babies."

Thomas bristled, "Mother, that's enough! Erasmus is a wounded veteran and a good worker and as far as I'm concerned, he can stay at our place as long as he wants to." He glowered at Brown, discouraging him from further comment.

The guests stirred uncomfortably. Brenda looked embarrassed and turned to feeding the baby more broth and Thomas stared down at his empty bowl.

Ivan rose from the table, collected the tureen and soup bowls, and retreated to the kitchen. He returned momentarily bearing a large platter of *sauerbraten mit spatzle*. Everyone dug quietly and industriously into the German-style pot roast, and little Tommy started cooing and rocking back and forth between bites of mashed peas and carrots being fed by his Grandpa.

Thomas stuck his fork into a slice of meat and looked across the table at his mother. "So, how's the birth control clinic doing?"

"Oh, just wonderful. Since opening at our new location we've had quite a few visitors. And Doctor Zitser is gathering all kinds of valuable information."

"Police haven't bothered you?" Brenda asked.

Emma shook her head adding, "Oh, and guess who came in last week?"

Brenda shook her head.

"Missus Garcia."

Thomas looked up from his plate. "Pedro's wife?"

Emma smiled and nodded.

"What did she want?" he asked, irritated that someone might be interfering with his farm help.

"What a lot of other women want, to stop having babies. She has four, you know, and feels too worn out to have any more."

"What did you tell her?"

"Doctor Zitser showed her how to keep from getting pregnant."

Brown chortled, "I hope she also told Pedro to sleep out in the vineyard!"

Emma blushed, Emil and his girlfriend laughed nervously, and Ivan asked, "How's Pedro feel about it?"

Emma replied, "Don't know. Guess that's between the two of them."

Thomas shook his head in frustration. "I just hope you haven't made Pedro unhappy when we need him the most." He reached for his glass of tea and drank it down.

With dinner finished, Ivan cleared the table, brought in a chocolate birthday cake and placed it on the highchair tray in front of Tommy. Ivan lighted the single candle and Brenda and Papa made huffing and puffing sounds trying to get the baby to blow it out. Instead, he drooled down his chin, reached out and stuck his fingers in the gooey frosting, then put them in his mouth. Everybody chuckled as Ivan removed the slightly bruised cake, cut individual slices and passed them around.

Afterwards, they retired to the parlor for coffee and to open presents. Papa Stuckey gave his grandson a toy truck he had made from wood, and Ivan and Emil went together on a jumping jack clown made of *papier mache* that could be hung in his crib so he could move the arms and legs by pulling a string. Emma and Becky each gave jump suits. Thomas and Brenda gave their son a set of Lincoln Logs and a teddy bear.

Eventually, when the little tyke started to yawn, Thomas and Brenda bid everyone goodbye and headed for home. It was after nine o'clock and even with the sun firmly settled behind the Diablos Mountains some one hundred miles to the west, the temperature was still in the nineties. Brenda, holding the sleeping baby in one arm and fanning her face with the other, asked, "What did you think of your mother's remarks about Erasmus?"

Thomas gripped the wheel tighter, "Pretty stupid."

"You don't think we should be a little wary?"

He glanced at her, scowling, "Why, what's he gonna do? He works hard, minds his manners around you and Tommy, keeps to himself when he's not working. What better help could we want?"

Brenda didn't comment further. Thomas, feeling a little embarrassed over the sharpness of his response, shifted in his seat before adding, "Frankly, I was surprised at Mother sounding so prejudiced. She never used to seem that way. My guess is she gets it from Brown."

She nodded absently, and he continued, "It's kinda scary to think of someone that intolerant as a deputy sheriff."

She sighed and cuddled the baby closer.

"Hard to understand what Mother sees in him."

"Maybe she thinks of him as a father figure, someone she can lean on."

He didn't respond as they motored along in silence past the roadside encampment of sleeping <u>braceros</u> and the makeshift Russian farmhouse, now battened down in the dark.

Abruptly, he raised his head and sniffed the night air. "You smell that?" he asked.

She inhaled, "What, the Mexicans?"

"No, no, the air. It smells electrical and feels prickly on my skin." He rubbed the hairs on his forearm.

She started to doze while he resumed focusing on the road ahead, then exclaimed, "Oh my, did you see that!"

Her eyes popped open. "Now what?"

"It looked like lightning." He pointed to the northwest far beyond the beam of the headlights. As he slowed and turned into the driveway, he saw another distant flash and in a few moments, heard the barely perceptible rumble of thunder. He shook his head, "Man, I hope that stays over there. We don't need rain around here."

He parked under the sycamore, unmoving in the still night, and stepped around to help Brenda. As he reached for the sleeping Tommy, he heard a faint, ghostly rustling, like a giant hand brushing across the tree's upper branches. Then all again was quiet.

He shivered involuntarily as he took the baby in one arm and Brenda's hand with the other and led the way into the house. He deposited the baby in his crib, joined Brenda in undressing and they crawled into bed.

But he found himself too concerned about the distant storm and too frustrated to sleep. The frustration came from the brief discussion during their drive home, which he vented slightly by commenting to Brenda lying beside him. "I've been thinking over what you said about Mother's relationship with Brown."

"How so?"

"Well, Father dominated their marriage for nearly twenty-five years. I just hope she's not slipping back into that kind of relationship."

"Let's face it, Thomas. It's pretty difficult for a woman to make her way in the world all by herself. Maybe she feels the need for whatever support Brown can provide."

"I guess that's OK as long as he doesn't try to run her life. She did such a good job of becoming independent with her Red Cross work, and I guess now with this birth control thing."

"I think you and your sister can take credit for that. After your father died, weren't you the ones who helped her find a new life?"

He nodded absently and plucked at his sweaty undershirt as a hot breeze suddenly stirred outside, causing the limbs of the boxwood and privet shrubs to scratch noisily up against the side of the house. When the wind curled the window curtains into their own little pirouette, Brenda rolled toward him, smiled and bussed him on the cheek. "You going to let me be independent when I want to?"

He smiled back sleepily and kissed her on the forehead, "Sure, why not?"

"Maybe you'll let me get a job in town?"

He tensed up, "What on earth are you talking about?"

"Just teasing. But I do think about it sometimes. I used to enjoy my old job at the department store and the chance to be where things are going on and you meet other people."

"I thought you wanted to stay home and raise babies."

She replied thoughtfully, "Maybe I could do both."

Thomas, too disturbed and confused by the remark, yawned and settled his head into the pillow. She kissed him again on the cheek and lay back on her side of the bed. He glanced toward the baby safely tucked into his crib, pulled the single sheet up over their sweating bodies and turned out the bed lamp. With his mind tumbling between Brenda's remark about taking a job and his decision to hold off on harvesting, he continued to toss and turn against the damp sheets. He occasionally opened his eyes and peered into the dark outside the window as the wind cooled and freshened and the ominous rumble of thunder came closer.

When he finally fell into fitful sleep, it was to again experience the nightmare he thought had left him. Once more, it was the flash and rumble of artillery and the rattle of machine guns as he hunkered down with his fellow Marines in a muddy trench. Suddenly, there was a blinding flash and deafening explosion as a heavy shell landed nearby and Thomas dreamed he was knocked to the bottom of the trench.

He awoke with a start, his underwear soaked with sweat, and found himself sprawling on the floor tangled in the sheet.

"Thomas, what on earth!" Brenda cried. She turned on the bed lamp while he groped to a sitting position, rubbed his eyes and tried to collect his thoughts.

He struggled to his feet and looked out through the wind-blown curtains as raindrops pattered intermittently on the roof. Another flash of lightening in the near distance, followed quickly by the crash of thunder, made him jump back from the window. Cautiously he peered out again, only to see a subsequent flash strike a distant grape post and set it afire. The next stab of lightening exposed PJ staring out from the corner of the bunkhouse, wearing nothing but his skivvies.

Thomas returned to bed and pulled Brenda close. "My, God, poor Boris. His whole crop's on the ground!"

She shook her head and cuddled up in the crook of his arm. In a few minutes they could tell from the direction of the thunder that the storm was passing away to the east. They laid back down on the bed, pulled the sheet up, curled together like two spoons, and fell into a restless sleep as the storm rumbled away into the Sierra Nevadas.

They were awakened early the next morning by an exceptionally bright sun pouring into their bedroom through a freshly-washed sky. A light breeze stirred the curtains and blew the sweet smell of damp earth through the room. The baby was in his crib quietly playing with his blocks and new Lincoln Logs.

Thomas got up, went to the bathroom, then to the kitchen door. He pushed the screen open to gaze out on the rain-dampened yard. The chickens were having a clucking good time scratching and pecking for bugs washed out of their underground fortresses. Returning to the bedroom, he pulled on his coveralls, socks and boots, clapped on his straw hat and advised Brenda he was going over to the Russians' to see how they had faired in the storm.

When he pulled up to the Menshikov's, he found the braceros gone and the yard unusually desolate looking. Their Ford truck and wooden wagon, both glistening wet from the rain, stood to the left in front of the small barn. The once stately green branches of the poplar trees along the western boundary were knocked askew from the onslaught of rain and hail, and the limbs of the big white oak to the right of the house were sagging and dripping forlornly.

The freight car house looked even more faded than he remembered from his earlier visits. There were no outward signs of life except for a wisp of gray smoke curling up from the stovepipe chimney. When he walked around to the rear and approached the partly open door, he was met by a haggard-looking

Sonia with the baby in her arms and two of the other youngsters hanging onto her skirt. Wordlessly she nodded toward the vineyard.

Looking out, Thomas could see the rounded shoulders of his neighbor slumped over at the end of one of the vine rows. As he walked past the smelly outhouse and approached the vineyard, he made out the shape of Yoseff seated beside his father, resting his head on his knee. Neither moved, and Thomas could quickly see why.

The vineyard rows were a shallow sea of muddy water and soggy grapes sloshing back and forth on their wooden trays. Some bunches still had their purple, partially sun-dried skins turned upward; others had been tumbled over to expose their undried green skins. Many clusters had washed completely off the trays into the mud. The leaves of the vines were drooping and dripping from the impact of the rain and hail.

Wordlessly, he pulled up an empty lug box, sat down beside Boris and put an arm over his slumping shoulders. He was surprised at how small the Russian's tall, ramrod physique felt to his touch. Neither said anything for a few moments until Boris picked up a handful of mud and flung it at one of the wooden trays.

"All lost," he mumbled.

Thomas couldn't think of anything to say. Actually, there was nothing that could be said to ease the pain of the moment.

Menshikov spoke again, "Boris no *goot* farmer... *goot* garbage man."

Thomas squeezed his shoulder, "You're good enough, Boris, just not lucky. You have to remember that farming is a 'next year' business."

"What mean?"

Thomas smiled wanly. "It means that no matter what happens this year, next year will be better. Sometimes, it's the only thing that keeps you going. And don't forget, you made good money with your peaches this summer."

They were silent for a few more moments, then Boris turned to Thomas. "You vant wodka?" Thomas shook his head.

"Come, have tea."

Thomas stood up and helped his neighbor to his feet, watched as he kicked at one of the drying trays, turned and accompanied him and his son to the house. Reluctantly, he entered the stuffy interior, still permeated with the faint, smoky odor of creosote used to preserve wooden boxcars. He doffed his hat, and watched Boris light the alcohol burner under a samovar at the end of the sink.

While the Russian busied himself slicing off slabs of a dark, rough bread, Thomas looked surreptitiously around the long, uninviting inside of the structure. It was depressingly dark, lighted only by the isinglass window on the south wall and a single electric floor lamp in the near corner. A rectangular wooden table covered with a white cloth was located in the right foreground. The mother was in a rocker feeding a bottle to the baby. The two middle youngsters, who were seated at the table eating cold cereal, were joined by their older brother.

A cast-iron Franklin stove stood against the wall to Thomas' left, and at the far end, a free-standing, wood-framed screen apparently served to separate the parents' sleeping area. Cots with feather mattresses on the near side of the divider seemingly were for the children. The walls were bare with no framed pictures, only a color print of a mountain scene nailed to one wall, a seascape tacked to another. A makeshift sink and gas range with several heavy pots hanging overhead lined the back wall at Thomas' right.

When Boris handed him a slice of bread and glass of tea, Thomas took a cautious sip of the fiery liquid and followed his host to a seat at the table. He fanned himself with his hat and watched mesmerized as the old Russian poured some of the tea into a deep saucer, stirred a few dollops of jam into it from a jar, and noisily slurped it down. Then he spread jam on his bread. Thomas followed his lead, marveling aloud at the richness of the whole strawberries in a heavy syrup. Boris pointed at the jar with a grin and spoke the word *varenie,* and his guest nodded at whatever that meant.

As Menshikov slurped and chewed, he leaned forward with his elbows on the table and began reminiscing in broken English about the family's prior life in Los Angeles. He told how as a newly married couple, he and Sonia had emigrated to America in 1906 after the Russo-Japanese war to escape religious persecution. They had joined a colony of several thousand other Russian Molokans in the eastern part of downtown Los Angeles. After a few years of seasonal work in foundries and lumberyards, they had saved enough to buy a horse and wagon, which Boris used to haul rubbish and garbage. This had provided a better income, up to two hundred dollars a month. It was enough to support their growing family and save for a down payment on the Fresno farm so they could move from the congestion and growing gang problems of city life.

During the long monologue, in which Thomas had hardly been able to insert a word or two, he began to worry about the time. He pulled out his pocket watch and realized he had been away from home for over two hours. Brenda would be concerned.

When he finally stood up to leave, Boris was still talking. Thomas interrupted to suggest he not do anything with the rotting raisins. In a few weeks, soon as he had finished his own harvest, he would send PJ over with the *Trak-Pull* and plow them under for fertilizer.

As he started toward the door, Menshikov stood up and wrapped his arms around him in a bone-crushing hug, and the son jumped up and grabbed him around the legs. Sonia smiled wearily from the background. Thomas finally extricated himself and, with tears in his eyes, returned to the Maxwell.

When he pulled into his own yard a few minutes later, he found PJ waiting for him. "How do the Muscats look?" he asked as he turned off the engine and got out of the car.

"Not too bad, Boss. Some of the top clusters on the yonder side got a little beat up from the rain but the pickers can cut those out."

"How about the Thompsons?"

"Me and Pedro checked 'em a little while ago, and they even look better. Worst of the storm apparently passed north and east of us."

"How about Erasmus, he got all the trays repaired and ready?"

PJ nodded.

"OK, let's wait a couple days for the ground to dry and get the pickers in. I want to wrap this harvest up before anything else goes wrong."

PJ touched his hat in agreement and headed off to the bunkhouse. Thomas turned toward a worried looking Brenda standing in the doorway in her cotton housedress and apron and holding a squirming baby. He took him in his arms and followed Brenda inside and sat down at the kitchen table.

"I was getting kinda worried," she ventured. "Seemed like you were gone so long."

"Yeah, I was trying to console Boris. Looks like the rain and hail knocked out his whole raisin crop." As he filled in the details, she shook her head in dismay and turned toward the sink asking, "You want some breakfast?"

"Cereal will be fine, and a bowl of peaches." When she brought the *Kellogg's* corn flakes, bowl of fruit and bottle of milk to the table, he lifted the baby into his highchair and asked, "What've you two been doing this morning?"

Brenda replied, "Oh, we had breakfast and I started a load of laundry. And now I'm preserving eggs. The chickens have really been busy the last few days." She reached into a wire basket holding some two dozen eggs, lifted one out and started rubbing it around in her hands.

"Mother used to do that, but looks like you're doing it differently." He mashed up a peach half and started feeding it to Tommy.

"I'm using the grease method recommended by the Department of Agriculture." She turned toward him, holding up a hand. "See, I put a little *Bailey's Fresh Egg Keep* in my hands, rub it until it's soft, and smear it all over the shell. When that's done, I wrap 'em in paper and put them in the icebox."

For Thomas, the sight of his new bride, her feminine curves still visible under the shapeless housedress, brought a sudden warm feeling. He kissed Tommy on the forehead and fed him another spoonful of mashed peaches.

Brenda smiled at him, apparently sharing his feeling of domestic tranquility, and remarked casually, "Better not feed him too many of those or I'll have to start another load of diapers!"

She returned to greasing eggs, "So what do you think the Russians will do now?"

He shook his head. "Dunno. Boris is obviously pretty upset. Have no idea if they have enough money to last another year or not." Tommy was starting to get droopy eyed in his chair so his father picked him up, carried him into the front bedroom and covered him with a sheet for his morning nap.

He returned to the kitchen, stepped up behind Brenda and slipped his arms around her warm body. "How much longer you gonna be?" he whispered, leaning down and nibbling on her ear.

"Just as long as it takes you to get out of your boots and coveralls," she replied, smiling and turning to the faucet to wash the grease from her hands.

Unmindful of the gathering, sticky heat, they chased each other into the back bedroom, closed the door and windows, pulled down the shades, undressed and tumbled into bed. The worldly worries over ripening crops, rain storms and the availability of pickers disappeared into the glorious escape of making love.

Chapter 13

It was the second Saturday in November and Thomas was returning to the farmhouse bursting with pride. That morning, after depositing Brenda and Tommy at the Stuckeys and phoning in sick to the Post Office, he had gone to the aerodrome to take the test for his aviation pilot's certificate, and passed.

As he skidded the Maxwell to a stop under the sycamore and entered the house, he noted by the wall clock that it was a little past noon. Too excited to think about lunch, he went to the bedroom for his typewriter and paper and returned to the kitchen table to prepare his letter of application for a pilot's certificate from the Aero Club of America. They in turn would appoint an official representative to supervise the same tests before granting the document.

He no sooner started writing than the phone rang. Annoyed at being interrupted, he waited to see if there would be a second ring. When it came, he stepped to the wall and picked up the receiver, "Hello."

"Hi, old buddy."

"Oh, hi, Brad"

"You know your Russian neighbor's in jail?"

"Oh, no! My God, what happened?"

"Sheriff claims he's a communist, along with about twenty others he's rounded up. According to the wire service, the Justice Department has arrested over nine hundred all across the country and plans to deport them to Russia."

"That's crazy."

"You know if Menshikov is a citizen?"

"Not sure. Seems like he told me once, but I don't remember."

"Well, a judge has scheduled a preliminary hearing for this afternoon. Can you meet me at the Court House by two o'clock?"

Thomas glanced at the clock. "Yeah."

"You better check with his wife if she's still home. If Boris is a citizen, we might be able to get the judge to release him."

Thomas hung up the phone, pulled on his jacket and cap and headed for the Maxwell. He had only seen Boris a couple times in passing since the September rainstorm had ruined his raisin crop, and now was feeling a twinge of guilt over being so neglectful. When he pulled into the Menshikov yard, he was struck by how forlorn everything appeared. The old yellow freight car looked even more washed out under the sunless fall sky. One of the double doors of the barn hung part way open, its hinges squeaking as it swung lazily back and forth on the breeze. A thin trail of smoke drifting away from the house into the cool air seemed to offer the only promise of life.

When Sonia opened the door in response to his knock, he was assailed by the odor of garlic. She looked bedraggled and red-eyed, like she'd been crying. Her hair was unkempt, and an old wool housedress hung loosely on her body. Against the background noise of the baby crying, she mumbled, "Boris no here...*polits* come."

Thomas nodded his awareness of the situation as he stepped inside the overheated room. The baby was in his crib, the two middle children eating and drinking milk at the kitchen table, the oldest boy sitting on one of the cots in the background. As the mother turned toward the baby, Thomas asked, "Did Boris ever become a citizen...you know...an American?"

Yoseff called out, "Ya, two years."

"Do you have his papers?"

The youngster jumped up, went to a cardboard box sitting against a wall and started rummaging through it. In a few moments, he approached Thomas and proudly held out a Certificate of Naturalization boldly inscribed in cursive letters with the name Boris Alexander Menshikov. Thomas noted it had been signed by a Federal judge in Los Angeles and was dated November 8, 1917, exactly two years earlier. He explained to Yoseff and Sonia that he wanted to take the certificate to the Court House to see if he could get the father out of jail. Turning to leave, he almost stumbled over the youngster, now grasping for his hand. "Wanna go."

"Um, maybe you should stay here and help your mother."

Yoseff shook his head. "Papa need help."

Acknowledging Sonia's nod of approval, Thomas took the boy by the hand and headed for the Maxwell. They drove to the Court House in record time, and found Brad waiting on the granite steps. Thomas waved the certificate and, with the youngster tagging along, followed him inside, asking, "What the hell's this all about, Brad?"

"I understand this was the idea of that idiot, Attorney General Palmer, and his new assistant, some guy named Hoover. They're still looking for 'Reds' around every corner."

"They think Boris is one?"

"Apparently he used to belong to an organization called the Union of Russian Workers. From what I've found out, most of their leaders went back to Russia a couple years ago after the revolution."

Thomas studied the certificate. "Looks like that's when Boris became an American citizen."

When they entered the courtroom, they found about a dozen people in the audience, mostly women and children, and six men sitting forward around the defendant's table. Brad led the way to the front row reserved for the press. As he handed the Naturalization Certificate to the defense attorney, Yoseff ran to the table crying 'Papa, Papa', and threw his arms around his father. A burly deputy pulled him away and escorted the tearful youngster back to a seat next to Thomas.

In a moment, the judge entered and called on the district attorney to present the charges against the six defendants. After that, the defense attorney produced the Naturalization Certificates as evidence that of the total rounded up, these particular individuals were American citizens. He described them as honest, God-fearing family men who were members of the Molokan religious sect and did not frequent saloons. For emphasis he added that the word Molokan was Russian for "milk drinker". He declared firmly that they were not communists, and were not proposing to overthrow the United States government.

The prosecutor then produced a booklet published by the Union of Russian Workers, which he claimed included a proposal to overthrow the government. He also charged that a number of the prisoners were suspected of having venereal disease, a claim that caused tittering from the audience.

The defense attorney, who could read Russian, rebutted with his own copy of the booklet. He pointed out to the judge that it was dated 1914, was written in Russian, and proposed the overthrow of the old Tsarist government in Russia, and not that of the United States. He also produced the results of medical exams indicating no presence of disease in any of the men. He finally concluded, "Your honor, the original leaders of the URW returned to their native country after the revolution two years ago. Quite frankly, the members remaining in America are nothing more than a group of friends who assemble occasionally to reminisce about old times. They enjoy the freedom of this wonderful country too much to ever propose the overthrow of our government. I request that all charges be dismissed and that they be released to their families immediately."

The judge motioned the two attorneys forward, reached for the booklet and studied it for a few moments, apparently thinking the strange Cyrillic lettering would shed some light on the situation. The defense attorney pointed out and interpreted the pertinent passages.

The prosecutor, who had been fidgeting during this discussion, finally interrupted. "Your honor, I believe there is another matter to consider relative to one of the defendants."

The judge glanced quizzically toward the six accused and back as the attorney continued. "The government believes one of them is a member of the radical Mensheviks, who participated in the Russian revolution in 1917. He has altered his name to Menshikov."

The defense attorney looked at his counterpart in open-mouthed disbelief and turned to the judge, "Your honor, my colleague only displays his ignorance. The Mensheviks were the minority faction of Russia's old Social Democratic Labor party. They favored a gradual, more democratic change in the government rather than the radical approach pursued by the Bolsheviks. Mister Menshikov could never have belonged to either faction because he and some six thousand other Molokans emigrated to America in 1906 after the Russo-Japanese War."

The judge paused, seemingly taken aback by the defense attorney's knowledge, then turned to the courtroom and asked if anyone would like to speak for any of the defendants.

No one responded until the words "I would, your honor" echoed through the room. In a second, Thomas realized the sound was coming from his mouth and he was standing.

He coughed, trying to clear the phlegm from his throat before continuing, "My name's Thomas O'Roark and I'd like to speak on behalf of Mister Menshikov, your honor." He leaned forward with his hands on the seatback in front of him, trying to steady his shaking knees, as the judge acknowledged him.

The words tumbled out of his mouth, "I...I've known Mister Menshikov as a neighbor for several months. He's an honest man...he's a...a...naturalized citizen of our great country...and...and a hard working fellow farmer trying to make a living for his family. I've never heard him say anything against our country...or...or anything in favor of Russia...or... or communism. He's an excellent example of the thousands of immigrants who came here to escape persecution and find a better life." As he paused for breath, he was conscious of Boris and the other defendants peering back toward him and of Brad and Yoseff, seated on either side, looking up at him.

With the pause, the judge asked if he had anything more to say.

"Yessir. I recently returned from that bloody war in Europe. My best buddies were an Indian, a...a Mexican, and...and...a Jew, a man of French ancestry and another white guy like me, all ready to fight for America. This demonstrates the...the differences that make America so strong. We need more good citizens like Mister Menshikov."

Thomas choked up and took a deep breath as ghostly memories flooded back. Finally, his throat tightening with emotion, he struggled to finish. "All of those guys were killed...or...or wounded fighting for you and me, your honor, and I'm sure Mister Menshikov would gladly do the same if he were called upon."

Thomas, his heart pounding, sat down awkwardly to the sound of scattered clapping, and turned to see Yoseff, staring back at him wide-eyed, then jumped back on his feet, "Your honor, I shoulda introduced his son...this young man beside me, and...and he has three more children at home." He finally sat down and took a couple of deep breaths as the judge advised he would announce his decision on Monday and rapped his gavel for adjournment.

While Thomas pulled out a handkerchief to blow his nose and wipe his eyes, Brad patted his shoulder, commenting, "Man, what a speech," and a smiling Yoseff reached for his hand. Thomas tried to calm his trembling while the bailiffs escorted the defendants back to their cells. His heart sank when he realized they were shackled at their hands and feet, and he saw how broken and dispirited his neighbor looked. He felt frustrated that he couldn't do more.

As they left the Court House with Yoseff still holding on to his hand, he spoke to his young companion. "How old are you Yoseff?"

He straightened his shoulders, "I'm twelve next month."

"Where do you go to school?"

"No school. Mama and Papa teach me at home, and I have tutor."

"You like that better than a regular school?"

Yoseff sighed, "Yes, kids tease me about my clothes and…and religion and my kosher food."

When they reached the Maxwell, Thomas opened the door for Yoseff, climbed in behind the wheel and started toward the farm. He thought of asking about the Molokan religion but hesitated, fearing he might be getting into a sensitive subject.

The youngster apparently sensed his interest. "You want to know about our religion?"

Thomas, feeling a little sheepish, smiled and nodded.

"We're Christians. We left the Orthodox Church many years ago."

Thomas, slowing to look both ways before crossing the Santa Fe tracks, then asked, "What did the attorney mean about you being milk drinkers?"

"That's why our ancestors were banned from the Orthodox Church, 'cause we drink milk every day, even during lent."

"If you're Christian, how come you eat kosher food?"

Yoseff shrugged. "I don't know. It's always been that way."

"What's different about kosher food?"

"We believe pork, horse or shellfish are *treyfah*, not fit. Our food has to be killed and cooked a special way."

"You like kosher food?"

The boy grinned and swung his legs. "Yes, honey cake and *varenie* jam *kharoshi*."

Thomas paused, impressed with how knowledgeable Yoseff was for a twelve-year-old. He resumed his questioning. "You have a church around here someplace?"

The youngster shook his head. "No, but we pray a lot at home."

They rode along quietly for a few moments before Thomas spoke again. "You like living on a farm?"

"I miss my friends in The Flats."

"Where's that?"

"Los Angeles."

"How about your mother and sisters and baby brother? Do they like living on a farm?"

He again shook his head.

Thomas, remembering when he was twelve years old, could empathize with his young companion. That was when he was living on a dairy farm in Michigan, doing chores from daylight to dawn and struggling through bitter cold winters and humid summers and pervasive poverty.

They continued their journey in silence until they passed the O'Roark farm and he noticed the kitchen light shining through the door window. He couldn't recall if in his hasty departure he had left it on, or if Brenda had returned from visiting her father. But he did remember he had left his pilot's license application on the kitchen table. He accelerated toward the Menshikovs and when he pulled into their yard, bid Yoseff goodbye with a few words of reassurance about his father, then hurried home.

When he opened the door and stepped into the kitchen, he knew he was in trouble. Tommy was in his playpen idly toying with his blocks. But Brenda was on the sofa, her arms folded across her chest, glowering at him with a bulldog look that reminded him of his mother.

"Where have you been all afternoon?" she asked ominously.

"I've been trying to help---"

She interrupted, nodding toward the table, "And what is all that flying stuff about?"

His eyes flitted to the table where it appeared that the typewriter, application letter, photos and Money Order were undisturbed. He sighed, "I've been taking flying lessons. And, I've passed the tests, so now I can apply---"

"Thomas, how could you do this without telling me? I've told you how I feel about those…those people buzzing around in…in those rickety machines."

He looked at her guiltily. "I was afraid you'd object and try to talk me out of it."

She responded sternly, sounding motherly, "Certainly I would. I'm worried about you getting injured…or…or worse."

"Oh, but Brenda, it's such a wonderful experience. I've dreamed about it ever since watching those lucky guys flying over the muddy trenches of France. I feel so free and relaxed up in the air."

"But people are getting killed in those contraptions every day!" She waved her hand around and continued, "It was in the paper…another one crashed just last week and killed two of those wing walkers, or whatever you call them!" She was starting to sound hysterical, causing the baby to stop playing and stand up in his playpen.

Thomas stepped over, picked him up and held him close. He turned toward her and spoke evenly, "People get killed in motor cars, too, Brenda, and falling off of horses. And some of my buddies got killed in the war.   But I'm not interested in wing walking or parachute jumping or any of that stuff. I'm being careful and---"

"Speaking of buddies, wasn't your friend Jack Lewis killed in one of those aeroplanes?"

The remark hit hard in his gut and stirred deep memories.   With Tommy still in his arms, he sat down at the kitchen table and took a deep breath. He struggled for a response, but none came as she jumped up from the sofa, crying, "How could you do this to me, Thomas?" She stalked into the bedroom and slammed the door behind her.

He carried the baby to the rocker and patted him soothingly as he wrapped his little arms around his neck, and both started to doze. When they awoke in about an hour, it was five thirty and their stomachs were growling in unison. Thomas placed Tommy in his high chair, started a bottle of milk warming and turned to build a fire against the chill of the evening. He returned to the kitchen cabinets to dig around for his brandy, poured a glass one-fourth full, and chipped in some ice and a little water.   He handed the baby his bottle, and they tipped their drinks up in unison. Then he started rummaging in the icebox to see what he could scrounge up for supper.

After supper, he finished addressing his application letter, put it in an envelope with a three cent stamp, and laid it on a night stand so he would remember to take it to the Post Office on Monday. That night he slept in the front bedroom with Tommy beside him.

On Sunday, with Brenda still pouting in the bedroom, he and Tommy enjoyed a late breakfast while he dawdled over the *Morning Republican*. He particularly noted the story of the roundup of over nine hundred suspected 'Reds' throughout the country, including the twenty or so in the Fresno area. The raids had been initiated by the Attorney General, A. Mitchell Palmer, and his new expert on communism, J. Edgar Hoover, and were hailed by many as a necessary step in ridding the country of subversives and other undesirable aliens.

Thomas also spent the day feeding, diapering and entertaining Tommy. During the afternoon, he even contemplated taking him for a drive for some fresh air but demurred when he stuck his head outside to find that the November weather had turned several degrees colder. He put a couple more logs on the fire, and they spent the afternoon playing with blocks and toys and napping. Throughout the day, he saw Brenda only briefly when, looking disheveled in her terry cloth robe and unkempt hair, she left the bedroom to use the bathroom. He thought of trying to open a conversation during one of these sojourns, but decided against it. She would come around, he hoped, when she thought she had punished him enough for his transgression.

Thomas awoke early Monday morning and scrunched down under the blankets to escape the coldness of the bedroom. He gently felt for Tommy, sleeping next to him, then reached out with one hand to push back a window curtain only to see the reflection of a pale sun against the frosty ground. He toyed with the idea of again calling in sick until the pressure on his bladder finally forced him to make a barefooted run to the bathroom. After he finished, he flipped on the floor heater and returned to the living room to rebuild the fire in the fireplace.

When he entered the bedroom for his robe and slippers, he caught his breath. Tommy was missing from the nest of pillows he had placed around him to prevent him from rolling out of bed. He turned to see that the door to the other bedroom was ajar, and pushed it open to find him cuddling in his mother's arms. He ventured a tentative "Good morning."

Brenda responded with a weak smile. "Hi. Would you mind warming his bottle?"

Thomas nodded and retreated to the kitchen. When he returned in a few minutes, mother and son were giggling and playing some game. He handed over the bottle and turned to the closet. "I need to get my clothes for work."

"Thomas," she called out.

"Yes."

"I'm sorry I behaved so badly. It's just that…well, I just don't want to see you get hurt. Will you forgive me?"

He turned back, confused and suspicious over her sudden change in attitude, and didn't know how to respond. Hesitantly, he sat on the edge of the bed, leaned over and kissed her on the forehead. "I don't want to get hurt either, Brenda. But flying is just such a grand adventure. I...I'm sorry, but I don't want to give it up."

She put her arms around his neck, pulled him close and asked, "Do you still love me?"

He nuzzled his stubbly cheek into her warm neck and they held each other close for a few moments before he replied absently, "Yeah, I still do." Then he sat up, commenting, "Guess I better get ready for work." He retrieved his suit, shirt and tie and underwear, laid them out in the other bedroom, and went to the bathroom to shave and bathe.

His day at the Post Office turned into a particularly long and boring one. He had trouble concentrating, partly dreaming about flying and partly feeling suspicious over Brenda's sudden turnabout on the subject. He finally perked up when he received a message from Brad advising that Menshikov would be released from jail late that afternoon.

When he entered the jail after five o'clock, he was a little taken aback to find that someone would have to pay a hundred dollar fine before Boris could be released. He pulled out his check book, then waited patiently for the old Russian to be brought out. He was shocked when he finally appeared. His hair was uncombed, his beard straggly and his eyes looked sad and forlorn. His broad shoulders were slumped forward and his clothes hung on him like he had lost weight. Thomas went to him, reached to shake his hand, draped the other arm over his shoulders and silently led him out to the car.

They rolled quietly through the traffic and bustle of the city streets until bumping across the railroad tracks seemed to jar them out of their reluctance to talk about the ordeal. Thomas finally ventured, "They feed you OK?"

Boris grumbled sullenly, "Horsemeat no *kharoshi*."

"You mean that's all they gave you to eat for three days?"

"Mush too."

They again fell silent until the Russian spoke, "Americanism no goot for immigrants...joost for natives."

"What do you mean?"

"Boris goot citizen, go jail anyway. Joost like Russia."

"Yeah, that doesn't seem right. But unfortunately that's the way the system works sometimes."

The Russian sat quietly for a few moments, contemplating the passing scenery, before speaking again, "Boris go back Los Angeles."

"What did you say?"

"Me move, take family. Boris goot garbage man, not farmer."

Thomas sighed, "Jeez, Boris, I hate to see you give up. You're a good farmer, just had a little bad luck this season. Next year's gotta be better."

Menshikov stared ahead. "Me move, you buy farm real cheap."

Thomas glanced at his passenger, "I don't understand."

"Sell farm thousand dollars. You help me move Los Angeles."

He shook his head, "Oh, I couldn't do that, Boris. Those forty acres are worth a lot more than that. Besides, I don't think I want to have that much land to worry about."

"You *kharoshi druk*. You take truck too."

Thomas smiled at being called a 'good friend' and offered the old rattletrap Model T. He could use a truck all right, but wasn't sure that would be much help. "You better keep that. You'll need it in Los Angeles."

"Nyet. Buy big truck. Haul garbage. Make goot money."

They had reached the Menshikov farm, and Thomas reached to shake his neighbor's hand as he climbed out. "I'll see you later, my friend," he called out as he turned the car around and watched the older boy and his sisters running to greet their father. Sonia stood at the corner of the house waving with one arm and holding the baby in the other.

When Thomas arrived home, he was met at the door by a smiling Brenda and the smell of chicken frying. She threw her arms around him and kissed him warmly, adding "I was getting kinda worried. Seems like you're later than usual."

He shrugged. "I'll tell you all about it over supper. Right now I'm starving." He removed his coat, tie and shirt collar and tossed them on the sofa. He kissed Tommy, wiggling and grinning in his high chair, and took a seat at the table. Brenda brought a big platter of chicken and mashed potatoes and gravy and canned peas. As she pulled up a chair, Thomas noticed that none of it was cooked German style.

He reached for a drumstick and took a bite. "Um, man, this is good. One of ours?"

"Yes. Erasmus killed and dressed it for me."

As he dug into the rest of his supper, he told all about Boris being put in jail, his appearance in court on Saturday, and bringing him back home. He turned to feed the baby a spoonful of mashed potatoes and commented offhandedly, "Funny thing happened on the way home. He offered to sell us his farm."

"Oh, my! Why'd he do that?"

"Said he doesn't want to farm anymore, wants to move back to Los Angeles."

"But can we afford that?"

"For a thousand dollars?"

"That's all he wants, for the whole forty acres?"

He nodded and reached to help the baby spoon up some of his applesauce.

"But can we even afford that much?"

"Yeah, we can take the money out of the bank. Trouble is, I'm not sure how serious he is." He added with a chuckle, "Probably change his mind after he talks to Sonia."

She took a bite of chicken and chewed pensively. "How much you think that property's worth?"

"Oh, at least forty thousand dollars in today's inflated market."

"Then why would he want to sell it so cheaply?"

"I don't know, Brenda, and I'm not taking it too seriously.   If he really wants to sell for a thousand dollars, he's probably talking about the principal on his loan.   We would have to make the payments on whatever balance he owes."

She rose from the table to get dessert, a peach cobbler, and brought it to the table, then removed their dirty dishes and replaced them with saucers. "Heavens, if we owned another forty acres we'd be rich!"

"Yeah, but who would do all the work?   Don't believe I could handle it with my leg, and besides, we'd have to buy a tractor and other expensive equipment."

She served up the cobbler. "Maybe if you gave up your Post Office job?"

He looked at her quizzically.   "I thought you wanted me to work there."

"Yes, I suggested it.   But you don't seem to be happy doing office work."

"You're right, I'm not.   But now that I'm used to that regular pay check, not sure I'm ready to trade it for the uncertainty of farm work."

After finishing the rest of their supper in silence, Brenda took Tommy to the bedroom to change his diaper and dress him in his pajamas. Thomas added logs to the fireplace and started washing dishes. With that chore over, he took a seat in the corner of the sofa and Brenda and the baby joined him, cuddling up close in the comfort of the crackling fire. It wasn't long before Tommy was asleep, and Brenda carried him to his crib. She returned for Thomas, guided him into the darkened bedroom, and helped him remove his clothes. They made love again that night like two newlyweds.

The next day was November 11th, the first anniversary of the Armistice, and a national holiday as decreed by President Wilson. There was to be an official dedication of the new Liberty Cemetery at eleven o'clock, the hour the Armistice had been signed in the forest of *Compiegne*, France, then that afternoon a patriotic parade through the downtown area and a band concert in Court House Park. Also scheduled was an afternoon of auto racing at the fairgrounds followed by a demonstration of wing walking and parachute jumping to be put on by a visiting aerial circus. A fireworks display at nightfall would wrap up the day's festivities.

When Thomas and Brenda initially had discussed the daylong celebration, they had decided not to participate. He didn't feel the planned activities were a fitting way to honor the thousands who had lost their lives. For him, they only brought back the ghosts of Tim Campbell and other buddies he was struggling to forget. Brenda was looking forward to the holiday so she could catch up on household chores.

But when she received a phone call from one of the women she used to know at Gottschalk's department store, she changed her mind. The friend advised of a particular visiting speaker scheduled as part of a Chautauqua to be held in Roeding Park in the afternoon. Thomas, rather than accompany Brenda to listen to some boring talk, opted to take Tommy to the auto races and flying demonstrations at the fairgrounds.

He returned home late that afternoon, arriving before Brenda. He deposited the youngster in his playpen, warmed a bottle for him, and turned to building a fire against the chill of the evening air. He sat down in the rocker and was thinking about having a brandy and cigarette when he heard an automobile, and Brenda came bursting through the doorway.

"Oh, Thomas," she enthused, "I just heard the most wonderful speaker!" She ran to the chair, leaned down and kissed him on his upturned mouth.

"Who was that?"

"A man named Wiggam. He's a journalist and author. You would have enjoyed meeting him."

"What did he talk about?"

She replied breathlessly, "Eugenics, and how it's all tied into the Bible and religion and…and…how eugenics is an extension of the Golden Rule into the stream of protoplasm. He said if Jesus came back now he would tell us to do unto the unborn as we would want them to do to ourselves."

Thomas shook his head, "Sounds like some kind of religious nut. Where's he from?"

"Some place back east."

She paused to catch her breath, pulled off her overcoat and hat, tossed them on the sofa and extracted some papers from her purse. "Look, he gave everyone family record blanks to fill out and send back to their office!"

"What the heck's that for, what kind of records you talking about?"

"Our family history, where we were born, where our parents and grandparents came from, our medical history, things like that." She moved to the kitchen table, pulled up a chair and spread out the papers.

She dug a pencil out of her purse and started scanning the papers. "Heavens, this is more complicated than I realized. I can fill in most of my family history and Papa can help with the rest. But how about you, weren't you born in 1899?"

He nodded weakly, and she pencilled in the blank.

"What town?"

"Near Battle Creek, Michigan."

"In a house or hospital?"

He hesitated. "To tell the truth, Mother found me in a garbage dump. It was a cold winter night and the snow was---"

She looked across the room to catch him grinning. "Thomas, stop teasing! I know you were born in June, so it couldn't have been a cold night."

Tommy had stopped playing with his rattle and blocks and stood up in his playpen, usually a sign that he had dirtied his diapers. Thomas stepped over to him and leaned down to feel. "Looks like we need a little repair work here." He carried him into the bedroom to change and when they returned, sat down at the table, holding him in his lap.

Brenda, still filling out the forms, asked, "Where was your father born?"

"Ireland."

"What did he die from?"

He shrugged, "Heart attack, I guess. Maybe it was from meanness."

She ignored the remark and asked, "Did he ever have any other diseases?"

"What do you mean, like the clap, or something like that?"

She put down her pencil, "Well, that would be important to know if he did. But I was referring more to something like tuberculosis, or pellagra or temperament."

"He had a bad temper, that's for sure."

"No, no. I don't think that's what the form is referring to." She looked down to read the directions more carefully. "It says here that temperament is determined by the four humors of blood, phlegm, yellow bile, or black bile, which cause a person to be sanguine, phlegmatic, choleric, or melancholic. Was he any of those?"

Thomas chuckled sardonically. "I'd say all of them!"

"Oh, Thomas, please be serious. This is important!"

He was becoming bored and annoyed, "Well, my dear, this all sounds like a bunch of hooey to me. Who wants all this personal information anyway?"

She looked down to read the heading at the top of the form. "It's the Eugenics Record Office in Cold Spring Harbor, New York."

"What are they going to do with it?"

"According to that Mister Wiggam they compile it all on three-by-five cards so they can do research on heredity. They analyze the data to see what causes feeblemindedness, or epilepsy, insanity or criminal behavior, or other kinds of hereditary degeneration, even alcoholism."

Thomas shook his head in disbelief, and started drumming his fingers on the table as she continued, "They can even match the cards between a man and woman to see if their proposed marriage will be eugenic."

"So what about us, are we eugenic, or should we get a divorce?"

"Don't be silly! We're from good northern European stock, we're native-born Protestants and we both survived the war...and...and we've already produced a eugenic baby!"

Thomas sighed resignedly and glanced at the clock. "Well, it's almost six o'clock, and Tommy and

I are hungry and thirsty. I guess he'll start with milk. But since I've inherited alcoholism, I'm gonna have something a little stronger." He lifted the baby from his lap into the highchair and walked over to the cupboard for his bottle of brandy.

She gave him a disdainful look, "Mister Wiggam said the same thing I did before, Thomas. That stuff's just going to weaken your germ plasm."

"It didn't seem to hurt my father's germ, or whatever you call it. He used to get pretty drunk every once in awhile but still managed to sire six offspring."

She put down her pencil and leaned back in the chair. "What do you mean six? I thought there was just you, Becky and your older brother."

He chipped ice into a glass, filled it up with brandy and water, and took a thoughtful swallow before replying, "It was a big surprise to me, too. Mother and Becky were talking about birth control a few months ago, and it just came out."

"Where are the others, they die or what?"

He scowled, "Not sure I remember all the details. Apparently, the first baby, a girl, was stillborn. Then she had Patrick followed by another boy who died at a young age from something, diphtheria, I believe. Next came Becky and me. She finally had another boy, who died just before we moved to California."

"Heavens, that's terrible! No wonder the poor woman is so interested in birth control!"

"Why do you need to know all this anyway?"

She motioned toward the questionnaire. "Well, it's important to know if they died from some kind of disease because that could make a difference in your family pedigree. It might indicate some trait that could be inherited through your blood plasma---"

Thomas blew his stack, "Christ, Brenda, what do you mean 'pedigree'? You think I'm some kind of animal...like...like a pig, or...or cow! What a bunch of crap!"

She gasped at his sharp outburst, grabbed her papers and disappeared into the bedroom, slamming the door behind her. He stalked over to the fireplace, picked up the poker and stabbed angrily at the smoldering logs. Then he returned to Tommy, now starting to whimper at the loud voices, lifted him from the highchair and carried him to the rocker.

Thomas took a deep breath and pulled out a package of <u>Lucky Strikes</u> his sister had given him. He lighted up, took another drink and rocked determinedly, sipping his brandy and carefully blowing the smoke away from the baby. That night, he and Brenda again would sleep in separate bedrooms.

CHAPTER 14

For Thomas, the return to work the day after the Armistice holiday started out as the same old routine. But it changed by late morning when he was summoned to the postmaster's office to take a phone call. He lifted the cradle to his ear and was surprised to hear Emmett Johnson, the bank president, offering him congratulations.

Thomas replied, "Er, what happened?"

"You're the new owner of forty acres."

Confused, Thomas didn't respond and Johnson continued, "Your Russian neighbor wants to give you his farm, practically speaking anyway."

"Uh, I don't understand."

"He's here in my office ready to sign his mortgage over to you for one thousand dollars. He's giving up on farming and moving back to Los Angeles."

"What's the catch? That place is worth a lot more than that."

"No catch. You'll have to take over his loan papers and keep up the payments. But it's still a heck of a deal because he originally put three thousand dollars into it and the place must be worth at least forty thousand."

Thomas glanced at the clock and spoke into the phone, "Mister Johnson, I'll be off for lunch in about an hour. I'll meet you then at the bank."

"OK, but don't delay. I wouldn't want to see you lose out on this deal."

Later, when Thomas arrived at the bank, he found Johnson and Menshikov waiting for him, the latter stepping forward with his usual bear hug greeting and blast of garlic breath. He slapped Thomas on the back and called him "goot friend, goot friend", as Johnson took his overcoat and hat and they moved to seats in his office. He again explained what was being offered and concluded, "Seems like this should be pretty easy, Thomas. You can just transfer a thousand dollars out of your savings account."

Thomas nodded. "Yeah, that part's easy enough. Problem is I don't want to take advantage of Mister Menshikov, and I'm not sure I want to be responsible for another forty acres." He was pensive for a moment before adding, "Jeez, that would give me a total of one hundred acres. That's a lot of fruit to take care of!"

"Actually, you'll be doing him a favor," Johnson responded. "Told me he needs cash to return to Los

Angeles and buy a new truck so he can get back into the garbage business."

"What kind of interest on the balance?" Thomas asked.

The banker stirred uncomfortably, "Well, we've got him at ten percent right now, but---"

"But you'll draw up new papers at seven?"

Johnson smiled guiltily and nodded, "You're getting to be quite the businessman."

The old Russian sat quietly as the two talked, turning his head back and forth and nodding occasionally, but giving no indication if he really understood.

Thomas looked at him for some sign, but got only a gold-toothed grin in return. He stood up, moved to the window and stared out pensively at the noontime throng of pedestrians bundled up against the unseasonably cold north wind knifing its way along Fulton Street. A big red streetcar, blue sparks cascading from its overhead trolley, was bullying for space against a plethora of motor cars, seemingly unguided with their occupants hidden behind protective side curtains. His mind drifted back to the first time he had met the Menshikovs and rescued them from the Klan attack, the crop ruined by rain and finally Boris' session in jail. Then he remembered when he drove Yoseff home from the Court House and the youngster's desire to return to Los Angeles. He turned toward Johnson and Menshikov, remarking, "OK, I guess we've got a deal." The whole transaction was completed in a few minutes, and after a round of handshakes and bear hugs, Thomas departed.

That evening as he left the Post Office for home, he was thankful he had worn his overcoat. The temperature had barely struggled into the fifties by noon, and now was dropping rapidly toward the low forties. He drove through the winter darkness past his own place and the warm welcome of the kitchen light shining through the window, and continued on to the Menshikovs.

He was surprised to find a Studebaker moving van in the yard. He stepped out, placed his fedora firmly on his head, pulled his coat close around his body and approached the house. He was greeted by Boris helping the movers carry out the samovar, followed by Yoseff lugging a box of miscellaneous items. Sonia stood inside the nearly empty structure, pink-cheeked from the cold, hunkered up in a wool coat, dress and sarafan, and holding the baby. The two girls were shivering and hanging onto her skirt. The beds, table and chairs, along with the floor lamp, gas range and Franklin stove had been loaded into the truck earlier, leaving the inside of the railcar as empty and cold as the outside.

As they reached the end of the loading, Thomas suggested the family come to his house for supper and to warm up. Boris shook his head, and Yoseff advised that the movers would take them into town where they planned to catch the southbound Southern Pacific's *California Limited*. Boris grinned, gave him a farewell hug and turned abruptly toward the truck. Yoseff, tears running down his cheeks, wrapped his arms around his legs and mumbled "Spasibo, spasibo." Sonia kissed him on the cheek, and he bent down so the girls could do the same. Then they piled into the back of the truck, the driver slammed the doors shut and they headed out the drive. As Thomas waved goodbye and looked back through the open door into the cold, tomb-like darkness of the abandoned freight car, he felt an emptiness that brought tears to his eyes. He shuddered against the cold, returned to the Maxwell and departed for home.

When he entered the house, he found Brenda in the rocker, a knitted shawl across her shoulders, a wool blanket wrapped around her legs, and nursing Tommy. "Oh, Thomas, thank goodness you're home. We're freezing to death, and I can't seem to get a good fire going."

He tossed his coat and hat on the sofa, knelt down before the fireplace and stirred the logs with the poker. "Looks like you got hold of some green wood. I'll fix it." With the prior argument over the eugenics questionnaire still lingering in his mind, he stepped to the chair, kissed the noisily suckling baby, and tentatively did the same to Brenda She smiled wearily and kissed him in return, shivering involuntarily at the touch of his cold lips. He turned to rebuilding the fire with newspaper and dry kindling.

A few minutes later when Tommy finished nursing, Brenda placed him in his high chair and Thomas went to the bathroom to wash for supper. When he returned to the table, the emptiness he had felt over the departure of the Russians quickly disappeared as he reveled in the warmth of his little family and the resurging fire.

Brenda began serving from a big pot of chicken noodle soup and produced a loaf of fresh-baked bread, still hot from the oven. She cooled a small bowl of the broth and placed that and a baby spoon in front of Tommy, then took her seat. Thomas cut off several slices of bread, slathered butter on one, tore off a piece of the soft center and handed it to the little one.

"How many teeth does he have now?" he asked.

"Six, the last time I counted," she responded, blowing on her soup.

"How come you're still nursing him?"

She shrugged, "Oh, I don't know. I still have milk and it seems to calm him when he gets fretful. Besides, the Children's Bureau recommends it."

"Who?"

"The Children's Bureau in Washington. Remember, I told you about their pamphlet on child raising?"

"He doesn't bite?"

She chuckled, "He's gotten me a few times. But I guess that's part of being a mother."

Thomas blew on his soup and slurped up a spoonful as he watched the baby chew contentedly on the piece of bread. He was caught off guard by Brenda's next remark, "I sure wish we could do something about better heat."

"Er, what do you mean?"

"On cold days like this the fireplace and those little electric heaters in the bathroom and bedroom just aren't enough. I'm afraid Tommy will catch the croup, or worse yet, the grippe, and I might get the chilblains." She massaged her hands over the heat from the hot soup.

He took a spoonful of soup. "You wanna buy more electric heaters?"

She shook her head. "All they do is warm your ankles. I really wish we could afford one of those new gas radiant heaters, at least in the bedroom."

"Well, maybe we can." He blew on another spoonful and served it to the baby, waving his little hands in anticipation.

"What do you mean?"

"As of today we're a thousand dollars poorer, or forty thousand richer."

Brenda stopped eating and looked at him in disbelief as he described his acquisition of the Menshikov farm. When he finished, she reached across the table and smilingly squeezed his hand. "Heavens, Thomas, that means we own one hundred acres...that's...that's more than Papa!"

He ate more soup in silence while he struggled with mixed emotions. On the one hand he marveled at the unexpected windfall of the Menshikov farm. But he also shuddered at the increased responsibility it would entail, and what direction it might be pushing their lives. He was partially stirred from his ruminations by Brenda refilling his bowl and serving more hot bread, then fully brought back to the moment by her seemingly offhand remark. "Goodness, maybe we could even afford a new house!"

"New house...uh, what's wrong with this one?" He glanced around.

"Like I mentioned before, it's poorly heated. And it's not very big. It would be nice to have a separate kitchen, and maybe another bathroom. An indoor laundry room would be good too so I wouldn't have to go out in the cold to do the washing."

This sudden interest in a new house came as a complete surprise to Thomas. Since his father's death, when he had modernized their current house with electricity, running water and an indoor bathroom, and added a lean-to on the back for laundry and storage, he had found it quite comfortable. But then he recalled that Brenda had come from a larger two-story house with a parlor, dining and living rooms, multiple bedrooms and bathrooms upstairs and downstairs.

He dismissed the subject with a non-committal shrug.

They spent the balance of the week struggling to keep warm. On several nights the temperature dipped into the thirties, forcing Thomas to drain the water from the Maxwell's radiator. He even had to get up from his warm bed during the night to rebuild the fire, and finally broke down and bought two more electric heaters. Daytimes weren't much better since the winter sun had weakened too much to penetrate the blanket of cold and fog that covered the landscape.

But by the end of the week, Thomas no longer was worrying about the weather. Rather, he was trying to deal with a situation he had never experienced before, gobs of money. The sudden wealth came with the first payment from the Growers Association on their 1919 raisin crop, which had totaled some one hundred twenty tons.

He was ensconced at the kitchen table with the family ledger going through the farmer's periodic ritual of paying bills. His feeling of satisfaction was magnified by the morning's ambiance. A fire was crackling in the fireplace, and Brenda was at the sink washing dishes after their Sunday breakfast of fresh-sliced oranges, pancakes, bacon and coffee. The baby had finished his bottle and dish of applesauce and was in his playpen absorbed in trying to stack his wooden blocks.

"Man, I never realized money could make you feel so good," Thomas said idly.

Brenda smiled, "Yes, doesn't it though."

"I've already paid PJ, Erasmus and Pedro, and gave 'em each bonuses. Now all that's left are these bills for fertilizer and water and the bank loans."

Brenda pulled the plug of the sink, picked up a dishtowel to start drying and turned toward her husband. "You remembering your mother and Becky?"

"Getting ready to write their shares right now. Not sure Mother deserves a full share, but Becky does for keeping the place going while I was away."

He got up to poke the fire and add another log, reached into the playpen to pat Tommy and returned to the table.

"So, how much you figure we'll have left over?" she asked.

He looked down at the ledger where he had been toting up the bills and rechecked the columns of numbers. "Well, our first payment came to almost fourteen thousand dollars and expenses about four thousand. So that leaves about ten thousand."

"Sounds like a lot, but I know it has to last all year."

"Yeah. 'Course, we'll get our final payment sometime next summer, but in the meantime we'll have to hire out the plowing and pruning and pay other bills. And we'll need to buy a tractor and other equipment. That extra acreage will be too much for our little *Trak-Pull*."

"So we can't afford to get too reckless."

He nodded in agreement while she wiped her hands on the dish towel, hung it up to dry and stepped over to check on the baby. She felt his diaper and wrinkled her nose. "Lordy, that stuff goes right through him." She departed for the bedroom as someone knocked at the door.

Thomas got up to answer and found PJ standing in his heavy jacket, hat in hand. That usually meant he was going to ask for something out of the ordinary.

"Mornin', Boss."

"Howdy, PJ." Thomas' voice sounded more wary than he intended, but it didn't look like it was going to deter the farm manager from his mission. He shuffled his boots in the damp dirt. "Reckon we've got a little problem."

"Yeah?"

"Yeah. 'Rass' is hankerin' to go to town."

Thomas smiled, "Guess that new money's burning a hole in his pocket?"

"That's part of it all right, but...but...well." PJ blushed and glanced to one side. "I reckon he's lookin' for a woman."

Thomas chuckled. "I'll be darned. Looks like he's human, just like the rest of us."

PJ nodded sheepishly.

"But, this is Sunday, PJ. I'm not sure if those old gals are working."

PJ frowned, "Oh, he don't wanna go there. He's talkin' about some niggra church over on the West Side."

"Well, I suppose that's the right place to meet a good woman."

"Yessir."

Thomas turned to look at the kitchen clock. "It's almost ten thrity. If he's ready, I'll drive him into town in a few minutes."

PJ smiled and put his hat back on. "Thanks, Boss. I'll git him right out."

Thomas closed the door, advised Brenda of his plans and asked if she wanted to accompany them.

She sighed. "I'll just stay here and try to get the washing and ironing done. What'll you do while you're waiting for Erasmus to come out of church?"

He paused for a moment, then grinned. "Guess I'll just take Becky's check to her. And I'll take Tommy so you can get your work done."

"Fine, just keep him bundled him up good so he doesn't catch the croup."

He picked up the baby, pulled his winter outfit over his squiggling arms and legs, then put on his own fleece-lined outer coat, gloves and cap with the ear flaps. He kissed Brenda goodbye, and with Tommy on one arm and carrying a teakettle of water in the other hand, walked outside into the crackling cold morning. He found a grinning Erasmus waiting beside the Maxwell. He was all decked out in a new plaid wool jacket with leather patch elbows, corduroy pants and a shiny new high-top shoe on his right foot. The grape stake leg and board foot still supported his left side.

"Mornin', Massa Thomas."

"Morning, Erasmus. I see you're all dressed for steppin' out."

"Yessuh," the old Negro grinned. He reached to take the baby as Thomas knelt to close the drain cock, then emptied the teakettle into the radiator.

"How's the little fella?" Erasmus asked, bouncing him on his arm.

"Fit as a fiddle right now. Full tummy and empty bowels."

Erasmus handed the baby back and hobbled around toward the left side of the car. Thomas pointed to the front passenger seat and called out, "Why don't you sit up here?"

"No suh, this wuks bess with mah peg." He opened the rear door, lifted his body backwards through the doorway and scrunched across to the opposite side so the unbending artificial leg could rest on the seat. "Ah can hold 'im back here."

Thomas carried the baby around to the other side, placed him in Erasmus' arms, climbed behind the wheel, started the engine and headed toward town.

As they rolled along, Erasmus began humming some obscure Negro lullaby and rocking Tommy back and forth. Thomas appreciated the effort to entertain the baby but at the same time found the soulful sound only added to his growing feeling of malaise. Even though his spirits had been temporarily buoyed by the welcome infusion of money, he still felt troubled by Brenda wanting to find a job in town rather than be a housewife. Or was it her sudden interest in building a new house?

His feelings were exacerbated by the dreary weather, the gray sky that blotted out the sunshine, and the ghostly appearance of the landscape. Peach, apricot and almond trees stood leafless and naked in their winter dormancy, the grapevines all blackened and gnarly, looking like they were trying to squirm away from the cold, sunless sky and into the earth's embrace.

He was snapped back to the moment by the car bumping over the Santa Fe tracks as he motored on toward the west side of town. Other than several motor cars, apparently heading for church with their occupants hidden behind winter side curtains, there wasn't much of the busyness that was characteristic of city life during the workweek. The relative silence was broken only by the sound of automobile tires swishing across wet macadam or splashing through occasional puddles of leftover frostmelt.

He steered the car across the Southern Pacific tracks into Chinatown, past the indecipherable signs and inscrutable joss houses and into the Negro section of town. He turned north on B Street and rolled to a stop in front of the African-American Pentacostal Church. Several dozen Negro men, women and children were gathered around the front and on the steps, making their way inside. He stepped out to take the baby and place him on the front seat as Erasmus squirmed out and closed the door.

Thomas smiled and reached to shake his hand. "Hope you enjoy the sermon, Erasmus. And you might say a little prayer for me. I'll be back around noon to pick you up."

"Yassuh." He hobbled off toward the church.

A few minutes later, after Thomas had knocked several times on the door of his sister's apartment, he was about to conclude she wasn't home. Finally she responded, calling out tentatively, "Who's there?"

"The President of the United States with a present."

She hesitated until she realized it was her teasing brother, and opened the door with a crooked grin, holding Ricky in one arm. A towel was wrapped turban-like around her head, her willowy body encased in a white, full length terry cloth robe belted at the waist. "You sure don't look like the President, all bundled up in that coat and cap with the ear flaps pulled down." She leaned up and kissed him and Tommy on the cheek. "My, he's got the warmest skin! Not sick, is he?"

"Don't believe so, just all wrapped up against this frosty weather."

She pulled Thomas into the apartment and closed the door as he asked, "What happened to your head?"

She reached up and plumped the towel. "Oh, nothing. Just trying out one of our new shampoos so I can tell my customers all about it."

She walked into the bedroom and lowered her baby into his playpen. Thomas followed with Tommy, removed his sweater, knit pants and booties, checked to make sure his diaper was still dry and put him down beside his cousin.

He gave each of the little tykes a rattle and returned with his sister to the living room. He took off his coat and hat, hung them over one of the bentwood chairs and settled into the Sheraton, commenting, "You've sure got it hot in here."

"Yes. I like to keep it warm when I'm washing my hair so I don't catch a chill." She moved to the corner to turn down the small radiant gas heater, and turned back to her brother, "What brings you to town on this cold, miserable day?"

He explained about taking Erasmus to church, adding, "I suspect his main interest is in finding female companionship."

She chuckled, "Not surprising. I imagine PJ is a pretty poor substitute."

He reached for his jacket, removed an envelope from the inner pocket and handed it to her. "Here, this is for taking good care of the farm while I was gone."

He watched expectantly as she put on her glasses, tore open the envelope, extracted the check, and stared wide-eyed, "Good heavens...what...what's all this for?"

"That's your share of our first crop payment."

"But fourteen hundred dollars?"

"That's ten percent. That sound fair?"

"Oh, my yes! Now I can start a real savings account, or maybe even buy a motorcar. Oh, this is wonderful, Thomas. I can hardly believe it!"

"You're not alone.   We couldn't believe the size of our payment either.   Hope these wartime prices last for a few years."   He picked up a magazine to fan his face and asked, "So, how's your business been doing?"

"Just great.   I made over three hundred dollars last month!"

"Good grief!   Maybe I should get a job selling cosmetics."

She laughed.   "You'd have to compete with the two women I have working for me, and they're pretty aggressive."

He waited patiently while Becky unwrapped the towel from around her head and rubbed it vigorously through her bobbed hair.   When she finished, he spoke nonchalantly, "I guess I've got some more good news."

"Oh, heavens, tell me!"

He told about the Russians deeding over their forty acres.

"My, that is exciting!"

"Not so sure, Sis.   It's gonna mean a lot more work for somebody.   Don't know if I'm up to it."

"How about PJ and Pedro...and...and Erasmus?"

"It's questionable if they can handle it or not. Guess we'll find out."

She didn't respond, but gave him a hand mirror and told him to hold it while she stuck bobby pins in her hair.   He held it obediently for a few minutes, then looked toward the kitchen. "I'm thirsty. Got anything to drink?"

His sister jumped to her feet, "Goodness yes, let's celebrate! I've got a bottle of champagne a customer gave me. Not sure if it's cold enough, but shall we open it?"

"Why not?"

She reached into the icebox, pulled out the bottle and handed it to her brother. "Here, you open it. These things always scare me." She turned to the cupboard for a couple of water glasses as he stood up and started struggling with the cork. Eventually it came free with a resounding 'pop', and he filled the two glasses. They touched the edges together in a salute to their financial good fortune and downed their first glassful of the bubbly liquid.

Thomas burped appreciatively, refilled the glasses, and sat back in the easy chair. He placed the bottle on the small table beside him as she returned to her chair. She gathered her robe around her knees, reached for a package of cigarettes on the side table and held it toward him. "Want a smoke?"

He pulled one from the pack, tamped the end on the chair arm and stuck it in his mouth. He found matches in his pocket and lighted both of them.

They puffed quietly for a few moments before she asked, "So what do you plan to do with all your money?" She took another swallow of the champagne, relishing its fizzy, cooling feel against the mild irritation of the cigarette smoke.

"So far we've just been paying bills."

"Nothing left over?"

"Oh yeah, about nine thousand dollars." He drank more champagne, picked up the bottle to refill his glass and topped off his sister's, still half full. "I thought we'd put some of that in our savings account. They're paying five percent now, you know."

"So did you?" She flicked her cigarette over the ashtray.

He took another puff followed by a drink, and returned his glass to the table before finally responding, a touch of sarcasm in his voice. "Thought I would, but my dear wife says she wants to use the money to build a new house."

"Oh, heavens, that sounds expensive!"

He didn't reply, but turned his head and stared vacantly across the room.

"Where's she talking about, on the farm?"

"Hasn't told me that. Just says she wants a bigger place with more bedrooms and an indoor laundry."

Becky smiled and held out her empty glass while he refilled it, "Don't tell me she's with child already?"

He poured more champagne into his glass and turned toward the bedroom where he could see the two babies playing and laughing in the crib. "Afraid not. Tells me she doesn't want any more, at least not yet."

"That's the trend nowadays. Lots of us younger women don't want to be burdened with large families."

She rose, went to the small kitchenette and returned with a plate of cookies.

He reached for one. "That's not the half of it. She also wants to get a job."

Becky looked perplexed. "Here in town?"

"Yep. Says she's bored on the farm. Wants to get back where life is more exciting."

"Who would take care of Tommy?"

He sighed without responding, then gulped down more champagne and poured the last few ounces into their glasses. He burped again, picked up a cookie and chewed solemnly.

Becky, recognizing they were getting into a sensitive issue, hesitated before venturing, "You want a sandwich, or something for lunch?"

He shook his head and asked, "Gosh, what time is it?" He reached for his watch and popped the lid open. "Quarter to twelve. I gotta leave." He took a final drag on his cigarette and stubbed it out in the ashtray.

"What's the rush?" She ground out her cigarette.

"It's almost time to pick up Erasmus." They went to the bedroom where they found both babies sound asleep. Thomas reached down to feel his son's diaper and turned to his sister. "You got an extra one? I forgot his."

He gently lifted the youngster from the crib, placed him on the bed and expertly changed diapers under Becky's approving gaze. "Maybe you should be the one to stay home, take care of him and the farm, and let Brenda get her job," she suggested.

"Don't know, Sis. That doesn't sound much like a man's responsibility, and you already know how I feel about farm work." He finished dressing Tommy, pulled on his own outer clothes and started toward the door.

"But that would be a nice quiet environment for writing."

He hadn't realized his sister knew of his interest in writing, gave her a surprised look but didn't respond further and turned to open the door. She waved as they disappeared down the hall, and Thomas called back, "Thanks for the champagne and cookies, and the smoke."

"Thanks for the check," she responded, and closed the door.

When Thomas pulled up to the church a few minutes later, he was surprised that he could hear singing, clapping and shouting all the way out in the street. He double-parked, turned off the engine and waited until the congregation started pouring out, many still clapping and dancing as if against the cold. He marveled at how well dressed they were, the men in dark suits and fedoras, the women in colorful dresses and overcoats and wearing the latest styles in millinery. Children, too, were all decked out in their Sunday go-to-church outfits.

He spotted Erasmus when he moved awkwardly out of the church and paused on the steps. He was talking to a woman, who in turn was holding a little pigtailed girl by the hand. From the distance, Thomas guessed the youngster to be three-to-four years old. He waited patiently while Erasmus shook the woman's hand, patted the girl on the head, hobbled down the steps to the car, and eased his big frame into the rear seat.

"Sorry, Massa."

"What for?"

"Keepin' you waitin.'"

Thomas ignored the apology. "Sounded like you were doing a lot of shouting and stomping in there. That how you keep warm?"

"Nossuh, thas jus' the way we is. The spirit jus' hits lak lightnin'. Ain't no holdin' back. Sometimes we jus' stomps to keep from cryin.'"

Thomas smiled, "The little guy's asleep. You want to hold him?"

"Yassuh."

He lifted Tommy from the seat and handed him to Erasmus. He started the engine, observing, "That was a mighty handsome woman you were talking to."

"Yassuh. Thas' Mizz Mandy."

"You knew her before?"

"Nosuh. Her man still missin' from the war."

"Did you know him?"

Erasmus shook his head as he cuddled the baby in his arms. "Same outfit as me, but did'n know him. Army say he jus' missin.'"

"Miss Mandy have a last name?"

"Yessuh. Reckon it's Slocum."

Thomas sensed he had probed enough, shifted into gear and eased the car away from the church. He fell silent as he steered across the Southern Pacific tracks and headed east toward home, straining to stay awake against the comforting warmth of the car. Condensation on the windshield and his champagne-bleary eyes didn't help, forcing him to hunker over the wheel to stay focused on the road ahead. Through the floorboards he could feel Erasmus stomping with his good foot while he hummed a hymn and rocked the baby.

When he pulled into the yard and got out of the car, he caught sight of freshly laundered sheets, pillowcases, diapers, work shirts, coveralls and underwear waving leisurely from the clotheslines. Brenda obviously had been busy in his absence, and he relished the warm, comforting feeling that came from having a dutiful wife.

As he retrieved the baby from Erasmus and wished him a good afternoon, he caught another welcoming sign, the aroma of a pork roast cooking in the oven. This was a particularly nice surprise because for the past several Sundays, Brenda had been preparing some of her favorite German dishes for their big midday meal. He had managed to struggle through such rich offerings as pig's knuckles with sauerkraut and potato dumplings; deep fried fish with boiled potatoes, cabbage and marrow dumplings; and creamed frankfurters with chicken and steamed vegetables. But the liver dumpling soup two weeks previously had almost done him in.

The one saving grace was the desserts, usually coffeecake or fruitcake or ginger cookies, and the occasional bottles of wine she pilfered from her father's fine cellar. The other was that they followed the heavy meal with an afternoon nap and, if the baby remained asleep, what Thomas referred to as "a friendly tussle in the hay."

"How are my two favorite men?" Brenda said cheerily as they entered the house. "I've been keeping dinner warm. Afraid you were going to be late."

The baby was wide awake now, smiling and waiving hungrily toward his mother's outstretched arms. Thomas handed him over, planted a chaste kiss on Brenda's cheek, and headed for the bathroom to relieve the pressure on his bladder and splash cold water on his face.

"Smells like you've been celebrating something," she called out.

"Yeah, Becky broke out champagne to celebrate the big crop payment."

"Well, hurry along. I've got a lovely pork roast ready to serve. And, I've baked a surprise for dessert."

"No German cake or cookies?"

"Rhubarb pie."

She placed the roast, potatoes and vegetables on the table along with a bottle of Zinfandel and waited patiently as Thomas held her chair for her. She sat down and unbuttoned her blouse so the baby could get to her breast. Thomas carved the roast and served them, then ladled the gravy after Brenda had mashed her potato and carrot together until they were smooth.

He uncorked the wine and poured each a glass, and they lifted them in a toast to their new wealth. With the comforting sounds of the suckling baby and a roaring fire for background music, they began a quiet and leisurely dinner on a bitterly cold and dreary November afternoon. Then the phone jangled with the O'Roark's one long, one short ring.

Thomas got up to answer, listened for a moment, and turned to Brenda. "It's some friend of yours, a Melba Bowers."

Brenda stood up with the baby in her arm, stepped over to the phone and listened, responding intermittently with "oh my", "heavens yes" and finally, "December first, yes, I believe I can." When she finally hung up and returned to the table, Thomas was taking a drink of wine and bristling inside. The negative feeling he initially developed toward Brenda's new-found friend had intensified when he realized she was getting her more involved in the eugenics movement.

Brenda spoke excitedly, "I've just been offered a job!"

He didn't respond, just glowered mulishly at his plate, firmly mashed a potato and carrot together and reached for the gravy.

She repeated. "Melba told me about a job at the Normal School, Thomas. It only pays forty dollars a month, but it's a start. Aren't you excited for me?"

"What'll you be doing?" he mumbled.

"Working in the office doing secretarial work… typing and filing and …and…things like that. They want me to start the first of December."

"What do you know about typing and filing?" He stuck his fork in a piece of meat, pushed it around in the gravy, poked it in his mouth and chewed sullenly.

"I studied it in high school. I'm probably a little rusty, but maybe I could practice on your typewriter."

He ignored her suggestion, "Who is this Melba, anyway?"

"She's the school's office manager. Remember, I went with her to the Armistice Day Chautauqua?" Brenda sighed and her voice turned bitter, "She used to work at Gottschalk's but then got laid off like all the rest of us German-Americans."

"Her name doesn't sound very German." He took another bite of roast, followed by a forkful of potatoes and carrots, and continued munching.

"Bowers is her married name. It used to be Birkenstock."

"What's her husband do?" he asked idly, reaching for his wine.

"He was killed in the war."

He squished the last of his mashed potatoes in the gravy and asked, "Didn't you tell me she's involved in that eugenics stuff?"

She nodded, "Yes, she's read a lot about it."

Abruptly, he pushed his empty plate to one side and drained the last of his wine. "So, you're gonna be talking about raising super people or some darn fool thing? We just whipped a bunch of damned Heinies who thought they were better than everyone else."

"Oh, Thomas. Please don't talk that way about the Germans."

He raised his voice, "You're not German, for God's sake! You're American!" You were born in this country!"

"You know what I mean." With Tommy finished suckling, she stood up and laid him across her shoulder to burp him, then placed him in his playpen and returned to finish eating.

But the raised voices and loud shouting had disturbed the baby, and he started to pucker out his lower lip. Brenda stepped back to the playpen, took him in her arms and tried to comfort him. She turned toward Thomas, who had gotten up and walked over to the fireplace. "Now see what you've done, you've frightened the baby."

He ignored her remark. "So how are you going to feed him and take care of him if you're working in town?"

She hesitated before responding, "I thought I'd take him to school with me. That's what Melba does with her little girl."

He turned back toward her, "So you can test them, and...and...perform experiments?"

"Oh, Thomas, of course not!"

He could sense he was losing another argument. He kneeled down in front of the fireplace, picked up the poker and jabbed angrily at the waning fire, sending a shower of sparks up the chimney. He grabbed another log and tossed it on the embers, then added a second one for good measure.

Brenda carried the baby into the front bedroom, changed his diaper, tucked a blanket around him and surrounded him with pillows for his afternoon nap. She returned to the living room to find Thomas seated in his father's rocking chair. He turned toward her, "So, who's going to take care of the vegetable garden, and do the cooking and washing and...and your other chores?"

She sat down on the floor in front of him, resting her arm across his knees. "I'll still have evenings and weekends for cooking and washing. And Erasmus is already taking care of the garden." He didn't respond, and she quietly laid her head against his knee.

In a few moments she continued, sounding more melancholy, "It just seems like during the war I spent so much of my young life cooped up on the farm, afraid to go into town. I missed seeing people, the hustle and bustle---"

He interrupted angrily, "God, Brenda. How about the time I spent cooped up in a muddy trench, dodging German bullets...and...and watching my buddies get killed!"

She sighed, " I guess you're right. We all had to make some kind of sacrifice."

They fell silent until he finally spoke, "Well, do we have to decide all this tonight?"

She raised her head, "I promised to give Melba an answer by next week."

He rocked forward in the chair and stood up, leaving her sitting on the floor. He went to their bedroom, closed the shades, kicked off his shoes and, still wearing his pants and shirt, crawled under the chenille bedspread for his Sunday afternoon nap. She returned to the table to finish her cold dinner. Afterwards, she pulled on her heavy coat and went outside to gather in the laundry, now hanging stiff from the frigid air.

In a few minutes she returned to the bedroom and, feeling chilled by the cold, crawled in beside him. Still somewhat befogged by his earlier consumption of champagne and wine, it took him a few moments to fully respond to the warmth of her body curled against his back. He reached his hand around to find her bare legs and buttocks. He rolled on his back, unloosened his belt and squirmed out of his pants and shorts to release his rising manhood.

As he rolled toward her and started to mount, she pushed her hand against his shoulder. "Don't forget your condom."

"Huh?"

"Put on a rubber, Thomas. I'm not ready for any more babies just yet."

He flopped back on the bed, barely able to control his mounting aggravation.   Like a tire losing air, his tumescence faded away and he rolled over on his side and stared silently and unseeing at the bedroom wall, eventually falling into a disturbed sleep.

CHAPTER 15

Thomas and Brenda and the baby were downtown on the second Saturday in December, struggling through the crowds to do their Christmas shopping. It appeared that every resident of Fresno was there, apparently drawn like fruit flies to the ripeness of prosperity and the first sunny but cool day the area had experienced in several weeks.

Many were package-laden or dragging wide-eyed children bent on seeing Santa Claus, grimly bumping into each other as they made their way along the sidewalks. Others were crowding sardine-like into the stores to grasp at merchandise, or waiting for tables at the Oyster Grotto, the Hughes Hotel or other popular eateries. The streets were jammed with motor cars, their honking and backfiring adding to the dissonance of street cars clanging and screeching against their steel tracks. A few braying, rearing horses, wild-eyed at the confusion around them, were trying to obey the commands of their buggy-riding masters.

Thomas and Brenda were taking Tommy for his first visit with Santa Claus. As they crossed Fulton Street and turned toward Gottschalk's department store, Thomas caught a glimpse up the street of Mister and Missus Fenton intermingled in the throng of shoppers moving toward them. He grabbed Brenda with his free hand and pulled her into the entryway to Stein's jewelry store.

She looked around nervously, "Why are we stopping here?"

"I'm trying to avoid the Fentons."

She struggled to pull away but he held her and the baby tightly while he whispered a reminder that the Fenton's younger son Ernie had been the Klansman killed by PJ, and how he felt guilty that he had not visited them to offer his condolences.

But he was too late. Mister Fenton called out, "Sergeant O'Roark!"

Thomas turned, "Oh, Mister and Missus Fenton, what a nice surprise!"

He reached for the hand proffered by the older man, nodded and grinned foolishly in response to the weak smile offered by his wife. They both looked haggard and uncomfortably dressed for the day, he with a black armband over his gray winter jacket, the brim of his fedora pulled down across his dark, bottomless eyes. She was wearing a black wool coat over her dress and matching cloche. A tiny American flag emblem was visible in her coat lapel.

"What a beautiful day!" Thomas ventured.

"Yeah, kinda warm," Mister Fenton responded, fanning his face with one hand, plucking at his shirt collar with the other. He eyed Brenda absently.

"Er, this is my wife, Brenda, and our little boy, Tommy. Brenda, this is Mister and Missus Fenton."

Brenda smiled weakly, and Missus Fenton replied, "What a cute baby! How old is he?"

"He's just fifteen months," Brenda answered.

Thomas shifted the squirming youngster to his other arm and added, "And he already weighs twenty four pounds…seems like a lot more!" After an awkward pause, he motioned toward the passing crowd and continued, "Everyone seems happy, like they're enjoying the Holiday season."

The older couple nodded unsmilingly.

"So how've you folks been doing?"

Mister Fenton opened his mouth to say something, but she interrupted, sadness in her voice, "We've lost both our boys now, you know."

Thomas, thinking she was referring to Ernie, caught his breath. He opened his mouth to reply, but the father broke in, "Now, Ethyl. We said we weren't gonna talk about that---"

She ignored him, "Army says they can't find our Earl."

Thomas scowled. He handed the baby to Brenda, took the older woman's arm and gently guided both of them further into the store's outer foyer away from the passing crowd. "What do you mean, they can't find him?"

Mister Fenton answered, "We got a letter from the Army Grave Registration Service. Said they've dug up a bunch of bodies where the Marines were in the fighting but couldn't find Earl."

"They call him an 'Unknown,'" she added, tears puddling in her eyes.

Thomas struggled to dig into unpleasant memories. "That's crazy. I…I remember right where he is."

She pulled a hanky from her purse and dabbed at her eyes. "You do?"

"Certainly. He was standing in the trench when… when a big shell exploded, and…and it caved in on him."

"That really killed him?" the father asked, looking puzzled.

Thomas nodded and tried to swallow the lump in his throat.

"Then, why can't they find him?" she asked plaintively.

"Probably looking in the wrong place. Might just be digging up bodies from the temporary grave where we buried a bunch of guys." He could feel his foregut constricting as he recalled the gruesome shock of his first burial duty after that bloody battle at <u>Belleau Wood</u>, the battered bodies with arms, legs or heads missing, some with their guts or brains spilling out on the ground. He burped and choked back the bile rising from his stomach and glanced furtively toward the curb as he fought the urge to throw up his breakfast.

The mother continued, "We want to bring him home so he can be buried in that new Liberty Cemetery like all the other soldiers."

Thomas shook his head vaguely, momentarily lost in the memory of how his old friend really had died, cowering in the trench when the rest of his squad went over the top. He wasn't comfortable with the thought of him being honored as a hero along with the rest of the city's war dead.

"Could you tell 'em where to find him?" The question came from the father and caught Thomas by surprise.

"Well, er...gosh, I don't know. The area's probably all changed by now, or covered over with dirt. Or...or planted in wheat." His recollection of the wheat field through which he had charged toward the Germans suddenly flashed across his mind.

"Would you try?" The plea from Earl's mother was so soulful that it brought tears to Thomas' eyes and more tightening of his throat.

"Uh, I...I guess I could," he stammered. "Not sure if I can remember it that well, but maybe I could sketch a little map."

Missus Fenton brightened and reached for his hand. Her warm touch completely unnerved him. He pulled a handkerchief from his pocket and wiped his eyes and blew his nose vigorously. He hesitated a few moments, waiting for the roiling in his mind, the churning in his gut to settle down, before adding, "OK, when I get home, I'll draw up a map. And... and... I'll mail it to you."

"We'd sure appreciate it," Mister Fenton said, reaching for Thomas' free hand and turning toward Brenda with a furrowed brow, "Didn't you used to work in one of the stores?"

Before Brenda could respond, Missus Fenton added, "Oh, yes, I remember now. You were a sales lady at Gottschalk's before the war. Weren't you that Stuckey girl?"

Brenda sighed, "Yes, I used to work there but like a lot of others, got laid off during the war." A strained silence followed, acknowledgement that anyone laid off during wartime labor shortages undoubtedly was a German-American or from some other suspicious background.

Thomas, hoping to break the awkward moment, turned part way toward the sidewalk and tried to extricate himself from two hands that didn't want to let go. Finally, he leaned over and kissed Missus Fenton on the forehead, then grasped the father's hand in both of his. He let go, took a step back, and blurted out, "I'm terribly sorry about your younger son, Mister Fenton. I...I...wish there was something---"

Fenton interrupted, his voice dropping to a growl, "So, who killed him, that nigger you're keeping?" His facial expression turned belligerent.

Thomas was so startled and angered by the question that he took a reflexive step back, choking out, "No, no, he doesn't even have a gun!"

"You then?" Fenton asked, his voice rising.

Thomas shook his head, "No, no---"

"It was PJ," Brenda blurted out before he could finish. Thomas eyed the older man warily and tensed up to defend himself, backed away a couple more steps, took Brenda's arm and pushed her further toward the sidewalk.

Just as suddenly, Fenton's expression softened, and he added calmly, "Don't worry, son, we understand it wasn't your fault. Guess it was just a tough break, wrong place at the wrong time."

"Well, I'm sorry anyway. I...I'm..." Finding himself at a loss for words, Thomas took the squirming baby from Brenda, and they muscled their way back into the jostling crowd. As they moved away, she looked over her shoulder and blurted out through clenched teeth, "Ugh, what a horrid man!"

"Yeah, scary"

"Did you see how he glowered at me?"

Thomas responded irritably, "Maybe if you hadn't made such a point about being laid off. You made it so obvious about your heritage---"

She cut him off, "No, no. He was staring at me before that!"

He took a deep breath, "Yeah, me too."

Thomas felt both relieved and guilty that the confrontation he had worried about for three months was finally over. He trudged on, leading Brenda toward the department store, trying to remember what it was they were shopping for. It all came back when they entered the store and found a line of several dozen children and parents waiting patiently for their turn with Santa. By the time they were able to deposit Tommy in his lap, the little tyke was squirming and whimpering. He poked out his bottom lip in a big pout, grabbed the beard held in place by an elastic band, and let it snap back askew across the old codger's face. As Santa struggled to regain his composure, Thomas grabbed the baby and mumbled an apology, and they executed an embarrassed departure.

A couple hours later, after they had completed their shopping, they staggered back to the Maxwell completely frazzled. Thomas handed the sleeping Tommy to Brenda, climbed in behind the wheel and started the engine. He jammed the car into gear and, unmindful of his gasping wife, honking horns and screeching brakes, spun a U-turn in the middle of Tulare and headed east toward home. It wasn't until they rattled across the wooden bridge over the Fresno Canal and onto the rough, gravelly farm road that, shaking his head, he spoke, half murmuring, "Guess I really don't give a damn."

"What'd you say?"

He glanced toward Brenda quizzically, almost like he had forgotten she was there beside him. "Earl. They can't find him."

Since he had told her little about his wartime experiences, she didn't understand what he was referring to. She responded vaguely "That's too bad."

He fell silent, prompting her to probe. "Who're you talking about?"

He responded irritably, "Earl Fenton. The guy who joined the Marines with me and got killed in France. The Army can't find his body."

She didn't comment further, recognizing from the tone of his voice that he was struggling with a painful memory she couldn't share.

He continued haltingly to describe the circumstances of Earl's death until they had motored past their house and were about half a mile from the Stuckey farm. He called out, "Looks like you had a visitor."

She sat up and stared ahead to see a vehicle pulling away from the Stuckey residence and turning toward them. She shook her head, "It looks like that fancy motor car of Jake's."

They tensed up as the car approached rapidly, bearing down on them and hogging the center of the road. "Hang on!" Thomas yelled, as he swerved to the shoulder and the Stutz *Bearcat* roared past, sending a cloud of dust and gravel rattling across the top and side window flaps of the Maxwell. Brenda cried out in fright and clutched Tommy to her breast as Thomas ducked and yelled "son of a bitch!" He eased the Maxwell back onto the road, mumbling, "Someday, I'll get even with that bastard."

When they turned into the yard, they found Emil and Elsie on the porch waving and laughing. As Brenda crawled out of the car, still shaking, she called out, "That Jake friend of yours sure is an idiot!"

Emil shook his head and hollered back, "Yeah, I saw what he did. He's a real cutup when he gets in that car!"

Thomas and Brenda walked into the house where they were greeted by Papa reaching for his grandson, and the pungent odor of *schweinekniestucke mit sauerkraut und kartoffelklosse.*

"Oh, my!" Brenda called out as she slipped into her father's warm hug. "Smells like pigs' knuckles and potato dumplings."

"Yah, yah," he grinned.

"And lots of good Riesling to wash it down," Ivan added as he entered the parlor carrying a bottle, corkscrew and glasses. Brenda excused herself, and in a few moments, could be heard upstairs arguing with Emil in German. Thomas could only catch an occasional unfamiliar word, and assumed Emil was catching hell over Jake's behavior.

During the heavy meal that followed, Thomas struggled to stay awake as the Stuckeys discussed their grand plans for an old fashioned German Christmas. Later, as they headed home through the night, it seemed to him Brenda had become particularly pensive. "Something wrong, or are you just tired?" he asked.

She pulled the sleeping Tommy closer, "Yes, it's been a busy day."

"What were you and Emil arguing about?"

"Oh, er, just a family matter. Nothing important."

"Nothing important, or nothing you're gonna tell me about?"

She sighed, "We were arguing over that Jake Stein. I told him he should stop seeing him, or he's just going to get in trouble."

"Did he agree?"

"I don't think so," she replied as he turned into their yard and parked the car under the sycamore. When they approached the house, they found an envelope stuck in the door addressed to Brenda. "Oh my," she enthused, "this must be the information Melba promised!"

They continued into the house, and Thomas carried the sleeping baby to his crib and returned to build a fire. Brenda was seated at the kitchen table perusing printed material. "Oh, honey, this is so exciting! This is all about the new Fitter Families Contest!"

"What the heck's that?" He kneeled before the fireplace, crumpled up old newspaper, added kindling and a log, and struck a match.

"It's a new contest being sponsored by the American Eugenics Society to recognize the better elements of society. The first one will be held this summer at the Kansas Free Fair in Topeka. Maybe we could go. Wouldn't that be fun?"

His guard was up the moment he heard the word 'eugenics', but he stepped to the table and pulled out a chair across from her as she continued reading from the contest brochure. "See, it says the time has come for the science of human husbandry to be developed on the principles of scientific agriculture."

He grimaced, "So, like I said before, we're gonna be raising kids like pigs and cows?"

She pursed her lips at the comment but continued reading aloud, "They're going to judge families in three categories; small, average and large. I suppose we would qualify for the small. The winners in each category will receive a Fitter Family Trophy awarded by the Governor." She paused for breath, "Oh, and listen to this, Thomas. The Grade A families will receive a Capper Medal named after the Kansas senator, Arthur Capper. Doesn't that sound exciting?"

He didn't respond, but reached resignedly for the brochure and started reading until he came to the entry requirements, "Good grief, Brenda! It says that to enter you have to provide the family's eugenic history and take some kind of psychiatric intelligence test. That's ridiculous!"

"But we've already sent our eugenic history into that record office, and you took the intelligence test when you joined the Marines, so that shouldn't be---"

He interrupted, "And take a Wasserman test. I'll be damned!!

"What's that for?"

"To see if we've got a sexual disease, syphilis or whatever!"

Brenda, momentarily confused, sat back, arms folded across her chest. Then she tried to bounce back, "Well, wouldn't that be a good thing to know?"

He jumped up, leaned forward with his hands on the table and glared at her, "The last thing they did before I got discharged from the Marines was give me another damned short-arm inspection. So, if I've got anything, my dear, it would have to be from you!" He turned his back on her and moved to stir up the fire while she sagged in her chair, hurt and confused by his response.

He grumbled, "Well, my leg is killing me and we're both worn out from a long day. Maybe we could talk about this another time?"

She didn't reply but slumped further into the chair and stared blankly at the table. He tossed another log on the fire for the night and headed for the bathroom. When he came out, she had disappeared into the bedroom, so he locked the kitchen door, turned out the lights and followed her into bed. When he ventured a little peck on the back of her neck, she brushed him away.

***

The full extent of Brenda's Holiday planning didn't hit Thomas until the following Saturday morning, the final weekend before Christmas. Since she had started work in town, they had been inclined to sleep late on weekends, whenever the baby would let them. But on this particular day, Thomas was awakened by the smell of bread baking. He squirmed deeper into the warmth of the covers, reached across to find that Brenda was missing and lifted his head to squint at the bedside clock, barely visible in the nearly dark room. It was a quarter to six.

He stumbled out of bed, pulled his robe over his pajamas and went to the kitchen to find his wife at the sink pouring boiling water from the teakettle into a large bowl. An open sack of flour, package of raisins, tub of butter and jars of molasses and honey were on the counter. Tommy was in his high chair, contentedly sucking on his bottle.

"Hi," he called out.

Brenda, an apron tied around her old calico house dress, glanced back at him, responding with a cheery "Good morning!"

"What are you up to?"

"Baking bread…can't you smell it?"

"When did you get up?" he asked, sauntering over to pat the baby.

"Oh, an hour or so ago."

"Good grief! Why so early?"

She now was leaning over the bowl and kneading a batch of dough. "Have to make about a dozen loaves, so thought I'd get an early start."

"How come so many?" he asked absently, his eyes focused on the moving contours of her body under the thin dress.

271

"I promised one each for PJ and Erasmus, and Pedro's family will want at least two. The postman and iceman each get one, and I want to take a loaf to the office for the principal and another for Melba. We'll need *Stollen*, too, and a couple loaves of *Tannenbaum Brot* for Christmas dinner at Papa's, but I won't bake those 'til later in the week."

"What's that?"

"*Brot* is Christmas Tree Bread and *Stollen* is Christmas fruitcake."

He nodded vaguely. Brenda had baked bread before, usually one or two loaves for their own use. But recently, especially since she had been working the past two weeks, she had been bringing it home from the bakery.

"How come you're including the postman and iceman?" He moved to tend the fire.

"Oh, I can't forget them. They were very kind to us during the war. Brought us stuff when we were afraid to go to town."

"What kind of stuff?" he asked as he returned from the fireplace and reached down to pick up the bottle the baby had dropped.

She continued kneading the dough. "The postman used to sneak in one of Papa's German language newspapers once in awhile. The iceman would bring flour or sugar. We usually gave them fresh eggs, fruit or meat when Papa butchered something, or sometimes a bottle of wine. But they always seemed to enjoy the fresh bread the most."

"How about us?" he asked, sounding a bit plaintive.

"Don't worry. I'll bake a couple extra." She stepped over to the oven, pulled open the door to check the progress of the first loaves, and turned toward him. "You want to help?"

"Sure." He went to the bathroom to relieve himself, splash cold water on his face, comb his hair and wash his hands, then rejoined her at the sink.

Before turning to remove the finished loaves from the oven, she pointed a flour-covered hand toward a second large bowl in which a mixture of rolled oats and yeast had been soaking in hot water. "Put two cups of flour in there, add the honey and raisins and stir it up real good," she directed. He did as he was told as she removed the loaves from the oven and placed them on the kitchen table, instantly filling the room with a heavenly fragrance and stimulating the baby to gleefully clap his hands.

She returned to the first bowl to give its contents a final kneading, shaped it into a single large mound, and draped a clean kitchen towel across it. She ladled the final two cups of flour into Thomas' bowl and told him to keep kneading. When he finished some minutes later, she also shaped it into a mound and draped it with another towel.

"Now, we'll wait for those two batches to rise," she commented as she leaned over the sink to wash her hands. "In the meantime, what would you like for breakfast?"

"How about a little tussle in the hay?" he responded throatily as he stood beside her to also wash his hands, and felt the warmth of her body, enhanced by the heat of the oven.

She smiled up at him, "You're not mad at me anymore?"

"Actually, I think you were mad at me," he replied as he put his arms around her and pulled her close. When his robe fell open, he could feel the warmth of her tummy, the firmness of her breasts through the thinness of his pajamas. She gasped over the sudden hardness she felt through the skimpiness of her dress, "Oh, my! Where did that come from?"

He leaned down and kissed the warmth of her neck. "I guess bread's not the only thing that can rise around here."

She turned to look at the baby, now banging his spoon on the tray of his chair, his bottle back on the floor. "Think he'll be OK for a few minutes?"

"Maybe you better give him something to eat."

Brenda reached in the icebox, pulled out a cold saucer of mashed peas and carrots and placed them in front of the little one while Thomas again retrieved his bottle from the floor. They headed for the bedroom, she untying her apron and letting it fall to the floor as they went.

He closed the door and pulled the shades to darken the room, peeled off his robe and pajamas and slipped between the sheets. She removed her dress up over her head then sat on the edge of the bed to take off her bra and underwear. He rolled toward her, kissed her soft, bare back and reached around to cup one breast in his hand. She quickly rolled toward him and they passionately made up for the love they had been missing for the past two weeks.

When they finished, they cuddled together like two spoons and started to doze until she remembered the baking bread. As Thomas rolled back to his side of the bed, she jumped up and ran to the kitchen, slipping into her robe on the way. In a moment she was back at the bedroom door, "Guess what your son did!"

"Humph?" he mumbled sleepily and scrunched down under the covers.

"Threw his peas and carrots all over the kitchen floor!"

Chapter 16

For Thomas, after more than two weeks of preparation and anticipation, Christmas Day almost seemed anticlimactic. The fact that it turned out to be a typical Fresno winter day, when the cold, damp fog ate through a person's warmest clothing, didn't improve his outlook.

But in Brenda's mind it was going to be the festive event she had been looking forward to for over two years. It was the one Stuckey family custom she had missed the most during the bleak and constrictive holidays of the war period.

After a late breakfast, Thomas pulled on his heavy sheepskin coat, cap and gloves and scooped up a pan of hot coals from the fireplace. With his breath making frosty puffs and his boots crunching against the frozen ground, he walked outside to warm up the

Maxwell. He leaned down to slide the coals under the engine, closed the drain valve on the radiator, and refilled it with water. When he tried to start it with its electric starter, all he got was a couple of weak, uncertain groans. He resorted to cranking it to life and, with the cold air tickling his nostrils and biting into his lungs, sat shivering in the seat while the engine warmed up..

When he returned to the house, he found Brenda brushing Tommy's hair, getting him ready for their visit to Grandpa's house. He peeled off his outer clothes and headed for the bathroom to shave and bathe.

An hour or so later, when they turned into the Stuckey yard, they found Emma's Overland already there parked alongside Brad's Model T Ford sedan. Papa Stuckey, waiting anxiously on the porch in spite of the cold air, greeted them with shouts of *"Frohlicher Weihnachten!"* Brenda returned the greeting as she carried Tommy to her father's welcoming arms and stepped back to retrieve her two loaves of fresh raisin bread from the car. Thomas picked up the peach cobbler and jars of homemade pickled figs, and followed her into the house.

Thomas and Brenda joined the others huddled around the embracing warmth of the living room fireplace where Ivan was ladling out glasses of eggnog. They were greeted by cries of 'Merry Christmas' from Emma and Major Brown, Becky and her baby, and Emil and Elsie. Brad, displaying his knowledge of French, took a swallow of his drink and called out *"Joyeux Noel"*. His lady friend Sarah Cohen added to the international flavor with *"Rozhdestvom Khristovym"* which nobody understood, but guessed it was Russian.

After a few minutes of everyone exchanging greetings and sampling eggnog, Papa gave Tommy back to Brenda and disappeared briefly before returning with his accordion. Encouraged by his daughter's exhuberent clapping, he slipped the straps over his shoulders, squeezed out a few preliminary notes, and launched into a rusty rendition of *O Tannenbaum*. With Ivan, Emil, Elsie and Brenda eagerly singing and following, Papa led the way out of the living room into the hall, past the parlor, back through a bedroom and around the kitchen and dining room. The others tagged along, dutifully humming or mouthing the unfamiliar words to the old German song. After a couple of circles, they ended up at the locked door to the parlor.

When Papa stopped at the door, he handed the key to Brenda with a flourish. With the baby on her arm and a giggle of anticipation, she turned the key and threw open the door to a darkened room. Papa moved in and stumbled around cautiously to plug in the tree lights, suddenly revealing an enchanting Christmas spectacle. A large fir tree they had brought down from the mountains dominated the far corner of the room and was surrounded by a melange of brightly wrapped packages. A smaller tree they had cut for Tommy and Ricky sat on an end table next to the larger one.

The trees were profusely decorated with a variety of glass ornaments, some ordered through the Sears catalog, others purchased locally from Woolworth's. Cascades of silver tinsel, strings of multi-colored lights and garlands of popcorn strung together were looped through the limbs.   Tiny figurines in the shape of doves, angels and stars, which Papa and Ivan had folded from colored paper and tin foil, were hung among the baubles.   A silver star adorned the top of each tree, and cotton simulated snow around the base.

Papa settled into the large leather chair, holding Tommy in his lap and Ricky on the right arm. Thomas and the others sat on the sofa or pulled chairs up for a better view, while Sarah relaxed on the floor at Brad's feet, as Emil's girl friend did at his.   Brenda served as hostess, pulling packages from under the trees and handing them to their intended recipients.

The gifts ran the gamut from pen wipers to clothing to books to *Victrola* records to games and toys, all opened and admired with a great deal of jollity.   A highlight was saved for near the end when Papa directed Brenda to unwrap two large gifts that stood against the wall next to the trees. They turned out to be gaily painted wooden rocking horses he had made for both babies. Each boasted a saddle, stirrups and reins fabricated from leather and glued-on real horsehair.

Papa finally motioned for Brenda to retrieve two packages from under the smaller tree and hand them to the children sitting on his chair arm. They tugged and tore at the colorful wrapping paper to expose identical books.

"Oh, look," Brenda exclaimed, "they're *Grimm's Fairy Tales!*"

Thomas glanced over from the sofa, "What's that?"

"They're old German folk tales...*Hansel and Gretal, Cinderella, Rumpelstilskin*." She reached for one of the copies, then gasped, "Oh, but Papa, they're in German...I won't be able to read them!"

He grinned and nodded, *"Yah, yah...ich buchen."*

Another unusual gift also came from Papa. It was three stock certificates, each for ten shares of General Motors Corporation, which he gave jointly to Thomas and Brenda and individually to Ivan and Emil. Thomas and Brenda were a little confused, having never seen such a certificate.

Emil was ecstatic. "Oh, Papa, this is great!" he exclaimed, waving the certificate around. "This is the way to make money nowadays, investing in the stock market. No more slaving away on the farm, praying for good weather and decent prices!"

Papa looked perplexed, and Ivan frowned and admonished his brother, "Er, where'd you think the money came from to buy that certificate, little brother?"

Emil looked a little piqued at the sobriquet, but wasn't ready to be completely contrite. "Yes, but the stock market is the wave of the future. I don't know what Papa paid for these but the last time I checked, they were approaching two hundred dollars a share!" Thomas and Brenda looked at their certificate a little more appreciatively. The rest of the room fell quiet, except for the two little boys, both squirming to get to their rocking horses.

Brenda gave Thomas a kiss that suggested bigger rewards to come in return for the new wool suit he gave her, an ideal addition to the wardrobe she needed for her job at the Normal School. She in turn presented him with a pair of black *Florsheim* wing tips that would go with his blue pin stripe. Thomas and Becky had teamed up to invest five dollars in an enameled butterfly-shaped pin from Norway their mother had admired at Warner's jewelry store. From her each received a copy of H.G. Wells' latest novel, *Mister Britling Sees It Through*, which, with over three-hundred-thousand copies sold nationwide, was still topping the best seller list. Major Brown happily tried on a pair of leather gloves from Emma. He in turn had given her a year's subscription to her two favorite magazines, *The Pictorial Review* and *Ladies' Home Journal*.

Emil smiled appreciatively when he opened his gift from his older brother, a leather-bound copy of Booth Tarkington's Pulitzer prize-winning novel, *The Magnificent Ambersons*. Papa received a wool cardigan sweater from Brenda and Thomas, and socks and slippers from his sons. Becky gave a dress shirt and tie to her brother and cosmetic sets to her mother, Brenda, Sarah and Elsie.

But the most surprising exchange came at the end. Thomas knew that Brad admired the writing of Joseph Conrad, and thus had given him a copy of his latest novel, *Arrow of Gold*. He, in turn, had opened Brad's present, which was wrapped in a large hatbox, to find a *Panama* hat. As he reached into the box, he smiled at the thought that Brad was playing some kind of joke by presenting him with a straw hat in the wintertime.

But as he lifted it out, a fleece-lined leather pilot's helmet complete with goggles fell onto the floor. Thomas' mouth dropped open and his face turned red. He was speechless, torn between the wonderful surprise and the apprehension over what kinds of reactions it would generate. As far as he knew, among those in the room, only Brad and Brenda were aware of his interest in flying.

A grinning Brad spoke first, "Don't you remember? I promised you a *Panama* like mine when you got your pilot's certificate."

Thomas cleared his throat and finally blurted out, "But...but the helmet...I don't have my certificate yet!"

"I'm not worried. O'Leary tells me you're one of the best he's trained."

Thomas tried to think of something else to say, but nothing came out. The room had become so quiet that even the two babies stopped playing with their rocking horses. Brenda, sitting on the floor next to him, was the first to react as her eyes flashed angrily at him and Brad. She stood up and left the room.

Emma looked confused and Major Brown frowned. The Stuckeys couldn't comprehend the meaning of the gift, so remained quiet. Only Becky reacted positively with a yip of surprise followed by, "Oh, my heavens, Thomas! What have you been up to?"

Finally, he found his voice and turned to Brad. "Thank you, my friend...what...what a thoughtful gift. You really surprised me!"

Brad smiled and looked apprehensively around the room. "Looks like I surprised a few others, too. Hope I haven't stirred up some kind of trouble."

Thomas shook his head. "Not at all. I'm sure it'll all work out."

The awkward moment was resolved when Papa rose and headed for the kitchen, and Ivan invited everyone to their seats in the dining room. Thomas had never seen such an elaborate table. It was covered with a needlepoint tablecloth and a centerpiece of yellow chrysanthemums bracketed by silver candlesticks. Each place setting featured sterling silverware, crystal glassware, a plate of fine china resting in a brass charger and a napkin that matched the tablecloth.

He picked up the plate to look more closely at the delicate flower pattern, then leaned close to Brenda and spoke quietly, "Looks like Papa's gone all out for this dinner." Still angry over his new pilot's helmet, she didn't reply, but Ivan did overhear and responded. "Yes, this tablecloth was made in Germany by our grandmother. Mama and Papa also brought the sterling and *Meissen* porcelain with them when they moved to America. We only bring it out for special occasions such as this."

While everyone settled into their chairs, Emil circled the table pouring Riesling into the crystal goblets. After Papa delivered his usual lengthy blessing, Ivan started ladling out liver dumpling soup and the guests reached for their spoons and stirred their bowls with various degrees of enthusiasm. Thomas, still not enamored of the rich concoction, dipped into his bowl slowly, interspersing it with generous swallows of wine. Peeking out the corner of his eye, he could see that others also were approaching their portions gingerly. The silence was broken only by Papa slurping lustily, and the rest of the Stuckeys leaning into their bowls eagerly and reaching for more.

The eating was interrupted by Ivan tapping on his glass. "I would like to propose a toast to Thomas and Brenda who now are the proud owners of forty more acres of prime farm land." Everyone raised their glasses, and Emma beamed proudly across the table at her son as Papa added his '*Goot, Goot*' and reached to pat his daughter on the shoulder.

Ivan looked at Thomas and continued, "It looks like the Russians left that old Maloney property in pretty bad shape. We're expecting you to turn it into a real showplace."

Thomas, surprised by all the attention, responded, "Well, thank you. Guess I haven't had time to think about it yet, but it's gonna take a lot of work."

Emma, still beaming, spoke up, "Goodness, that means you now have a total of one hundred acres. Father would be so proud of you!"

Brenda, still moping over Brad's gift, forced out a thin smile and reached to pat Thomas on the arm, adding a little weakly, "I'm proud of him, too."

Brad asked, "Think you'll be able to keep the Post Office job?"

Before Thomas could answer, Major Brown interjected, "That's good steady pay. Better hang on to that job."

"How bout PJ?" Becky asked. "Can he handle that much more responsibility?"

Ivan interrupted before Thomas could respond, "Looks like you're gonna have to invest in your own tractor, plow and spreader. Haven't you been jobbing out that heavy work to someone?"

Thomas looked up from his bowl of soup and nodded, "Yeah, old Iverson and his horses from over in Sanger. But he keeps upping his prices."

Brad added, "Guess you can't blame him. Horses are more valuable now since so many were killed in the war."

Emil spoke, "That's one reason why everyone's switching from horsepower to motor power. According to a government study, you can plow for ninety-five cents an acre with a tractor compared to a dollar forty-six with a horse."

Brad spoke, "Yeah, but I understand you gotta be real careful with a tractor. If you catch the plow on a rock or tree root or something solid like that, those *Fordsons* will rear up and roll over on you!"

"That's right," Major Brown added. "We picked up some poor farmer out near Clovis last week. One of those contraptions rolled over and killed him."

Emma gasped and looked at her son, "Oh, my! Maybe you'd better stick to horses."

Thomas put down his glass of wine. "Don't worry, Mother. I've hardly had time to think about that extra property, so I don't know what I'll need yet."

Everyone became silent, and Ivan arose to remove the nearly empty tureen while Emil started collecting soup bowls. They returned with a platter bearing a roasted goose, its juicy golden brown skin glistening in the light of the flickering candles and overhead chandelier. A second platter, which Thomas recognized from Brenda's cooking as pigs' knuckles, sauerkraut and potato dumplings, followed. The first one was placed in front of Papa, the second at the other end of the table.

Glancing across the table, Thomas caught his mother leaning toward Brown with a questioning nod at the strange-looking food Ivan was starting to serve into individual dishes. He sought to enlighten her. "That's *schweinekniestuke mit sauerkraut und kartoffelklosse*, Mother," he said, mangling the German badly enough to bring an embarrassed sigh and translation from Brenda, "It's pigs' knuckles, sauerkraut and potato dumplings, Missus O'Roark."

Emma nodded and smiled apprehensively, and along with the others turned to watching Papa expertly carve the goose as Emil circled the table refilling glasses. Brenda passed a plate of her Christmas and raisin breads for sopping up the rich sauces, and they all dug in. Even the two babies seemed to enjoy the mashed potatoes and carrots spooned up by their mothers, interspersed with swigs from their milk bottles and judicious samples of the sauces.

Emil broke the silence when he directed a remark to Brad. "Judging by the *Republican*, it looks like all of the labor strikes are finally winding down."

Before Simpson could respond, Brown opined forcefully, "It's about time! My God, the country's had over three-thousand strikes this year!"

Brad nodded, "Yeah, and several million people out of work."

Emma, looking a little embarrassed at Brown's outburst, added, "One of the worst was the one last summer by the local telephone workers. It sure interrupted our work."

Sarah joined in, "I understand some are making six dollars a day now."

"That's just for linemen and cable splicers," Elsie interjected. "I was a student operator before I left for the university, and we only got increased to twelve dollars a week."

Thomas took a swallow of wine and joined the discussion. "Six dollars a day is a lot of money. That sounds like wartime wages."

"And more than us deputy sheriffs are making," Brown added irritably.

Brad, wiping his mouth with his napkin, asked, "How about the American Federation of Labor agitating for a forty-four hour week? That should anger a few more capitalists."

Ivan responded, "We sure can't run our farms on forty-four hours. And I'm worried about what those pay increases will do for our labor needs next summer. The pickers will be wanting more than forty cents." He pushed his chair back, and he and Emil rose from the table and started carrying empty dishes to the kitchen.

Becky agreed with Ivan, "I can't run my cosmetics business on forty-four hours either. I have to serve my customers whenever they're available."

Brown asserted himself again. "Far is I'm concerned the Commies are behind the unrest. Patriotic Americans wouldn't be stirring up so much agitation."

Brad shook his head. "That's not really true, Major. Most of the strikers I've interviewed are good, hard-working Americans who just want the business owners to pay a fair return for their labor."

Brown replied firmly, "I can tell you that a lot of the ones we've arrested are real imbeciles, even mentally incompetent." Defiantly he downed the rest of his wine.

Brenda, who had been wiping up a spill on Tommy's chair tray, joined the discussion. "It seems like if they're mentally incompetent we should sterilize more of them. At least they wouldn't be producing more feeble-minded children."

Her statement brought the conversation to a dead halt until Emma, looking around the table, added innocently, "That certainly would help our birth control program. It seems like the poor and unfit are the ones who need the most help controlling the size of their families." Thomas was too taken aback to think of anything to say, while the others looked down in embarrassment or reached quietly for their glasses.

Brenda tried to defend her remark, "Well, California's already sterilized over two thousand in our mental hospitals without any problems...and... and some of them are murderers and robbers...and... and even sexual deviates!"

Silence followed until Brad finally ventured, "I know that's the solution supported by the eugenics leaders, Brenda, but that sounds pretty severe for the people we're talking about."

Emil added, "Yeah, Sis, that seems a little radical to me. A lot of people aren't really nuts, they just act that way!" Several chuckled nervously at the weak joke, then again fell silent as Ivan entered with Brenda's Christmas fruitcake and a pot of coffee. Generous portions were quietly dispensed and everybody returned to eating and sipping coffee.

Papa removed the napkin tucked under his chin, pushed back his chair and suggested they adjourn to the parlor for a liqueur. As Major Brown rose from the table, he turned to shake hands with Papa, Ivan and Emil and beg his leave so he could return to work. Emma dutifully turned to follow, but Becky, who had ridden out from town with them, protested. "I don't want to leave yet. We're having too much fun!"

Thomas spoke up, "Why don't you stay, Sis? I'll drive you in later."

"Yes," Sarah added, "or you can ride with us."

With the Major and Emma on their way, Papa, Ivan and Brenda went to the kitchen to wash dishes and put away leftover food, and the others moved to the parlor. Emil removed a humidor from the shelf and offered each of the men a big Cuban cigar and teasingly held them in front of Becky.

She demurred as she glanced toward Ricky and Tommy, now on the floor playing with their gifts. "Well, maybe it would be OK if I smoke just one little cigarette. Since the babies are down on the floor, it shouldn't bother them." She reached in her purse, pulled out a pack of *Lucky Strikes* and held it out toward Sarah and Elsie. Sarah declined with thanks as she reached into her suit pocket to retrieve her own pack. Elsie produced a tin of rope-like Turkish cheroots, and she and the other two women waited patiently for someone to produce a light. Emil smilingly obliged as the other men sat nonplussed, still not used to the idea of women smoking.

Emil then settled into the big leather chair with Elsie on the arm. Sarah took another chair, and Brad sat on the floor beside her. Thomas and his sister pulled up two other casual chairs and were idly watching their babies tearing into the inviting piles of colorful ribbons and wrapping paper. Ivan entered the room with a sterling epergne of colorful Christmas cookies and passed it around the room. He left and returned in a moment with six glasses and a narrow, square-shaped bottle of liqueur.

"What surprise do we have here, Ivan?" Thomas asked as some of the liqueur was poured into his glass.

"Peppermint *Schnapps*," Ivan replied. "Couldn't get any during the war, so this is our last." He held the blue colored bottle up to the light to show that it was less than half full.

Thomas sniffed the sweet, minty-smelling liquid and waited while the others were served. After everyone raised their glasses in a toast to a Christmas in peace, he took a tentative sip. "Gosh, that's a refreshing taste," he added as the soothing liquid trickled down his throat, and the others nodded their agreement. Ivan pointedly took the bottle with him as he returned to the kitchen.

Thomas settled back in his chair, sipped his *Schnapps* and took a few contented puffs on his cigar. When his eyes fell on the cigarette pack Sarah was returning to her purse, he leaned forward, asking, "What's that you're smoking?"

She held up the pack, "Oh, these are my favorite French brand. They're called *Gauloises*." Thomas almost choked on his cigar as he recognized the distinctive package showing a French soldier and gypsy woman superimposed on the pale blue of a poilu's uniform. It was the same brand Lillian smoked in Paris.

"Where'd you get those?" he asked.

"That tobacconist on Mariposa near Court House Park. He has these and several other foreign brands."

Elsie added, "That's where I bought these Turkish ones."

Everyone fell quiet for a few moments, sipping the liqueur and idly watching the two youngsters play with their new toys. Thomas opened his mouth to say something, but was stopped by Brenda shouting, "Thomas, what on earth are you doing!" She suddenly had appeared at the doorway and was standing defiantly with hands on her hips.

"Huh...what...what's the matter?"

"You're exposing Tommy to all this smoke! You'll stunt his growth!"

Thomas chuckled, "It's Emil's fault. He passed out the cigars!"

Emil grinned, "Sorry, I didn't realize Irish babies were such sissies."

"They're both part German, Emil, as you well know!"

"But they both have---"

Brenda, her voice almost hysterical, cut him off, "Emil, that's enough!"

Thomas and Becky, flabbergasted by this heated exchange between brother and sister, remained silent.

Brenda crossed the room, picked up her son and turned toward Becky. "I'm surprised you would expose Ricky to smoke like this, Becky. You should be ashamed of yourself!"

Becky was too startled to respond and guiltily stubbed out her cigarette, as did Sarah and Elsie. Brad and Emil doused their cigars, but Thomas stuck his in his mouth and defiantly tried to suck it back to life. Brenda paused at the door and called out, "Come on, Thomas, it's time to go home."

Thomas, embarrassed and angry, glared at Brenda and growled, "I'm not ready to go yet!"

"Tommy and I are leaving. I don't want to expose him to all this smoke."

He still didn't move from his chair until he noticed the others had fallen silent and were looking awkwardly down at the floor or at the walls. He shook his head in frustration and without further word stood up, gathered up their gifts and stalked out to the car.

Brad picked up the rocking horse and followed him, adding, "Don't worry about Becky. We'll take her back to town." Thomas nodded and climbed behind the steering wheel as Brenda struggled into the other side with the baby. As they pulled out of the driveway onto the farm road, he removed the dead cigar from between his clenched teeth, pushed the side flap open, and tossed it out. He stared ahead into the empty blackness of the night, struggling to focus his boozy vision.

He turned and spoke menacingly, "Don't ever do that to me again."

"Do what?"

"Embarrass me in front of my sister and friends."

"I didn't mean to embarrass you, but I was worried about Tommy and all that smoke."

"That little bit of smoke didn't hurt him one damn bit!"

"It's not good for his lungs, and the eugenics people say---"

"I don't give a damn what that bunch of oddballs says. I've got as much right as you to raise our son, at least you claim he's ours." The angry words tumbled out before Thomas could stop them, and he immediately felt the bile of remorse surging up from his gut as Brenda started dabbing at her tears.

He turned into their yard and brought the Maxwell to a skidding stop under the sycamore. He stepped around to help Brenda out but she brushed him aside and carried the baby into the house. He followed, turned on the lights and bent to building a fire as she disappeared with Tommy into the bedroom and slammed the door.

Thomas returned to the car to retrieve their gifts, carried them into the house and dumped everything in a corner of the living room. That was with the exception of the *Panama* hat and pilot's helmet and goggles, which he placed beside his father's rocker. He reached into the kitchen cabinet for his bottle of brandy, chipped some ice in a glass and poured in a couple fingers worth. Next, he wandered into the front bedroom closet and reached into his coveralls for his cigarette makings. Returning to the rocker, he pulled out one of the thin papers and curled it around his index finger, tapped in some tobacco, ran the edge across his tongue and stuck one end in his mouth. He removed a stick of kindling from the fire, touched the glowing end to his cigarette and inhaled deeply. When the smoke exited his lungs in a lazy arc toward the ceiling, he washed away the acrid taste with a cooling swig of brandy over ice.

He picked up the *Panama*, hefted its light weight, plopped it on his head and ran his hand around the brim to snap it down at a rakish angle. Then he reached for the pilot's helmet and goggles and carefully examined the pliant leather, the precise stitching and the soft fleece lining. After several drags on his cigarette, he returned to the bedroom where he could see himself in the mirror. With a smile of satisfaction, he removed the straw hat and substituted the helmet, finding it a perfect fit when he pulled it over his head and lowered the goggles into place. With the cigarette dangling casually from his lips, he admired himself from the front and sides. When he tired of this, he went back to the rocking chair, gazed distantly into the lambent flame of the fireplace, and dreamed of the day he would be awarded his pilot's certificate by the Aero Club and be free to fly away from all his troubles.

Chapter 17

As 1919 drew to a close, most Americans were looking forward to putting the thousands of labor strikes, the "Red" scare, the race riots and other painful reminders of the Great War behind them and embarking on a new decade.

Thomas and Brenda celebrated by attending a New Year's eve dance at the new Pavilion Ballroom. It was an especially gala affair that went on well past midnight with everyone enjoying the continuing prosperity and trying to figure out how to live with the specter of Prohibition due to take effect in mid-January. While some discussed the best recipes for converting raisins into brandy or gin, or where local stills were being set up, others simply seemed bent on consuming enough liquor to carry them through the possibility of a dry future.

Although Thomas had agreed to go to the dance reluctantly because he believed it would aggravate his leg wound, he finally caved in when Brenda proposed that they reserve a room for the night at the Hughes Hotel. Ostensibly they did this so they wouldn't have to drive back to the farm in marginal weather after an evening of drinking. But Brenda also had hinted coyly that they could recreate the joy and abandon of their wedding night.

The dance had indeed turned into a big celebration, but not a particularly happy one for Thomas. Much to his annoyance, Brenda had invited her co-worker Melba and her new boy friend to join them.

As Thomas feared, the dancing did cause his leg to drain; additionally, the new wing tips Brenda had given him for Christmas pinched his feet. The end result was that he had left the party before midnight, taken a taxi to the hotel, woosily signed the register, and ridden the elevator to the suite they had reserved on the top floor. He took an antipyrine for his pain, squeezed out of his shoes and flopped on the bed with most of his clothes on.

Later, he could only vaguely recall Brenda entering the room. But he could remember the breakfast in bed on New Year's morning and the crackle of sleet from a winter storm slashing against the windows while they soaked away their hangovers in the oversize bathtub and downed another bottle of champagne. He also had fond memories of their romp in the big double bed that followed.

But now it was mid-February and they still were trying to settle into a new lifestyle. Brenda was getting used to driving the Maxwell into town five days a week for her job at the Normal School, usually taking Tommy with her. This gave him the benefit of finding new friends to play with in the school's nursery and of having his mother available for his occasional breast feedings.

Thomas was adjusting to his return to farm work after quitting his Post Office job at the end of December. He finally had recognized that with the addition of the Menshikov place, he now owned too much acreage to entrust solely to hired help, even individuals as reliable as PJ, Erasmus and Pedro.

He also had anticipated that spending quiet time alone at the farmhouse would make it easier to pursue his elusive goal of writing. Even more important, the extra time had given him the opportunity in January to replicate his flying tests for the Aero Club inspector and be issued his pilot's certificate. And Brenda was none the wiser.

So on this bleak morning of Friday the 13th after another freezing night, and with the outside temperature still hovering in the low 40s, Thomas had settled himself at the kitchen table with his typewriter. He had enrolled in a course in short story writing from The Home Correspondence School in Springfield, Massachusetts. Now, with no one around to disturb him and the house quiet except for the crackling and popping of the fireplace, he sat down and rolled a sheet of paper into the typewriter. Since Brad had given him the machine, he had taken it out of the closet several times to try to learn the random location of the letters of the alphabet. He still found himself pretty awkward with the 'hunt and peck' system.

He scanned the first assignment from the school, which was to write several paragraphs of action that would form the basis for a short story of some three thousand words. He had collected a few thoughts, so felt like he was ready to start. He leaned expectantly toward the typewriter and rested his fingers on the keys, only to be interrupted by the sound of a vehicle pulling into the yard.

He pushed his chair back with a scraping sound, went to the door and glanced out to see the iceman in his Studebaker panel truck preparing to make his regular semi-weekly delivery. Thomas opened the door and called out, "Good morning, Gus."

"Mornin' Mister O'Roark." The short, stocky deliveryman, his tongs locked into a twenty-five pound block of ice resting against the leather apron that protected his shoulder and back from melting ice, stepped effortlessly into the room. As he deftly removed the small remaining chunk of ice and loaded the new block into the icebox, he never stopped talking. "How about that Jackie Powell...won another fight Saturday."

Thomas, who hadn't followed the progress of Fresno's promising young welterweight very closely, mumbled a vague response.

"Looks like he's gonna be champ one of these days."

Thomas nodded. "Yeah, you're probably right."

With a casual "don't forget to empty that drip pan," the iceman departed and Thomas settled back in front of the typewriter. He tapped the space bar to move the carriage toward the center of the paper and with the forefinger of each hand, slowly filled out the title page supplied by the correspondence school:

```
Name: Thomas J. O'Roark
Address: Route A,
Box 345, Fresno, Calif.
Course: Short Story
Lesson Number: 1
ID Number: 92261
```

He scanned the letters he had typed onto the paper, encouraged that he had done so without an error. He positioned his fingers above the keys to resume typing, but was brought back to the moment by the iceman's parting words, "don't forget..."

He stepped over to the icebox and lifted the hinged door underneath the side that held the ice. Sure enough, the darn thing was full and about to overflow again. Hadn't he just emptied it yesterday?

Carefully, he slid the pan out, lifted it to the sink, and poured the meltwater out. He put the pan back in place and used the dishrag to sop up the water splashed on the floor. Wondering to himself if anyone ever emptied the pan without spilling some, he returned to his typewriter, tapped the space bar to center the carriage, and typed out the title:

Actiom For A Shorr Story To Be Titlexx
The Fimal Day.

He peered proudly at the words he had transferred from his mind to his fingers to the paper in front of him, then shook his head at the typographical errors. He again positioned his fingers over the keys but once more was distracted, this time by an intermittent popping noise emanating from the front bedroom.

Struggling to control the annoyance of this third break into his concentration, he rose and went to the bedroom to find that the sound came from a windowpane expanding from the slowly rising outside temperature. He returned to the typewriter and started searching out and punching each key with determination, occasionally missing his intended letter:

A young Marine sdrgeant, weary from too
mut/ch war,
leads his squad dogg//edly toward another
bombed-out
village in northezastern France. He wonders
how //// much
longwr this senseless carnage will continue as
he guides his

comrades into the relative secusrity of an anciant cathedral.

The soldiers roll out their bedrools sfor the night and fire up

///containers of canned heat to warm up their cold bully beef.

When the sergeant wanders into the adgoining graveyard

/to relieve himself, he runs into an officer.

He asks the officer What days it is.

The lieutenant tells him it is November 10, just anosther

day.

The sergeant asks what the orders are for tomorrow,

and is told they will be pushing the Heinies across the

<u>Meuse</u> River, and then on to Berlin.

The sergeant nods numbly when told his squad will

get to lead the attack.

Thomas paused in his typing, thinking he heard the toilet water running in the bathroom. He went in and jiggled the pull chain, then decided to relieve himself. When finished, he flushed the toilet and stood there buttoning his *Levis* and watching disinterestedly as the water sluiced around in the bowl. He washed his hands and returned to the living room, noticed the fire needed tending, poked at the embers and tossed on another log. He poured a cup of cold coffee left over from breakfast and returned to the typewriter.

He lifted up the paper to review what he had written, shook his head dejectedly at the typing errors and resumed pecking away at the story concept:

> The sergeant returns to his ///squad and tells then of
> their orders to crosa the river in the morning. He notices
> sthat his Corporal, who has gotten thru the war without
> a scratch, has become very di//sconsolate. Upon
> questU/ioning, he learns that the Corporal is worried
> about croxsing the river beca//use he cannot swim.

Thomas was disturbed by a knock at the door. With a sigh of frustration, he again pushed his chair back and went to the door, where he found PJ. "Sorry to bother you, Boss, but I reckon we've got a problem."

"What's the matter?"

"Some of them trees at the Russian place. Bark looks all white and scaly, like maybe somethin's eatin' at 'em."

"Where abouts?"

"That first row closest to the old house."

Thomas tried to conceal his irritation, "What do you want me to do?"

"Thought maybe you oughta have a look, maybe call the farm advisor."

Thomas sighed and leaned back in the room to glance at the wall clock. "OK, PJ. It's almost noon, so I'll grab a bite and we can drive over together."

He turned back to the typewriter and contemplated continuing with his writing, but decided to give up. His creative juices had been shut off by the reality of everyday life on the farm. He removed the typewritten page, folded it in with the assignment papers, put the cover on the machine, and stashed it all in the bedroom closet. He returned to the kitchen and fixed himself a cold chicken sandwich, glass of milk and a slice of leftover apple pie.

When PJ returned after lunch, Thomas banked the fire, pulled on his heavy outer coat and fleece-lined cap, and walked out to the Ford truck he had acquired along with the Russian property. Having the vehicle had given him the excuse he needed to teach his farm manager how to drive. But because of his short stature and the pointy toed, high-heeled boots he always wore, he had trouble working the clutch and brake pedals, which often resulted in jerky starts and stops. At least he could handle the vehicle adequately for the endless hauling of sacks of fertilizer, drying trays, packing boxes and miscellaneous tools required between the family's three farm locations.

Thomas motioned PJ toward the driver's seat and stepped in front to turn the crank.

"Don't you wanna drive, Boss?"

"Naw. You can take 'er."

The wiry little farm manager climbed into the driver's seat, turned on the switch and set the spark and throttle levers.

"Ready?" Thomas asked, laying his hand on the crank handle and pulling it through until he felt the engine compression.

PJ nodded a bit uncertainly.

Thomas gave the crank a quick turn and felt a touch of satisfaction as the little engine popped to life. He always took pride in keeping his vehicles running well. So when he inherited the neglected truck, he had devoted a day to tightening the engine bearings and tappets, installing a new magneto and spark plugs, and adjusting the brakes and clutch bands.

He climbed into the passenger seat and watched warily out of the corner of his eye as PJ leaned forward in the seat and advanced the throttle lever on the idling engine. He depressed the left foot pedal, then abruptly let it out, sending the wheels spinning and chickens flying as he launched the truck around the sycamore. Thomas grabbed the seat back in his left hand, the windshield frame in the other, and hung on tight. He fought the urge to reach over and reduce the throttle as they headed out the driveway, bounced onto the farm road and turned east without PJ glancing one way or the other. Fortunately, no other vehicles were in sight.

With PJ hunched over the steering wheel and staring straight ahead, Thomas pulled the ear flaps down on his cap and hunkered into his heavy coat. He folded his arms across his chest and tucked his hands under his armpits, cursing that he had forgotten his gloves. Through chattering teeth he ventured a compliment, "Your...your driv...driving seems to be improving."

"Yessir. Still a little shaky on the starts. But reckon I'm gittin' there."

They reached their destination in record time, and PJ brought the truck to a skidding stop next to the yellow freight car abandoned by the Russians and cut the engine. They climbed out and trudged toward the diseased trees. Off to the east alongside the continuation of the farm road they could see two huge bonfires where workers were continually adding scraggly dead limbs freshly cut from the dormant grapevines and fruit trees. Dark gray smoke from those fires and many others around the eastern part of the valley was rising against the unyielding blanket of fog and hanging there like a giant funeral pall.

PJ led the way to the edge of the orchard and knelt down beside the first tree. He rubbed his gloved hand up and down the trunk and peeled off some of the white, scaly looking bark. Thomas reluctantly pulled a hand from the warmth of his pocket, squatted down to pick up a piece of bark and turned it back and forth. "Yeah, this doesn't look so good. Looks like some kind of bug or insect is getting after it, maybe in the roots, or maybe it's the gophers."

PJ stood up and walked deeper into the orchard, kicking at elongated mounds of dirt characteristically made by burrowing gophers as he approached several more trees that appeared diseased. After viewing the last one, Thomas shook his head in dismay. "Guess you better boil up a batch of lime sulfur, and paint all these trunks. Hopefully we can still save 'em."

"OK, Boss. And I'll git 'Rass' to fix up some boxes for the owls to nest in so's they can git after them gophers."

"What's that?"

PJ held up his hands to outline the shape of an oversized bird house with a peaked roof and a large, round hole in the front. "We'll hang em around in some of the trees for barn owls to nest in. They'll come out at night and gobble up them gophers right quick like."

Thomas glanced sideways at his farm manager, not sure if he was pulling his leg or not. "You're sure about that, huh?"

"Yessir. Worked right good back in Texas. Used to eat up them field mice and spit the bones and fur all over the place."

Thomas stuffed his hands in his coat pockets, and they turned and walked back toward the truck and past the outhouse, now smelling pretty ripe. They paused as they reached the abandoned freight car. Although Thomas had visited the property once since the Menshikovs had moved out, this was the first time he felt the urge to look inside the structure.

Hesitantly, he reached for the half-open door, pushed it further and stared into the dank, semi-dark interior. Aided by the pallid light from the single window on the opposite wall, he could barely make out the outlines of the empty, cavernous interior. The sink remained attached to the wall, and a few scraps of paper and miscellaneous pieces of clothing were scattered around on the floor.

He stepped back from the doorway, turned and walked around the railcar to look at the skeletal remains of the old Maloney house. The concrete foundation, edged by the dry pedicels of last summer's weeds, was still there along with the former plumbing pipes poking their limbless stalks toward the sky. The two-story stone fireplace was standing sentinel-like over the few charred pieces of wood that remained. He speculated the Russians had used most of it for firewood.

He turned back to his farm manager. "PJ, let's bring a crew in here and get rid of this old reefer. Sell it, haul it away or burn it down, I don't care. Just get rid of it. You can keep any of the stuff you want or give it away." He paused to blow his warm breath into his cupped hands, then waved his arm in a semi-circle. "That privy too, and clean up the yard and barn. Any old junk that's in there you can sell or keep. Just get it out of here and clean the place up real pretty."

"Yessir."

He doffed his cap, ran his fingers through his tousled hair and put it back on. "I'm thinking we could build a new house here, a nice two-story one like the Missus talks about."

PJ nodded as Thomas became pensive for a few moments, then spoke again, "Don't suppose you've got a tape on you?"

"Got one in the tool box." PJ went to the truck, returned shortly with a tape measure and handed it to Thomas.

He took the tape and motioned to PJ to hold one end as he proceeded to measure around the perimeter of the foundation, pausing to make a rough sketch with a stub of pencil and scrap of paper he had taken from his coat pocket. He marked the location of the fireplace, the plumbing pipes and protrusion for the front porch. He penciled in the various rooms as best he could remember from his visits to the house prior to the fire.

Finally, with a satisfied smile, he turned and led the way back to the truck.

It was mid-afternoon by the time they returned to the home farm, and Thomas was surprised to find the Maxwell parked in the yard. Brenda usually didn't get home from her work until after five o'clock, but he speculated that this being Friday, she might have gotten off early.

He entered the house to the sound of the baby crying lustily and hastened toward the back bedroom, noticing on the way that the bathroom door was ajar. He found Tommy standing bare-assed, hanging onto the edge of his crib, tears streaming down his cheeks. As Thomas approached and patted his son solicitously, his nose identified at least part of the problem, confirmed by the crappy diaper kicked off in one corner.

He tossed his coat and cap on the bed, picked the baby up by the armpits and cuddled him to his chest. He was rewarded with the warm feeling of urine dribbling down and through his wool shirt. He carried him to the bathroom, pausing by the door at the sound of moaning.

"Brenda?" he called out anxiously.

In response, he heard the toilet flush and more groaning. He pushed the door open farther then jumped back, embarrassed at finding his wife sitting on the toilet, her bloomers down around her ankles, leaning forward with her head in her hands. He called out, "My God, Brenda, what's the matter?"

"I'm sick," she mumbled.

Still cradling Tommy in his left arm, he entered the bathroom and turned toward the sink to grab a washcloth. It was then that he noticed a half-full bottle of calomel, an empty glass and spoon sitting on the shelf.

"Why are you taking this stuff? You coming down with the grippe?" He dampened the cloth with cold water, placed it in her hands and felt her forehead. "You don't feel feverish."

She pressed the cloth against her head without comment.

"Maybe you better go to bed. I'll turn the covers down."

He carried Tommy with him into the bedroom, pulled back the bedspread, blanket and top sheet and returned the baby to his crib to clean him up and put on a fresh diaper and rompers. He pulled off his own pee-stained shirt and undershirt, tossed them in the corner, and donned fresh ones from the dresser. After warming a bottle for the baby, Thomas returned to the bathroom to help Brenda to her feet and escort her to bed. He tucked her in and leaned down to kiss her soothingly on the forehead.

He started to leave, but when she called he turned and sat down on the edge of the bed.

She looked up at him, tears in her eyes. "Thomas, I'm so sorry…and…and frustrated. I'm"…she paused.

"What on earth's the matter?" He pulled a handkerchief from his pocket and dabbed gently at her tears.

She blushed and smiled weakly. "Guess we should have been more careful after that New Year's dance."

"What do you mean?"

She hesitated before answering, her voice rising. "I'm afraid I'm pregnant!"

He caught his breath, and a look of puzzlement came over his face before he responded. "Well, isn't that good news, don't we want another child?"

She turned away before answering. "I was hoping not for a while."

He leaned down to kiss her cheek and sat back up. "Are you sure?"

She nodded. "I missed my monthly period. Usually that's a pretty good sign. I just don't understand. The girls in town said I couldn't get pregnant as long as I was nursing Tommy."

Thomas, not comfortable with the thought of Brenda talking to strangers about their personal matters, stiffened. "So, why were you taking so much calomel?"

She didn't reply, fearing the reaction that would come if she answered.

"That's supposed to be for cleaning out your bowels. You stove up or something?"

She turned her head away and started crying again before finally blurting out, "I was trying to abort. Your mother said that sometimes…"

Thomas jumped up, "Mother! My God, what's she got to do with us?"

Brenda tried to explain, but he interrupted, his face flushed in anger. "Don't tell me you went to her damned birth control clinic!"

She bit her lip in an effort to control her sobbing and buried her head in the pillow, and he stalked out to the living room. He stopped in the middle of the room, his hands jammed in his pockets, struggling to control the emotions threatening to overwhelm him. The anger he felt toward his mother becoming involved in their personal lives and the frustration over Brenda's unhappiness were fighting to replace the joy and pride he wanted to express over the prospect of becoming a father. And he felt guilty over venting his anger against his wife.

Realizing it was becoming cold in the house, he turned to see that the logs in the fireplace had nearly burned out. He picked up the poker and jabbed at the coals, stirring up a flurry of ash and a few wobbly sparks. He rolled up some newspapers, piled on kindling and a log, and stared blankly as the fire was re-ignited by the slumbering embers. After he cleaned up the mess Brenda had left in the bathroom, he went to the cupboard for his brandy, poured some in a glass, splashed in a little water and ice, and settled into the rocking chair. The first drink tasted so good that he had another and began to doze.

Soon snapped awake by his head bobbing to one side, he glanced at the clock to see that it was after four o'clock. He stood up and yawned, rubbed the crick in his neck and stepped over to the partially open bedroom door to watch and listen to Brenda breathing softly, rhythmically. Tommy, quietly playing with his toys, stopped and raised his arms toward his father.

He tiptoed into the bedroom, lifted the baby out of his crib and carried him to his highchair in the kitchen. He opened the icebox in search of milk and his eyes fell on the chicken carcass from which he had been slicing sandwich meat for the past several days. A bright idea crossed his mind; chicken soup was just what Brenda needed! He rummaged around some more until he found a bowl of lemon custard, which he figured would make a good dessert.

He fixed a bottle for Tommy, then set about preparing the soup. He filled a large pot half-full of water, dumped the carcass in, added some carrots, onions and celery, and turned on the stove. He sat down at the kitchen table to admire the colorful, abstract squiggles the baby was making with his crayons.

Glancing at the colored scrawls suddenly reminded him that the next day was Valentine's Day. Earlier in the week, he had stopped in Gottschalk's department store and purchased a cloche hat to match the outfit he had given Brenda for Christmas. He also had invested fifty cents in one of the fancy German-style cards with a pink heart made of ruffled paper that popped out when the card was opened. Impulsively, he decided they would celebrate tonight over a bowl of chicken noodle soup, *Saltine* crackers, hot tea and lemon custard.

When the soup started bubbling he tossed in a handful of noodles. He rummaged around in a kitchen drawer until he found a used candle, stuck it in a holder on the table, set out silverware and cups and saucers, and went to the bedroom door.

He found Brenda sitting on the edge of the bed, her hair tousled from sleep, her eyes red from crying. "How'r you feeling, honey?" he asked.

She shrugged and turned toward him. "Better, I guess."

"Would you like a nice bowl of chicken noodle soup and cup of tea?"

She signaled her approval, pulled on her robe and slippers and shuffled across the living room into the bathroom. When she came to the table, she bent down to hug and kiss Tommy, then took the chair Thomas was holding for her. He set a steaming bowl of soup in front of her and a plate of crackers and poured tea. He ladled some of the cooled broth into a small bowl, placed it before the baby and took his seat. He raised his cup to Brenda, "Happy Valentine's Day, my dear."

She smiled weakly. "Goodness, did I sleep that long?"

"No, it's tomorrow. But I thought we might celebrate early." He reached inside his shirt and pulled out the card, and smiled with self-satisfaction as she opened it and grinned appreciatively when the pink paper heart popped out.

Before she could say anything, he reached under the chair for his gift package and put it on the table in front of her.

"Heavens! There's more?"

"Yeah. I hope you like it." Tommy, seeming to sense the moment, waved his arms and banged his spoon on the high chair, spilling some of his soup.

Brenda opened the package and lifted out the hat. "Oh, Thomas, how attractive! And it's just the right color to match my new winter outfit." She took a moment to admire the hat, then protested, "But I haven't gotten you anything yet."

He pushed his chair back, stepped over and put his arm across her shoulder and kissed her warmly on the cheek. "I think you have," he grinned. "It just won't be delivered for about nine months!" She responded with a wan smile.

He went to the sink for a cloth to wipe up the soup the baby had spilled, remarking to Brenda. "I'm sorry I snapped at you this afternoon. I'm really happy we're going to have another child. Hopefully you will be too."

She didn't reply as she bent forward to taste the soup. He retook his seat and they ate silently for a few moments until there was a knocking sound, so quiet they almost didn't hear it.

"Someone at the door?" she asked.

He went to the door, flipped on the outdoor light and peered out to see PJ, with Erasmus standing behind him. Feeling a little irritated over his supper being interrupted, he opened the door, letting in a blast of the cold winter air. "Hi, PJ, what can I do for you?"

The little man stood there, half hidden under his big Stetson, hands stuffed in the pockets of his winter coat, looking a little sheepish. Erasmus was behind him to one side, an embarrassed grin on his face, hat in his hands.

"Could we talk to you for a minute?" PJ asked.

"Er, sure. Come on in before we all freeze to death."

PJ clumped his dirty boots on the stoop, removed his hat and stepped inside. Erasmus held back with his hat in his hand, then with a motion from Thomas, knocked the dirt from his one boot, hopped up the step on his good leg, and hobbled into the house. They both nodded respectfully to Brenda.

"So what can I do for you?" Thomas asked.

PJ hemmed and hawed for a moment, glancing back at Erasmus and down at the floor, finally blurting out, "We wanna git married!" The black man, twisting his hat in his hands, grinned in agreement.

Brenda let out a little gasp, and Thomas' breath caught in his throat. He looked at PJ, then Erasmus, and back to his manager for a sign of whether or not they were playing a joke.

Finally, he responded, "You mean to each other?"

PJ broke out with a nervous chuckle while Erasmus' eyes widened and he shook his head vigorously.

"No, no!" PJ replied firmly. "I want to marry Missus Harrington. 'Rass' plans to marry up with that Miss Mandy."

Thomas glanced at Brenda for her reaction and back at his two farm hands. "Well, I think that's great! When's this gonna happen?"

"We were thinking about sometime in the next few weeks."

Brenda spoke up, "How about the two ladies, they say yes?"

PJ nodded; Erasmus appeared more uncertain.

Thomas suggested, "Gosh, maybe we could have a double wedding right here at the farm." He again looked at Brenda but only got a quick frown.

Erasmus, still twisting his hat in his hands, spoke for the first time. "Mizz Mandy say she wanna marry up in church."

It suddenly dawned on Thomas that marriage might lead to the loss of some good farm help. "Uh, where do you plan to live?" he asked apprehensively.

PJ nodded toward Erasmus. "He says his woman wants him to move in with her. She has a nice house over on the west side. Missus Harrington and I haven't decided. She plans to turn her farm over to her two boys, so moving in there probably wouldn't be a good idea."

Thomas hesitated as a thought formed in his mind. "Well, how about right here?" He turned to catch a surprised look on Brenda's face.

PJ looked flummoxed.

Thomas continued, "Yeah, you and Missus Harrington would be very comfortable in this house. And I'll build a new one for Missus O'Roark!"

Brenda, completely vague on what her husband was talking about, sat back in her chair, arms akimbo, waiting for more details.

He turned toward her. "I was going to tell you later, dear. I've sketched plans for a new house we can build on the old Russian property. It'd be a nice two-story one with two bathrooms and...and a modern kitchen."

Brenda, non-plussed, looked at him warily.

Thomas, sensing he had gone too far too fast, turned back to PJ and Erasmus. "Guess we can talk about this some more tomorrow. In the meantime, congratulations. We're happy for both of you."

After they departed, he closed the door, flipped off the outdoor light, and stepped over to the fireplace to poke the waning embers back to life and add a couple more logs. He realized his idea about a new house had caught Brenda by surprise and thought it best to let it sink in before pursuing it further. He went to the stove to reheat the pot of soup.

She hesitated before breaking the silence. "So where'd you get the idea I wanted a new house?"

He shrugged his shoulders as he offered her more soup and ladled some into his bowl. He retook his seat, "Well, last fall you talked like you were unhappy here, like maybe you wanted something bigger, more modern." He blew on his soup and downed a spoonful.

"But, out here in the country?"

He frowned. "Why not? Long as we're gonna be working the land we should be close to it."

She rose silently and went to the icebox. She returned with the bowl of custard and saucers, scooped some out for the two of them and reached across the table to feed a spoonful to the baby.

Thomas continued, "If we build on the Russian place you'll be closer to Papa."

She took a bite of the dessert before responding, "Can we afford it?"

"Sure. There should be enough from last fall's crop payment to cover the lumber and other materials. If we need more, we can borrow it from the bank."

Brenda brightened. "How big a place you thinking about?"

"We probably can't afford one as big as Papa's. But I'm thinking of two stories, probably three bedrooms, nice dining room, modern kitchen, bathroom downstairs and upstairs, a screened sleeping porch for summer." He waved his arms expansively then added, "Oh, and an enclosed laundry room so you won't have to go out in the cold."

"No parlor...or...or window boxes?"

"Oh yes. Lots of window boxes for flowers, like Papa's, and a nice parlor, maybe even big enough for a piano." When she didn't respond, he added, "You said you'd like to give Tommy lessons when he gets a little older."

She reached over and took his hand. "Well, if you're sure we can afford it, it sounds good to me."

He leaned across the table and kissed her on the cheek. "I'll sketch it out next week."

Chapter 18

The weekend after Valentine's Day turned into an ideal one for Thomas and Brenda to plan their new house. With a warming fire to offset a cold, unrelenting rain drumming on the roof, he had taken a pencil and ruler and spread a large sheet of brown wrapping paper on the kitchen table. He laid out to scale the exterior walls based on his measurements of the old Maloney house. Then, with Brenda's input, he struggled to fit in the various rooms they wanted.

On Monday, he saw Brenda and the baby off to town, then lost no time trying to find a contractor. Because of all the post-war construction going on, it took several phone calls before he found a willing candidate and set a future date to visit the site to review their plans and provide a cost estimate.

After conferring with PJ and Erasmus over their work plans for the week, he went to the closet and hauled out his typewriter. He was anxious to finish the descriptive paragraphs for his proposed short story, *The Final Day*, so he could submit his first assignment in the home correspondence course. He placed the typewriter on the kitchen table, opened it up and reviewed his earlier draft. He rolled the paper back in the machine and started typing:

> After their meager supper, the Marines xxxcrawl into their bedrollss fsor sthe night. But the Corporal can't sleep. He keeps the Sergeant awake as sthey reminsce about their previous R and R in Reims. They are awakened at 0;500 the next morning by the start of the allied arstiller barrage preparisng the way for their advance. They go withour breakfast because the chow wagons didn't make it again, and scatter under cover when German artillery lands in the courtyard. They finally double-time march to the river where in the thin dawn light they struggle across sthe wobbly pontoon bridges. The Corporal is knocked in the river and presumably drowns. The Sergeant makes it across sbut is severaly wounded. Tshe Armistice takes effect five hours later.

Thomas stopped and lifted the paper in the typewriter to review what he had created. He continued on through the morning, stopping only occasionally to drink some coffee, stoke the fire, or go to the bathroom. He was interrupted first by the milkman knocking to signal that he was leaving his regular Monday delivery of milk and butter on the stoop, then later by the iceman lugging in a block of ice.

By noon Thomas had completed a first draft of the several paragraphs called for in the assignment. He decided to stop for lunch and devote the afternoon to trying to type an error-free copy. First, he pulled on his coat and cap to venture out to the mailbox where he found a couple of advertising flyers, a bill from Pacific Gas & Electric, and an envelope with a foreign stamp and postmark. Recognizing the feminine handwriting, he caught his breath, then tore the envelope open to find a letter from Lillian Branson.

> *Paris, France*
> *January 2, 1920*
>
> *My Dear Thomas:*
> *They say bad pennies always show up, so here I am again! Hope you don't mind? This time I'm enclosing a photograph, so you won't forget what I look like! I'm the one in the middle. The picture was taken last spring after the French government decorated several of us Red Cross nurses for helping stamp out a typhoid epidemic in the village of Buzancy, about fifty miles east of Reims. We were happy to help but it was so depressing to see the villages and countryside and*

that magnificent cathedral, all so devastated from the war.

Thomas paused in his reading to glance at the photo, easily recognizing Lillian in the group of nurses. A lump caught in his throat as he remembered her halo of soft blond hair, still visible under her nurse's bonnet, and her soft, full lips. He could even recall her perfume from that night on the train to Tacoma nearly two years ago. He sighed and turned back to her letter:

> *I started to write a couple months ago, hoping you would receive it by Christmas. But we just got too busy. It's been a very cold winter with lots of sick people, including a few doughboys still waiting to go home. Sometimes we're not sure if they're really ill or just homesick, but still have to take good care of them. So anyway, hope you know that I was thinking of you over the Holidays, and maybe this will get to you in time for Valentine's Day. Hope you had a nice Christmas. My friend Mary and I (you met her one night in that little cafe) moved out of the American Hospital last fall into a small two-bedroom apartment. So we were able to set up a little tree and exchange gifts and share a bottle of good French champagne.*
>
> *They also had a large tree at the hospital, and the patients exchanged funny gifts and French children came in to sing carols. Mary and I are getting pretty good with our French, so we were able to understand most of the words.*

As you may recall from my last letter, Mary and I thought we might return home last year, but we changed our minds.

We've finally decided this summer will be a good time. It's a difficult decision because there's still so much sickness and suffering here, especially among the children. Many French women also seem especially vulnerable to disease and serious illness, and we suspect it has a lot to do with the war. It so decimated their male population that there are very few men left, and most of those have arms or legs missing. I'm also hoping I'll get to see you again. I think of you often and the time we met on that wonderful train ride to Tacoma. I even remember fondly the fun part of our weekend in Bakersfield, and try to forget the regrettable ending. Also that memorable night in the little Left Bank hotel before you returned home. Hope that's not a harbinger of our future, that it will end sadly. I also hope you haven't done something silly, like get married?!

Well, it's getting late so better sign off. Mary and I both have to go back to work in the morning, ending our nice two-day holiday to celebrate the New Year. Didn't do much except drink another bottle of champagne and watch the fireworks from our window. And we did drink a toast to the start of a new decade. Hope it brings much prosperity, and no more terrible wars.

Much love,

Lillian

P.S. Wondering how you are coming with your writing?

When he finished reading the letter, he stood by the mailbox trying to swallow the lump in his throat, the cramps building in his stomach. He wasn't sure if his trembling was from the freshening midday breeze, now turning cold enough to bite through his heavy coat, or his reaction to Lillian's letter. He had almost put her out of his mind, although occasionally something unexpected, like a stray whiff of perfume or the distant wail of a train whistle would bring her memory back. And she did reappear from time to time in his dreams.

He wiped a tear from his eye and took a deep breath, nearly choking as the cold air cut into his lungs. After glancing again at the photo before putting it and the letter back in the envelope, he returned dejectedly to the house and tossed his coat and hat and the mail on the sofa. He added more wood to the fire, jabbed the embers to life and sat down before his typewriter. He typed determinedly throughout the rest of the afternoon, finally finishing a first draft of *The Final Day*. He rolled the last page out of the machine and leaned back in his chair to scan what he had written, shaking his head in frustration at the typos. He carried the draft and typewriter to the closet, slid Lillian's letter under the bed next to the previous one and the writing set, and went to the kitchen to prepare the meatloaf he had promised Brenda for supper.

***

On Saturday, Thomas and Brenda awoke to an unseasonably warm and sunny day. They hurried through breakfast before piling themselves and Tommy into the Maxwell and heading for town. Thomas was anxious to meet with Emmett Johnson about a loan and Brenda wanted to start looking at new kitchen appliances and furniture.

They eventually found a parking place on Van Ness Street across from Court House Park, and started walking toward Fulton Street. When they reached the First National Bank, Brenda continued on, pushing the baby in his new wicker buggy toward the Pacific Gas and Electric showroom to look at gas ranges. They would regroup later to start their search for furniture.

As Thomas entered the bank, he was met by a friendly wave from Mary and Johnson stepping out from his office. "My goodness, if it isn't Thomas O'Roark!" he called out, extending his hand. "What a wonderful surprise! Haven't seen you since…well…since November. You've been keeping well, have you?"

Thomas grinned sheepishly, taken aback by the effusive greeting.

"How's the baby?" Mary asked.

"Oh, he's fine," he replied, "growing like a weed, saying his first words."

"I'll bet it was 'Papa' wasn't it?" the bank president ventured.

He chuckled, "Yeah, right after 'Mama.'"

"Well, come on in," Johnson urged, reaching for Thomas' arm and guiding him to a seat in his office. Johnson squeezed his ample weight into another chair beside him. "So tell me what you've been up to.   I've been hearing pretty big things about you."

"Like what?"

"First of all that you've been cleaning up that old Russian place, and you're learning to fly those aeroplanes."

Thomas replied with a grin, "Yeah, got my pilot's certificate last month."

"I hope you'll be careful.   Too many people been getting hurt in those infernal machines."   Thomas didn't respond, and the bank president changed the subject, "So, what brings you into town on this beautiful sunny day?"

He told about Brenda's pregnancy and their plans to build a larger house on the former Russian property.

Johnson caught on quickly, "So, I assume you're looking for a loan?"

Thomas, feeling a little tentative, nodded.

"How much?"

"I was hoping for about three thousand."

The banker raised an eyebrow and hesitated for a moment before responding. "That sounds like quite a bit, but I guess with today's crop prices and your new acreage you should be able to handle it all right."

Thomas, hoping to reinforce his request, added "We're in a pretty strong cash position, Mister Johnson, but wanted to save that for this year's expenses."

The older man nodded as Thomas pushed ahead, "Besides, we've been investing a little in the stock market, trying to diversify."

"That seems wise, particularly with the market growing so rapidly, and your loan request sounds reasonable to me." He stepped out of his office to give Mary the information for typing up the loan papers, then returned to his desk to respond to a phone call.

Thomas waited for Mary to complete the papers, signed them and with an appreciative wave to the still-occupied Johnson, departed. He caught up with Brenda at the Owl Drug Store all enthused. "Oh, Thomas, I found the cooking range I want! It's a new model with four burners and a raised oven on the side so you don't have to bend down to put stuff in it. And a new *Hurley* electric washer with a wringer that doesn't have to be hand cranked."

"That sounds nice," he replied non-commitally as they moved to a booth. He took the baby from her and held him on his lap. "How much will those cost?"

"The salesman said we could have both for ninety five dollars!"

"That seems reasonable enough. But maybe we should wait to see how much the other furniture is going to cost before we make a decision."

Brenda, her spirits a little dampened, nodded. Silently they took the menus brought to them by the waitress. They ordered sandwiches and coffee along with milk and fruit for Tommy, and Thomas told about his successful meeting with Johnson.

Afterwards they lost no time in finding their way to the Western Furniture store where, somewhat to Thomas' dismay, Brenda went directly to a large display of Victorian style tables, chairs, sofas and headboards. He had never paid much attention to any style of furniture, having been brought up in a home of simple straight-leg, pine wood tables and ladder back chairs, a plain sofa with lumpy cushions, and square-shaped four-poster beds with feather mattresses. The old Morris chair, his father's wooden rocker and mother's ornate bric-a-brac cabinet were the only luxury pieces in the O'Roark house.

But he quickly recognized the heavily ornamental Victorian style from the Stuckey house and realized that any decisions about furniture for their new home probably were out of his hands. As Brenda became engaged by a friendly salesman, Thomas pushed the dozing baby in his buggy while he strolled toward a separate display, identified by small placards as Mission style. He sat down in one of the chairs, rubbed his hand over a smooth tabletop and quietly admired the simple, straight lines of the heavy, dark, ruggedly designed furniture. Another salesman sidled up to him to advise that the various pieces in this collection were patterned after furniture found in

California's old Spanish missions. Thomas nodded appreciatively although the reference was lost on him, since he had never been to one of the crumbling adobe structures.

His daydreaming was interrupted by Brenda calling for him to join her at the Victorian display. "Oh, Thomas, isn't this beautiful?" she called out as he drew near. "Just feel the lovely shape of these chairs and the velvet upholstering. And I really love the marble top on this dresser." She paused to take a breath, then moved deeper into the display. "And aren't these the cutest little cupid decorations on this headboard, and…and look at this pier glass mirror." She did a coquettish turn in front of the mirror.

Thomas nodded unenthusiastically and dutifully rubbed his hand over the lustrous finish of the black walnut frame of a casual chair. He sat down and bounced a few times to test the feel, and watched disinterestedly as the salesman tipped over a companion chair to show the quality construction.

"And Thomas, it's all on sale!" Brenda gushed. "The salesman says we can have this whole display for seven hundred and fifty dollars!"

"And that includes free delivery to your new home," the salesman added.

Thomas, taken aback by the total price, stood up, "Well, we haven't built it yet. Probably be another couple months or---"

The salesman interrupted, "That's not a problem, Mister O'Roark. With a small down payment, we'll hold it in our warehouse until you're ready."

He was a little surprised the salesman knew his name, but surmised that Brenda had told him. He pulled out his checkbook, and wrote a check for one hundred dollars, which earned him a hug and kiss on the cheek from Brenda.

They returned to their motor car and headed east toward the farm, lost in their private thoughts. While the baby snoozed in the arms of his drowsing mother, Thomas hunched over the steering wheel and tried to concentrate on the road ahead as he worried about their ability to pay for the new house and furnishings. She shuddered awake at the freshening breeze, pulled her coat around her and the blanket over the baby, and asked, "What kind of heat will we have in our new house?"

The question surprised him. "Well, uh, I figured a fireplace in the parlor and another in the kitchen."

"Can't we have gas central heat like other new homes so we don't have to stoke the fireplace all winter long?"

He felt annoyed that she was challenging his planning. "That would cost more, and we'd have to find a place for a furnace and run ducting to each of the rooms. Undoubtedly cost quite a bit more." He glanced sideways for her reaction, saw her bottom lip pucker out in a pout, and feared he was about to lose another discussion.

He ventured another tack, "How about if we put radiant heaters in the bedrooms and maybe some of the other rooms?"

"But Melba says her house has central heat, and she stays so comfortable during the coldest winter days, and doesn't have to mess with all that wood."

He tensed up at the mention of Melba, then sighed resignedly as they entered the driveway and rolled to a stop under the sycamore. "OK, I'll talk to the contractor and see how much more...Jesus Christ, what the...! Brenda gasped at the sharp language, stared at him apprehensively, then followed his gaze toward the bunkhouse and cried, "Oh, my heavens!"

Across the east wall someone had crudely slathered the words '*Nigger Go Home*' in bright, yellow paint. Fuming in anger and frustration, Thomas gripped the steering wheel and mumbled half aloud, "The dirty rotten bastards. Who the hell would do something like---"

"Oh, Thomas! What on earth are we gonna do?" She clutched the baby protectively to her breast as he started to awaken from the loudness of their voices.

Gritting his teeth, Thomas turned off the engine and stepped around to the side to take the baby, and help Brenda out of the car. As they turned toward the house, they paused at the sound of PJ pulling into the driveway and skidding to a stop at the sight of the glaring yellow paint. "Who in tarnation done that, Boss?" he called out.

"Damned if I know. Guess you didn't see anybody messing around?"

PJ shook his head, "Nope, been helping Pedro tie up vines all afternoon."

"Where's Erasmus?"

"Supposed to be paintin' lime sulfur on the peach trees."

"I'll take the Missus inside, then I'm gonna have a look around." PJ climbed out of the truck and waited until Thomas returned, and they walked over to the bunkhouse. They stared in disbelief at the crudely lettered words and the rough rendering of a pointy headed Klan mask below them. Thomas touched the paint to find it still tacky in several places.

PJ spoke apprehensively, "Kinda looks like lime sulfur."

Thomas shook his head, "Yeah, but it's not, it's real paint. You can smell the turpentine." He turned to search the surrounding area for footprints or other signs that might have been left by the intruder. Initially, they found nothing but old tire marks from the Maxwell and Ford truck and scuffed up dirt. But when they moved closer to the sycamore, Thomas stopped and squatted down for a closer look at unfamiliar tread marks. He mused out loud, "These look like they're from those expensive *Dunlop* Cords I saw advertised last week in the *Republican*." Standing up he added, "Whoever the bastard was either had a lot of guts or knew the Missus and I would be in town today."

"And me and 'Rass' would be out workin' the fields," PJ noted.

As they wandered back toward the house, they looked up to the 'putt-putt-putt' sound of Erasmus returning astride the *Trak-Pull*, his wooden leg poking awkwardly out to one side. He pulled to a stop under the tree and stared wide- eyed as Thomas pointed toward the desecration, "Oh, hebens, who doan that?"

PJ replied, "We don't know."

"Guess you didn't see any strangers around?" Thomas asked.

Erasmus, his eyes saucer-like in fright, shook his head.

Thomas ignored the response as he glanced idly into the two-wheel trailer attached to the little tractor. It contained a large empty bucket, its interior caked pale yellow with dried lime sulfur. A yellowed paintbrush and empty sacks of lime powder and sulfur also were there.

"You get a lot of trees painted?" he asked

"Yassuh, the whole fust row 'til ah run out ub sulfuh." He held up his yellow-streaked black hands to emphasize the extent of his work.

When Thomas reached over and patted him on the shoulder, he could feel how tense he was. "Try not to worry, Erasmus. Looks like this was the work of one person."

Erasmus nodded weakly and responded with an uncertain "Yassuh."

Thomas turned to his farm manager, "Wait here a minute, PJ. I'm gonna get the shotgun for you fellows to keep in the bunkhouse." He stepped into the house, came back with the gun and box of shells and handed them to Erasmus, who responded with an uncertain look and took the gun tentatively. He shook his head, "I doan know, Massa, ah ain't shot at nothin' since the war."

Thomas again patted him reassuringly. "Don't worry. We all damn sure have the right to protect our property and our lives." He turned to PJ, "With the shotgun and your trusty .44 and my father's old pistol, we'll be ready for 'em if they show up again, won't we PJ?"

The little man grinned and nodded, "Yessir."

When he returned to the house, he found the baby in his playpen and Brenda sitting on the sofa, her arms folded across her chest. He surmised from her glowering look that he was going to catch hell for something, perhaps about the need for a fire to ward off the gathering coolness of the late afternoon. As he knelt to build a fire, he was surprised by her opening comment, "I'm sure glad Erasmus is getting married and moving."

Taken aback by the abruptness of her remark, he chuckled anxiously, "Why, for Pete's sake?" He struck a match to the paper and kindling he had stacked in the fireplace.

"Because he's black and just brings trouble."

He stood up and turned toward her, "What on earth are you talking about? He's a good worker… and…and a crippled veteran!"

She raised her voice, "I don't care what or who he is.. He's the reason someone painted those words on the bunkhouse and the reason the Klan came here last September when we nearly got killed. And if you'll remember, they threatened to come back. Someday they're going to hurt us…or…or Tommy."

Thomas, feeling a rising mixture of annoyance and anger, couldn't think of a response.

"And he's not good for the baby. He's genetically inferior, and…and…he's intellectually limited, too!"

"Inferior to a baby? That's crazy, Brenda. Tommy loves Erasmus. You can see that when he plays with him!"

She again raised her voice. "I don't care. Our son should be brought up around people of superior intelligence, not inferior."

He shouted back in frustration, "One thing I don't understand, Brenda, is how you can be so damned prejudiced after all the harassment you went through during the war! Don't you believe we all should be treated equally like it says in our Constitution?"

Brenda glared back at him without replying. Since the loud talking had disturbed Tommy, she rose from the rocker, lifted him from the playpen, stalked into the bedroom and slammed the door. Thomas just stood there looking blankly at the closed door.

He was at a loss to explain the sudden outburst, the unexpected negative attitude toward Erasmus.

Resignedly, he moved to the rocker, dug around in his coat pocket for his cigarette makings and lighted up. The burning of the smoke in his lungs and the warmth from the fireplace gradually brought him a small level of relaxation.

CHAPTER 19

The Monday morning after the argument over Erasmus, without an alarm in the front bedroom, Thomas overslept. He finally was awakened by the ring of the telephone, stumbled out of bed into the kitchen, lifted the receiver and mumbled a bleary "Hullo."

"Good morning, my friend, how've you been?"

"Oh, hi, Brad...er fine," Thomas responded absently as he turned and looked toward the rear bedroom where the door was ajar. Standing in his skivvies and bare feet in the cool morning air, he shivered involuntarily. He sensed the house was empty and he was alone.

Brad's voice came over the phone, "How'r you doing with your flying?"

"Great! I've been up several times since getting my certificate. Even flew to Madera and back last week all by myself."

"I've got the day off. How about taking me up for a spin?"

"OK. I'll have to call to see if a plane's available."

"I'll pay for the gas and oil and rental."

"No, no. After all you've done for me, I'll be glad to take care of the expenses." Ignoring Brad's protestations, he looked at the clock to see that it was a few minutes after nine. "If there's a problem, I'll phone you right back."

"I'll pick you up soon as I can, and I'll bring a thermos of coffee."

"Sounds good."

Thomas pulled on a robe then pushed the door open to the back bedroom. It was empty, the bed unmade and Tommy's crib in disarray. Although annoyed that Brenda had left for work without awakening him, he didn't delay in phoning the aerodrome to reserve a plane. He downed a bowl of cereal, dumped the dishes in the sink, shaved, and dressed in record time. He thought briefly about leaving a note for Brenda, but decided against it. She undoubtedly wouldn't understand and besides, he should be home before she returned from work. So what she didn't know wouldn't hurt her.

He was waiting on the stoop when Brad pulled into the yard. He jumped in the Ford and they headed toward the airfield, chatting amiably about the bright, sunny March day, the freshness in the air from the recent rain, the fruit trees and grapevines showing their first spring growth. Thomas was particularly proud that his good friend had enough confidence in him to become his first passenger.

They turned into the fairgrounds, entered O'Leary's office and exchanged greetings. Thomas led the way to the wall map of the San Joaquin Valley. Tracing his finger across the map with Brad looking over his shoulder, he said, "I suggest we follow the SP tracks north to the river, head west to where the Kings River joins the San Joaquin then cut back to Fresno, sort of a big triangle."

O'Leary concurred in the flight plan, and they turned to finding a two-piece, fleece-lined leather flying suit, helmet and goggles for Brad. Thomas squeezed into his flying suit and in a few moments they were standing beside the 'Jenny' and Thomas was carefully going through the pre-flight routine of checking the oil, water and fuel levels, and the free movement of the rudder and ailerons. He guided Brad into the front cockpit, made sure the seatbelt was properly fastened and admonished him to keep his hands and feet free of the controls. Finally, with a wry grin, he pointed to the brown paper bag on the floor. He climbed into the rear cockpit, buckled his seatbelt, pulled down his goggles and signaled to O'Leary that he was ready. With a spin of the prop the big OX-5 roared to life, O'Leary pulled the chocks and they were on their way.

After takeoff, Thomas eased the plane into a climbing turn toward downtown Fresno and leveled off at five hundred feet. He flew along the south side of Tulare Street and dipped his right wing to give Brad a view across the *Republican* building toward the copper dome of the Court House glistening in the morning sun and surrounded by the broad park of trees and grass. He angled across Fulton Street and the Bank of Italy building, its ten stories thrusting up toward them, picked up the Southern Pacific depot off his left wing, and pointed northwest parallel to the twin silvery rails falling away toward the flat, endless horizon of the valley floor.

When they came in sight of the parallel railroad and highway bridges crossing the San Joaquin River, he banked west, passed over the old steamboat terminal at Skaggs Bridge and followed the general direction of the river as it wound snake-like between the banks of cottonwoods and sycamores. He eased the plane lower when they could see the river turn northwesterly, and flew between it and a dirt road lying to the left. West of the road there were sun-seared empty vistas of sagebrush, cactus and tumbleweed reaching all the way to the Diablo Range of mountains. To the immediate east, between the road and river and beyond, were wide swaths of green pastureland and fields of newly planted cotton.

Thomas vectored the 'Jenny' toward the west and made a broad half-circle over the flat, desolate landscape. He skirted south along the foothills to give Brad the thrill of a few thermal bumps, and dipped down to chase several jackrabbits and antelope through the sagebrush. Then, banking around to an easterly direction, he waggled his wings at two farmers waving from the ground, and climbed to five hundred feet as he crossed the Kings River where it meandered lazily toward its confluence with the San Joaquin. Since he could see the sun reflecting off the windows of Fresno's tall buildings some twenty-five miles away, he decided to take a direct route. Brad passed the thermos over the windshield and they settled into their seats, comforted by the steady drone of the engine.

In his previous flights, Thomas had followed the pattern of approaching the airfield from the northwest and cutting a path between it and the O'Roark farm as he headed into his final descent toward landing. When he eased the plane down to two hundred feet and started the pattern, he peered forward to see that the airfield was clear, then to his left toward the farm. The sun's reflection from the windshield of a car caught his eye and he looked more intently to see it speeding toward town on the farm road, followed by a rooster tail of dust.

When he got a fleeting look at white Klan robes in the vehicle, he tensed up. He eased the throttle forward and banked toward the home farm for a closer look. As he flew along the south side of the road, he could see a strange car near the sycamore, with a white-robed Klansman lying next to it on the ground and another crouched beside it. Looking farther back he caught a glimpse of Erasmus peeking around the corner and pointing the shotgun.

"Jesus Christ!" he yelled above the roar of the engine. "What the hell's going on down there?" Brad heard enough that he turned and followed Thomas' pointing arm and shook his head, trying to comprehend. When they passed to the east of the farmhouse Thomas had a clear view across the open backyard toward the bunkhouse and the vineyard some one hundred yards to the north. Two other Klansmen, one lying down, the other crouching, were visible and they appeared to be pointing pistols at the bunkhouse. Then he saw a puff of smoke from the bunkhouse, and the crouching individual slumping to the ground.

Thomas became consumed with rage. He circled back toward the farm, pushed the throttle all the way forward and pointed the nose down at a thirty degree angle, aiming directly for the two men on the ground. As the plane accelerated past its red line speed of seventy-five miles per hour, he was oblivious to the ominous hum of the wing bracing wires, and to Brad waving his arms and shouting in fright and bewilderment. When he was about twenty feet above the ground he leveled off and watched one of the strangers, his white Klan robe and head covering now clearly visible, jump up and run toward the vineyard. He roared over the top of the bunkhouse, pulled into a climbing turn and looked back to see wooden drying trays and a chunk of roof fly off in the prop wash.

He continued to circle around until he could see the would-be escapee running between the vineyard rows. Like a hawk after a gopher, he turned the plane toward him, gunned it downward until the wheels were skimming just above the tops of the grape stakes, and chased the man as he stumbled through the rows until he fell face down in the dirt.

Once again, Thomas pulled into a gradual turning climb, and looked ahead to see Brad slumped down in the cockpit. He shouted his name but received no answer; apparently he had fainted in fright. As he looked back toward the farmhouse, he heard a sharp 'twang', and turned to examine apprehensively the maze of struts and wires supporting the two wings. Nothing seemed awry until he noticed the dragline that ran from the engine frame to strengthen the lower right wing had snapped and was whipping in the wind. His heart jumped into his throat as he saw the leading edge of the wing pull away slightly from the fuselage.

Hoping to ease the pressure on the wing, he cut back on the throttle and made a wide, cautious full circle to the right, eventually heading west along the farm road. He lined up over the roadway at a steady forty-five miles per hour, holding his breath as he strained to return to the airfield before the wing gave way completely. There didn't appear to be any vehicles in his path until, peering through his goggles against the glaring sun he saw a motor car coming directly at him. And was it…Oh my God! It looked like the Maxwell with Brenda and Tommy returning from town! As the car veered into the roadside gully, he jerked back on the joy stick and heard the snap of the right wing spar.

He yanked the throttle back and reached down to turn the fuel shut-off valve as the 'Jenny' banged down hard on its right landing wheel, bounced once, settled back down and spun into a ground loop. The big wooden propeller dug into the dirt 'ca-chunk, ca-chunk, ca-chunk', and broke into splinters, killing the engine. Thomas slumped in the cockpit, unconscious from the impact of his forehead slamming against the thin cockpit padding.

When he regained consciousness, two passersby had removed his helmet and were struggling to lift him out of the plane. He grimaced at the pain in his left shoulder and forearm and from both ankles, and at his throbbing head. He could feel a warm, wet stickiness in his lower right leg, indicating the impact of the hard landing had reopened his wound. When he finally got free of the cockpit, the two men helped him sit down at the side of the road next to Brenda, who was standing, anxiously holding Tommy in her arms.

She kneeled down and put her arm across his shoulder and the baby crawled into his lap as they watched the passersby lift Brad out. Thomas heaved a sigh of relief when his friend yelled out in pain; at least he was still alive. He tensed up, anticipating a lecture from Brenda, but instead she pulled a hanky from her blouse, wiped her eyes and blew her nose and kissed him on the forehead, asking anxiously, "You all right?"

He groaned in pain as she leaned against his left shoulder, "Yeah, I think so, except for my shoulder and wrist, and my head." He bent forward a little, trying to rest his painful left forearm across his lap, and rubbed his throbbing head with his right hand. Brad, without his helmet and eye glasses, his arms draped over the shoulders of the two passersby for support, was hopping toward him on his left leg. He struggled to a seat beside Thomas, asking, "You OK?"

Thomas shook his head uncertainly and turned at the sound of a vehicle approaching then skidding to a stop. PJ jumped out of the Ford truck and ran to him, "Jesus, Boss, what happened...you OK?"

He nodded, "How about you and Erasmus?"

"I'm OK. I was over at the orchard when I heerd the shootin' and that airyplane buzzin' around. By the time I got to the house, the fun was all over."

"Erasmus?"

"They clipped him in the shoulder, but it don't look too serious. Man, he sure can handle that shotgun."

"What about the Klansmen?"

"One's dead and two wounded. 'Rass' is guardin' 'em."

"How about the one I chased in the vineyard?"

"Didn't check on him yet."

"You better get back to the house and call the sheriff. The Missus can take us to the hospital." PJ nodded and returned to the truck while Brenda picked up Tommy and went to help back the Maxwell out of the gully.

One of the passersby brought Brad's broken glasses, and he and Thomas, still clad in their bulky flight suits, struggled painfully into the rear seat of the car. As they bounced along toward the hospital, scrunching around in a fruitless effort to ease their pains, Thomas finally spoke, "Sure sorry, Brad. "Guess I really screwed up."

His companion winced as he responded with a wry grin, "Well, it was more adventure than I bargained for, but what the hell, we survived didn't we?"

Thomas nodded weakly, "Guess I kinda lost it when I saw those damn Klansmen back at our place again."

Brad mused out loud, "Looks like some people didn't get enough of harassing other folks during the war." Thomas nodded and they fell silent as the car bounced across the Santa Fe tracks and Brenda turned toward the hospital.

***

The next morning, the two friends awoke in a hospital room in adjoining beds, both still groggy from the morphine that had been administered the night before. Thomas had suffered a broken left forearm and dislocated shoulder, apparently from bracing himself against the crash. Both ankles were sore and his leg wound had broken open from the impact. He had a big headache and two black eyes from striking his head on the forward edge of the cockpit.

Brad had sustained a broken right ankle from the force of the landing gear being jammed part way up into the forward cockpit. He also had several cracked ribs on that side and a big ugly bruise on the right side of his face. Like Thomas, it seemed that his whole body ached from the uncommon twisting and strain against muscle, tendon and bone.

They were propped part way up in their beds and had just finished breakfast when Brenda showed up at the door holding Tommy. "Good morning!" she called out brightly while putting the baby down so he could toddle over to his father's bedside. Thomas returned the greeting and reached to help the youngster crawl up on the right side of the bed.

Brenda acknowledged Brad and stepped closer to Thomas, squinting, "What happened to your eyes?"

"Oh, that's from banging my head against the cockpit padding. They'll be all right in a few days."

She leaned down and kissed him on the forehead. "I've been so worried about you...couldn't sleep all night. Did you break anything?"

He nodded toward the sling supporting the plaster-of-Paris cast around his left forearm, mentioned the dislocated shoulder and briefly described Brad's injuries before asking, "How's everything at home?"

"Pretty quiet this morning."

"Erasmus OK?"

She nodded. "Yes, he got wounded, but it didn't look too serious. I bandaged him up last night."

"Did Thorsen and his deputies show up?"

"Apparently. They were gone by the time I got home."

Brad spoke up, "Any idea who the Klansmen were?"

She hesitated and looked away before replying, "Uh, I don't know. Like I said, the sheriff and the dead and wounded were gone when I got home."

Everyone fell silent until Brenda sat on the edge of Thomas' bed and asked plaintively, "Honey, you're not going to fly any more are you?"

He was caught off guard. "Well, 'er, I don't know. Guess I'll have to think about---"

"I told you it was dangerous, now look what's happened. You coulda been killed, and you almost ran into Tommy and me!" She patted the baby, adding, "And think about your son...and...and now that we have another baby on the way."

Thomas finally responded, "Mister O'Leary told me once if I ever have an accident I should go up again right away so I won't be afraid to fly. Guess we'll just have to wait and see."

Brenda sighed and looked at her watch, "I need to get to work. Any idea when they'll let you out of here?"

"Doctor said probably tomorrow, so when you come back would you bring my coveralls? I won't be able to get into my flying suit with this sling."

She acknowledged his request, reached for Tommy and rose to leave, pausing in response to another question from Thomas, "By the way, how come you were going home in the middle of the day anyway?"

"Oh...er... I was going to get some papers I promised Melba." He didn't react as she added, "I'll come by this evening on my way home." She kissed him on the forehead, turned and left the room.

An orderly entered the room to remove their breakfast trays and plump up their pillows, then brought them a pitcher of fresh water. After he left, Brad broke the silence. "Looks like you've got a little problem."

"What do you mean?"

"Brenda. Seems like she doesn't like the idea of you flying."

Thomas lay back against his pillow and gazed out the window. "Yeah, not sure how I'm gonna handle that. But right now, I'm thinking how proud I am of the way Erasmus fought off the damn Klan all by himself."

"Yeah, pretty impressive."

"But I'm also concerned about how to get that bunch of goons off my back." He told of the <u>Nigger Go Home</u> words being painted on the bunkhouse and how he suspected the Klan.

Brad sat up on the edge of his bed, "You want a suggestion?"

"Sure."

"I think you're being naïve. You need to get rid of Erasmus."

Thomas bristled and turned toward his friend, "What do you mean, get rid of him after what he just did to protect his life and my property?"

"I know, that was very gutsy. But you really need to help him move over to the West Side so he would be among his kind of people."

"But…but…what would he do? There's no work for him over there."

"He could still work for you daytimes."

Thomas, annoyed and taken aback by his friend's suggestion, couldn't think of what to say. He stared blankly out the window for a few moments, then turned back with another thought, "But, I'd have to pick him up and take him home every day. Besides, he's happy staying at the farm."

"How do you know he's happy? Don't forget he's subservient in nature. He comes from a background of slavery. He's not used to telling his boss what he really thinks."

Thomas, grimacing in pain from his sore ribs and shoulder, scrunched on to his right side while Brad continued, "Like I said before, those Klan people are still fighting the war. They're ready to persecute Negroes, hyphenates, Catholics, Jews, Commies, anyone who doesn't fit their concept of Anglo-Saxon, white, Protestant teetotalers born in America."

Still straining for a more comfortable position, Thomas again rolled on his back and ended up staring absently at the ceiling as Brad added, "The scariest part is that the Klan movement is getting bigger every day. Right here in Fresno, lots of our community leaders are becoming members. A couple of judges and lawyers, the police and sheriff, merchants and even some of our God-fearing ministers have joined. And your bank president; he's one of their leaders."

Thomas sighed, "Yeah, I heard that about my old boss. He tends to get involved in some pretty questionable activities sometimes." He paused, then turned toward Brad, "What do people see in the Klan anyway? I thought they were just active in the South."

"People join them because they claim to be a Protestant organization fighting for one hundred percent Americanism, the same crusade that made the war so popular. They're expanding into several eastern and mid-western states, even my old home state of Indiana. Also up in Oregon and now California. First thing we know they might be running our government."

They were silent for a few moments until Thomas spoke, "Well, to tell the truth, I've been wondering what to do about Erasmus. I'd hate to lose such a good, loyal worker, but he's talked about getting married, so maybe that will take care of the problem."

Later, after finishing their lunches and taking a long nap, they were awakened by a knock at the door. Thomas rubbed his eyes open to see Major Brown in his deputy sheriff uniform, his face twisted into a wry grin. "How'r you two barnstormers doing?" he asked.

Thomas, anticipating a harangue of some sort, tensed up and nodded without comment. Brad stretched and yawned widely and acknowledged Brown.

"I've got some news for you." Brown waved a yellow file folder. "We've identified your visitors."

"Yeah?"

Brown opened the folder and read from one of the papers, "The one you chased through the vineyard was some old Kraut named Werner von Karman."

Thomas sat up abruptly, blurting out, "My God, are you sure?"

Brad turned to Thomas, "Didn't he used to be a professor at the Normal School?"

Brown answered, "That's the one. According to our records he was deported in January of '18. He slipped back through Canada and returned to Fresno last summer."

Thomas stared at Brown intently, "You say 1918? I thought he was deported the previous November."

"He escaped from jail around Christmas of '17 before the sheriff could turn him over to Immigration. He hid out at the Stuckeys for a few days until deputies finally found him staying with some Heinie friends out north of town."

Thomas shook his head, exclaiming, "Son of a bitch! You're telling me he's been back in town since last summer. That means he could have been one of those who attacked our place in September."

"You might be right 'cause when the doc pulled off his boots and pants to put a cast on his busted ankle he found several buckshot scars on his legs."

Struggling to absorb all the conflicting information, Thomas again fell quiet and stared out the window. In a moment, he turned to Brown, "So when did the bastard break his ankle?"

"When you chased him through the vineyard with the aeroplane. He apparently stepped in a gopher hole."

Thomas smiled without parting his lips, "How about the others?"

Brown again consulted his papers. "The dead one and the two wounded used to work at that old German brewery, the one they closed up during the war."

Thomas looked at Brad, "That's the one that used to belong to Brenda's relatives."

"That's right," Brown acknowledged.

Brad asked, "How about the other carload, the one we saw from the aeroplane/"

Brown shook his head, "No idea. Looks like they got away."

Thomas asked, "So where's von Karman now?"

"We've turned him over to the Immigration Service," Brown replied. "This time we put him in cuffs and leg irons so he won't escape again. I imagine they'll be sending him back to Germany pretty quick."

Thomas stared blankly out the window, mumbling bitterly, "Too bad I didn't fly lower. I coulda chopped off his goddamn head!"

Brad cried out, "Yeah, and I would have crapped my pants!"

Brown stepped closer to Thomas' bed. "I'm afraid I've got more bad news." He pulled a photograph from his folder and handed it over. "You recognize this?"

Thomas scanned the photo and nodded, "Looks like this was taken at that New Year's dance. That's Brenda and me, and her friend Melba and boy friend. Where'd you get this?"

"From von Karman's personal things." Brown then showed him a second photo, "How about this one?"

He stared at the second scene, then blurted out, "That's von Karman...and...and Brenda! And...and he's got his arm around her! What the hell!...when the devil was this taken?"

Brown spoke, "Must have been after you left the party and von Karman showed up later. After the dance was over, and I hate to tell you this, Thomas, he escorted her to the Hughes and it looks like they took a room."

Thomas groaned, struggling to control the cramping in his stomach. He sank into his pillows and stared unseeingly at the ceiling.

Brad, fearing for his young friend, sat up on the edge of his bed with the thought of trying to console him, then realized there was nothing to be said. Idly, he asked Brown, "You sure about all of this?"

The deputy nodded, "Yes, I talked to the night clerk at the hotel. Said he remembered seeing them get on the elevator because they came in so late, around one o'clock."

They were interrupted by a hospital orderly carrying in afternoon tea and cookies. Brown left the photos with Thomas, retrieved his other papers and apologized for bringing bad tidings. He shook hands with both of them, promised to keep Thomas posted on any new developments and departed.

Later, after Thomas' tray had been removed untouched, and a long silence, he finally spoke, "What the fuck am I gonna do, Brad?"

He shook his head. "Don't know what to say. I've never been involved in anything like this." He shrugged, "Maybe Brenda has an explanation. Maybe there's been a mistake?"

Thomas laughed sarcastically, "Yeah, there's an explanation, all right. She's so full of that damn eugenics crap and her love for anything German she just had to spread it around. What a bunch of shit!" He crawled out of bed and started pacing back and forth in the small hospital room, then looked out the door and up and down the empty hall. He stepped back into the room, reached into the closet for the heavy flight suit he was wearing when he entered the hospital, and started removing his pajamas.

"What are you doing?" his roommate asked worriedly.

"Getting the hell out of here."

"We're not supposed to check out until tomorrow."

"To hell with it." With his forearm in its heavy cast, Thomas struggled to pull on the pants of the leather flight suit and finally got them to where he could cinch up the waist. He leaned over to put on his shoes with his good hand.

"You're not going to do something stupid, are you?"

He stood up and replied bitterly, "You mean like shoot someone?"

Brad didn't comment further as Brenda suddenly appeared at the door with a friendly "Good afternoon. You ready to leave already? Here, I brought the coveralls you wanted."

Thomas ignored her, reached to shake Brad's hand and with the leather flight jacket slung over his good shoulder, headed down the hall with Brenda dragging the coveralls along in confused pursuit. When they reached the car, he silently pointed her toward the driver's seat, tossed the jacket in the rear and climbed in the passenger side. As they pulled away from the curb and motored east toward the farm, they both were quiet. She seemed to sense something was troubling him; he was struggling to control the pain and loathing building inside.

Finally, he spoke, "How's our baby?"

"Oh, he's with Papa having a grand time, but missing his fath---"

He interrupted, barely concealing his bitterness, "I mean the one growing in your belly."

She glanced at him warily, "Uh, it's fine. Starting to kick occasionally."

"That's a German kick, I suppose?"

"Thomas, what are you saying, is something bothering you?"

He raised his voice, "That baby inside you. Does it belong to me or your Kraut friend, von Karman?"

She gripped the wheel in shock and cried back at him, "Thomas...what on earth...!"

He interrupted again his voice tightening, "And how about Tommy, you really sure he's mine?"

"Thomas!"

"I understand you spent New Year's eve at the Hughes with that Heinie bastard. What did you do, play tiddlywinks?" He looked directly at her and felt a twinge of sympathy as all expression drained from her face.

But his feeling was quickly replaced by one of disgust. "I guess that makes you a harlot, Brenda, or...or a goddamn German whore. They used to be free in France!"

She gasped at the crude reference, steered the car to the side of the road and stopped. She turned toward him pleading, "Thomas! What are you talking about? I...I don't---"

"I understand von Karman joined you at the dance after I left?"

With a startled expression, she responded, "How'd you hear about that?"

He took a deep breath, trying to relieve the pressure building in his chest before he answered, "Major Brown came to the hospital and brought this." He pulled the photo out of his pocket and held it up in front of her.

She stared open-mouthed at the photo, reached into her purse for a hanky, and dabbed at the tears welling up in her eyes. "Yes, von Karman stopped by the table and...and---"

"And put his arm around you?"

She cried out, "Thomas! He's an old family friend. What was I supposed to do?"

"And he drove you to the hotel?"

She glanced at him furtively before replying, "Yes. He let me out at the front door and...and... I took the elevator right up to our room."

Thomas paused as her positive answers brought on a touch of doubt, "But, the night clerk said he saw you both get on the elevator."

She shot back, "That's not true! Who's telling you all this anyway?"

He described Brown's hospital visit revealing the fact that von Karman was the Klansman Thomas had chased through the vineyard, and the source of the photos from the New Year's dance.

Brenda blew her nose, cleared her throat and tried to assert herself, "Well, someone's lying, Thomas. Von Karman did stop by our table, someone used his camera to take our picture and we all left a few minutes after midnight. He volunteered to drive me to the hotel, so I agreed, thinking that would be quicker and…and safer than waiting alone for a taxi that late at night."

He hesitated before asking, "He didn't stay at the hotel?"

"I have no idea. He said he was staying with friends out north of town."

Thomas, his anger and confusion now slipping into embarrassment and guilt over his jealousy, fell silent. He took a deep breath, trying to ease the emotional pressure building in his chest as Brenda pulled back onto the roadway and continued slowly toward home. When they reached the driveway, she stopped and asked if he wanted to accompany her to Papa's to pick up Tommy.

He ignored the question and responded sarcastically, "How about the Christmas of '17? Did you give von Karman the same 'present' you gave me?"

She turned toward him sharply, wide-eyed in disbelief, her voice rising hysterically, "What do you mean...what are you talking about?"

"Didn't von Karman escape from jail and stay at your house in December of '17?"

"How did you hear about that?"

"Brown told me. So what did you do during that visit, play more tiddlywinks, or maybe take care of his physical needs?"

She cried out, "No, no! What on earth are you saying? He slept down stairs in...in the parlor!" She took a deep breath, trying to steady her voice, before continuing weakly, "He hid out at our house for a week or so before Christmas. Papa was afraid if the sheriff found him we'd be arrested, so he made him leave."

Thomas, feeling weak and partly guilty from seeing his young wife so distressed, paused and tried to control the pounding of his heart. Then he decided on one more test of her veracity, "What were you and Emil arguing about that time before Christmas when we saw Jake Stein leaving your father's house?"

She hesitated, attempting to dig back in her memory. Finally, with a sigh of despair she replied, "I don't want to tell you."

He glared at her intently, "So, another secret, huh? How do you expect me to believe anything you say about von Karman when you won't trust me with some little family secret?"

She gazed absently through the windshield, now almost too weak to respond, before mumbling resignedly, "I told Emil he shouldn't be hanging around with Jake 'cause he's a bad influence. He said I shouldn't have married you because we're just going to end up with another Irish baby in the family."

Thomas continued to glare at her. "What the hell kind of remark is that? What damn business is it of Emil's who you married, or if we have a baby?"

Speaking just above a whisper, she replied, "It doesn't mean a thing, Thomas. Sometimes, Emil just says crazy things like that."

Shaking his head in anger and frustration, Thomas grabbed his flight jacket, stepped out of the car, slammed the door shut and crossed the road toward the house. Brenda, tears streaming down her face, shifted the Maxwell into gear and continued uncertainly toward the Stuckey residence.

Absently, Thomas removed the mail and *Morning Republican* from their roadside boxes and walked to the house. He breathed deeply of the cool evening air in a fruitless effort to ease the physical pain of his injuries, worsened by an embarrassing brew of confusion and self-doubt. He stepped inside to find his typewriter sitting on the kitchen table.

He stood motionless for a moment, trying to recall whether or not he had left it there after working on his short story. He moved to the table and found the machine surrounded by brochures and application forms for the Fitter Family contest; Brenda had been using his typewriter without asking. In a rage, he grabbed every scrap of paper on the table, tore it into shreds and threw it in the fireplace. He took a deep breath, put the oilcloth cover on the machine and with his one good hand, lugged it to the closet. He returned to the living room to pour himself a tall glass of brandy, ice and water, and turned to building a fire. He settled into his father's rocker to watch the scraps of paper turn black and flame briefly before they curled into embers and blew away up the chimney.

Chapter 20

For Thomas, the bitter argument over von Karman had placed an almost irreconcilable strain on his eight-month marriage. He was jealous of any relationship that might have existed between Brenda and the old German and resentful that she hadn't been more communicative about it. These feelings had stirred up his initial doubts about Tommy's paternity, which further annoyed him because he finally had started accepting the youngster as his own.

Fortunately, with spring approaching, he was entering an especially busy time, which gave him an excuse to avoid trying to resolve their differences. He ignored the matter by cranking up the new *Fordson* tractor and fertilizing the peach trees on the former Russian place. This was a particularly pleasant chore since it meant working among the plethora of delicate pink blossoms bursting from the once dormant winter limbs, and drinking in their intoxicating perfume.

So on this cool Monday morning in late March, Thomas awoke groggily to the sound of voices and dishes clattering in the kitchen. He struggled up on the edge of the bed, rubbed his eyes and yawned several times. Finally, he sauntered out to find Brenda feeding Tommy his *Cream of Wheat*. It was seven fifteen, almost time for her to leave for work.

"Mornin'," he said listlessly.

She returned the greeting without emotion; the baby calling out 'Dada' was more enthusiastic.

He patted the little one on the head and continued into the bathroom. When he returned, Brenda asked, "You want to keep Tommy today or shall I take him into the nursery?"

He poured a cup of coffee, carried it to the table, pulled out a chair and sat down before answering sullenly, "Maybe you could take him. I need to finish fertilizing the orchard and want to work on my short story."

She didn't respond but wiped the baby's face with a damp cloth, lifted him out of the highchair and carried him into the bedroom. When she returned, they were dressed for town and heading for the door. She paused and turned back, "Don't forget, next week is Holy Week, then Easter Sunday."

He grunted and stared at her blankly, trying to remember if he was supposed to do something. Before he could respond, she and the baby were out the door, and in a few moments he could hear the Maxwell pulling out of the yard.

With a sigh he poured himself more coffee and filled a bowl with corn flakes. Idly, he made toast and added milk and sugar to the cereal and sat down at the table. He topped that off with a saucer of his mother's home-canned apricots.

When he was through, he placed the dishes in the sink, dressed in his comfortable coveralls and headed for the orchard. At noontime, when he returned to the farmhouse for lunch, he stopped first at the roadside mailbox where he found several advertising flyers and a letter postmarked from San Diego. He glanced at it then caught his breath when he noticed it was addressed to Sgt. Thomas O'Roark. He tore open the envelope to find a typewritten letter:

San Diego, Calif.
March 19, 1920

Dear Sarge---

Remember me? I'm the guy you slogged around France with for seven months. Betcha thought I was dead---most people did.
I'm back home now with my dear Emily and beautiful baby daughter. We got married last week and I'm back delivering mail for the Post Office. I drive a rural route, which works out pretty good since I have to drive on the left to fill the boxes, which I still can do with my good arm. Worst part was learning how to wipe my ass with my left hand!

Guess I forgot, you don't know I lost my right arm when I got hit by Heinie shrapnel and knocked in that river. Damn near drowned or bled to death but some Frenchies found me unconscious on the bank with my arm all mangled. They took me to one of their docs who cut it off. Right side of my face got tore up too but Emily don't seem to mind. Maybe you can come visit us sometime soon. We had some good times in spite of all the mud and hell, but I sure am glad to be home. Hope you got home OK and will write real soon.

Your buddy,
Tim Campbell

Thomas read the letter again, shook his head and wiped tears from his eyes with the back of his hand. He remained silent for a few moments, reliving the last time he had seen Campbell stumbling across that pontoon bridge and being blasted into the river. He walked slowly to the house, dropped the letter on the table and turned to opening the windows in the kitchen and bedrooms and started preparing a quick lunch. The house was quiet except for the normal background noises of a day on the farm; the distant put-put-put of a tractor as it moved back and forth through a vineyard, the soft rustle of a wind-blown curtain, the chirping of birds in the sycamore, or the hysterical cackling of a hen being chased by a horny rooster.

Finishing lunch, he used his cast-free hand to laboriously lug the heavy typewriter from the bedroom closet to the kitchen table. Expectantly, he stared at the partially finished manuscript, including the half-page still in the machine. But no words would come; his mind kept drifting back to his service in France with Campbell and his other Marine buddies, and than to his memories of re-connecting with Lillian in Paris.

Impulsively, he rolled the sheet out of the typewriter, walked into the front bedroom, rummaged around underneath the bed and pulled out Lillian's two letters and the sterling writing set. He sat on the floor and opened the set, picking up and admiring the individual pieces, then put them back in the box. He returned to the typewriter, rolled in a clean sheet of paper and started typing:

```
Fresno, Calif.
March 22, 1920


Dear Lillian---

Sorry to be so slow in responding to your
letters. I can't believe it's been xxxx over a
year since youxr first one and that very thoug/
tful antique writing set. I thought about using
it to ///// write this letter, but as you can see am
trying out my new typewriter instead.    You
probably couldn't read my hand/riting anyway!
The typewriter's a used one that my friend
b//Brad Simpson gave me when he got a new
one.    It works fine except that I'm not very
good at usingit.    I make too many mistakes,
but am getxing ////// better.    Have been using
it to write my first short story.    I enroll//ed in
```

a correspondence course for writers and am about to send them a concept for a fir//st story. So I'm trying to type a clean copy.

Maybe some day I'll be a famous author! Been very bus/y on the farm. I now own one hundred acres, which is a lot to ake care of. Still have PJ as a manager //// plus two other full time helpers. Now that spring is here we'll really be getring busy. But fortunately, we're finally recexxing decent prices for our crops, including record payments last year. Long as that keeps up, I don't mined the hard work so much. In my spare time, I've been le/ernin to fly an aeroplame and received my pilot's certificate a couple months ago.

Sure is a wonderful way to get away from all your troubles. Maybe when you get back to Bakerssfield, I can fly down and gib you a ride. Happy to hear about your award from the French government---I'm sure it was xxxx well deserved. Also glad to receive your photo---you look even more lovely than I remembered---and to learn from your last letter that you'll be coming home soon. Sure would like to see you again.

He stopped typing and looked back over what he had written, shaking his head in dismay at the typos. But he was more concerned over how to finish the letter. He couldn't quite bring himself to tell Lillian he was married or that he had a son and another child on the way. He had about decided he would close by telling about the status of his leg wound but was interrupted by a knock at the door. As he pushed his chair back from the table, he glanced at the clock to see that it was almost three o'clock. He answered the door to find PJ.

"Hi, PJ. What can I do for you?"

"Reckon we've got a problem."

Thomas sighed irritably, "What now?"

"Pedro's quitting. Says his wife died."

"Oh, Jesus, that's terrible! How'd that happen?"

PJ shrugged. "He didn't say. Just said she's <u>muerto</u> and he's quitting so he can take her back to Mexico to bury her."

"Is he coming back?"

"Can't tell. Said he wants his *dinero pronto* so he can leave."

"OK, come on in. I'll see if I've got enough cash on hand."

PJ doffed his Stetson, stepped inside and waited while Thomas went to the bedroom to retrieve the ledger in which he kept the farm's financial records. He returned with the book, opened it on the kitchen table and thumbed down through the various entries.

"Looks like we're current except for this month. I'll pay him that and add twenty dollars to help with his expenses." PJ nodded his approval as Thomas returned the ledger to the closet and withdrew the money from a metal cash box, and they walked out to the Ford truck.

When they pulled into the driveway of the West Forty and stopped in front of the small, yellowed wood frame house, they found Pedro sitting on the porch in an old wicker chair. He was holding a bottle of beer, and his four children, all looking pretty doleful, were seated or standing around him.

Thomas turned off the engine, climbed out of the truck and with PJ at his heels, approached the old Mexican. *"Hola, Pedro. Lo siento por su esposa."* Never too confident of his limited Spanish, he glanced at PJ and back at Pedro for some reaction.

PJ shuffled his feet and Pedro nodded, but didn't comment. The children stirred, and the oldest turned and entered the house.

Thomas continued, *"Lo siento su regresar a la Mexico, pero yo comprendo."* With still no reaction from Pedro, he decided to switch to English. "I'm real sorry, Pedro, but I understand. I hope you'll come back. We'll sure need your help cause we've got some big crops coming on."

Pedro, still expressionless, took a swig of his beer. Thomas, sensing he was not communicating very well, started feeling helpless. He again looked at PJ for support, but he just shrugged. He stepped closer to the porch and held out his hand. "I brought your pay for March, plus extra to help with your expenses."

The older man took the money, smiled weakly and mumbled *'gracias'* as he folded the bills and stuck them in a pocket of his coveralls. Thomas spoke, "We hope you'll come back soon. We'll keep your job open as long as we can."

Pedro nodded slightly, but Thomas didn't get the impression he understood. Either that or he was too saddened or preoccupied with the death of his wife.

Thomas started to depart then paused. *"Cuando su dejar?"*

This time Pedro spoke up. *"Mañana."*

"Que hora."

"Seis."

Thomas, hesitant at the thought of the early hour, replied, "OK. We'll drive you into the train station."

Pedro shook his head, *"No, no…paseo en camion!"*

Puzzled, Thomas peered at the old Mexican, then PJ, then back. "You're gonna drive your truck…<u>su camion</u> all the way to…to Mexico?"

Pedro nodded.

"But…but…that's a long, rugged trip over the mountains…*las montañas!*" He turned to PJ, "You think that's a good idea in …in that old truck?"

PJ sighed uncertainly, "Don't seem right to me, Boss. But I reckon that's how he got here from Mexico."

Thomas shook his head, unable to comprehend the spectacle of Pedro and his kids driving over five hundred miles in their battered Chevy. Then another thought hit him, *"Vaya con su esposa en…en…*her coffin?"

"Si, si."

Too confounded to pursue his questioning further, Thomas shook his head, bid Pedro *'adios'* and returned to the Ford truck with PJ following. He climbed in, set the spark and throttle levers and waited for PJ to crank the engine. As they headed toward home, Thomas spoke, "I can't believe he's gonna drive that old truck with the loose tappets and worn tires clear down to Mexico with four kids and…and his dead wife in a coffin in the back, can you?"

The little farm manager just shook his head and stared straight ahead.

Thomas continued, "Something seems to be bothering Pedro, something more than his wife dying."

"Yeah, I reckon, Boss. He's butt-sprung about somethin.'"

"How'r we gonna make out without him?"

"Not sure. Gonna play hob with our sprayin' and weedin.'"

"You wanna bring in some temporary help?"

"Naw, let's see how things go for a spell first."

When Thomas returned home, he was surprised to find the Maxwell parked under the sycamore. It was still mid-afternoon, too early for Brenda to be home from work, so he speculated that she or Tommy might be ill. But when he stepped inside, he found out differently.

The youngster was in his playpen, but Brenda was sitting sternly on the sofa, arms folded across her chest, legs crossed with the top one swinging back and forth ominously.

"Er, hi," he ventured, "you're home early. You sick or something?"

She didn't answer the question, but nodded toward the kitchen table, "So who's Lillian?"

His eyes flitted to the table and back to the sofa and he felt the blood rush from his face. He had left his letter to Lillian in the typewriter on the table.

"Uh, she's nobody, just a nurse I met in France."

Brenda raised her voice, "Doesn't sound like 'nobody' to me if you're planning to fly to Bakersfield to meet her!"

"Well, she was very helpful in the hospital...guess I just..."

"Just what, Thomas? You accused me of being unfaithful before we were married, so what were you planning to do, get even after we're married?"

Too embarrassed to respond, he shook his head dejectedly and looked at the floor. She jumped up from the sofa crying hysterically, "How could you do this to me, Thomas? I'll never be able to trust you again!" She stalked into the bedroom and slammed the door.

He went to the table and slumped down in one of the chairs. When the phone jingled the familiar long ring followed by a short one, he ignored it. But when it repeated the ring, he reluctantly stepped over to the wall, picked up the receiver and mumbled, "Hullo."

"Thomas, this is Becky."

"Oh, hi Sis."

"You all right? You sound kinda down in the dumps."

He sighed, "Yeah, I'm OK. What can I do for you?"

"I just heard about von Karman."

"Yeah, but far as I'm concerned, he had it coming. Shouldn't been messing around in that Klan business."

"Kinda scary to think he was back in town and I didn't know about it."

"How about in December of '17, just before I went off to war? You know he stayed with the Stuckeys then?"

She cried, "Heavens no! I thought he had been deported before that!"

"He escaped from the sheriff. They didn't catch him till a month later."

"My gosh, that's really scary!"

He fell silent, trying to clarify something that was bothering him.

"Thomas, you still there?"

"Yeah. I want to ask you something."

"What?"

"If a woman is...er...you know with more than one man in a one or two week period and gets pregnant, how does she know which one is the father?"

Becky paused, trying to comprehend the question. "What are you asking, Thomas? I don't understand."

"Well, as I think you know, I spent a night with Brenda just before Christmas of 1917, and that's when von Karman was staying at her house. God only knows what they were---"

She cut him off, "Oh Thomas, Thomas, stop torturing yourself. Brenda's in love with you, not von Karman. And you're the father of that little boy and nobody else."

He hesitated, then asked, "But, how can you be so certain?"

"A woman just knows. Besides, you were the only man she talked about during the war."

He sighed resignedly and opened his mouth to comment further. But he stopped as he recalled that von Karman was the one who had impregnated his sister in the summer of 1917 and later tried to kill her. He decided to change the subject, "Uh, how's Mother doing these days?"

"She's pretty upset about Pedro's wife."

"How does she know about that? I just came from seeing Pedro!"

She paused before continuing, "You didn't hear what happened?"

"Er, she died. What else?"

"She died from abortion surgery at the birth control clinic."

He caught his breath, "God! What...when---?"

She interrupted, "Apparently they tried to perform an abortion and sterilization procedure and something went wrong. It was that Doctor Zitser from the clinic."

"Oh Jesus! Don't tell me Mother was involved in this?"

"No, no. But Pedro's wife was the second one of Zitser's patients to die in a month."

Thomas raised his voice as shock quickly turned to disbelief, "Damn, I had a feeling Mother shouldn't get involved with that bunch of quacks!"

Becky tried to calm her brother down. "Try to relax, Thomas. Mother didn't have anything to do with the surgery. She's resigned from the clinic, and the police have closed the place and arrested that doctor."

He took a deep breath. "That's nice, but it won't do Missus Garcia much good now, or Pedro and the kids, either. They're all pretty unhappy and heading back to Mexico."

"Mother's suffering too. She thought she was doing a good thing helping women to not have so many babies."

"I think that whole idea is stupid. Women are supposed to have babies and stay home and take care of them…and…and their husbands too."

Becky sighed before replying resignedly, "That's easy for you to say. You men don't have to go through all the discomfort and misery of being pregnant and giving birth. You just…just…well, you just have your moment of fun and you're on your way."

He opened his mouth to respond, but stopped when he again remembered Becky's unhappy experience with von Karman.

She spoke again. "Well, Thomas, you have a right to be angry, but we need to be pretty careful with Mother. She's really upset over this. I'm worried about what she might do."

He replied resignedly, "Yeah, I guess you're right. I'll try not to be so judgmental." He bid his sister good-by, hung up the phone, returned the typewriter to the closet and shoved the Lillian letter and short story manuscript under the bed. He returned to the kitchen for his bottle of brandy.

***

After Brenda found the Lillian letter, she and Thomas didn't speak to each other for several days. Thus, the full significance of her earlier reference to Holy Week didn't register until the following Wednesday. That was when he entered the house dog-tired and sweat-stained and hungry enough to chew weeds. He had spent a long day plowing at the West Forty, struggling to steer and shift gears on the tractor and work the plow handle with his one good hand. But instead of cooking dinner, Brenda was at the sink coloring eggs.

"Whatcha doing?" he asked as he tossed his hat on the sofa and ran his hand through his sweat-matted hair. He stepped toward Tommy in his playpen.

"Coloring eggs. Tomorrow's Maundy Thursday, you know. We need to carry them with us all day for good luck."

He turned to her, "But, so many, and it looks like they're all green!"

"That's part of the old German custom, and some are for Papa and my brothers, and to take to Melba."

His gut tightened at the mention of Melba, and his voice rose in frustration, "Well, how about the old Irish custom of fixing supper for your starving husband?"

"After awhile. Soon as I finish this."

Angrily he walked to the cupboard for his bottle of brandy, poured a stiff drink, added water and ice, and retreated to the bathroom. He filled the tub with water, peeled off his sweaty coveralls, underwear and socks and carefully held up his arm cast as he settled into the tepid water. He soaked and scrubbed for about an hour, periodically reaching for his drink.

After finishing, he found that Brenda and the baby had disappeared into the back bedroom. Gritting his teeth resignedly, he opened a can of pork and beans, cut a slice of bread and poured a second brandy. Afterwards, he settled into the comfort of the old rocker and, with a cool spring breeze wafting through the room, had a third brandy and a cigarette for dessert, and eventually retreated into the front bedroom for still another sleepless night.

When he awoke the next morning, he found that Brenda and Tommy had finished breakfast and were ready to leave for town. As he took a seat at the kitchen table, they moved toward the door and she called back, "Don't forget, we're going to Papa's for Easter dinner."

His response jumped up from his stomach along with the bile as he sat straight up, "Like hell we are!"

She turned around, surprised, "What do you mean?"

"I've had enough of all that damn German family crap!" Stabbing the table with his forefinger, he emphasized each word, "I'm-staying-right-here-and-having-dinner-in-my-own-house-with-my-own-family! And...and cooked-by-my-own-wife!"

She glowered at him and answered sarcastically, "You might have better luck asking Lillian to cook your dinner." She picked up a basket of green eggs, took the baby's hand, and left the house, letting the screen door slam behind her. He pounded his fist on the table and slumped down against the unyielding wood of the ladder-back chair.

CHAPTER 21

Thomas lost the argument over Easter, and spent a discomfiting Sunday at the Stuckeys. .The celebration certainly didn't help his manly ego, and it took another blow the following day. That was when Brenda announced she would be traveling to Los Angeles with Melba the following weekend to attend a meeting of the Eugenics Association. He toyed with the idea of challenging her, but then decided he really didn't give a damn. Besides, her absence would give him an opportunity to work on his short story and spend more time with Tommy.

But today was the Monday of her return. As he motored into town to meet her at the Southern Pacific depot, it was with a feeling of uncertainty. When Melba had picked her up the proceeding Friday to start their trip, Brenda and Thomas had exchanged only cursory good-byes, not even a chaste kiss.

So now as he stood with a fidgeting Tommy on the station platform, he was surprised to find her overflowing with excitement. She ran smiling from the train, threw her arms around his neck,, and kissed him firmly on the mouth. He kissed her back and experienced a touch of pride as he felt her rounding breasts and protruding tummy under her travel-wrinkled linen dress.

With one hand holding her wide-brimmed straw hat in place, she knelt to hug and kiss Tommy as he clamored for attention. Then, standing up, she exclaimed, "Oh, Thomas, "I had the most wonderful time!"

"Uh, great! What'd you do, win some kind of prize?"

"No, no, silly. There weren't any prizes. But I met some of the most impressive people, even Doctor Popenoe."

"Who's he?"

"He's one of the leaders of the eugenics movement in California."

"Sounds pretty important."

"Yes. And another man, a Mister Gosney, who's done research on sterilization with Doctor Popenoe. His first name is Eugene, just like our Tommy's middle name."

"I'm glad you had a good time. How was the weather?"

"Nice and cool until we crossed the mountains coming home to the valley," she lamented. "Then it got so stuffy on the train we had to open the windows." She paused to brush particles of soot from her dress.

She extracted a claim ticket from her handbag, and they made their way through the milling crowd of arriving and departing passengers toward the baggage counter. As they recovered her wicker suitcase and walked to the Maxwell, he asked, "You need to go to work today?"

"Oh, no. Melba said I could take the day off."

"Good. I'm anxious for you to see the new house. The painters are ready for us to select the interior colors and wallpapers. A lot's been done since you saw it last."

She nodded vaguely as he opened the passenger side door, helped her into the seat and lifted Tommy up on her lap. He placed her suitcase on the rear seat, climbed in behind the wheel, started the engine and backed away from the curb. As protection against the bright spring sun, he had left the top up but taken down the winter side curtains.

While he patiently guided the car with his good hand through the noontime dissonance of honking motor cars, clanging streetcars and chattering citizens Brenda resumed talking. "Do you have any idea how many people in the United States have been sterilized since the first laws were passed ten years ago?"

Taken off guard by the question, he chuckled nervously. "I guess not."

"Over three thousand."

He winced, "You're kidding!"

She shook her head, "And the highest percentage are right here in California."

The revelation gave him a stab of pain in his groin. He halted the car at Fulton Street while a streetcar negotiated the turn east on Tulare Street and a phalanx of pedestrians crossed in front of him. She removed her hat and fascinator and started fanning herself and Tommy against the hot air beating up from the pavement, and resumed talking. "The society leaders believe the lowest ten percent of the population should be sterilized."

He chuckled again, "You're making me nervous."

She smiled back at him. "Oh, you needn't worry. They're just talking about the feeble-minded, the mentally retarded and the unfit. They're trying to keep them from having more babies." She shifted Tommy in her lap.

Thomas mulled that over for a moment. "Gosh, that sounds like a good deal. The nuts of the world can just get together and have fun and not worry about getting pregnant."

She shook her head, "You shouldn't be making fun, Thomas."

They fell silent as they left the downtown hubbub and he accelerated the car toward home, welcoming the cooling breeze occasioned by the forward motion. He reached over and patted his son, contentedly playing and babbling to his teddy bear in a language only the two of them understood.

Brenda broke the silence, "Oh, and another thing, Thomas. The association is pushing for tighter immigration restrictions for America. They believe that people from northwest Europe are superior and make the best citizens and need to be conserved."

He peered at her quizzically, "That include us?"

"Yes, of course. It includes Germans, Irish, Scottish, English and French, but not eastern or southern Europeans like Slavs and Italians. And speaking of Germans reminds me, the association is planning to invite the leading German eugenicists to an international congress in New York next year. Wouldn't that be wonderful?"

Thomas scowled, "From Germany?"

"Yes. Before the war, Germany praised America for its bold leadership in eugenics and patterned its programs after ours. The problem now is that they refuse to come to America as long as foreign soldiers occupy parts of their country. And they're insisting that German be accepted as one of the conference languages."

He flushed in anger, "Well, far as I'm concerned, you can tell 'em to go to hell!"

"Oh, Thomas, what a thing to say!"

"Those bastards started a goddamn war, Brenda, and killed a bunch of Americans, including some of my buddies. And they put a bullet hole in my leg, in case you've forgotten!"

The baby became frightened at his father's sharp language, clutched his teddy bear in one hand and snuggled closer to his mother.

"Now see what you've done, you've scared Tommy."

"I'm sorry about that, but I wish you'd be more sensitive to some of my feelings. You forget I've still got friends buried over there who they can't find."

She remained silent, looking straight ahead pouting, cuddling the baby.

"I also wish you would remember that we're Americans, not Germans, or Irish, or Italian, or whatever. We're all part of a big melting pot and should be learning to live together, and not trying to put down one ethnic group or another."

He also fell silent as they left the pavement of the city street and continued along the familiar farm road, already turning dusty from lack of rain. As they passed their forty-acre vineyard Thomas, still bitter over the inanity of their conversation, spoke out, "When you talk of sterilization, you might remember that's what killed Missus Garcia when she went to that damn birth control clinic."

She sighed, "Yes, I heard. That was unfortunate."

"And she was the second one in a month," he added bitterly.

Brenda didn't respond.

"So now Pedro's stuck with four kids and no wife, and I'm missing some good help. Maybe they'd been better off with another child." He looked at

Brenda, but still got no response. She just stared ahead blankly as they passed their current house and continued on to the site of the new one. As they pulled in the driveway, she brightened at the view of the handsome two-story structure. Since she last had seen it, the workers had finished painting the outside white with a contrasting light brown trim on the window frames and door frames and around the foundation. Glass in the new windows was glistening and reflecting sunlight. A painter was putting a coat of white paint on the gingerbread railing of the porch that surrounded the front and eastside.

"Oh, no!" Brenda cried out.

"What's the matter?" Thomas asked, looking toward the house.

"That railing is supposed to be brown!"

The painter had stopped at the sound of their arrival and welcomed them with a friendly greeting as they climbed out and approached the house.

"Afraid that's the wrong color, Mister Jason," Thomas called out.

The painter looked at the railing and shook his head. "Thought you wanted that in white like the rest of the house."

Brenda looked like she was on the verge of tears. "No, no. I want it trimmed in brown like Papa's house!"

Thomas looked at the painter resignedly. He got the message and shrugged, "Guess I better change that."

He laid his brush atop the paint can, turned and led them up the steps and into the entryway where they marveled at the sight of the beautiful walnut paneling. They followed the painter through the damp odor of freshly plastered walls into the parlor and dining room. Since these rooms also faced south, they too were to be finished in walnut to help keep them cool during the hot summer months. They continued through the hallway, stepping around two carpenters installing hardwood flooring, and paused to peer into the bathroom with its shiny porcelain bathtub and toilet. The wainscot portion of that room was to be completed in a light oak paneling and the balance of the wall painted a cream color. They ended up in the kitchen where the painter had placed rolls of wallpaper on a workbench.

After Brenda made a preliminary selection and Thomas acquiesced, they carried the sample rolls upstairs where they settled on a subdued floral print for the master bedroom. In the bedroom that would become Tommy's, the painter rolled out a sample featuring a striped blue pattern with pictures of small animals. When the baby became engrossed in the pictures, signaling his approval, they moved into the third bedroom, which at a future date would be occupied by the second child.

The painter partially unrolled three different patterns and alternately held them up against the wall. "Oh, Thomas, don't you just love that?" Brenda enthused, pointing to one with pink and purple flowers.

"Um, yeah, that's nice.   But aren't those girl's colors, pink and purple?"

She nodded with a smile.

"What if it's a boy, wouldn't they look kinda sissy?"

"Oh, it's going to be a girl, I just know.   And we'll name her Eugenia."

He frowned, "What on earth type of name is that?"

"It's the feminine version of Eugene, Tommy's middle name.   It means 'well born'. Don't you think that's a lovely name?"

He shook his head, partly in dismay, partly because he didn't want to get into an argument in front of the painter.   They made their way outside to find the contractor waiting and offering assurances that all work would be completed for them to move in by late May.   They could go ahead and plan their long-awaited house warming.

They returned to the car and started toward home, chatting idly about the best date for the house warming and who should be invited.   As they pulled into the driveway, they found Erasmus working in the vegetable garden.   "What's he doing?" Brenda asked irritably as they pulled up and parked under the dappled shade of the sycamore.

"Looks like he's getting it ready for spring planting," Thomas replied nonchalantly, turning off the engine and walking around the car to help Brenda and lift Tommy out to the ground. He held the youngster's hand as they stepped over to the edge of the garden.

"Afternoon, Erasmus," Thomas said.

"Afternoon, Massa, Mizz 'Roark." The old Negro stopped chopping with the hoe, shifted his weight to his good leg and wiped the sweat from his forehead with a large checkered handkerchief he removed from his coveralls. He grinned as the baby pulled away from his father, ran over and wrapped his arms around his good leg. He reached down and patted him gently on the head.

"Kinda warm for this early in the spring," Thomas ventured as he scanned along the neat, weedless furrows Erasmus was carving into the dark loam, rich with the compost he had spaded in during the winter.

"Yassuh."

"What are you planting?"

Erasmus took Tommy's hand, led him to the end of the garden plot and returned with several packages of *Burpee's* seeds. He shuffled them in his hands, looking studiously at the pictures. "I'se got pole beans an'…an' cone…and peas, and thisn's carrots and okra, and---"

Brenda interrupted, crinkling her nose suspiciously, "What's okra?"

"It's, it's"…Erasmus struggled for an answer and handed her the packets.

Thomas tried to come to his rescue. "It's a tall plant, something like corn. Southerners use the pods to make gumbo soup."

Brenda dismissively tossed the packets on the ground, scowled at Thomas, turned and stalked away toward the house, dragging Tommy by the hand.

Thomas glared at her disappearing backside, bent down to pick up the packets and returned them, "Sorry, Erasmus, she's with child, you know."

"Yessuh, ah knows."

Thomas, still embarrassed, asked, "How about my beets and spinach?"

The old Negro shuffled the packets again, then showed two to Thomas.

He smiled his approval, "Yeah, those look like beets and spinach."

He retrieved the luggage from the car and followed Brenda into the house. As he entered, she turned toward him, hands on her hips, and spoke sharply, "I don't like the idea of that darkie planting our vegetables with his old black hands!"

"What on earth are you talking about?"

"We'll be eating those some day, and the thought of his dirty hands---"

He cut in, "For God's sake, Brenda! You're not making any sense!"

"I don't care. He comes from an inferior race. He shouldn't be touching food we'll be eating!" The baby turned at the loudness of her voice, moved over beside his playpen and reached between the spindles for the comfort of one of his toys. Thomas slumped into a chair at the kitchen table, too bewildered to think of anything to say.

She continued boring in. "Besides, I thought you were going to move him away."

His bewilderment turned to anger and his throat tightened as he glared at her, barely able to control the urge to jump up and slap her. He finally replied in firm, measured words, "I told you he would move when he wants to, not one damn minute sooner. Now shut up, and don't bring up the subject again!"

She glowered back at him, then as her lower lip started to pook out in a pout, she turned and disappeared into the bedroom, slamming the door behind her.

Thomas sighed resignedly and picked up a magazine to fan himself against the growing heat of the day. He looked up in a few moments as she returned wrapped in her robe, entered the bathroom and started filling the tub. She stepped back to take Tommy's hand and lead him toward the bathroom.

"What are you doing? Thomas asked irritably.

"Taking a bath," she replied curtly, removing the youngster's clothes.

"He just had one this morning!"

"I don't care. I want to wash away those old black hands."

Thomas shook his head in disbelief and went to the bedrooms to open the windows, hoping a breath of fresh air would blow away the heat of the day and his increasing feeling of helplessness.

***

For Thomas and Brenda the balance of the week following the argument tumbled by in a blur. They escaped from each other by going their separate ways, she to her job in town, he by staying on the farm to work the land, dabble with his writing and take care of Tommy. He drove over to the new house early in the week and wandered around disinterestedly, watching the workers as they hung wallpaper or finished installing the hardwood flooring. He noticed that the porch railing had been repainted brown.

On a couple of days, he took over the plowing at the West Forty to ease the burden on PJ and Erasmus created by the absence of Pedro. These were especially enjoyable occasions because he carried Tommy with him and let him pretend he was driving the tractor and helped him splash cool irrigation water in his face to wash off the dirt and sweat of the warm weather.

But he continued to fume about what he considered Brenda's intransigence over Erasmus. His feelings became particularly acute when he was working in the field where he could observe the old Negro softly humming some ancient gospel song as he chopped weeds, repaired furrows and tied up wayward grapevine tendrils. Thomas' admiration increased as he watched him hobble around on his grapestake peg, a poignant reminder of what could have been the result of his own war wound.

At mid-week Thomas tried to inaugurate a truce by cooking *Kalbsbraten*, one of Brenda's favorite German dishes, for dinner.   He had phoned for the veal shoulder to be delivered in their regular grocery order, but forgot to include the beef bullion the recipe called for.   Brenda didn't seem to appreciate the end result, possibly because he had substituted chicken broth for the missing bullion.   She did appear to relax some, chatting casually about the weather and the status of the new house and even playing briefly with Tommy.   But she retired early, not yet ready to discuss her differences with Thomas over the status of Erasmus.

On Friday after lunch he decided to drive into town to pick up some supplies.   Since Brenda had the Maxwell with her, he gathered up Tommy and they headed for the Model T truck.   They found PJ sitting under the sycamore dejectedly picking off pieces of the red and brown mottled bark and tossing them in the dirt.

"Afternoon, PJ," Thomas called out as he settled Tommy in the front seat.   "You look like something's troubling you."

The farm manager shuffled his feet and looked down at the ground before he responded, "Ol' 'Rass' is gone...quit."

"What do you mean?"

"He done quit.   Said he was movin' over to Niggra town."

"You two have a fight?"

PJ looked to one side, apparently reluctant to make eye contact before he finally blurted out, "No, but reckon he did with the Missus."

"Missus O'Roark?"

"Yessir, over by the vegetable garden. I seen 'em yesterday afternoon, looked like she was havin' a hissy fit about somethin'. Afterwards, 'Rass' come into the bunkhouse and packed up his things. Said he wasn't feelin' good." PJ, still avoiding eye contact, again looked away.

Thomas stared down at the diminutive farm manager, disbelieving what he was saying, "Well, where was I? Why didn't I see them?"

"Reckon you was workin' the West Forty."

He nodded in acknowledgment then kicked the dirt and took a deep breath, striving to control his rising anger. "How the hell did 'Rass' get to town?"

"Missus carried him in the car this mornin'."

Thomas, too confused and angry to comment further, climbed into the driver's seat and waited while PJ struggled to his feet and cranked the engine to life. With a half-wave, he let out the clutch and spun out of the yard. Later, as he and Tommy rolled into town, he decided on impulse to do something he had not done before, visit Brenda at the Normal School. Perhaps she could offer a reason for her confrontation with Erasmus.

Much to his surprise, at the entrance to the red brick building he found a sign advising the school was closed for the afternoon for a teachers' conference.

He peered through the glass of the entry door into the shadows of the empty hallway in disbelief, and Tommy tried to help by reaching up and rattling the doorknob. They turned and walked a few steps down the sidewalk before Thomas stopped and looked blankly back at the door, trying to recall if Brenda had told him they would be closed or if perhaps he had missed her returning home.

He motored back to the downtown area and pulled into a parking place next to Epstein's department store to use a telephone to call home. When there was no answer, he also tried the Stuckey residence, but Ivan didn't know where she might be either.

As they stepped back out into the warm afternoon, Thomas could see his young son was getting tired and restless, and squirming like he needed to go potty. He glanced up and down the block for an inspiration and noticed the Hughes Hotel at the corner. Lifting him up to his right shoulder, he said, "Come on, Tommy, let's go to the bathroom then we can get an ice cream soda or sarsaparilla. Doesn't that sound like fun?"

The little tyke rested his head on his father's shoulder as he carried him through the busy sidewalk crowds and into the cooling, restful atmosphere of the hotel's lobby to the registration desk "Where's your men's toilet?" he asked.

The clerk pointed around to his left, "Over on the other side of the elevator. You can't see it from here."

Thomas carried his son across the lobby into the toilet, and they took turns emptying their bladders.

As he leaned down to re-button the child's rompers, the words 'can't see it from here' suddenly caught up to him.

He returned to the registration desk and looked around to his right to confirm that indeed, neither the elevator nor the toilet entrance could be seen from there. He turned back to the clerk. "Uh, could I have a look at your register?"

"I beg your pardon?"

"Er, yeah. The wife and I spent a delightful New Year's eve here. Just thought I would bring back some great memories."

"Well, that would be in our December or January book, depending on what time you signed in. Both are filed away, and I'm afraid it would be highly irregular to let you see them."

Thomas responded with a half-smile, extracted a couple of dollar bills from his wallet and waited for the clerk to return with the registers. Silently he turned to the last page of the December volume and scanned down to see where he had signed himself and Brenda in for the evening. He then opened the first page of the January register and ran his finger through the guest signatures. He did not find von Karman's name or any others he recognized.

With a chill running down his spine, he thanked the clerk and led Tommy outside into the bright sunlight and returned to the truck. During the drive to the farm, his mind roiled and his stomach churned. One moment he felt guilty that he had accused Brenda of spending New Year's eve with von Karman. But then who misled him or lied in the first place, Major Brown or the night clerk? Or had von Karman registered under an assumed name? And he remained angry over her apparent confrontation with Erasmus.

By the time he reached the farm, he could hardly remember the return home. He entered the empty house and settled Tommy into his highchair at the kitchen table. He turned to the icebox and pulled out a cold *Nehi*, popped the cap off, poured the fizzy contents into a glass with a piece of ice and handed it to him along with a couple of cookies. He poured himself a brandy over ice and a little water and drank it down. It tasted so good he had a couple more quick ones before he picked up the baby starting to doze and carried him into the bedroom for his afternoon nap. Then he sat down at the kitchen table and idly flipped through a couple of old issues of the *Ladies' Home Journal* while waiting for the Maxwell to pull into the yard.

When Brenda did arrive around six o'clock, he was in high dudgeon and ready to confront her. He got up from the table to peer out and could tell she was tipsy by the haphazard way she parked the car and her wobbly walk toward the house. He opened the screen door to let her in and watched without sympathy as she glanced furtively from under her hat, sitting askew atop her head, stepped unsteadily up on the stoop and crossed the room to flop down on the sofa.

"Where the hell have you been?" he asked, letting the door slam shut.

She hiccuped. "Wha' do you mean?"

"This afternoon. Where were you?"

She looked puzzled. "At work, why?" She reached up awkwardly to remove her hat and dropped it on the sofa.

"Like hell. We came looking for you and the damn school was closed!"

She snapped out of her boozy state and shot back in anger. "Wha' were you doing...spy...spying on me...like...like during the damn war?"

He hesitated for a moment, surprised to hear his wife swear, confused over the reference to spying. "Stop lying to me, Brenda. You were out someplace getting drunk! And I want to know what you did with Erasmus."

She struggled to focus her memory, "I took...uh drove him to town...where he said, 'hic', said he needed to...er... see...to see a man about something."

He raised his voice, "I don't believe that! Why the hell would he go to town without telling me?"

She shook her head vaguely without replying.

"Where'd you leave him?"

"In fron'...of...front of Court House Park."

"For God's sake, Brenda, how could you do that? He's not familiar with the downtown area. He'll probably hobble around on his peg until the Klan grabs him or the police pick him up."

She opened her mouth to respond, then blurted out, "Oh, I'm gonna be sick." Hand to her mouth, she stood up woozily and staggered toward the bathroom. He started to follow her, but caught himself, reasoning she should suffer by herself. He turned to find that Tommy had awakened and let himself down from the bed in the front bedroom, and was standing by the door rubbing the sleep from his eyes.

"Come on little fella," he said as he reached out and guided him to the kitchen table and lifted him into his highchair. "Mommy's not feeling well so us guys will just fix our own supper." His casual comment seemed to overcome any concern the youngster might have shown over the sound of his mother heaving in the bathroom.

Thomas removed the leftover veal from the icebox, cut off a few slices, dropped them in a frying pan to warm, and dumped the gravy and a couple of boiled potatoes into a pot. He heated the leftover peas, carrots and cauliflower in another. When the food was ready he dished out two servings, carefully mashing the potatoes and slicing the meat into tiny bites, and carried them to the table. He poured Tommy a glass of milk and himself one of iced tea. They both dug in industriously as Brenda exited from the bathroom, staggered to the bedroom and closed the door.

After supper, while the baby played on the floor with his toys, Thomas washed the dishes as best he could with his cast-free right hand. He ended the evening reading nursery rhymes to Tommy until bedtime when they both climbed into bed.

Thomas slept late the next morning, finally awakening to the bright sunlight of a glorious spring day. When he realized Tommy's side of the bed was empty, he sat up with a start and called to him. Receiving no answer, he got out of bed and walked out to see that the door to the back bedroom was partially open. As he pushed it open a little farther, he was assaulted by a strange odor. Tommy was standing beside the bed trying to wake his mother, visible only as a formless lump under the cover of blankets and a tuft of hair poking out the top.

Thomas entered the room, put his arm around the baby to comfort him and called to Brenda. She responded with a barely audible mumble. As he reached to pull the bedding down from her face, he realized she had covered herself in two heavy wool blankets. "Are you sick?" he asked.

She stirred slightly and spoke weakly, "Oh, Thomas, I'm having terrible chills…and…my head aches and my lower back."

He smiled, "You sure it's not the booze?"

She didn't respond.

He felt her forehead. "You feel like you've got a fever." He went to the bathroom for a thermometer and stuck it under her tongue. "You want something cold to drink?" he asked, waiting for the instrument to register.

She nodded and replied weakly, "Yes, please. I'm so thirsty."

In a few moments he removed the thermometer and exclaimed, "Oh, my, your temperature's a hundred and three! I'll get you an antipyrine."

He brought her the powder and a glass of water. As she sat part way up and swallowed the medicine, he added, "I noticed a bottle of Mother's *Lydia Pinkham's* still in the cabinet, and one of *Dr. Hostetter's Bitters*. You want either one of those?"

She shook her head and snuggled back down under the covers.

Thomas and the baby retreated to the kitchen to prepare and dawdle over their breakfast, occasionally poking their heads into the bedroom to check on Brenda. But by early afternoon, when Thomas found that her temperature had risen to one hundred and four and she still was complaining of chills, sweating and lower back pain, he decided to phone Doctor Bandy.

The doctor arrived about an hour later in his familiar green and black Chevrolet roadster. Thomas went to the door and watched as he extricated himself from the car, bent his short, ample body over the rear compartment for his medical kit, and waddled toward the house. Thomas called out "Good afternoon", and Bandy responded with his usual greeting, "Got a sick one, have we?"

As the doctor entered the house, he paused and sniffed. "What's that unusual odor?"

Thomas looked perplexed, "Uh, well, I've been painting. Maybe---"

"No, no. That smells like smallpox."

Thomas caught his breath. He had never experienced the dread disease but had heard enough about it to be concerned.

Bandy excused himself, walked back to his car and returned, pulling on a full-length raincoat. "Trying to protect my clothing from contamination," he explained as he re-entered the house and went to the bedroom.

When the doctor emerged a few minutes later, he frowned and shook his head. "Looks like your wife is pretty sick, Mister O'Roark."

"Is it the pox?"

"Can't tell for sure at this early stage. Might be the measles or even the flu. Hope it's not 'cause that took a lot of good citizens a couple years ago."

Thomas nodded, reached down and picked up Tommy.

Bandy motioned toward the youngster. "Can't remember if I scratched him for smallpox last year or not. How about you, you been vaccinated?"

He nodded, "Yeah, couple years ago when I joined the Marines."

Bandy continued talking as he removed a pot from the cupboard, added water and placed it on the stove to heat. "I'm afraid California made a big mistake awhile back when they rescinded compulsory vaccination for children." He retrieved two needles and a vial of vaccine from his satchel, dropped the needles in the pot and resumed talking while waiting for the water to boil. "I want to vaccinate both of you as a precaution. Then I believe I better take Missus O'Roark with me back to the hospital."

In a few moments, the doctor plucked a needle from the boiling water, dipped it in the vaccine and scratched it into the arm of a grimacing Thomas. He repeated the process on Tommy as he cried and cuddled in his father's arms. When he calmed down, Thomas placed him in his playpen and went to help the doctor bundle up Brenda and assist her to the car. He felt a sudden emptiness as they pulled out of the yard.

The next morning, after a restless night of feeling very much alone, Thomas deposited the baby with Grandpa Stuckey and drove to the hospital. He was directed to the isolation ward where he met Doctor Bandy, just emerging. He spoke solemnly from behind a gauze mask that covered his nose and mouth. "Mister O'Roark, I'm afraid it's smallpox all right."

He shook his head, "You sure?"

Bandy nodded. "Yes, her face has broken out in a rash and her body is giving off the distinctive odor of the disease. She still has a high fever and rapid pulse, and the nurses report that she vomited twice during the night and experienced some delirium."

"Can you do anything for her?"

"I just gave her a shot of morphine to ease the pain and have ordered cold compresses. We may add a cold bath if we can't bring down her temperature. And we'll be treating her eruptions with *Vaseline* to ease the itching and reduce later scarring."

Thomas shuddered as the mention of the familiar petroleum jelly brought back memories of his wartime surgery and the accompanying odor of ether. He turned away from the doctor, fighting back nausea and a feeling of helplessness.

Bandy, fearing that Thomas was about to faint or become sick to his stomach, guided him to a chair, sat down next to him and waited for him to collect himself before continuing, "Mister O'Roark, I believe your wife has been with child now for what, four months?"

He nodded absently as he leaned forward in the chair to rest his left forearm and its heavy cast on his lap, and stared at the floor.

"I don't mean to unduly alarm you but that makes this illness especially serious. It often has a negative effect on pregnant women and the fetus."

Thomas shook his head, unable to think of anything to say.

Bandy continued, his voice turning even more ominous. "This is very worrisome because it's the first smallpox case we've had for some time. It usually takes ten to twelve days after a person has been exposed to become ill, then another day or two to break out with the rash. We need to remember all the people she's had contact with over the past couple weeks so we can try to determine the source and vaccinate against any further spread of the disease."

Thomas continued sitting with his head down, embarrassed at the tears that kept clouding his eyes, barely able to think clearly. He searched his memory for a moment, then jumped to his feet. "Damn! I knew she shouldn't have gone to that conference in Los Angeles last week!"

"Sounds like that was too recently. She probably didn't contract it there. How about the week before?"

Thomas shrugged, still scratching his memory, "We didn't do anything special. I worked around the farm and she went to her office."

"Any other folks come to mind?"

He thought some more before continuing, "She's had contact with the people and the students she works with at the Normal School." He paused, struggling to stir more deeply into his memory. "Also, the workers at our new house. And, her father and brothers and of course, Tommy and me."

"We need to get word to all of them so we can vaccinate---"

Thomas interrupted, "And I just remembered, PJ and Erasmus."

"Who are they?"

"Our farm manager and his helper."

"That name sounds like he might be Negroid."

Thomas nodded.

"Smallpox is especially bad for colored folks. You need to make certain you warn him, and that he's been vaccinated. I'll notify the Public Health agency so they can place a quarantine sign on your house."

Thomas glanced at the doctor wistfully. "Can I see her for a moment?"

The doctor shook his head. "You can observe her through the glass panel, but we can't let you in the room, son. That would be too risky." He stood up and patted him on the shoulder. "Try not to worry too much. We'll do our best to pull Missus O'Roark through this, and we'll keep you advised."

Thomas rose and crossed the hall to peer through the glass panel into a long sterile-looking isolation ward. Although all the window shades were drawn to keep out the bright morning sunlight, a single light bulb in the center faintly illuminated some two dozen empty beds lined up along both walls. All were neatly covered in a blanket and sheet with the top folded down, patiently awaiting the next victim of some dread disease.

The sight of his wife lying helpless and alone in the nearest bed sucked at his gut, and he instinctively reached for the doorknob. Finding it locked, he turned and walked despondently out of the hospital. He returned to the Maxwell, occasionally pulling a checkered handkerchief from his pocket to wipe away tears or blow his nose. One moment he was fighting the guilt he felt over their argument and the bitter things he had said; the next he was struggling to remember what the doctor had told him to do.

He drove home slowly, his mind churning, oblivious to the carloads of people headed for Sunday church in their spring finery. When he walked into the house, the silence and emptiness were almost unbearable. He glanced into the back bedroom, pungent with the odor of Brenda's sickness, the blankets and sheets still in disarray. He closed the door, entered the other bedroom, flopped fully clothed onto the bed and dropped off to a restless sleep. The pounding of the Public Health officer attaching the quarantine sign outside the door finally awakened him, and he was advised to burn or boil all the bedding, towels and clothing Brenda had used and to avoid contact with everyone for fifteen days.

The visit reminded him of the doctor's advice to warn anyone who had been in contact with Brenda. He went to the bunkhouse to tell PJ and said he would phone Miss Mandy so she could alert Erasmus. But when he reached her, she reported she had not seen him for over a week. He advised the Stuckeys when he picked up Tommy, stopped by the new house to tell the contractor and made a mental note to call the Normal School office the next day.

For the next two days, Thomas operated like an automaton. He arose and fixed breakfast for himself and the baby, washed dishes and made their beds as best he could with one free hand. He deposited Tommy with the Stuckeys whenever he drove in to check on Brenda, only to find that her condition had not changed. Then he returned home to another empty afternoon. An attempt to get back to his writing failed because he couldn't concentrate. He visited the new house, now nearing completion, but could only respond with disinterest when the contractor asked him for advice on a particular matter. One afternoon he returned to plowing the West Forty but had to give up when, from lack of concentration, he inadvertently cut into several vine roots. He tumbled into bed early each night, only to lie awake staring into the darkness.

On the fourth morning, he awoke from another restless sleep to a particular sense of foreboding. He had kicked off the covers, even though it had been a cool night, and now felt chilled under the sheet that was damp with his sweat. Apprehensively, he put his hand to his forehead, but didn't feel like he had a temperature.

He struggled out of bed, looked at Tommy, still covered and sleeping in his crib, and touched his little forehead, which felt normal. He cooked up a batch of *Cream of Wheat*, awakened Tommy and fed him, took him to Grandpa Stuckey's and drove purposely to the hospital.

He walked into the building past the station where two nurses were working and up to the door of the ward. He peered inside and caught his breath when he found that Brenda's bed was empty. Panic stricken, he shouted her name, then irrationally reached for the locked door and tried to pull it open.

Suddenly, the two nurses were by his side calling his name.

"Where's my wife?" he shouted. "Where's Missus O'Roark?"

"Oh, Mister O'Roark. We're so sorry."

"No, no, don't tell me!"

"We're terribly sorry. We couldn't save her. She passed on about an hour ago."

As Thomas sagged at his knees, the nurses grabbed him and steered him to a chair. One ran for a swab of ammonia to wave under his nose, and they knelt down and massaged his free hand, trying to console him. In a few moments, Doctor Bandy joined them and expressed his regrets as Thomas, unhearing, lowered his head into his free hand and sank into the deep pain of sudden loss.

CHAPTER 22

For Thomas, the month of April would be remembered as one of the most painful of his young life. Although the trauma started with Brenda's death, it intensified when he went to the funeral home to make arrangements for her burial. Seeing what the smallpox had done to her once beautiful face was emotional enough, but the vision of some young male mortician pawing over her naked body and bulging belly tortured him. The overpowering odor of flowers made him nauseous, and he could feel his gut churning further as he accompanied the unctuous funeral home director to a room full of caskets. His mind drifted back to Brenda's wartime lament that they couldn't bury her mother in a nice copper or bronze one, but when advised of the price, he rationalized that it wouldn't do her any good now.

He decided on a taffeta-lined wooden coffin, and agreed that her burial should be limited to a simple graveside service with the casket sealed.

Today, as he guided the Maxwell toward her interment at the Mountain View Cemetery, his feeling of loss was magnified by the leaden sky overhead, its ponderous, low-lying clouds releasing their burden of moisture as a warm, gentle spring rain.

He steered mechanically with his right hand. His left forearm, still encased in its heavy cast, rested in his lap. Becky, seated in the passenger seat, alternately reached over to sweep the windshield wiper back and forth, or pushed open her side window flap to blow condensation from the windshield. PJ was riding solemnly in the back.

The drive on this humid day was particularly uncomfortable for Thomas because he had decided to wear his blue wool pinstripe suit and the ill-fitting wing tips. He had seldom donned the suit since his days at the Post Office and now, after work on the farm had bulked up his shoulders, it was a snug fit. The starched shirt collar and tie added to his discomfort.

No one else in the car was any more comfortable. Becky had foregone one of her stylish new spring outfits for a winter wool suit and hat because she thought it looked more somber. PJ had on his best blue jeans, western style snap-button shirt and a black string tie. He topped it off with the ubiquitous Stetson. To protect their sons from the sadness of the occasion, Thomas and Becky had left them with Emma, who had begged off attending the service.

When they pulled into the cemetery a few minutes before eleven o'clock, the scheduled starting time, no other vehicles were visible except for a long, black Cadillac hearse and a companion limousine. Several individuals were inside, their shadowy figures barely discernible through the rain-splattered windows.

"Where's everybody, Boss?" PJ asked as Thomas parked behind the hearse and turned off the engine.

"We might be the only ones, PJ."

Becky added, "The obituary in yesterday's paper was very brief, so some of her old friends might not know about it. Others are probably afraid because of the smallpox."

PJ, obviously agitated, asked, "How about her Papa and…and brothers? Ain't they comin'? And them folks where she worked?"

"Afraid not," Thomas answered bitterly. "The Stuckeys are mad because I wouldn't bury her next to her mother. And I could care less about that school bunch."

Becky, ignoring her brother's remark, interjected, "I phoned their office and found out they're afraid to attend because they might be exposed to the pox."

PJ stuck out his chest, "Hell, my arm's been scratched. I ain't afraid of no little bug."

"Smallpox is a pretty mean little bug, PJ," Thomas said. "Let's hope no one else catches it."

While they were talking, a preacher arrived in his Model T Ford and conferred with the funeral director, who then turned toward the Maxwell to signal they were ready to begin. The director opened the back door of the hearse, and the pallbearers climbed out of the limousine. Grasping the heavy casket in one hand, each held a black umbrella in the other to form a moving testudo during the slow, uneven march across the muddy grass. Thomas, with Becky's umbrella held loosely in the fingers of his left hand, his right hand gripping her arm, followed along solemnly. While the pallbearers positioned the casket over the open grave, Thomas, Becky and PJ sat down in the wooden folding chairs set up under a protective canopy.

As the minister opened the service with a prayer, Thomas unbuttoned his suit to relieve the tightness he felt building in his chest. He stared blankly at the casket, then averted his eyes down to the mud collected on his *Florsheims*, then away to the roadway to see a familiar Chandler sedan rolling to a stop. He watched in disbelief as Ivan got out and turned to assist Papa from the front passenger seat. They walked slowly toward the gravesite, Ivan obviously supporting his faltering father, and sat down in the second row of chairs. While the minister continued, Papa could be heard sobbing softly.

Thomas tried to force his mind away from the weeping, the sound of his sister sniffling and blowing her nose and the preacher's meaningless words. His thoughts wandered over the brief months of his marriage, the fun and abandon of their honeymoon, the promising future in their new house, the unborn child still in her womb, and of the little boy she had left him with. What would their future have been like, he contemplated, living under the cloud of doubt represented by von Karman or the lingering guilt over his relationship with Lillian.

He didn't return to the moment until he heard the words 'ashes to ashes, dust to dust' and stared vacantly at the handful of mud being tossed on the casket. He stood up and picked a carnation from the single floral decoration and placed it on the casket, and Becky and PJ did the same. Papa and Ivan did likewise, and everyone started walking to their motor cars.

When Thomas glanced through tear-moistened eyes toward the in-laws, his pain was magnified by the sight of Papa sobbing so uncontrollably that his son almost had to carry him to the vehicle. He wondered why Emil wasn't there to help, and felt the urge to say something but nothing would come out of the emptiness he felt inside. Morosely he let Becky guide him into the passenger seat, and she walked around to the other side to drive them home to the farm.

As they pulled away from the cemetery, he loosened his tie, removed the stiff shirt collar, slumped dejectedly in the seat and mumbled, "That was shitty."

Becky nodded silently and gritted her teeth at the crude language while her brother continued, "I guess Mother's right about one thing."

"What's that?"

"It's better to have a lot of people at your funeral."

Becky didn't respond as he continued grumbling, "Hope somebody shows up when I kick the bucket."

She smiled grimly at the remark as she steered the car back onto the main road, and reached over and patted his knee. "Just don't be in any big hurry, dear brother. You've got a little boy who's really going to need you now, and me too."

PJ added from the rear seat, "Me too, Boss."

Prior to departing from the farmhouse, Becky had started a ham cooking in the oven. Now upon their return she added the potatoes, carrots and onions and suggested to her brother that he change into his more comfortable blue jeans and plaid shirt and take a nap. She invited PJ to join them for dinner, then stretched out wearily on the sofa.

She was starting to doze when she was awakened by the phone ringing. She got up groggily, picked up the receiver and spoke, "O'Roark residence."

"This is Sheriff Thorsen. Is Thomas there?"

Becky summoned Thomas from the bedroom and handed him the receiver, "Hello, Sheriff, what can I do for you?"

"I reckon we found your nigger."

Thomas caught his breath at the blunt statement, the crude reference, "What do you mean…I…I didn't know he was miss---"

Thorsen cut him off, "We found his body jammed up against a weir in the Houghton Canal west of town. Looks like Willie Slocum cut him up pretty bad."

"Oh, Jesus! You sure it was Erasmus?"

"Weren't part of his left leg missing?"

"Well, yeah…but…but." Thomas struggled to ease the tightness building in his chest and turned toward his sister, trying to comprehend the enormity of what the sheriff was saying.

The sheriff continued, "He was wearing one of them military ribbons pinned to his shirt and some kinda cord twisted around his left shoulder."

Thomas strained to recall, then asked, "Was the ribbon red and blue with a couple of white stripes down the middle, and the cord red and gold?"

"Yeah, I reckon. They were kinda washed out from the water."

Thomas fell silent, still trying to digest the tragic news.

"You still there?" Thorsen asked.

"I'm here. Who the hell's Willie Slocum, anyway?"

"He's another black dude. Married to that Mandy Slocum. Claims he caught her and your man messin' around."

"Jesus, I thought he was missing in the war."

Thorsen chuckled, "He ain't missin' now, he's in jail. Army wants him for killing another soldier in France."

Thomas again became quiet until the sheriff spoke, "What was your nigger's name anyway? Weren't any ID on him."

Thomas, flushing at the insulting reference, replied, "Erasmus. Erasmus Jones."

"Any kin around these parts?"

"Not that I'm aware of."

"What should we do with the body?"

"Beats me. But I'll be glad to pay for the funeral." His offer sounded hollow and left him feeling embarrassed.

Thorsen hung up abruptly, and Thomas flopped down on the sofa with his head in his hand and blurted out the words, "Erasmus has been killed." Becky sat down beside him, hoping to bring comfort as he told what little he had learned from the sheriff.

Both became quiet, lost in their respective thoughts, until she stood up and went to the oven to check on the ham. "Guess we better eat this before it burns up. You want to call PJ?"

He nodded and made his way to the bunkhouse to summon the farm manager and advise him of Erasmus' death. He noted in passing that the rain had stopped and the dark clouds were drifting away to the east, allowing a warm sun to suck wisps of moisture up from the damp earth. He breathed deeply of the balmy air, trying to ease the pain of the moment, the vague feeling that somehow he was partly responsible for the demise of the old Negro.

When he entered the bunkhouse and broke the news, PJ jumped up and kicked the wall with his boot, "Goddamn, if that don't beat all. I just knowed somethin' was wrong when we didn't hear nothin' from old 'Rass.'"

Thomas nodded as the farm manager continued to vent his anger, "Who the hell would do a thing like that? Hell, 'Rass' never hurt no one."

"Sheriff says it was that Miss Mandy's husband. He just got back from the war."

"Damn! I figgered there was somethin' funny goin' on there. 'Rass' was actin' kinda peculiar the last few weeks." PJ stuffed his arms in the sleeves of his jacket and clapped on his Stetson, and they walked silently to the farmhouse.

They entered and took seats around the table while Becky served the ham and vegetables, poured iced tea and sat down. With a collective sigh, they dug silently into their meal, lost in their thoughts until Becky asked, "Any idea what you want to do next, Thomas?"

He stared at her blankly and took a drink of tea before responding sullenly, "Yeah, I'm thinking about selling out."

PJ paused in mid-bite, looked at him in surprise, then stared down at his plate. Becky stopped eating with her fork in mid-air. "What are you talking about...you mean the farm?"

He nodded, "Yeah, with today's prices I'd probably get a hundred thousand for the whole hundred acres, maybe even more with that new house on the Russian place."

"But…but… this used to be our home, we grew up here!"

"Yeah, but think of it, Sis, what I could do with that much money. 'Course, I'd have to pay off the bank loans, but there'd still be enough to live on comfortably for a long time." He glanced at his farm manager, staring silently at his plate. "I could even give PJ a year's pay so he'd have plenty of time to find a new job."

Becky put down her fork and responded nervously. "But don't you remember how much fun we used to have here?" She waved her hand toward the outside, "That old tire swing on the sycamore where you pushed me so high I would scream, and---"

"I wouldn't have to work so hard. I could move into town and concentrate on writing and taking care of Tommy and---"

She cut him off, her voice almost hysterical, "And remember the time we rode 'Old Blue' over to the canal so you could teach me to swim, and…and he broke his tether and trotted home and…and we had to walk all the way back over the hot dirt in our bare feet!"

Thomas, taken aback by her strong reaction, could see she was on the verge of tears. He reached across the table to pat her arm reassuringly. "Don't get too excited, Becky, I haven't decided anything yet. Just trying to figure out what to do with the rest of my life."

She pulled out a hanky, dabbed at her eyes and blew her nose. PJ, recognizing he was in the middle of a family discussion and realizing he might be losing his job, remained quiet and poked listlessly at his food.

Thomas stabbed idly at a potato and continued, "Hell, I really don't know what I want to do. The farm represents a lot of hard work, even with good help like PJ. And the record crop prices we're getting can't last forever, especially now that we have Prohibition. It just seems like I could find an easier way to make a living."

Becky sighed, "Maybe you could sell the Russian property or the West Forty if you really want to. But, I'd hate to see you get rid of this place. I have too many memories."

"Unfortunately, I don't remember those days the way you do. I mostly recall a father who was always angry, an overly-demanding mother and fighting with my brother."

She didn't respond as she rose and went to the counter to retrieve the apple cobbler she had baked earlier. She served them and they ate in silence for a few minutes until Becky spoke, "Well, it seems to me Thomas you have to deal with another problem before you do anything."

"What's that?"

She motioned toward the back bedroom. "You've gotta clean out all the bedding, towels and clothing from that room. And you need to open the door and windows and air the room out."

He looked away, averting her gaze. The thought of the room and the memory of blissful nights that eventually turned to pain and tragedy tore at his gut and started the bile churning. Abruptly, he got to his feet and walked to the back bedroom and shoved open the door. With the odor of Brenda's fatal illness still palpable, he walked through the semi-darkness, rolled up the shades and opened both windows. He grabbed the bedding and dragged it through the living room and out the door and tossed it behind the house. He made a couple more trips to retrieve armloads of clothing.

When they finished their meal, PJ thanked them for dinner and returned to the bunkhouse. Thomas and Becky washed and dried the dishes, then he drove her to her apartment. He had promised to get her back so she could resume the cosmetics business she had been neglecting for several days.

As they motored along in the gathering dusk, she reopened the earlier conversation, "You sure worried me, Thomas, talking about selling. And I think you scared PJ pretty good."

"Sorry about that. I'll apologize when I see him."

"Any thoughts on what you really want to do now?"

He shook his head, "Not a clue."

"You've got a little boy who's going to need you all the more without his mother."

He nodded absently.

"And a lot of crops coming on."

He sighed and nodded again.

Becky, recognizing the future was something her brother was not ready to deal with, didn't pursue the subject further, and they continued on in silence. When they pulled up in front of her apartment, she reached over and patted him on the knee. "Just remember," she said, climbing out of the car. "I'm here if you ever need me. Don't hesitate to call."

He smiled vaguely. "Thanks for everything.."

He drove home silently, barely able to see as he became consumed by the feeling of quiet and loneliness building up over the loss of Brenda and Erasmus. When he parked the car under the sycamore, he looked up to see PJ coming toward him, waving his arm for attention, yelling, "Hey, Boss, I found somethin' I can't reckon on."

His heart sank. The last thing he needed was another problem to deal with, but he climbed out of the car and reluctantly approached the farm manager.

PJ motioned him forward, "Come here. Somethin' you better see."

When Thomas followed around the side of the bunkhouse to where they stored wooden drying trays, PJ pointed toward the ground, "I was stackin' them trays and found that paint can hidden under the pile."

Thomas stepped forward and squatted to more closely examine the rusty can, runners of dried yellow paint down the sides, a used paintbrush lying stiffly beside it in the dirt. A faint whiff of turpentine caught in his nostrils and throat.

PJ broke the silence. "You reckon old 'Rass' painted them words on the bunk house hisself?"

Thomas stood up and glanced to where the offensive words were still barely visible as a ghostly reminder, defying PJ's earlier effort to cover them with a coat of white paint. Bewildered, he shook his head. All the obvious questions paled against the most important one...why? Why would Erasmus paint a message that would threaten his comfortable life at the O'Roarks; the steady pay, regular meals and relative security from discrimination? He reached down to touch the can, picked up the brush, pushed it against a wooden tray and listened absently to the crackling of the dried bristles.

Finally, he stood up and turned to PJ, "Guess I'm gonna have to try to figure this one out, PJ. Damned if I have any answers. But, I guess you can just throw the can and brush away. 'Rass' won't be needing paint for anything now."

As he turned to leave, Thomas kicked at the dirt, exposing something glistening in the sunlight. He bent to pick up a mud-encrusted metallic object about the size of a quarter and half an inch thick, with a thin chain attached. He held it out, "This something of yours, PJ?"

The little man glanced at it and shook his head. Thomas turned and, head down, shoulders slumping, walked slowly back to the house as he rolled the strange object around in his hand. He flipped on the kitchen light, went to the sink and held it under the faucet to wash off the mud, revealing that the outer sides and attached chain were gold. Turning it over in his hand, he noticed it was hinged on one end, and pushed it open to find a tiny magnifying glass. He turned it over again to see the initials JS engraved in the gold surface of one side. He also observed that the chain's clasp was broken.

Thomas carried the object to the sofa and flopped down, struggling to focus his mind on the day's events; Brenda's funeral, the murder of Eramus, the can of yellow paint and the mysterious magnifying glass. He dropped the glass on the side table and returned to the kitchen cupboard for the new bottle of brandy PJ had brought him a few days earlier. He pulled the cork with his teeth, chipped some ice into a glass, poured in a generous amount and sat down at the kitchen table. After an hour or so with his new companion, he fell asleep with his cast-bound wrist and head on the table.

He eventually was disturbed by the phone ringing, went to the wall and picked up the receiver. It was Brad. "Hi, my friend, how'r you doing?"

The brightness of his voice was in such contrast to the way Thomas felt that he had to struggle for a response. "Oh, I'm hanging in there."

"Sarah and I were sure sorry to hear about Brenda. She was a great gal."

"Yeah."

"I found out about Erasmus this morning, Sorry about that, too."

Thomas, trying to control the wrenching in his gut, didn't comment.

Brad continued, "There is some good news. It looks like the doctors have managed to keep the smallpox from getting out of hand."

"How'd they do that?"

"They vaccinated with what they call a concentric pattern, starting with Brenda's immediate contacts and branching out from there. Doc Bandy told me it's taken over a hundred vaccinations, but it looks like they prevented the disease from spreading."

"That's good."

"So, I assume you're still under quarantine?"

"Yeah, for a few more days."

Brad chuckled, "Guess that means you're not getting into any mischief."

Thomas didn't respond, and Brad broke the silence, "By the way, I got my cast taken off yesterday. Sure feels good to have my leg back to normal."

"Supposed to get mine off tomorrow," Thomas replied laconically. Reflexively he tried to move his left wrist back and forth and wiggle the fingers.

"I assume you'll be ready to go flying again?"

Thomas sighed, "Not sure. Hopefully one of these days." A long pause followed, finally broken by Brad, "Well, I gotta get back to work. Don't hesitate to call if I can do anything for you."

***

The next day, Thomas motored into town to have his cast removed and pick up Tommy, who had been staying with Emma. When they returned to the deathly silence of the farmhouse, he was hit by an instant reminder of the roller coaster of emotions he would be subjected to when his son ran toward the back bedroom, calling, "Mommy, Mommy."

Thomas' heart jumped into his throat as he raced to catch up, dropped to the floor and pulled the youngster close. "Oh, Tommy, Tommy, I'm sorry. Mommy's not here. She...she's gone to...to..." His throat tightened around any further words and tears puddled in his eyes.

"Go office?"

He held his son closer and buried his face in his warm little neck. He finally was able to blurt out the word 'heaven'. Then he added, "Mommy's gone to heaven, Tommy, and she won't be coming back."

They held each other close for a few moments until the youngster silently pulled away, toddled to his playpen and started playing with his toys. Thomas sat on the floor for a long time, trying to regain his composure, too weak to get up.

For the following week, he concentrated on caring for the youngster, feeding him, playing games, bathing him and cuddling him when they slept. He ventured outside occasionally to collect the mail and daily *Republican* and chat briefly with PJ.

One night late in the week, with Tommy asleep in the front bedroom, he once more reached for the elusive comfort of his bottle of brandy and his cigarette makings. He fixed a drink, rolled a smoke and settled into the old rocker. But he soon found that he couldn't relax. With a sudden inspiration, he flipped the unfinished cigarette into the fireplace and went to the bedroom to retrieve his typewriter and manuscript for *The Final Day*. He spread everything out on the kitchen table, settled into one of the ladder back chairs and took a sip of his drink.

He perused the manuscript to refresh his memory and found that, with the exception of the typing errors, he was pleased with what he had created. He rolled a clean sheet of paper in the *Royal*, positioned his fingers over the keyboard and started pecking slowly, one key at a time. He paused after a few lines, lifted the typewritten sheet to scan his work and sat back in the chair, satisfied at his error-free effort. He took a swig of brandy, and resumed typing.

When he came to the end, he pushed his chair back from the table with a scraping sound and reached his hands up to massage his shoulders, weary from leaning over the typewriter. He glanced at the wall clock to see that it was past midnight. He placed the finished manuscript in an envelope, covered the typewriter and returned everything to the bedroom closet. Then he tumbled into bed and fell sound asleep.

Chapter 23

The next morning, after again depositing Tommy with Emma, Thomas drove into town and parked a few doors from Stein's jewelry store. When he walked up to the entryway, bright sunlight was pouring into the windows, adding an extra sparkle to the watches, rings and jewelry on display. He paused outside to peer through the glass, waiting for Jake to appear by himself.

When he did step out from behind a beaded curtain, Thomas quickly moved inside and approached with a forced, "Good morning. You repair jewelry, do you?"

Jake responded from behind one of the rear counters, "Yes, we certainly do." Then his eyes widened as he recognized who had entered the store and added, "Er, good morning."

Thomas stepped forward, pulled the tiny magnifying glass from his pocket and dropped it clattering on the glass counter top. "The clasp is broken on this chain. Think you'd like to fix it?"

Jake looked down at it, mumbling, "I, uh, I...yeah, that's my jeweler's loupe." He chuckled nervously, "Uh, where'd you find it?" He looked up, his swarthy complexion turning pale, eyes darting to one side. He moved around behind the counter, stumbling over an umbrella caddy in the corner, while Thomas followed, as months of anger and frustration boiled to the top. "I found it next to that can of yellow paint you left at my place, you miserable bastard!"

Jake turned toward him and raised his voice, "Get the hell out of my store! We don't serve nigger lovers in here!" Thomas reacted instantly, hitting Stein with the back of his right hand across his open mouth, sending spittle flying.

Jake swung back with a weak blow against Thomas' cheek. Thomas slammed his left fist flush into Jake's face, knocking him back against the wall, blood spurting from his mouth and nostrils. He reached across the counter to grab him by his coat lapels, oblivious to an ominous 'click' followed by a sharp pain across his right forearm. He yelled out in shock, released his grip and looked down to see blood seeping through a cut in his shirtsleeve and the reflection of a switch-blade knife.

"You son of a bitch!" Thomas yelled as he swung wildly with the back of his left hand and followed that with a right cross that knocked Stein slumping to the floor. He ran around the end of the counter and, unmindful of the blood seeping through his sleeve, pounded Stein with both fists until he heard a woman crying out, "Jacob, Jacob!, *Mein Gott!!*

Stein yelled, "Mama, Mama...get the gun...*der waffe!*

The woman disappeared through the beaded curtain and returned in a moment waving a large pistol. Thomas ducked below the counter as she pulled the trigger, filling the interior with an ear-splitting explosion and sending a slug smashing into the store's bowl-shaped chandelier and a shower of crystal shattering onto the floor.

Thomas stood up to see that Jake had struggled to his feet and was advancing with an umbrella held high. He threw his arm up defensively and flattened himself against the wall as it bounced off his arm and crashed down on the counter top, scattering shards of glass into the glistening display of jewelry.

Thomas jerked the umbrella away and threw it to the floor. He stepped closer to Jake and struck him with a solid left and right, sending him sprawling on the floor. He leaned over him and growled, "You Heinie bastard, if I ever see you anywhere near my place again, you're a dead man!" Then, ignoring the mother screaming in the background and with his shoes crunching across broken crystal, he stalked to the door as Jake cried out, "Emil did it!

Thomas turned back, "What the hell did you say?"

Mumbling through his bleeding mouth, Jake replied, "Emil painted those words on your bunk house. Ask Ivan it you don't believe me."

Thomas jerked open the door, slammed it shut behind him and strode toward the Maxwell, oblivious to passersby watching the fracas through the store windows. He climbed in the car and headed toward home, staring ahead blindly, his mind roiling over Jake's parting words.

With a handkerchief wound tightly around his right forearm and keeping it elevated to staunch the oozing blood, he drove toward home. As he approached the farm, he made a decision. He would drive on to confront Emil over Jake's claim. When he entered the Stuckey yard and cut the engine, he looked up to the porch to see Ivan standing behind the screen door.

"Morning," he ventured, stepping out of the car. "I'm looking for Emil."

"I've been expecting you." Ivan answered. "Understand you paid a little visit to Jake."

Thomas nodded, "I believe my business is with Emil."

"Emil's not here. But I think you better come in and let me fix that cut. Besides, we need to talk."

Thomas moved forward cautiously and followed Ivan through the door, down the hallway and into the bathroom. Silently, Ivan handed him a washcloth to clean off the dried blood, daubed *Mercurochrome* across the cut and wrapped it with a bandage, finally commenting, "Well, that doesn't look too bad."

Ivan then led Thomas to the parlor and pointed him toward the leather chair. He pulled up a chair across from him and spoke wearily, "Emil's not here, Thomas. "He's in the state insane asylum in Napa."

Thomas stared back at Ivan. "What did you say?"

"We had to commit him when Brenda died. He went so berserk that Papa and I couldn't control him. It took me and two deputies to put him in a straightjacket so they could take him to the hospital where the doctors said there was nothing they could do. They sent him to Napa for professional help."

Thomas sat dumbfounded, not sure what to say or do. He opened his mouth to speak, but nothing would come out.

Ivan continued, "I'm sorry to say that Emil did paint those words on your bunkhouse. Jake drove him there, and both of them have been involved in the Klan. We learned that recently when Papa found a white robe and mask in the barn along with a couple cans of yellow paint. We even believe now that he was the one who painted our house during the war."

"Jesus, but why?"

Ivan shrugged, "Who knows? During the war, he was very disturbed over the persecution and harassment of German-Americans. He got into several fights in town and at the university, and was terribly upset when I was called up and he had to return home to help Papa with the farm."

Thomas rose from the chair and walked across the room, then turned back. "But, why attack me, his sister's husband, and…and his own sister, for God's sake?"

"Well, for what it's worth, Thomas, you weren't the only ones. From what we've learned, he and Jake and their fellow Klan members were responsible for several attacks around town including the one on your former Russian neighbors."

Thomas just shook his head as Ivan continued, "In your case, in his twisted mind, you represented the enemy. You went to France and killed Germans and you gave his sister an Irish baby. He became especially upset in February and got into an argument with Brenda when he learned she was pregnant with your second child."

"How much did Brenda know about Emil's condition?"

"She was aware of it, but like Papa and me, hoped he would get over it."

"I guess you realize how ironic this is with her interest in eugenics?"

Ivan nodded.

Thomas sighed, "So how's Papa taking all this?"

"Not very well. He's upstairs under sedation now. Between the loss of Brenda and this, he's in pretty bad shape. He seems to have lost his will to live."

Thomas shook his head then took a deep breath. "Is there anything I can do to help you or Papa? I feel so helpless."

"As a matter of fact, there could be. It might help cheer him up if you could bring Tommy over sometime to visit."

Thomas crossed the room and shook Ivan's hand. "I'll bring him over in the morning. And thanks for straightening me out. I hope Emil gets better." He returned to the Maxwell and drove home, barely able to see for the tears welling up in his eyes.

When he pulled into the driveway, he found a familiar Model T parked under the sycamore and its owner, Brad, sitting on the stoop. He turned off the engine and walked toward his friend's friendly wave, calling out, "Hi, Brad. What brings you out here on this sunny day?"

Brad stood up and stuck out his hand, "I thought it was about time to check up on...my gosh, you look like you've been in a fight!"

"You've got that right. Come on in and I'll tell you about it." They entered the house and took seats at the kitchen table, and Thomas massaged his sore knuckles and told about his fight with Jake and meeting with Ivan.

When he finished, Brad commented, "Sounds like you've had quite a morning. But I guess it feels good to get it off your chest."

"Yeah, it's good to know who's been hassling us all this time, but I'm sorry to hear about Emil's situation."

He turned to look at the clock to see that it was almost noon, "God, I'm famished.   You want something to eat?"

"Oh, no thanks.   I need to get back to work.   But I'm anxious to talk to you about something."

"What's that?"

"How would you like to go with me to Chicago?"

"Chicago…what for?"

"The Republican National Convention."

Thomas chuckled, "Afraid that's something I haven't been thinking about.   When is it?"

"June eighth through the twelfth."

"Sounds like quite a trip.   How come you're going?"

"My publisher feels like Senator Johnson will win tomorrow's primary.   He wants to give him as much support as he can for the presidential nomination, so he's sending me all expenses paid, and said I could take an assistant."

"But what would I do?   I've never written a newspaper story and never been to a convention, not even a state one."

Brad laughed, "I've never been to a convention either!   But there will be a lot of things going on with several hundred delegates and half a dozen possible candidates.   So I figure you could help me keep track of what's happening and running down information."

"You say it's in June.   I'll have to figure out when my peaches will be ready for harvesting, hopefully not until late that month.   And if Pedro doesn't come back from Mexico pretty quick, I'll have to find some new help."

Brad stood up to leave, "Well, let me know soon as you can. If you can't make it, I'll have to find someone else."

When Brad left, Thomas went to the hall cabinet between the two bedrooms and rummaged around until he found the family atlas. He opened it up and scanned his finger across the route from Fresno north to Sacramento and east to Chicago. He shook his head as he laid his thumb against the scale to calculate the distance, over two thousand miles, and remembered they would be traveling in the heat of summer. As he returned the atlas to the cabinet, the phone rang the familiar long ring followed by the short one.

When he picked up the receiver, the operator intoned, "Long distance call for Thomas O'Roark."

"Speaking."

Then the throaty feminine voice came over the line, "Thomas, this is Lillian!"

His response caught in his throat, stopping his reply from coming out, and she spoke again, "Thomas, is that you?"

"My God, yes! Is this Lillian…Lillian Branson?"

"The one and only!"

"Where on earth are you?"

"In Bakersfield. Mary and I got back a few days ago."

"Are you as beautiful as I remember?"

She responded with that familiar throaty chuckle, "I guess that's for you to find out!"

Thomas fell silent for a few moments, causing her to speak, "Thomas, are you still there?"

"Yeah. I have an idea. Why don't I fly down to see you tomorrow?"

"You say fly?"

"Yes. And I'm going to bring someone with me."

"Not a wife, I hope?"

"No, no. A man, a very young one."

"My, that sounds interesting."

"OK, it's a deal. I'll plan to arrive at the aerodrome around noon. Can you meet me there?"

"Certainly. You'll be careful, won't you?"

"By all means. See you tomorrow."

They hung up and Thomas stood motionless for a few moments, hardly able to catch his breath. Was he really going to see Lillian again, and what was he going to tell her? Certainly he would have to explain Tommy, and his marriage to Brenda and her tragic death. And...and his battles with the Klan and...and...all his new acreage. And his faltering efforts to write.

And how about Lillian?. Presumably, she hasn't married, or she wouldn't have phoned.

Finally, he removed his smoking material from his pocket and thoughtfully rolled a cigarette. He rummaged around in a kitchen drawer for a match, lighted up and took a seat in his father's old spindle-back rocker. Absently, he reached for the pile of newspapers Becky had stacked up and rummaged through them until the following headline in the lower right corner caught his eye:

HARDING CALLS FOR RETURN TO NORMALCY

Boston, Mass: Senator Warren G. Harding (R-Ohio) today called for America to return to "Normalcy." In a speech in Boston, he said "America's present need is not for heroics, but healing; not revolution but restoration; not surgery but serenity; not nostrums but normalcy." The 55-year-old senator has announced he will be a candidate for President at the Republican National Convention, which will be held June 8-12 in Chicago.

Thomas sighed contentedly, dropped the newspaper on the floor, flipped his unfinished cigarette into the fireplace, and quietly rocked himself to sleep.

About the Author

"A novelist with much passion and conviction." "His work is extremely appealing for its historical relevance and worthy theme". "His writing is solid."

That's how editors have described the writing of Richard K. Moore. *A Struggle for Normal* is his second novel, following his first work, *A Loss of Freedom*. Mr. Moore has been writing professionally for over forty years. He is a native of Fresno, California, where he graduated from Fresno State College with a degree in Journalism. He is retired and currently lives with his wife Willis in Waco, Texas.